Irish author **Abby Green** [obscured] career in film and TV—[obscured] of a lot of standing in th[obscured] trailers—to pursue her lo[obscured] she'd bombarded Mills & [obscured] manuscripts they kindly accepted one, and an author was born. She lives in Dublin, Ireland, and loves any excuse for distraction. Visit abby-green.com or email abbygreenauthor@gmail.com.

USA TODAY bestselling author **Natalie Anderson** writes emotional contemporary romance full of sparkling banter, sizzling heat and uplifting endings—perfect for readers who love to escape with empowered heroines and arrogant alphas who are too sexy for their own good. When not writing, you'll find her wrangling her four children, three cats, two goldfish and one dog… and snuggled in a heap on the sofa with her husband at the end of the day. Follow her at natalie-anderson.com.

Also by Abby Green

Heir for His Empire
'I Do' for Revenge

Brazilian Billionaire Brothers miniseries

The Heir Dilemma
On His Bride's Terms

Also by Natalie Anderson

My One-Night Heir

Billion-Dollar Bet collection

Billion-Dollar Dating Game

Convenient Wives Club collection

Their Altar Arrangement

Discover more at millsandboon.co.uk.

THE BILLIONAIRE'S LEGACY

ABBY GREEN

NATALIE ANDERSON

MILLS & BOON

All rights reserved including the right of reproduction in whole or in part in any form. This edition is published by arrangement with Harlequin Enterprises ULC.

This is a work of fiction. Names, characters, places, locations and incidents are purely fictional and bear no relationship to any real life individuals, living or dead, or to any actual places, business establishments, locations, events or incidents. Any resemblance is entirely coincidental.

This book is sold subject to the condition that it shall not, by way of trade or otherwise, be lent, resold, hired out or otherwise circulated without the prior consent of the publisher in any form of binding or cover other than that in which it is published and without a similar condition including this condition being imposed on the subsequent purchaser.

® and TM are trademarks owned and used by the trademark owner and/or its licensee. Trademarks marked with ® are registered with the United Kingdom Patent Office and/or the Office for Harmonisation in the Internal Market and in other countries.

First published in Great Britain 2025
by Mills & Boon, an imprint of HarperCollins*Publishers* Ltd,
1 London Bridge Street, London, SE1 9GF

www.harpercollins.co.uk

HarperCollins*Publishers*, Macken House, 39/40 Mayor Street Upper, Dublin 1, D01 C9W8, Ireland

The Billionaire's Legacy © 2025 Harlequin Enterprises ULC

Rush to the Altar © 2025 Abby Green

Boss's Baby Acquisition © 2025 Natalie Anderson

ISBN: 978-0-263-34465-3

05/25

This book contains FSC™ certified paper
and other controlled sources to ensure responsible forest management.

For more information visit www.harpercollins.co.uk/green.

Printed and Bound in the UK using 100% Renewable Electricity
at CPI Group (UK) Ltd, Croydon, CR0 4YY

RUSH TO THE ALTAR

ABBY GREEN

MILLS & BOON

CHAPTER ONE

Lili Spirenze had just been awoken by a frantic phone call to alert her to the fact that her boss, Cassian Corti, the owner of the Corti villa and estate where she'd been housekeeper for almost a year now, was due to arrive within the hour at the small pier that lay on the other side of the huge ornate wrought iron gates that opened directly from the lower garden onto Lake Como.

The faintest trails of dawn touched the sky. As Lili hurried through washing and throwing on some clothes, a knot of apprehension formed in her gut at the thought of meeting her boss for the first time.

She'd been hired by an executive assistant and someone on Corti's legal team. Her job was to oversee the general running of the villa and the cleaners, chef, gardeners and maintenance people who variously made up the numerous staff.

Something else joined the knot of apprehension as she made her way down from her quarters to the main part of the villa—irritation. Couldn't he have given more notice? And then Lili reprimanded herself. The man had a right to turn up at his own home when he wanted. Luckily she'd taken it upon herself to keep things in a state of readiness for just such an occasion, although she didn't feel smug now, she just felt…a sense of disquiet.

It was silly but as time had passed since she'd started working here with no sign of her boss appearing, she'd become a little complacent. She'd gotten used to feeling free to roam as she pleased and enjoy the isolation and sense of security that living in a private estate in one of the world's highest value property locations could afford one.

The furthest she'd gone from the Corti estate had been into the nearby city of Como to pick up supplies. For the first time in years, she'd felt a measure of peace unlike anything she'd ever experienced before. And, blessedly, anonymity.

But that peace was to be shattered now and she had to remind herself that this wasn't *her* home. She was merely caretaking it for its elusive billionaire owner. An owner who had clearly not had any inclination to spend time in his serene Lake Como home because he'd been too busy living a glamorous playboy social whirlwind, his every move breathlessly followed by the insatiable press. And, much to Lili's embarrassment, *her*. She'd told herself she was only doing due diligence in researching her boss so as to be better able to deal with anything that might come her way.

Like this impromptu visit. But now that his arrival was imminent, Lili's apprehension surged back to the fore. She was in the kitchen, moving efficiently around the large gleaming space, preparing some breakfast items and fresh coffee.

How did one deal with a man who was considered something of a legend? Not to mention routinely named as one of the most gorgeous and sexy men on the planet.

Scion to one of Italy's oldest and wealthiest families, he'd been hit by a terrible tragedy when still a young boy. His parents and younger brother had all died in a horrific car crash. Cassian Corti had walked away without a scratch—the sole remaining member of a vast familial dynasty stretching back into Medieval times when the Cortis had been mentioned in the same breath as the Medicis.

Since then, he'd been a figure of intense tragic interest, growing up under a spotlight with everyone watching to see what he would do.

His astounding good looks, physicality and wealth had almost predestined him to become a part of the debauched and glittering European social scene, which he'd entered with a predictable and resounding explosion—getting expelled from his exclusive boarding school in Switzerland after attending a famous debutante ball in Paris, only to be found in bed with the mother of his debutante date.

Embarking on a career racing the fastest cars on the planet had only enhanced his already rapidly growing reputation for risk-taking and scandal. He hadn't raced recently as he was getting over a minor injury. The press had breathlessly speculated over the years whether or not his fascination with cars had something to do with the awful tragedy he'd suffered as a child. Certainly his skill and control in that dangerous arena only fed the endless speculation and while Lili instinctively shied away from reliving trauma, maybe he was drawn to it to exorcise his own demons?

So now, he was not only a champion driver but he was also involved as one of the major shareholders of the worldwide body that owned formula racing cars. He was investing heavily in making the sport more sustainable. This was aside from his family business, the Corti Group, which encompassed a myriad of interests from tech innovation to real estate and banking. The Corti name was still over the door of some of Italy's oldest financial establishments.

His other properties included a palazzo on the Grand Canal of Venice, penthouse apartments in all the major cities, holiday homes in Costa Rica and Malaysia.

His personal life matched his professional life in terms of excitement and glamour, even if he had dialled down some of the more scandalous acts of his youth.

Sipping some fresh coffee, Lili sat down at the wide kitchen table and looked at her phone, searching for her boss. Immediately about ten pictures surfaced of him in a tuxedo at an event in Rome with a stunningly beautiful willowy blonde on his arm, a silver silk dress hugging toned curves and endlessly long tanned legs.

Lili sighed a little enviously. She was average height and with a figure that ran less to willowy and more…pillowy. Her hair was unfashionably long and she couldn't remember the last time she'd put on make-up.

Then she noticed something about the pictures and nearly dropped her coffee. They'd been taken at an event the previous evening and yet somehow his arrival was imminent.

Lili suddenly had visions of not only her boss arriving but also the stunning blonde. Maybe she was his girlfriend? Maybe he was bringing her here to show her his family home?

At that moment the gardener poked his head around the door. '*Buongiorno*, Lili, the boss is arriving by speedboat in a few minutes, I'll go down and open the gate?'

Lili stood up and smiled at Matteo. She knew his arthritis was acting up, making him slower, especially in the mornings. 'No, it's fine, I could do with the walk and I've never met him before, it'll be a way to introduce myself. Maybe send down Tommy to secure the boat?'

Lili knew what it was like to be around people like Cassian Corti; they generally left a trail of things to be picked up/attended to in their wake and she didn't want to be responsible for the boat floating back out into the lake.

'Of course, thanks, Lili.'

She quickly rinsed out her cup and after giving instructions to Maria, the young housemaid, set off through the villa, out into the back courtyard and down the steps to the level of the middle garden and then down more steps to the lower garden.

Even though it was still early, Lili could feel the latent heat of the coming day. Birds were calling in their dawn chorus. The dew-laden grass and flowers scented the air. It was incredibly peaceful and calm even as she walked across the gravel crunching under her feet. She felt a prick of regret that it would be shattered now.

She got to the beautiful elaborately designed wrought iron gates and unlocked them with the key she'd brought. She pushed them outwards with a little *huff* of effort.

This was her favourite part of the villa. This gate and the wide stone steps leading down, straight into the lake, with the small landing pier to the side, along the stone wall. The water lapped gently against the stone. There was a mist across the lake and the faint outline of land on the other side could be seen. The rising sun was sending out a hazy pearlescent sheen across the water.

Whenever Lili stood on this spot, she always felt a mixture of terror and temptation. To just get in a boat and leave, explore the world, or go back, close the gates behind her and never leave this place. It was like standing on a precipice… a precipice she always walked away from.

Coward, whispered a harsh voice. *No*, Lili told herself now. Not a coward. She was just protecting herself, and after what had happened to her, she had a right to protect herself however she wanted. She didn't owe anyone anything. She'd cut all of her ties—

She startled when a stone was kicked onto the steps beside her. She whirled around to see Tommy, Matteo's gangly teenage son.

'Hi, Tommy.'

The young man blushed. 'Morning, Lili.'

Tommy went down the steps to the little stone pier and started to get the rope ready to secure the boat. Just when Lili was wondering if the boss *was* even on his way she heard a faint sound that grew stronger and louder.

She saw the outline of a small boat slicing through the small waves of the lake, someone standing at the helm. Tall and broad. Dark. She shivered and it wasn't from the morning chill. She couldn't shake the sense that once this man arrived, nothing would be the same.

Cassian could see the familiar outline of the Corti villa rising up on the hill above the green and lush foliage. One of the less ornate villas in the area, it was still impressive with its cream walls and three stories. The terracotta roof. The whimsical wing that had been added at the turn of the last century with a turret.

The gardens were famous, designed by an iconic British landscape gardener back in the 1800's.

Cassian wished that he could look upon this view and feel nothing but it was impossible. It thrummed inside him like a second pulse. *His home.* The place where he'd been so happy and the place that filled him with the most pain because that happiness had been brutally shattered.

As he drew closer to the small pier memories and voices whispered over his skin and into his ears. *Cassian and Lorenzo, come inside now! I won't call again and we will eat all your gelato!*

Giggling and laughing so hard his stomach had hurt. Tugging his baby brother behind him as they'd climbed up through the gardens, mucky and aching all over from climbing trees and exploring…

His mother's voice now: *It's been so long, Cass...we've missed you.*

No. He would not let this return after more years than he liked to admit to unsettle him. This was just a place. It did not have any power over him. He'd carved out a life apart from it. Apart from his tragic past.

He had a decision to make now—to endeavour to keep the villa with all of its poignant and painful memories and past, or let it go, which he would have to do unless he complied with the strict and demanding rules of inheritance.

But even as he thought of cutting ties with his past and his family legacy, his insides clenched painfully and guilt burned like acid in his gut.

Sufficiente! He was a rational, intelligent man. He would decide on the course of action that made the most sense.

He could see the pier now and the slight figure of a young man. Cassian squinted. A very tall young man. Was that Tommy? He must have shot up since he'd seen him last. More guilt.

And there was another figure. Cassian could see it was a woman with long brown hair. But apart from that he couldn't make out much else because she was dressed in something cream, and long and loose with what appeared to be an equally long cardigan pulled over her chest, under crossed arms. She was wearing sneakers.

The new housekeeper. It must be. What was her name again... Lucy? Something like that. Cassian knew he should care more but his head was still throbbing slightly and all he wanted was a coffee strong enough to stand in. The Lake Como air had done little to clear it. On some level he knew that he'd had to have a fuzzy head to come here and he hated himself for it.

He killed the engine and the boat bobbed gently to the

pier wall. Tommy called out a greeting and Cassian forced a smile at the young man. 'Ciao, Tommy, you've grown!'

'Grazie, Signor Corti.' The young man went brick-red but he was smiling. Cassian jumped athletically from the boat to the pier and handed the rope to Tommy, letting him secure it. He walked towards the woman who seemed to be watching him warily.

He took in details. Long dark hair. Not styled. Average height. Indeterminate shape under the loose clothes. Nice enough face. Big eyes, that he saw were a startling shade of blue, as he got closer. That realisation jolted something to life inside him but he dismissed it. He was tired and hung-over.

He stopped and saw how her eyes widened, looking him up and down. Why did he suddenly feel defensive? Aware of his stubbled jaw and creased suit? His dry mouth.

'Buongiorno... Miss...' He searched his brain frantically, cursing himself for not remembering he'd be meeting his newest staff member.

Her eyes moved back up to his face. They really were arresting. Like bright blue jewels. With long dark lashes. No make-up. It had been a long time since Cassian had seen a woman with a bare face. It felt curiously...intimate.

She spoke. 'I'm Lili Spirenze. Your housekeeper.' Her voice was immediately pleasing. Low and slightly husky.

She stepped back. 'I've prepared some breakfast.'

'Coffee?'

'Of course. It's on the terrace.'

It was only when Cassian was walking ahead of her up to the house that he realised they hadn't shook hands. He turned around to remedy this, and she almost ran into him. She stepped back so hurriedly that she almost fell over. He reached out and she flinched back. Suddenly she looked flustered. 'Sorry, I wasn't looking where I was going.'

Cassian put out his hand. '*I'm* sorry, I'm forgetting my manners.'

She looked at his hand and went pale. He noticed how beautiful her skin was. Peaches and cream complexion.

She looked at him, and then held up her hands. 'Please, forgive me, I picked up some weeds on the way down, my hands are dirty.'

They looked fine to him but Cassian just shrugged and turned around again. Maybe she was a little eccentric. She certainly dressed like it. As she fell into step almost beside him he said, 'Weren't you furnished with a uniform?'

She said a little breathlessly, 'I was told that trousers and shirts would be favourable as well as practical but I'm afraid I got a little complacent when there was no one in residence for so long.'

It wasn't remotely a rebuke but it stung Cassian nevertheless.

She said, 'I could change if you like.'

'That won't be necessary, I won't be here all that long, maybe twenty-four hours.'

'Do I need to prepare for any…guests?'

Cassian sent her a glance. There had been something about the inflection in *guests* but her hair was falling forward covering her face. He had to curb a strange urge to pull it back so he could see her.

'Just my solicitor,' he replied, looking forward again. 'He'll be joining me for lunch.'

'Anything in particular you'd like to eat? I can let chef know.'

'Antipasta, bread and salad will be fine.'

'Very well.'

They were at the terrace now and Cassian could see the table with breakfast things laid out and a pot of coffee. He cursed himself for not sending instructions ahead that he did not want to eat outside. His previous housekeeper had known, because she'd been with them since he was a baby and he'd told her expressly never to set a table outside again.

But his previous housekeeper had died suddenly. Cassian hadn't made it back for her funeral. More guilt.

This terrace was where his parents had always loved to dine once the weather had got warmer. He had memories of long dusk-laden evenings, falling asleep in his father's arms with the sound of his deep voice and laughter rumbling against his cheek.

He brutally pushed down the memories. He was tempted to tell Miss Spirenze to move the breakfast things indoors but stopped himself. He was being ridiculous, he was only going to be here for twenty-four hours and after his meeting with his solicitor, whatever he decided to do, he wouldn't have to set foot on this estate ever again if he so wished.

But, Cassian didn't feel a sense of liberation at that prospect. What he did feel was far more complicated and unwelcome.

Lili cursed herself. She was still trembling in the kitchen after that near collision with Cassian Corti on the way up to the villa. He'd arrived on that boat looking like the sexy villain in a movie in his creased tuxedo with bow-tie dangling open from around his neck, top buttons open showing a hint of dark chest.

Thick, wavy hair. Dark brown. Luxurious. When he'd stepped onto the pier Lili had had to force herself not to move backwards. He'd been so tall and broad. She hadn't expected him to be so physically imposing. Powerful. Muscular.

Beautiful face, all sharp, hard lines. Patrician nose. Deep-set eyes. Strong brows. Surprisingly full mouth. Dark hair liberally stubbled across his cheeks and jaw, only adding to his masculinity.

She'd been too intimidated to look at him for too long but she'd noticed that his eyes weren't dark. They were some shade of grey. Unusual.

She could still see his hand stuck out towards her, waiting for her to do the most natural thing in the world. Take it and shake it. And her immediate reaction had been to recoil from his touch. Like she recoiled from anyone's touch.

Lili stopped what she was doing and forced herself to take deep breaths to restore her equilibrium.

She had a pathological fear of being touched. Or of anyone getting too close to her. Crowding her. Because she'd been kidnapped when she was a teenager. Sixteen years old. Full of gawky adolescence and self-consciousness. Her father was a well-known millionaire entrepreneur—money made from his real estate company. He'd never been shy about displaying his wealth all while currying favour with the monied classes, trying desperately to attain a social status that he hadn't been born into, coming from a small town in Southern Italy.

Lili had been on her way home from school one day in Rome when she'd been grabbed near the train station by a group of men who had thrown a cover over her head, and tied her hands before brutally manhandling her into a van and on to some unknown location.

They hadn't touched her apart from moving her around but the threat of it had hung in the air, heavy and oppressive. The worst thing for Lili had been the not knowing when someone would grab her or pull her up or march her forward or push her down. She'd had no control, or privacy.

She breathed deep now. Years had passed since she'd

managed to escape, and she'd carved out a life for herself where she was in control. This place had become a sanctuary to her. Safe. Behind closed gates. With security. A handful of staff who respected her space and never came too close.

She actually felt like she'd healed in the past year and then Cassian Corti had turned to face her and put out his hand and she'd almost had a panic attack on the spot. Somehow managing to mutter something about dirty hands.

He'd looked at her as if she'd had two heads. She was a freak.

'Lili?'

Lili looked up. It was Maria holding an empty coffee-pot. She said, 'He wants more coffee.'

Lili took it from her and forced a smile. 'Thank you, I'll bring it up, you can go and check that his office is ready for his meeting. They'll need paper and pens. Make sure there's water.'

'Of course.'

The girl left and Lili pushed all the memories aside and filled the pot with fresh coffee. She took a deep breath and went back up to the terrace to find Cassian Corti with shades covering his eyes now, face turned towards the lake. She made her presence known. 'It's going to be a beautiful day. Any plans aside from meeting your solicitor?'

He turned away from the lake and towards her. She refilled his cup with coffee. He said, 'The coffee is good, you know how to make it well.'

She put the pot down. 'I'm a bit of a coffee snob. I like it strong.'

He lifted his cup towards her. 'Me too, this is perfect, *grazie.*'

He was still looking at her but Lili couldn't see his eyes.

Her skin prickled but it had nothing to do with fear. It was awareness and it was so surprising that Lili couldn't name it for a second. When she did she told herself she was being ridiculous. She was a woman with a pulse, her reaction was that of a straight female reacting to an Alpha male. Basic biology and chemistry at work. Nothing more.

But, he was the first man to spark that awareness, which was disconcerting.

He said, 'Actually, after I've freshened up I'll meet Matteo in the gardens and have a look at how they're being kept, if you'd let him know?'

'Of course.' Lili seized on the opportunity to escape and told herself that her tripping pulse had more to do with the sudden activity after months of inactivity than anything to do with her charismatic boss's arrival.

About an hour later when Lili felt sure that her boss must have freshened up and gone out to meet Matteo, she went up to his bedroom suite with the small overnight bag that had been with him on the boat, delivered by Tommy after they'd got back to the villa.

So used to navigating the villa on her own without fear of running into anyone, Lili pushed open his bedroom door and went over to the massive four-poster bed that dominated the room. The French doors that led out to the terrace were open, curtains moving gently in the breeze.

She put the bag on the bed just as she also noticed his discarded tuxedo. He had a fully stocked closet full of clothes here so he'd obviously changed into something else.

Lili picked up the suit and his scent hit her nostrils. Leather and amber notes mixed with something sharp, citrusy. Tantalising.

A movement out of the corner of her eye made her turn

her head and it was only then she realised that a full length mirror in the bedroom was showing a reflection of the shower in the bathroom, and it was too late to turn away. What she was looking at would be burnt onto her brain forever.

Cassian Corti was in the shower, his back to her, arms lifted, hands in his hair. The water sluiced down over his body, perfectly honed muscles moving under sleek olive-brown skin.

His shoulders were broad, as was his back, narrowing down to lean hips and down to strong thighs. But she couldn't take her eyes off his powerful and muscular buttocks. Slightly lighter in colour.

Lili was filled with a longing, yearning sensation that started in the very pit of her being and spread out to every limb, making her blood pulse. She had the strangest urge to take off her clothes and step into the shower behind him and slide her arms around him and press close to his back—

Her blood ran cold. She *never* ever imagined touching someone else. But she suddenly had the ground-shifting realisation that if she was the one doing the touching, the prospect was exciting, not terrifying.

It was too much to unpack. Cassian Corti had been at his villa for barely an hour and Lili was unravelling all over the place. She turned and fled before he could find her gawping at him as if she'd never seen a naked man before, which, she hadn't.

The thought of him witnessing her arrested moment was enough to galvanise her out of the villa and back down to the gates at the lake to make sure they'd been locked again.

CHAPTER TWO

A FEW HOURS LATER, after lunch had been served on the terrace and Cassian Corti was in his office with his solicitor, Lili carefully juggled a tray of coffee and knocked lightly on the door.

Her boss sounded irritated when he called, 'Yes, come in.'

Lili pushed the door open with her foot and went in avoiding looking directly at the men, one in particular, her boss, who had changed into faded jeans and a shirt. She did however, manage to notice that he'd rolled his sleeves up. He was standing by the window that looked out over the gardens rolling down to the lake. This was one of Lili's favourite rooms, the library/office.

The solicitor, an older man, was sitting in a chair and stood up politely when Lili came in. Corti said, 'Just put the coffee down anywhere, *grazie,* Miss Spirenze.'

She smiled at the solicitor who sat back down and busied herself tranferring the pot and cups from the tray to the table, along with the freshly basked biscotti.

They seemed happy to resume their conversation with her still in the room. Corti said, 'I just don't know if I want to sacrifice my freedom for the sake of the villa, it's no secret that I have an ambiguous relationship with it.'

'Of course, and no one is denying how much this place must remind you of what happened…'

Lili ascertained they were referring to the tragic crash that had killed Corti's entire family. It had happened somewhere not far from here. She couldn't even imagine what a loss like that would do to someone.

Corti made a non-committal sound, and the solicitor went on. 'But you can't ignore the fact that Cortis have owned this villa for generations. The last thing locals want is for some celebrity to move in, or a hotel chain to snap it up and carve it into pieces.'

Lili took the tray and moved silently to the door, pulling it behind her again. She noticed one of her laces was undone on her sneaker and rested the tray against the wall before bending down to retie it.

The solicitor was speaking again and it was audible through the door. 'Cassian, you've always known about this rule of inheritance—if you're not married with an heir by the time you turn thirty-three in a year's time, you forfeit the right to keep the villa and it must be sold.'

He went on, 'All you need to maintain ownership of your inheritance, is a wife who is willing to give you an heir. She could reside here and never set foot outside the gate if she so wished.'

Corti snorted incredulously. 'As if such a woman exists. Who on earth would want to hide away here forever?'

Everything inside Lili went very still. He'd literally just spoken her fantasy out loud. Living a quiet life here, feeling protected and at peace.

Now the solicitor snorted. 'Haven't you got a Rolodex of women lining up to bear a Corti heir? What about that blonde from last night?'

'She wouldn't last ten minutes in this villa without complaining about having nothing to do, and I can't think of any woman who would willingly destroy their figure to bear my child. A child I do not want, by the way, nor a marriage. I lost my family once, I won't ever take that risk again. I'm a racing car driver, I couldn't be less suitable to be a father.'

'Cassian, what happened was an awful tragedy but you can't let that stop you from having a family of your own. Don't turn your back on a legacy that is hundreds of years old. You won't always be racing.'

'I have a duty, is that what you're telling me, Giorgio?' He sounded bitter.

'In a word, yes. A duty to at least try.'

Lili couldn't move. It was as if she was frozen into that position, on her haunches, fingers on her lace. She was in shock. Stunned by what they were discussing and also shocked by Corti's palpable grief. Not to mention cynicism. *I can't think of any woman who would willingly destroy their figure to bear my child... I have a duty, is that what you're telling me?*

Lili stood up, reeling. Her hand automatically went to her belly. She had always wanted a child. Above almost anything else. A child of her own that she could lavish with all of the love and attention she'd never received from her parents. Because the fundamental flaw in their ability to bond with her had been because they'd adopted her.

They'd tried to have children for years before eventually adopting and from what Lili had gathered over the years, her mother had just never bonded with her, not helped by the fact that Lili hadn't been the delicate, petite girly girl she'd wanted for a daughter.

And then, a couple of years after adopting Lili, they'd got pregnant through IVF, and had twin boys. Lili's brothers. Almost overnight, all attention and any scant care she'd received had been deflected to their biological children and Lili had been more and more neglected.

Her biological parents hadn't loved her enough to keep her and her adopted parents hadn't loved her enough either. A double rejection that had clung to her like a bruise her whole life.

Through those horrific days of the kidnapping, she'd fantasised about living in some idyllic place, with a child. Just the two of them, protected from the evils of the outside world. She would ensure no harm came to her child. She would protect them with every fibre of her being, showing them that *she* loved them. If they were ever in danger she wouldn't hesitate to lay down her life for them.

She was well aware that a psychoanalyst would probably tell her that the child she wanted was *herself* and that she was just trying to heal that part of herself that had never got over the sheer cruelty of her parents' negligence.

But, her deepest unconscious motivations aside, she had always felt the need to be a mother. To nurture someone outside of herself. To care for a life. To give and receive unconditional love.

The solicitor spoke again and this time he sounded like he was admitting defeat. 'Are you really going to walk away from the legacy your ancestors and parents nurtured for you?'

Corti's voice was cold. 'That was an archaic rule set down in a time when the world worked very differently.'

'And yet no Corti has failed to secure the next generation's inheritance, until now.'

'That's a low blow.'

'It's the truth.'

Lili picked up the tray and left, walking blindly back down to the kitchen. Her head was buzzing with all she'd heard.

She could empathise with some of what Corti had said. As much as she *wanted* a child, she also had no desire to marry. The thought of being intimate with someone—emotionally or physically, made her break out in a cold sweat.

She'd learnt very young from her competitive siblings and cold parents that any show of emotion could be used to exploit vulnerabilities and weaknesses.

The ultimate example of how toxic it had been was when her own parents hadn't wanted to hand over the ransom the kidnappers were demanding for her release. They'd said afterwards to Lili that if they'd gone public and paid the ransom, it would put the boys in danger, not to mention take the risk of further kidnap attempts. But the truth was that they hadn't cared enough, and they'd been too mean.

Lili had been humiliated by her own parents. When she'd managed to escape the kidnappers and the police had brought her home, her parents had barely looked up from their dinner party. She would never forget the pitying look from the female police officer who had left her there like an unwanted returned puppy.

In that moment Lili had vowed that as soon as she was of age, she would walk away. She had, two years later, and sometimes she wondered if they'd even noticed.

Lili pushed painful thoughts of her family aside. She wondered now if she had just dreamed up that conversation between Corti and his solicitor? Because living here and being handed a licence to have a baby all of her own was almost too good to be true. She loved this place. She would happily nurture it for the next generation to fulfil the dictates of his inheritance. Cassian Corti wouldn't even have to be involved. After all, she knew how easy it was for some parents to turn their back on their children and he'd stated explicitly that he didn't want children.

She could also tell that he'd been torn about the decision. Obviously, if he'd been happy here with his family, this place must hold painful memories, but it was probably those very memories that were holding him back from fully letting go.

Lili's gut churned with a mixture of excitement and trepidation. Did she really have the nerve to go to him and suggest...herself? As a candidate to be his wife, the mother of his heir? They were complete strangers. *You saw him naked.* A flash of heat went through her. *Not all of him.* She felt a wildness thrum inside her at that prospect, and then the reality of what that would mean hit her. Being naked. Together. Her excitement drained away.

What was she thinking? She couldn't do this. It was nuts. She hadn't come into contact—willingly—with another human being in years. *You don't have to sleep with someone to get pregnant.*

She shook her head at herself. She was losing it. She pushed all such rogue notions out of her head and got on with her chores and told herself that no matter what happened—even if Corti ended up having to sell the villa because he wasn't willing to marry or have an heir to guarantee inheritance, then she would move on elsewhere.

She'd grown so much stronger in the past eight years since her kidnapping and then since she'd walked away from her family and any inheritance she might have been due. She didn't need anyone. But, even as she went about the rest of her day and caught glimpses of Corti walking around the villa's gardens talking to Matteo as dusk drew in, the tantalising vision of what she could have if she was brave enough to suggest it wouldn't leave her head, or his words: *As if such a woman exists. Who on earth would want to hide away here forever?*

Cassian sat in the shadows outside, a bulbous wine glass resting in his palm, the dregs of the red wine he'd been drinking with his dinner at the bottom of the glass. A bold Barolo, his favourite. From his own cellar.

Dusk had given way to night and the stars were out. The evening air was like velvet. He could hear the faint lapping of the water down below.

As much as being here caused him pain, he also couldn't deny the deep level of peace he always felt. Two contrasting states that battled inside him, making his insides feel jagged and tight.

Was he really going to give this place up? Because of an ancient clause demanding that he marry and have a child, or forfeit the villa—a jewel in the Corti crown, primarily because its very existence was a testament to the enduring legacy of the Corti family, passed down from heir to heir.

But, that enduring legacy had died for Cassian the day his family had died.

Did he really care if the community cribbed behind his back that he'd sold out on his ancestors? *On his parents and little brother? And the little sister in his mother's belly?* That detail had never made it into the public domain.

His mother had told them the day of the accident that she was pregnant and that they'd have a little sister by the end of the year. Cassian and his brother had made *ugh* sounds at the prospect of a girl but he had been secretly delighted and so excited at the thought of being a big protective brother.

And then within a mere second, it had seemed, he'd been orphaned and his care taken over by a series of guardians, schools and nannies, approved by the board of trustees. They'd believed that sending him to a boarding school in the UK would be the best distraction for him. Cassian still had nightmares about those first rain-sodden months in a grim school in the middle of nowhere miles away from his beloved Italy and utterly grief-struck.

At that moment a soft sound nearby made him tense. He was about to call out when he saw the shape of someone in a short toweling robe walk towards the pool, not far from where he sat in the shadows, nursing his wine.

He squinted. It was female. He could tell by the small waist, flare of hips. Long legs. Slim. Pale in the moonlight. Long dark hair rippling down her back.

His housekeeper. Lucy...? No. Lili. But she'd been shapeless under those voluminous clothes earlier. A long dress and cardigan. And yet, her eyes, those distinctive blue eyes popped into his head.

She stopped on the edge of the pool and was perfectly illuminated in a shaft of moonlight. Cassian wasn't sure why he didn't call out, or make his presence known but for the first time since he'd arrived his mind was blessedly diverted. He felt a need. To see her.

As if answering his silent thought she unbelted the robe and let it drop to the ground. She was wearing a plain white one-piece. Cassian stopped breathing for a second. Far from shapeless, he'd never seen anyone shapelier. The curve of her waist and hips and the toned length of her thighs ignited a spark in his blood. Her bottom was like an upside-down heart, perfectly plump. The spark ignited into a fire.

As he watched, she lifted her arms over her head, and executed a graceful dive into the deep end of the pool, barely making a splash.

Lili swam length after length until her limbs were aching. Eventually, she flipped over on her back and let herself float. This was her favourite time to swim, at night. When everything was still and the warmth of the day lingered.

A throat being cleared somewhere near the pool made her almost flip over again and she swallowed some water, coughing and spluttering. A deep voice said, 'I'm sorry, I didn't mean to startle you. I wasn't sure if you were training to swim the lake from end to end, you were doing so many lengths.'

Her boss. Cassian Corti. Standing at the side of the pool. He was still dressed in those worn jeans that molded far too lovingly to his thighs. And the shirt. A few more buttons open now. Hair messy. She couldn't make out the expression on his face in the dark.

She tread water. 'I'm sorry, I probably should have checked this was okay, I've got used to having the pool at my disposal.'

He gestured with a hand. 'Of course, it's fine. You're free to use the amenities.'

Lili's heart was beating fast and it had nothing to do with the exertion. She swam to the shallow end but, suddenly aware of her undress, she didn't stand up fully. Hoping her boss would take the hint she said, 'I'll leave you to your peace.' She could see her robe on the ground and hoped he would just walk away but he walked over to her robe and picked it up, holding it out for her.

Lili froze all over at the thought of appearing in front of him in just a swimsuit. But then she remembered pictures she'd seen of Corti on yachts with far more scantily clad women and told herself she was behaving like a shy nun.

She took a breath and stood up and walked up the steps with as much dignity as she could muster, practically snatching the robe out of his hand, careful not to come into contact. She avoided his eye and moved back and pulled the robe on haphazardly, belting it tightly. Wishing it was longer. It felt positively indecent. And why did her breasts suddenly feel so large and heavy? Her skin hot all over when it should be feeling cool.

'Do you normally swim late at night?' he asked.

Lili shrugged. 'Sometimes. I'm a night owl.'

'Me too.'

Lili stepped to the side. 'I'm sorry for disturbing you.' She went to walk away, back to the sanctuary of the villa but then remembered her responsibilities. She stopped and looked at him. She could see his face now in the moonlight and almost lost her breath at the sheer masculine beauty. His eyes gleamed like pewter.

'I should have checked with you earlier but you were on the phone after dinner...will you be leaving as planned tomorrow?'

'I'm not sure. I have some things to think about, I might be here for a couple more days.'

Some things to think about. Like finding the woman who didn't exist who would be willing to marry him and have his baby and live here in blissful peace and solitude.

Something about the time of the evening and the fact that darkness enveloped them like a cloak, made Lili feel a sudden sense of daring. It was now or never. She'd never have the nerve to do this in full daylight.

As if being prompted by a rogue devil inside of herself, she blurted out, 'I couldn't help overhearing your conversation with your solicitor earlier. I didn't mean to but I had to tie my lace outside the study and you were...talking quite loudly.'

Corti's mouth tipped up on one side and that tiny sign of humour added about another ten hundred percent to his appeal. For a second Lili felt dizzy.

He said, 'I would have expected that to be a privilege in the privacy of my own home. What was it you heard exactly?' He folded his arms now but that only drew attention to the corded muscles of his forearms.

Lili swallowed. 'About how you have to marry and have an heir if you want to keep this villa.'

'And this is interesting enough for you to bring it up...why?'

The night breeze skated over Lili's bare skin making it prickle into goose bumps. She was very aware that she was wearing just a swimsuit and a tiny towelling robe, her wet hair streaming down her back. The sense of daring fizzled away, she was being ridiculous.

She shook her head. 'It was nothing, I shouldn't have mentioned it.'

'But you did.'

There was a charge between them now. Something that felt almost tangible. 'Yes, I did,' Lili had to admit. But she felt too vulnerable half-dressed. 'Would you mind if I changed into my clothes?'

Corti uncrossed his arms. 'Only if you come back and explain why my conversation earlier was of interest to you.'

Hoist by her own petard. Lili said a little desperately, 'But I'm keeping you up? If you'd prefer to go to bed—'

'I can wait.'

Lili cursed her big mouth. But it was too late to go back now. 'Okay, it'll only take me a few minutes.'

She went back inside and speed-washed and changed into a dress and long loose sweater. She loosely plaited her damp hair and left it hanging over one shoulder. She caught a glimpse of herself in the mirror before she left her room.

She looked about as shapeless and colourless as a blob. She scowled at her reflection. There was no way that a man like Cassian Corti would ever agree to think about her as a prospective bride. But she'd opened her mouth and now she would have to see this humiliation through to the end.

Cassian was sitting down again with a refilled glass of wine. He was still absorbing the fact that underneath her voluminous clothes, his housekeeper was hiding an extremely alluring shape. He'd watched her walk up the steps out of the pool and his brain had gone blank for a long second, all of his blood migrating to his groin in a very base and uncontrollable response of a healthy virile male to a female who embodied lush sensuality.

Her legs were long and toned. Soft belly. And beautiful breasts. Full and high. Even with the robe on and firmly belted around her small waist, he'd seen the deep and tantalising valley of her cleavage.

It had been a long time since Cassian had seen a woman with such a full figure. It wasn't fashionable in the circles he ran in, even with the body positivity movement. He'd almost forgotten how a woman should look and now that he'd seen his housekeeper like this he couldn't *un*see it.

That's why he was intrigued to hear what she had to say after admitting that she'd overheard his conversation with his solicitor. That didn't bother him unduly. He was so used to being under a glaring spotlight since the worst day of his life when his family were killed, he'd long given up any attempt to control his privacy. He'd leant into the insatiable interest of the world's curiosity, bringing them along with him as he'd lived fast and partied even faster.

It wasn't that he had a death wish so much as no reason not to live life to the max and at full throttle. But he had to concede that he found the energy required to keep people entertained with his fast driving and fast living was becoming...harder to manufacture. These last few weeks, recuperating from a small bone fracture in his hand had been surprisingly pleasant. A respite. Stepping off the relentless merry-go-round. And yet as pleasant as that had been, it had also highlighted the void in his life, usually covered up by maintaining that relentless busy schedule.

He was bored. So bored in fact that when he'd faced the

prospect of a debauched few days in a desert at an infamous annual party which was the stuff of legends, he'd opted to finally give in to his solicitor's increasingly panicked demands for a meeting, here in Como, because despite his great reluctance to engage he'd known time was running out. He had a year from now to fulfil the terms of the inheritance or be the first Corti to fail to keep the villa in the family.

He heard a soft sound and looked up from his glass to see Lili hovering a few feet away. She was dressed in another loose dress, covered by an even looser sweatshirt. Long dark hair over one shoulder. Sneakers.

And yet now that he'd seen her, he couldn't stop his pulse tripping. It was completely unexpected and unwelcome, obviously. She was his employee. He exerted as much control as he could over his rogue hormones. He put it down to the fact that his recent sexual encounters had left him feeling dissatisfied.

He stood up. 'Please, sit down.' He gestured to the chair on the other side of the table.

Lili came forward and sat down, looking as if she might bolt at any second. Cassian held up the bottle of wine. 'Care to join me?'

She looked at the extra glass he'd placed on the table. Her skin went a pleasing shade of pink. 'I don't think that would be very appropriate.'

He arched a brow. 'And yet, why do I suspect that what you're about to say will push the boundaries of that propriety?' He was no fool. He knew that not many woman could have heard that conversation today and not been tempted to think that they could put themselves forward for the position of his wife. He was just curious to know what her reasons would be. Apart from the obvious, of course. A lifetime of wealth and prestige.

She looked at him, eyes going very wide. They really were stunning. Bright blue, with long lashes, finely etched brows.

She bit at her lower lip and Cassian felt a wave of heat move over his skin and into his blood. Again. Her mouth was wide and generous. Lower lip as plump as—

She held out her glass. 'Okay, just a small amount, please. I'm not much of a drinker.'

Lili watched as he poured the rich red liquid into her glass. As soon as he'd hinted that he might know what she wanted to talk about, she'd realised she'd need all the bravado she could muster.

She took a sip of the wine and winced a little at the strong robust flavour, but then it smoothed out as it went down her throat.

'Not a wine aficionado?'

Lili's face felt hot. Another reason why this was crazy. She might have come from a wealthy background but the difference in sophistication between them was as wide as the Grand Canyon. She felt gauche. She'd never felt as if she fitted into the world her parents had aspired to. Compounded by the fact that she knew she was adopted. She'd been too buxom and hippy as a teenager to be trendy and then the kidnap and the terror of what those men might do to her had shut down her burgeoning sexuality completely.

She was still a virgin. And that hadn't bothered her. Until she'd seen this man naked, or as good as, and he'd just seen her as near to naked as she'd ever been in front of a man. Her breasts still felt heavy, under all the layers she was hiding under.

He sat back. 'So? Would you like to elaborate on why you brought up the conversation you overheard?'

He sounded cynical, as if this was *so* unsurprising to him. It made her feel defensive, as did her awareness of him. 'I think you already know that I might be interested in asking if you'd consider marrying me so that you can retain the villa. But it's not for the reasons you might think.'

He took a sip of his own wine. His eyes were dark now. Hard to read. 'Go on.'

'It's not for your wealth or anything like that. I love it here and would feel honoured to be given the opportunity to help you keep it in your name.'

Now an expression crossed his face, something between scorn and sheer disbelief. 'Are you truly the one woman on the planet who doesn't want me for my unlimited funds and the social status I bring with me?'

Lili lifted her chin. 'I'd be willing to sign an agreement to prove that I want nothing more than a chance to live here in peace. You could get on with your life and never return if you so wished. You'd have the satisfaction of knowing the villa remains in your family for the next generation.'

'Ah, the next generation. You'd also be willing to be the mother of my child?'

Lili forced out a sudden flash of this man's naked body in the shower with water sluicing down over powerful muscles. She nodded. 'Yes, I heard that bit too.'

'And?'

'I've always wanted a child of my own, so yes, I'd be willing to…' She faltered, wondering how best to word it.

'Have marital relations?'

Lili wanted to squirm. She put her glass down. 'Well, not exactly. I'd be willing to discuss using IVF which I think would be appropriate given that we don't know one another.'

She couldn't read his expression and rushed on before he could say anything. 'Maybe that would suit you better too? The marriage and having a baby, an heir, need not impact your life all that much at all? You could get on with your usual routine…' And she'd remain a virgin. Possibly forever. That made her feel cold even though she couldn't countenance the alternative.

'I heard what you said about not wanting a child after… what happened. This way, you could fulfil your duty and have as little contact as you want.'

'Hardly an ideal scenario for the child, is it?'

Lili squashed the yearning inside her for the kind of scenario that featured two loving parents. Two parents merely doubled the risk of not being loved. Better to have just one parent who adored you.

'I would love this child and protect it above anything else.'

He asked, 'It's a lot to sacrifice just for a child.'

'It's not a sacrifice for me. My parents were wealthy but cold and unloving, obsessed with status. I've always wanted to have a child of my own, to do it differently. Give them a better experience than I had.' Lili stopped. It was more than she'd revealed to anyone, ever.

Cassian stood up, towering over the table and then he walked over to the edge of the terrace where the rest of the garden was in darkness, leading down to the lake. He had to turn his back to this woman who was making him reel with her suggestion. Everything she was saying. He'd suspected what she wanted to talk about but she'd still surprised him. Maybe she really was someone who just wanted a quiet life. A child to love. Because of her own experiences.

And, he was no different really, wasn't he a product of his experiences? Cassian lifted his wine glass and took a sip. His hand was trembling slightly. The thought of a child was something he'd managed to push down deep ever since he'd known about this requirement for keeping the villa in the family. Because it came loaded with terror. The thought of something so small, and vulnerable depending solely on him when he hadn't managed to save his own family.

To his shame he knew this was probably at the heart of why he'd prevaricated over doing something about securing his Lake Como inheritance before now. The fact that he would have to have a family to do so.

But if what Lili was saying was true, then maybe, just maybe there was a chance he could contemplate it. If she could love the child and keep it safe. Clearly her experience with her parents made her want to lavish a child with the love she hadn't had.

Cassian had had that. The love of two adored and adoring parents. They'd made him feel so safe and secure, like nothing bad would ever happen. But it had. The worst thing. So maybe someone like Lili would be a good mother, because she hadn't had that experience. She wouldn't fear the worst.

This child would be kept safe at the villa. Secure. And they would inherit the Corti legacy and Cassian would keep his distance, and they wouldn't be tainted by his demons. The demons that still haunted him because he'd walked away from that crash without so much as a scratch. He'd survived an inferno and his family hadn't and he still didn't know why that was.

He turned around to face Lili again. 'So, let me get this straight, you're willing to sign a prenuptial agreement that gives you none of my fortune except the right to live here with our child. You'd be willing to go through IVF to have this child and you'd be happy for me to continue taking lovers?'

Lili nodded. 'Yes. That's why I couldn't help listening

when I heard you say how impossible it would be to find a woman who would be happy to stay here and who wouldn't want more. That's exactly what I want.'

He came back closer to the table shaking his head, genuinely curious about this woman now. 'Forgive me but in spite of what you've said, I still find it hard to believe a young woman of…?'

'Twenty-four.'

He continued. 'Of twenty-four, would be prepared to give up her life for a marriage in name only and hide away with her child in a secluded Lake Como estate.'

CHAPTER THREE

LILI WANTED TO fade into the background, not be the focus of this man's silvery-grey gaze, narrowed so intently on her face. Her very bare and unremarkable face. 'I'm afraid it really is that simple. I want nothing more than peace and security. A child of my own.'

He sat down again, long legs spread under the table. Lili pulled hers together and slanted them away in case they touched.

'And it would be your child too,' she pointed out.

Something flashed across his face for a second but then disappeared. 'Our child then.'

Lili's heart beat a little faster. *Our child.* 'I really don't need much. I could be happy here with our child.'

'Your parents, you don't see them?'

She shook her head. 'We're not in touch.'

'Siblings?'

Lili avoided his eye. 'Two brothers, but again we're not close.'

'You mentioned a wealthy background, yet you're working as a housekeeper. Didn't you receive any inheritance?'

Lili shook her head. 'No, I didn't want anything from them.'

Corti made a sound. 'It must have been bad. What happened?'

The last thing she wanted was to reveal how two sets of parents hadn't deemed her lovable enough. She looked at him reluctantly. 'The truth is that they valued my brothers over me and my brothers valued taking their place in the family business over a relationship with me. They had no use for me so I decided to cut ties as soon as I was old enough.'

'So it's just you now?'

Lili nodded and tried not to let that impact her like a barb. It *was* just her and had been for some time. And she was okay with that. And now, if she was lucky enough to have a child of her own…maybe she could finally start to heal that wound of abandonment and ensure that her own child never felt the lack that she had.

He said, 'I'm sorry that you've had to walk away from your family, I can't imagine it was easy.'

Afraid he thought she was looking for sympathy, she said, 'I'm not angry or resentful or sad about my experience. I'm happier now that I've cut ties. Unfortunately I didn't have a positive childhood but that's one of the reasons why I want a child, to show them the love I never received.'

'And maybe find someone who will love you back?' Corti said quietly.

Feeling prickly and exposed she said, 'Is that so bad? To want to feel loved?'

He shook his head. 'Not at all, it's something everyone should experience. I had it with my parents but then it was taken from me and I learnt not to look for it again. Loving and losing is not something I would recommend.'

'I would ensure our child knows only love and security,' Lili said fervently.

Corti was silent for a long moment. And then he said, 'Well, you've given me a lot to think about.'

He was dismissing her. Lili put her hands on the arms of her chair. 'I'll go then, leave you in peace.' She stood up. 'Goodnight, Signore Corti.'

He stood up too. 'Goodnight, Lili.'

She walked away quickly, her skin prickling all over as the full enormity of what she'd just done landed in her belly. Of course there was no way he would choose her. He would undoubtedly find some titled Italian socialite who would be only too happy to bear the Corti heir. He was probably chuckling into his wine right now at the very thought of allowing his family lineage to be tainted by a woman who had chosen menial work over an inheritance.

But at least he hadn't laughed in her face.

'Signore Corti wants to see you in his office, Lili.'

Lili looked up from where she'd been sitting in the villa's managerial office. She'd been ordering supplies online. Her insides went into free fall. She'd seen Corti at breakfast briefly but he'd been on his phone speaking in rapid French and had barely acknowledged her.

Maybe, Lili had thought to herself, her suggestion last night had been so outlandish that he wasn't even going to countenance it? But now he wanted to see her. Maybe he'd had time to reflect on the audacity of her behaviour and was going to fire her?

She went up through the villa and once outside his office she heard voices. She recognised the solicitor's voice from yesterday. *She was going to be fired.*

Before she lost her nerve, she knocked lightly on the door. The voices stopped, and Corti said, 'Come in.'

Lili pushed the door open and the solicitor stood up again to greet her, except this time he held out his hand and said, 'Buongiorno, Miss Spirenze, I'm Giorgio Macchi.'

Lili looked at his hand. She had no choice but to touch it or seem incredibly rude. She steeled herself and let their hands touch for as brief a moment as possible before pulling her hand back and putting it behind her back. Her heart was beating too fast.

She looked at Corti who was frowning slightly but then his expression cleared and he said, 'Join us, Lili, take a seat.'

She sat down in the empty chair beside the solicitor, hands in her lap. Corti was standing by the window, tall and imposing. Dressed a little more formally today in dark trousers and a tucked-in light blue shirt, top button open.

She was a little surprised to realise that the man in front of her didn't really resemble the partying playboy she'd read about in the papers. There was an air of…something like boredom about him. Jadedness.

He said, 'I've been talking to Signore Macchi about our conversation last night. I need to know if you were serious?'

Lili's throat felt dry under the gazes of the two men. It had been a long time since she'd been the center of anyone's attention. If she ever had been. Even the kidnappers hadn't really noticed her, apart from manhandling her and making crude comments.

She nodded. 'Yes, I was.'

'Well, in that case, I accept your proposal.'

Lili blinked at Corti and then repeated a little breathlessly, 'You accept…my proposal.'

There was a flicker of amusement at the corner of his mouth. 'Weren't you the one who came to me and offered yourself in marriage?'

'Yes, I guess I was.' She felt light-headed again.

The solicitor beside her cleared his throat. Lili tore her gaze from Corti to look at the man who was taking out a sheaf of papers from a briefcase. 'In that case, if you are serious about becoming Signore Corti's wife and potential mother of his child, you'll need to sign a prenuptial agreement.'

Corti said, 'The agreement is pretty straightforward, protecting Corti assets naturally, but you will receive a generous allowance and leave to live here if we are successful in having an heir. We will share custody of our child but he, or she, will reside here with you as the main carer. We will both have a say in major decisions to do with schooling etc. If there is no child, you will also receive a generous settlement and you will be free to seek a divorce and move on with your life.'

Lili looked at the solicitor and back to Corti, a little bewildered with all of that information. 'It's that easy?'

Corti shrugged. 'Pretty much. We'll need some documents from you of course, and if the prenuptial agreement is to your satisfaction then we'll proceed with the marriage. It'll take place here in a month's time.'

'A month!' Lili squeaked.

'There's no need to delay is there? I'm not due to race again until Monte Carlo in a couple of months, and that should give you enough time to interview a new housekeeper.'

Lili felt like a parrot. 'A new housekeeper. Why would we need a new housekeeper? I thought the whole point was that I could stay here?'

'You can, but you'll be my wife, so you'll be the chatelaine of the villa, not an employee.'

She said falteringly, 'I...yes of course, it wouldn't be appropriate.' She hadn't even thought that far ahead but now it seemed to be hurtling towards her with the speed of a train.

The solicitor stood up and said, 'I'll leave the agreement here for you, Miss Spirenze. When you've looked it over you can let me know and I'll come back to witness your signature. Here's my card so you can contact me.' He held out a card and Lili plucked it from his fingers, careful not to touch him again.

He left the room. Now it was just her and Cassian Corti. He came to the other side of the desk and sat down in a louche sprawl. Now he did more resemble the playboy figure.

He said, 'If you're having second thoughts, Lili, I'd prefer if you could let me know now before we invest any more time in this.'

Lili shook her head faintly. She knew this was an outrageous thing that she was offering to do but after this last year in the villa she knew that this was where she wanted to be. And if she had a child too, she would have all she could possibly need. Security, love and peace.

She looked at her boss. 'Are *you* sure?'

A hard expression flitted over his face. 'You heard the conversation yesterday. This is what I have to do if I want to keep the villa in the Corti name and family. As much as I have ambivalent feelings towards it, I don't want to be the one who is responsible for letting it go.'

Lili knew the value of the properties in Lake Como. Clearly he didn't need the money from a sale.

She forced her mind to think, to ask some pertinent questions. 'But what if you change your mind? What if you want to marry someone else?'

'That won't be an issue because I never had any intention of marrying, or having a family.'

'But haven't you always known about this rule?'

He looked a little sheepish. 'Yes, but I have to admit that when the time came I thought I'd be able to let this villa go.'

'But you can't.'

His expression shuttered again. 'If I have the option to keep it then I will try.'

Lili stood up now, feeling too agitated to stay sitting. She put herself behind the chair, hands on the back of it. 'But if I can't have a child then you'll lose it all.'

Corti shrugged. 'Then I'll have done my best. I'll let it go and become even wealthier. You'll be well compensated for your time.'

'But you'll lose this connection to your family.'

His eyes flashed dark silver for a moment, as if she'd pressed on a nerve. He said, 'I lost that connection the day they all died.'

Lili cursed herself. 'Of course you did, I'm sorry, I didn't mean to suggest—'

He held up a hand. 'I know you didn't.' He dropped his hand. 'The truth is that it's my own fault that there's only a year left to secure the villa in my name.'

'Maybe you hoped you'd find someone who would change your views on marriage?' Lili suggested.

He barked an unamused sounding laugh. 'A cute but naive idea. No. Not in a million years. I knew what would be involved in keeping the villa and I hadn't relished the prospect of finding the elusive woman who would agree to a marriage in name only. *And*, agree to have a child.'

He continued, 'But then I returned here yesterday and met you and now I have the very real prospect of keeping the villa in the Corti name. An unexpected, but welcome, development. You couldn't be more perfect for what I need right now.'

And potentially, forever. Lili swallowed. 'If this does work out, what would your day-to-day involvement be?'

'Minimal. I have a busy life and work schedule. I'd check

in with you, naturally, and the child, but I'd be happy for you to be his main carer.'

'It could be a girl,' Lili pointed out, feeling a need to press against that nerve again. He sounded so…sanguine. As if they were not discussing an actual potential human being.

'Whatever the sex of the child, it will want for nothing.'

Except a father, Lili felt like pointing out. 'You really meant it when you said you didn't want to have children, a family.'

'Yes. I had a family and I lost them. A child is integral to keeping the villa but I will not be involved. I will be more like a benevolent guardian protecting his, or her, inheritance until they come of age.'

Lili really couldn't argue with that. She was willing to agree to an arrangement where she was going to be a sole parent. And he had explained his reasons which were pretty compelling. To suffer a trauma like he did, it would put anyone off risking that kind of loss again.

They were both guilty of fulfilling their own needs. But Lili knew she could love a child enough for two parents. It *would* want for nothing. She'd make sure of it.

'Okay,' she said.

'Okay?' Corti lifted a brow.

Lili nodded. 'I'll read over the agreement but I'm sure it'll be fine, Signore Corti.'

'I think that you can call me Cassian. After all, you know all my secrets now.'

Lili gulped. That felt very intimate, which was ridiculous after what they'd just been discussing. She responded, 'I…okay.'

Then she reiterated, 'I really don't want anything more than a place to live and a child of my own.'

'What was it you said last night? Peace and security?'

Lili nodded, feeling slightly defensive. No doubt he must think her very unambitious or parochial. 'You have your wishes and desires and I have mine.'

As Lili's words sank in, Cassian had to admit to a sensation of hollowness inside him. *Did* he have wishes and desires? Professionally, he was still passionate about racing but he couldn't deny that the relentless pace and schedule was becoming wearying. He was realising that he wanted to spend more time improving the sustainability of the motor racing industry.

And, the board of the Corti Group had been making increasingly frequent noises about needing his more consistent involvement.

But outside of that not much had caused him to desire much or wish for anything. He had everything. He could literally afford *anything* he wanted.

Nothing was unobtainable. Not even a convenient wife who was prepared to have his child so he could hold onto his inheritance. Without even making love. Which wouldn't be a problem if the potential wife in question hadn't sparked this current of awareness ever since he'd seen her stepping out of the pool.

It confounded him that he found her attractive when she was wearing another shapeless ensemble today. Dress, or skirt, he wasn't sure which it was, falling almost to the ground. Sneakers. A loose cardigan. Long hair. Unstyled.

But now he knew what was underneath. A voluptuous and full-bodied woman. Why was she hiding herself like this? Under clothes and in the confines of a vast villa?

He wanted her. But did she want him? His instinct said *yes*. She was skittish around him. Colour stained her cheeks and she looked at him as if she'd never seen a man before.

Fascinated and also something else he couldn't quite put his finger on.

He'd had dreams all night about peeling the white one-piece off her body and baring her to his gaze, dreaming of her breasts and nipples. Dreaming of spanning her waist with his hands and positioning her between his legs so that he could explore her breasts and taste her.

The awareness that had been humming in his blood since she'd entered the room, threatened to ignite fully. He did have a desire. He desired this woman. He clenched his jaw in a bid to control it, not welcoming this completely unexpected development.

He had the sense that Lili was the one woman who he might not be able to have but he wasn't even going to test that theory. There was too much at stake here. And if they could work this agreement the way she seemed to be happy to, it couldn't be better for both of them. He'd done business deals with more emotion involved than this.

He said, 'Take the agreement and have a look at it, if you want to engage your own solicitor that's fine.'

Lili picked up the sheaf of papers and held it to her chest. Cassian noticed the line of her jaw. He sensed a steeliness about her then and had to admire her for her balls in suggesting this audacious plan.

She said, 'I'm sure that won't be necessary but I'll let you know if there's anything I'm not happy with.'

'I'm leaving this evening, I have to go to a motor race meeting in Miami.'

'But you're not racing?'

He shook his head. 'No, as I said, not until Monte Carlo. I'll be in Miami in my role as shareholder of the governing body and to have some meetings about new sustainability measures.'

'I'll get in touch with you...via your assistant as usual?'

Cassian pulled out a piece of paper and scrawled a number. 'This is my private cell phone, use this if you need me.'

He handed it over the desk and saw how Lili looked at his hand for a moment before taking the very tip of the edge of the paper and snatching it out of his fingers. She'd looked at his hand like that yesterday and he'd noticed that she'd been slightly funny about shaking the solicitor's hand too.

He pushed it aside. He was imagining things. Lili was perfect. He'd hardly ever see her once they were married, especially if they used IVF to have a baby.

Lili was at the door now but she stopped and turned back to face him, not quite looking him in the eye. 'Um, obviously you're going to continue to live your life...in all aspects... I would just ask that if we marry you'd be discreet?'

It took Cassian a moment to realise what she was saying and then he welcomed the interruption to thinking about the reality of a child.

But he was surprised to find that the first thing he felt was not relief that his prospective wife was giving him free rein to keep taking lovers. Lovers who had singularly failed to ignite much more than a spark lately. Yet she was igniting a spark. More than a spark.

He assured himself this attraction was an anomaly. An aberration. He said smoothly, 'Of course, and I would ask the same of you.'

But the thought of *her* taking a lover, of some other man peeling that swimsuit from her body...gazing at her luscious curves instantly sent something dark and heavy into his gut.

Her eyes met his and they were very blue. There was almost a kind of a wry smile on her mouth and Cassian suddenly wanted to know what she would look like if she smiled properly. She said, 'That really won't be an issue.'

And she'd slipped out of the door before he could ask her to elaborate on that enigmatic response or wonder why the hell he wanted to see her smile.
Two weeks later

'Signore Conti?' said the voice into Cassian's ear. He felt a frisson of awareness go straight to his groin. So much for this desire being an anomaly or an aberration.

Cassian responded, 'Didn't we already have this conversation? It's Cassian.'

There was a pause, and then, 'Okay... Cassian.'

The frisson of awareness got even stronger to hear Lili say his name in that low voice. Man, he was losing it. He looked out of his office window in Rome. From here he could see the Colosseum and it never failed to give him a sense of satisfaction but today he barely noticed it.

'What can I do for you, Lili?'

'Is it really necessary for a stylist to come and fit me for a new wardrobe and a wedding dress? I can go into the boutique in the village and get a dress. I'll try not to embarrass you if that's what you're concerned about, I know my sense of style is a little, um...outdated.'

Cassian could agree with that when pictured the long flowing garments she wore and could well imagine her choosing the same but slightly different in cream or white for the wedding. He wanted to see her body revealed, like he had that night when she'd been swimming. That white swimsuit that had become an almost talismanic image, invading his thoughts at the most inappropriate moments.

'A photographer will be there for the wedding and the pictures will be sent out globally.'

'Oh.'

'And, as you will no longer be the housekeeper, I thought

it could be an opportunity to wear clothes a little more befitting the mistress of the property.'

'But no one will be seeing me except the staff.'

Cassian shook his head mentally. No woman he knew would be turning down a chance to spend his money on clothes.

'Your duties will be different now.'

Lili sighed audibly. 'I guess so.'

Cassian found himself biting back a smile. She really would prefer to remain the housekeeper. 'Have you picked the new housekeeper yet?'

'Yes, a local woman called Eloisa. She seems to be working out well.'

'Good.'

Cassian's assistant appeared in his office and he said with more reluctance than he would have expected, 'I have to go.'

'Okay, goodbye Signore Cor—' she stopped herself and amended, 'Cassian.'

'Goodbye, Lili.'

Cassian cut the connection. It was strange, because he barely knew Lili really, but in the two weeks since she'd agreed to marry him and they'd had a couple of phone conversations like this, he'd found himself thinking about her and wondering what she was doing.

Even more disconcerting, he'd found himself feeling a sense of anticipation at seeing her again. Surely she wouldn't have the same effect on him?

'Signore Corti?'

Cassian frowned and looked at his assistant. He'd not even noticed the man waiting to talk to him. Feeling prickly now he said, 'Yes?'

'It's Allesandra Amante on the phone. She wants to know if you'd like to go to dinner this evening?'

Cassian felt an immediately negative response to that idea even though she was someone with whom he'd enjoyed a no-strings arrangement over the years. 'Tell her I'm busy.'

'Very well, sir.'

Cassian turned back to the view. Even he knew it would be in bad taste to have announced an engagement and then be seen out with a woman, even though he could ensure it was done discreetly. But he had no desire for any woman. *Except for your frumpy housekeeper.* He scowled.

No. That had been an anomaly. Once they were married and they'd embarked on their IVF journey and she was ensconced in the villa securing his inheritance, life would go back to the usual routine.

But instead of a sense of relief at that assertion, all Cassian could see in his mind's eye was an image of the Villa Corti, a place he'd spent years avoiding as much as possible, rising up out of the lake, and that provocative image of his housekeeper—*fiancée*—emerging from the pool under the moonlight, every dip and hollow and curve of her body burnt onto his brain like a brand.

Damn.

Two weeks later

The wedding day had dawned bright and serene. Cassian—Lili still had trouble thinking of him as *Cassian*—had arrived yesterday but after a brief conversation, he'd been in his study most of the time working.

Lili had since, reluctantly, moved herself into a guest suite near Cassian's bedroom. She knew it was appropriate to do but it still felt as if she was transgressing.

It was now nearing midmorning, and time for the service in the chapel on the villa's grounds. The stylist Cassian had organised, a woman called Carlotta, was fussing around Lili smoothing the dress. Lili was putting up with the attention, gritting her jaw as the woman's hands fluttered around her.

Because of the wedding she'd had to endure being touched but to her relief, it hadn't been too stressful.

Lili had chosen the most covered up dress, much to the stylist's obvious dismay. She'd said, 'You have a beautiful figure, Signora Spirenze, you mustn't be afraid to show it off.'

Lili had still chosen the dress that covered her from neck to toe and shoulder to arm—and crucially, a dress that she could remove easily without having to ask for help. She liked it, even though the lace did cling to her figure in a way that she wasn't entirely comfortable with.

The stylist had arranged for someone to trim Lili's hair and while it was still comfortably long, the weight had been taken out of it and layers added, making it feel much lighter and move in a flattering way around her face and shoulders.

To her surprise, a few days ago the solicitor had arrived with a velvet covered box saying, 'These are family jewels from the vault. Signore Corti said to choose an engagement ring and jewelry for the wedding.'

Feeling like a total fraud, Lili had gasped when the box was opened, showcasing a glittering display of what had to be priceless antique jewels. She'd chosen the plainest ring she could see—with a gold band—three white diamonds in a row in a slightly raised setting. Yet even that seemed too ostentatious to her.

The ring felt heavy on her finger now. The solicitor had had it resized for the wedding and it fit snugly. She'd chosen a simple pair of pearl drop earrings.

She wasn't wearing a veil. Maria, who Carlotta had tasked to help with preparations, had pulled Lili's hair back into a loose chignon, securing it with a homemade garland of flowers from the garden. She'd also done her make-up, thankfully nothing too clownish. Lili had blinked at herself in the mirror—she looked…pretty. Her eyes seemed huge and very blue, and had her mouth always had that pouty look? Her cheeks glowed as if she'd just taken a brisk walk outside.

There was a knock on the bedroom door and Eloisa, the new housekeeper, put her head around the door. 'They're ready.'

Butterflies erupted in Lili's gut. More than butterflies. Was this really happening? Had she really been so bold as to suggest her boss marry her so he could keep his ancestral estate?

Feeling slightly as if she was in a dream, she was led out of the villa and down the steps where Matteo the gardener was waiting with a golf buggy used normally for getting around the estate. Maria appeared and handed Lili a simple bouquet of flowers from the garden, matching the flowers in her hair.

She clutched it gratefully.

Matteo was wearing a suit, as was his son, Tommy, and the buggy had been adorned with bunting and flowers. Lili felt ridiculously emotional. These people had become almost like family to her in the last year.

She got into the buggy with the help of Carlotta, making sure her dress was safely tucked in and then in that buggy and another behind, they made their way to the chapel in a secluded corner of the estate. Lili had always liked to come here—not out of any particular religious sentiment—but because it was peaceful and a place to savour a feeling of safety.

Ironic now that it was going to be the location of possibly the scariest thing she'd ever done in her life.

Her little entourage went into the small chapel and then Lili took a deep breath and walked out of the sunlight and into the cool interior.

CHAPTER FOUR

Cassian heard the sounds at the back of the small chapel. People arriving. He looked around to see his staff entering and taking seats. There were a few witnesses up at the front. His solicitor and his executive assistant.

And then, the sunlight coming into the chapel was momentarily eclipsed when Lili walked through the door.

For a second, Cassian felt as if someone invisible had just punched him in the stomach. He couldn't breathe. She was encased from head to toe in white lace. He'd never seen someone so covered up, and yet every delectable curve was lovingly outlined by the dress and it was more provocative than if she'd turned up wearing that one-piece swimsuit.

It immediately made him think of uncovering her.

She seemed to hesitate at the top of the aisle for a moment and then she started to walk down it, on her own, chin tilted up. Something about that caught at Cassian, making him feel a tug of...pride? He almost had an urge to go and meet her halfway but she was already there, beside him.

She looked at him and her eyes were very big, cheeks a little pink. Mouth looking even plumper than usual and slightly glossy. The expression on her face was somewhere between wary and serious. Something he really wasn't used to. It unsettled him a little because he'd got so used to dealing with women trying to charm their way into his life. And bed.

She's marrying you, reminded a little voice. Charm isn't required here, on either side. And yet, as Cassian tore his gaze from Lili to look at the priest, he found that he almost regretted that fact.

After speaking words she couldn't recall, Lili and Cassian emerged back into the sunshine. Her cheek burned where he'd placed his mouth in a dry kiss. When they'd faced each other at the altar, Cassian had bent his head towards her and she'd been struck with vying desires—to pull back and to reach up and press her mouth to his. Terrifying.

In the end she'd offered her cheek and had pulled away quickly. And by holding on to her bouquet with a death grip she'd managed to avoid touching hands.

She reassured herself now that no one would have expected a sham of a kiss. She wasn't even sure why he'd looked as if he was going to kiss her. But the fact that she'd even wanted to know what it might feel like…still made her feel a little wobbly and very exposed.

He drove the buggy back to the villa, the guests following behind. Lili still clutched the bouquet. When he came to a stop outside the main entrance he jumped out and Lili managed to absorb fully what he was wearing for the first time. It had been so overwhelming stepping into the small ornate chapel and facing the reality of setting this whole thing in motion that she'd focused mainly on his face.

She could see now that he was wearing a three-piece suit in steel-grey with a white shirt and grey waistcoat. A slim matching tie. A cream flower attached to a buttonhole matching the flowers in her bouquet. A whimsical touch that impacted her somewhere vulnerable.

Why go to that trouble?

The official pictures. It occurred to her just as he held out his hand to help her out of the buggy and said, 'The photographer is waiting to take our photos.'

Lili ignored his hand, saying, 'I can manage, thanks,' and used a handhold to help herself out of the buggy.

She didn't look at him for fear of seeing something on his face. They walked around to the side of the villa where a photographer was waiting with an assistant and a young woman in a suit who introduced herself to Lili as Cassian's PR manager. She was blonde and efficient.

They stood close together and were directed to look this way and that and then Silvia, the PR manager said, 'These are all great, but can we get one with you holding hands now?'

Lili tensed. Her skin was hot all over to be standing so close to Cassian and it wasn't entirely from the discomfort of his proximity. How could she say no, though?

She moved the bouquet from her two-handed grip to her right hand and Cassian took her left hand in his. Immediately Lili wanted to pull away but she forced herself to let him hold it, letting the fact that it felt cool distract her.

Cool, and large, fingers wrapping around hers.

'Now, can you look at each other please?'

Lili turned and looked up to find Cassian staring down at her. His beard was neatly trimmed, hugging his jaw. His lower lip looked hard, but soft.

'That's lovely, thank you, now can we get a kiss?'

Cassian must have seen something on Lili's face because he said, 'I think that's enough for now, Silvia. We'll use one of these ones.'

'*Bene*, okay guys, you can wrap it up.'

Cassian moved so that he was in front of Lili blocking the PR team. He was still holding her hand and she could feel her pulse thundering from a mix of fear and excitement.

He held up their hands and said, 'You don't like this, do you?'

Her mouth went dry. She shook her head jerkily, 'I...not really, no. I'm not very tactile.'

His grey gaze was narrowed on her face, his eyes even more silvery because of his suit. 'Is it just me? Because I could have sworn that you can feel it too.'

'Feel what?'

Cassian's thumb moved so that it sat over her pulse point at her wrist. He said, *'That.'*

Lili swallowed. He wasn't wrong, but he had no idea it was also fear. Not of him, but fear from the past from the sense of being powerless and at the mercy of threatening men.

She pulled her hand away and put it behind her back. 'I don't know what you're talking about.'

There was the sound of a throat clearing nearby and Lili saw Eloisa. She said, 'The wedding lunch is ready.'

'Grazie, Eloisa,' Cassian said.

Before they went inside Lili asked, 'The photos, where will they appear?'

'Some of the papers, and the magazines will likely pick them up too.'

Lili bit her lip. She hadn't really considered that. She imagined her family seeing the photos but reassured herself that they would probably refuse to acknowledge it was actually her. But it was ironic because she'd now married into exactly the level of society that her father had always sought validation and acceptance from. The fact that Lili had done something he'd never managed felt like a very hollow victory. She'd never wanted to better her parents, she'd just wanted their love.

Cassian stood aside to let Lili precede him into the villa

but she could feel his eyes boring into her back the whole way as if he was privy to her thoughts. She really hoped he wasn't. She hadn't deceived him—she *was* legally Lili Spirenze but that was the name she'd taken in a bid to distance herself from her family. She reassured herself now, there was no way that the world of Antonio Bagiotti would intersect with Cassian Corti. He moved in circles far removed from her parents.

The wedding lunch was being held in one of the formal dining rooms. Parquet flooring and frescoes on the walls and ceilings with gold trim made it one of the more opulent rooms.

The windows were open to let the breeze through and Cassian and Lili sat at the top of the table with their dozen or so guests—well, Cassian's guests—on either side of the table.

At one point Lili said *sotto voce* to Cassian, 'You didn't need to go to all of this trouble, it's not as if anyone here thinks this is a real wedding.'

'It's as real as any other wedding. We're just not deluding ourselves that it's built on anything more than practicality and good judgement. If more weddings were like this then the world might be a better place.'

Lili looked at him. 'Your parents were happy though, no?'

He blinked and Lili noticed that he had very long lashes. They didn't prettify his face though, the lines were too stark and hard for that.

'Yes, they were. Very much so.'

Lili turned to face him more. 'Well then, how can you say what you just did?'

He looked at her and she sucked in a breath at the flat look in his eyes. 'Because ultimately it didn't save them and having witnessed that love only to lose it forever was the cruellest blow. I would never want to put a child through that again.'

Lili bit her lip. 'I'm sorry.' Maybe he was right. In some ways it had been easy to break with her family because there was no love lost. She had no memory of what that must feel like. She only knew that she'd know it when she had a child of her own.

He shrugged. 'There's nothing to be sorry for. What we're doing is perfect. We will be giving our child a solid foundation of security and respect. They won't grow up believing in a myth only to have it torn from them.'

Someone on Cassian's right-hand side spoke to him then and she absorbed that. But what had seemed like such a brilliant idea two weeks ago suddenly felt a little…flawed. She could promise to love their child enough for two parents but how would they fare once they knew that their father intended to keep them at arm's length?

Was she going to inevitably end up doing to her own child what had been done to her, with an indifferent parent?

Although…as she studied Cassian's profile now—he didn't seem like the type to be indifferent. And she could understand his reasons for wanting to be. But maybe even he was underestimating the effect of actually having a child. Lili couldn't get an incendiary image out of her head, of Cassian with a small child with dark hair out in the gardens of the villa, running around and playing…throwing the child high in the air, making them squeal with joy…

She shook her head at herself. That was precisely the problem. He'd known that joy here already and he wasn't prepared to risk it again for fear of losing it. It would be *her* in that fantasy, not her husband, and she would have to come to terms with that because it was her reality now.

The following morning Lili found Cassian already dressed and sitting at the breakfast table, reading a newspaper. He was wearing a navy polo shirt and she couldn't see under the table but she didn't have to to imagine he would look good in whatever he was wearing. Tall and vital. Lean.

He looked up and then down, and her cheeks got warm with self-consciousness. She had skipped over the new clothes in the dressing room this morning, weakly pulling out a familiar loose dress and cardigan. As if it was some kind of armour against the massive changes *she'd* instigated.

She couldn't help wondering though, if theirs had been a traditional wedding and she didn't have her issues, would they still be in bed right now?

In spite of choosing a wedding dress that would be easy to remove on her own, Lili had found herself contorting into ridiculous shapes to get out of it and all night she'd had lurid dreams of Cassian peeling it slowly from her body, uncovering her skin inch by inch and dropping his mouth to kiss her exposed flesh. She'd woken hot and sweaty and frustrated and angry, because in her dreams she wasn't held captive by her fears.

Not helpful Lili, when her newly minted husband was now standing and pulling out a chair. 'Come in, have breakfast.'

She walked over to the table and slid into the chair. Cassian sat back down. He asked politely, 'Good night's sleep?'

Her cheeks felt even hotter. Could he read her mind?

She blurted out, 'I'm sorry I disappeared yesterday evening. I didn't mean to, but I got to the bedroom and I felt hot and sticky so I had a shower and then I laid down and… fell asleep.'

'It's no big deal, the guests weren't expecting you to throw the bouquet or anything.'

'I know but I should have been there to say goodbye.'

'They all know it's a business deal.'

For some reason that stung even though it shouldn't. Had

they looked at Lili and known that there was no way he'd ever choose a woman like her if he had a choice? And why was that bothering her now?

Then he said, 'That fertility specialist you saw last week in Milan?'

Lili nodded. He had arranged for her to visit the consultant in Milan so they could do a general examination and check her fertility. Cassian had undergone similar checks in Rome.

'She's going to call me in an hour to talk with us. She's got your results and mine, from my doctor in Rome. I thought this would be the most expeditious thing to do and then we can hopefully get started on the process.'

'Okay.' The doctor had told Lili last week that she didn't foresee any big issues, her menstruation cycle was regular and she'd never—thankfully—had any issues with painful periods or the like.

She'd asked Lili about sexual partners though, so she knew Lili was a virgin. Her insides twisted now, she hoped she'd be spared the humiliation of revealing that to Cassian.

Cassian took a swig of coffee and stood up. 'I have to make a couple of calls, come to my office in an hour?'

Lili nodded and sagged back into the chair when he was gone. The man made her feel about a million and one things at once. Fear—not that he would touch her or hurt her, but fear of how he made her feel when no one had managed to crack the impenetrable wall she'd put around herself for years.

And excitement which didn't make sense. Excitement for what? Once they'd decided how best to proceed with the IVF, he'd be gone back to his life and Lili would be left here in peace. *With nothing to do.* Which was exactly what she'd wanted, wasn't it? So why was the life that she'd so audaciously asked for suddenly looking a little...empty?!

***

'Come in.'

Lili pushed open the office door and tried to embody more of a sense of being entitled but it felt very alien to her. Cassian was behind the desk, hair messy as if he'd been running his hands through it.

He looked up. 'Come in, sit down, Dr Lombardo is going to call any—' he broke off when his phone rang as if on cue. He put his cell phone on speaker and answered, telling the doctor that he was with his wife. That sent an illicit thrill through Lili.

Lili sat down and leaned towards the desk, greeting the doctor. After some pleasantries had been exchanged, the doctor—a no-nonsense warm woman that Lili had liked—said, 'I have both of your results here and everything is showing me a healthy, fertile couple. Lili, your tests and the timing of your last period show that you should be ovulating around now, or very soon.'

Lili blushed at that intimate information. She did a quick mental calculation and figured the doctor would be correct. 'Okay,' she said, avoiding Cassian's eye.

The doctor went on. 'I know you want to go the IVF route and it's not my business to ask why, but I can't emphasise enough how much more beneficial it would be to try and conceive naturally. Not to mention infinitely cheaper. All of the signs are there to indicate that you have every chance of being successful and if it doesn't happen then of course we can talk again.'

She continued after a moment, 'You're welcome to go to another fertility specialist if you don't like to hear what I am saying, but when I have two young people come to me in perfect health and with no signs of having difficulty, I cannot in all conscience advise IVF. It can be an arduous process and time consuming. There is no guarantee of success even with all of your healthy indicators.'

She went on. 'So what I am advising is that you talk about it for at least twenty-four hours, and then if you want to proceed with my clinic we can of course help you. But I have to let you know that right now, is an optimum time to conceive naturally.'

Lili reluctantly looked at Cassian. His eyes were dark grey. Unreadable. A strange twisting sensation was making her belly tight. And her skin prickle. He said, 'Thank you, Doctor, for your time, we appreciate your advice and we'll be in touch.' He terminated the call.

Lili couldn't sit still. Something was fluttering inside her, and she wasn't sure if it was panic or that excitement. But it couldn't be excitement because there was no way—she stood up from the chair and went over to the window, arms tight around herself.

'Lili?'

She bit her lip and turned around. Cassian was leaning forward in his chair, hands loosely clasped between his legs.

He said carefully, 'We don't have to do as she is suggesting. We can continue with the plan.'

Guilt and shame knotted inside Lili's chest. This was on *her*. 'You heard what she said. It would obviously be better if we could do this...naturally.'

'But that's clearly a problem...you're as white as a ghost.' He stood up and came over to her but Lili instinctively backed away. He held up his hands. 'I'm not going to touch you. But you look as if you're about to faint, please, sit down.'

Lili went back over and sat down. She could feel her breath becoming shallower and forced herself to take deeper breaths. Cassian went over to a cabinet and poured a dark golden drink into a glass. He brought it over to her. 'Whiskey, take a little, you'll feel better.'

Lili took the glass and watched as he went back to the cabinet and poured himself a drink. He lifted his glass towards her and said, 'Saluti.'

She faintly echoed his cheers and took a sip, wincing as the liquid burnt its way down her throat and into her chest. But he was right, it sent out a warm, comforting glow, immediately making her feel less on edge.

Now he went over to the window and looked at her. He said, 'Can I ask you a direct question?'

Lili swallowed another gulp of whiskey and then nodded. 'Okay.'

'Do you find me attractive?'

Lili nearly choked even though she'd swallowed the drink. She felt like laughing and almost put a hand to her mouth to stop a slightly hysterical giggle coming out. When she felt she could speak she said, 'You must know how attractive you are.'

His mouth quirked. 'Flattering but not what I asked. I asked if *you* were attracted to me.'

Now Lili wanted to scowl. Instead she thought of the best way of defusing this line of conversation. She asked, 'Are you attracted to me?' Because of course he was going to say—

'Yes, I am.'

Lili nearly dropped the glass from between her fingers and had to grip it. She stared at Cassian. 'Did you just say…?'

'That I find you attractive? Yes I did. Distractingly so. Ever since we met, I think, but more so since I saw you emerge from the pool that night. For some reason you are hiding the body of a bombshell under those shapeless clothes and the more I see them the more I want to put them on a bonfire.'

Now Lili felt agitated. She stood up and went behind the chair as if that could afford some kind of protection from what he was saying. A suspicion occurred to her. 'You're just saying that because you agree with the doctor and want to convince me that conceiving naturally will be quicker and easier.'

'Believe me, if I didn't want you, I would not sleep with you.'

Of course not. Because he probably had a mistress waiting for him in Milan. Or Rome. Or Paris. Lili shook her head. 'Why are you saying this?'

'Because I think the doctor is right, we're both healthy and there shouldn't be any reason why we can't conceive naturally and there's no reason why we shouldn't try to when we both want each other.'

Lili's mouth opened. She shut it again. Opened it. 'How do you know I want you?'

Of course he does, jeered a voice, *he's vastly more experienced and every emotion you feel is written all over your face.* She cringed. Was she that obvious?

'I wouldn't be so arrogant as to assume that you do, but I can feel it between us, like an electric current. And the way you look at me, as if you're terrified I'll eat you up but you're equally terrified I won't. Your pulse races if I come near you. It was racing when I put my finger on it after the wedding.'

Lili's legs felt weak, she could remember how it had felt, his finger against her skin. A pulse throbbed between her legs and she clamped her thighs together. She did not want to think of how it might feel if he were to touch her there.

'I'm not saying I don't find you attractive, but—' Lili

faltered. How could she explain that they could never have normal relations?

'But what?'

They were married now and it might not be a conventional marriage but he deserved to know some of why she couldn't do this because the longer she prevaricated, the longer before they started the IVF and the doctor was right, it would take time and might not even work the first couple of rounds.

'I have a problem.'

Cassian frowned. 'What kind of problem.'

'I don't like to be touched.' That sounded a bit meager. Lili clarified. 'Well, what I mean is that I'm sort of phobic about it.'

Cassian looked at Lili, tense behind the chair. Face pale. Long hair falling around her shoulders, not as heavy as it had been. Silky. And as if things were slotting into place in his mind he recalled how she'd avoided shaking his hand that first morning. How she tensed if he came near. How she'd looked when she'd had no choice but to shake his solicitor's hand or appear unconscionably rude. How she'd avoided kissing him on the mouth, presenting him with her cheek, in the chapel.

The shapeless clothes. Something occurred to him. 'Did something happen to you?'

He saw her throat work. 'Yes...you could say that.'

Cassian tensed inwardly. 'Were you attacked?'

She went even paler. 'I don't really want to talk about it.'

Cassian almost couldn't frame the question because it was so horrific but he had to know. 'Were you...abused? Did someone—'

She shook her head, eyes huge. 'No...that didn't happen.

But I went through something when I was sixteen and ever since then I've had this...fear. I've avoided being touched since then.'

To Cassian's surprise, on hearing that he felt something almost protective rise up and an urge to fold her into his arms. She cut a lonely figure. As she had walking down the aisle. He pushed it down. No one got to him like that.

'How does it manifest exactly?'

Lili took a breath. She'd never had to articulate it before, it had been her shameful secret. 'I don't like being crowded, or being too close to people. I don't like shaking hands if I can help it. I don't like the idea of anyone's hands on me in any capacity.'

He put his glass down on the table and ran a hand through his hair. 'Okay.'

'Okay?'

He looked at her. 'Do you think this is insurmountable?'

She bit her lip. He noticed she did that and it was fast becoming a little quirk that had the ability to send sizzling heat into his blood.

'I'm not sure...it feels that way. The thought of...being intimate like that automatically makes me feel panicky. Claustrophobic.'

Cassian had never thought about it like that before but now he recognised that whenever he'd finished making love with a woman he always had the urge to get away as soon as possible for fear they'd want to cling to him. That had obviously only added to his love 'em and leave 'em playboy reputation. But he really hadn't done it to be cruel.

Another thing was happening to him as he absorbed what Lili had just told him—the fact that knowing he couldn't touch her was making him even hotter for her. He should be ashamed of himself. She'd shared this obviously very traumatic thing with him and all he could think about now was how much more he wanted to touch her because she'd told him he couldn't.

He looked at his watch and said reluctantly, 'I have a meeting at the Monza racetrack. I said I'd test drive a new car.' An idea ocurred to him. They needed to get out of this villa. It was as if he could feel the walls and gardens encroaching on him, never mind on Lili who hadn't strayed further than Como by all accounts.

'Why don't you come with me?'

She blinked at him. 'Go with you to the racetrack?'

He nodded. 'Why not? Have you ever been before?'

'No.'

'Well then, what else have you got going on?'

'Nothing, I guess. But...don't we need to talk about this?'

'I'm not sure if talking about it right now is going to make all that much difference and I need to be there by a certain time. We can continue the conversation later?'

'I...okay.'

He looked her up and down. 'Can you change into something a little less...flowy? Maybe jeans? And a jacket?'

Cassian almost smiled. She looked as if she desperately wanted to say no but she knew she couldn't. Eventually she seemed to huff out a breath and said, 'I don't really have a choice, do I?'

'It'll be fun, I promise.'

CHAPTER FIVE

WITHIN HALF AN HOUR, Lili had changed into a pair of jeans and a blue shirt, under a light jacket. She'd pulled her hair back into a low ponytail. She was ensconced in the passenger seat of a low-slung silver bullet of a car, going at a fearsome speed around the circuitous bends of the roads bordering the southern end of Lake Como. It was terrifying but it was also thrilling.

'Okay?'

She glanced at Cassian and nodded. 'Fine.'

'If I'm going too fast just tell me.'

She shook her head and looked back to the road. He *was* going fast but he wasn't driving carelessly. She felt safe. He was wearing jeans like her and a long-sleeved top, under a worn leather bomber jacket. He looked sexy and powerful. Her eyes kept going to the way he moved so fluidly, powerful thighs under denim moving as he used the brake and clutch. And his hand on the gear stick. Long fingers. A masculine hand. Not soft. She wondered what it would feel like on her skin and quickly turned her eyes back to the road. She wouldn't know because the thought of allowing that to happen…brought with it such a sense of overwhelm that she had to breathe deeply.

In a bid to distract herself she asked, 'It's okay for you to drive? With your injury?'

Cassian lifted his right hand from the wheel and flexed it, drawing Lili's attention again to long fingers, blunt nails and very masculine hands. *Damn.* Bad subject to bring up.

'It's fine for what I'm doing today, but with health and safety in the main motor racing industry they won't permit me to drive again until the requisite time is up. It's no big deal, I'm quite enjoying the time off.' He slid her a glance and Lili felt herself blushing. He'd certainly made the most of his time, acquiring a wife.

Before too long they turned off the main road into the town of Monza. Cassian said to her, 'You've heard of Monza?'

Lili nodded. 'One of my brothers was obsessed with motor racing when he was younger. He would hog the TV for the entire weekend that a race was on.'

She looked at Cassian's profile. 'I have to admit it didn't really interest me all that much, sorry.'

He put a hand to his chest as if wounded and glanced at her. 'You mean to tell me you're not one of my biggest fans?'

Lili's heart thumped unevenly. This man was surprising her on lots of levels and she was very much afraid that it would be all too easy to become a fan. More than a fan. He'd taken what she'd said earlier with equanimity. He hadn't run screaming from the room at her embarrassing phobia. He'd just suggested taking this day trip.

They were driving through gates now, being waved through by a beaming security guard. 'Ciao, Signore Corti!'

'Ciao, Enzo, va bene?'

'Bene! Grazie.'

They drove through and Lili could make out the race-track in the distance. Cassian parked outside an administrative building and got out, coming around to open her door.

It was hard to get out of the car and he put out a hand. Lili looked at it and at him. He pulled it back. 'If it's too much—'

Angry with herself for something so small being such a big deal, Lili said, 'No, thank you, I'd like a hand.' She could handle touch like this, she just didn't like to encourage it.

She put her hand into his and noted how he was careful to let her grip him. Something about that consideration caught her but she tried to hide it. She stepped out and pulled her hand back, feeling more breathless than she should be. 'Thanks.'

'Follow me.'

She did, and they went around the building to a thoroughfare that was lined with buildings either side. Cassian said, 'When the race weekend is on, this is where all the teams have their hospitality and media rooms. We're going trackside.'

Wordlessly she followed him through one of the buildings and they emerged in the huge arena. The track was there and Lili could see the stands full of seats. Empty now but she could imagine what it must be like when full. Terrifying and exhilarating all at once. And to be the focus of all of that attention? She couldn't even imagine.

Cassian was greeting an older man and hugging him. 'Ricardo, good to see you.'

'You too.'

Cassian pulled back. 'Please meet my wife. Lili.'

The man's hands were covered in some kind of oil so he didn't try to shake her hand but his smile was warm. 'So you're the mystery woman who has taken the world's hottest, richest bachelor off the market, hm?'

Lili blushed. Before she had a chance to answer Cassian was saying, 'Is the car ready?'

Ricardo nodded. 'One of the mechanics is bringing it around now. Thanks for doing this.'

'No problem.' He turned to Lili. 'I'll have to go change, you stay here with Ricardo and he'll tell you what's happening.'

Ricardo had someone bring Lili a coffee and after that she was put on a stool near a bank of very complicated-looking computers and screens and machinery. The car arrived with a loud throttle of the engine, a classic motor racing car, in red with a distinctive name and logo that even she'd heard of.

And then Cassian emerged from somewhere in the back in a close-fitting driving suit and she nearly fell off her stool. The suit was molded to his powerful body like a second skin, and she couldn't look away from him. Watching as he pulled on some sort of protective head covering and then the helmet.

He got into the tiny space of the driving seat, sunk low into the car, and within seconds he was out on the track, engine revving. Lili noticed someone with headphones and a microphone was talking to him and looking at data on a screen.

And then he was gone, starting his laps of the track. The noise was deafening and Ricardo handed her a pair of headphones. It was only when she had them on that she realised she could hear the conversation between Cassian and the engineer. Nothing she could remotely understand, about enabling DRS and other incomprehensible things.

Then Ricardo touched her arm briefly to get her attention and he led her out to walk up into a stand above where the engineers were based. Here Lili could see Cassian's car zooming around the track at what seemed to be the speed of light.

She was surprised to find it absolutely thrilling. Especially when he passed where they were and every bone in her body seemed to rattle. But then she thought of other cars being on the track at the same time and realised just how dangerous it must be.

'Okay, Cass, we have all the information we need, you can come back, thank you.'

'Copy.'

And then Cassian was returning with the car. Lili went back down and saw him contorting himself to get out, pulling off the helmet and snood, a big grin on his face. It was the first time she'd seen him smile like that and it was as if someone had punched her in the chest. It made him look younger. And even more gorgeous.

Ricardo chuckled. 'You're looking forward to Monte Carlo, eh?'

Something Lili couldn't decipher crossed over Cassian's face and his smile faded slightly. 'Of course, can't wait.'

If she didn't know better she'd almost have guessed he seemed...resigned. Not exactly as joyful as he had been just now, driving the car for no other purpose than to test it out.

Cassian caught her eye. 'I'll change and be back in a minute.'

His face was flushed after the activity and his hair was messy, and a little sweaty. Lili found herself battling the curiosity to know if this is what he'd look like after sex. She nodded jerkily. 'No rush.'

When he'd disappeared again and Lili turned away from the men to try and get herself back under control she wondered if she was thinking like this because of all the stuff the doctor had said: *Young, healthy, fertile...no reason why it can't be done naturally*...and now her brain seemed to be helping Lili to redirect itself towards the possibility that she might actually get naked with the man. Her, a woman who had shared only the most fleeting of touches with anyone else in eight years. Still a virgin, and destined to stay that way if they used IVF.

The sound of a throat clearing nearby made Lili startle. She turned around to see Ricardo. She handed him back his headphones with a smile, grateful for the interruption. 'Thank you, that was fascinating.'

'You liked?'

She nodded. 'I've never seen anything like that before. It's exhilarating.'

He made a gesture with his finger to encompass the area. 'Here, it is *life*. Everything.'

Lili could well imagine these stands full of fans. Locals. Cassian appeared then, redressed in his jeans and top, jacket slung over his shoulder. Ricardo said something to him but Lili couldn't make out what over the sound of one of the mechanics driving the car away again. When Cassian looked at her quizically. Lili said, 'What?'

Cassian asked, 'Do you drive?'

'Yes. I use the little Fiat at the villa to get around.' She liked driving. She always had. Seeing it as a way to escape her family whenever she wanted, until she was of age. And, it was how she'd escaped the kidnappers.

'There's a karting track just around the back of here, do you want a go?'

Lili blinked. Completely nonplussed to be asked such a thing. And she couldn't think of a reason to say anything else but, 'Why not?'

'Okay, come on.'

A short while later, Lili was sitting in a driving seat of a contraption like the racing car she'd seen before but this was open and it had some kind of a buffer ring on the outside, so it also kind of resembled a boat, on land even with its four big wheels.

They'd given her a driving jacket and it was a padded thing, buttoned up to her neck, close-fitting.

Cassian was leaning in, explaining how to use the accelerator and brakes. The steering wheel. It was simple. Then he put a helmet on her head. He said, 'Go as fast or slow as you like, just have some fun.'

Fun. It had been so long since Lili had had anything resembling *fun* that it caught in her throat. She nodded, glad of the helmet hiding her too-exposed emotions. It was because she was out of her comfort zone. The villa.

'Okay, let's go!' Cassian called out as he hit his accelerator and his kart shot forward. Lili did the same and her heart nearly came out of her chest when her kart moved forward. It took her a little while to get used to and she went at the pace of a snail but once she had the hang of it, she started moving faster. And faster. And faster.

Soon, she was zipping around the track at such a speed that she could feel the rush of air. It was more than exhilarating. She couldn't think of anything else but focus on what she was doing and it was incredibly liberating.

She passed Cassian on a straight and let out a whoop. She was sure he was allowing her to pass but she didn't care. A laugh bubbled up and out. Eventually she realised that they were slowing down and Cassian, ahead of her, came to a stop. She braked behind him.

He got out and pulled off his helmet and came over. She somehow levered herself out of the kart and realised she was trembling all over after the overload of adrenaline. She pulled off her helmet and realised she was grinning stupidly. But she couldn't stop.

He was smiling too. 'You're sure that was your first time karting?'

Lili nodded, still beaming, unable to speak.

'You're a natural.'

Eventually she managed to say, 'That was amazing. Thank you.'

Cassian took her helmet. 'I'm glad you enjoyed it.'

They walked back to the car after Lili had given back the driving jacket. She still felt a little wobbly all over, amazed by how good it had felt to have to focus so intently on one thing. Usually she was so scared of people and anyone noticing her quirks that she felt exhausted. That's why the villa had been such a balm. But now, she felt lighter, as if something had been sloughed away from her epidermis.

In the car, Cassian said casually, 'I thought we could have a late lunch in Como before going back to the villa?'

'Sure, that sounds nice. I've only been into Como a couple of times.'

On the way, Lili couldn't hold back her curiosity. She looked at Cassian. 'You obviously have no intention of retiring from racing any time soon, you love it.'

She noticed that his hand tensed on the wheel momentarily but then he said, 'Well, today wasn't racing.'

'I know that.'

He shrugged. 'I don't have any intention of retiring in the short term but I can't deny it's something that's been on my mind. I'm well aware I never should have been any good at being a racing driver. I'm too tall, for a start. And I've lasted a lot longer than I thought I would.'

'Why do you think you're so good?'

He looked at her. 'You know they say I have a death wish?'

'Do you?'

He made a face. 'Not a death wish so much as a...not caring wish.'

Lili felt a burst of compassion. Her family hadn't died tragically but she could sort of empathise with that feeling of being beholden to no one. 'That sounds a little like a death wish to me...'

'Maybe. I've always told myself that as soon as I lose my edge, I'll take it as a sign to go, but that hasn't happened yet.'

'You've won...six world championships?'

He nodded. They were driving into Como now, the old town. Cassian pulled into a seemingly tiny car parking space with enviable expertise. He came around to help her out again and when he held out his hand, Lili noticed that she only hesitated for a second before letting him pull her out. She let go though, as soon as she could, but she noticed that it wasn't coming from her discomfort of being touched so much as her awareness of him and how nice it felt to have his fingers wrap around hers.

They walked down a cobbled street and Cassian stopped in front of a boutique. Lili followed his eyeline to a dress in the window. Slinky and shiny. Dark green. Straps with a deep vee and a cutout over one hip and a slit over one thigh. A dress like that filled her with equal parts awe and horror.

Cassian glanced at her. 'You'd look good in that.'

Lili could feel heat rise, a mixture of desire and embarrassment. The thought of the sheer amount of skin on display...she shook her head. 'No, really I wouldn't. I'm too... big for a dress like that.'

To her relief, Cassian turned away and they continued walking, into the Piazza Duomo, a beautiful central square dominated by Como's massive and impressive Cathedral.

They stopped at a restaurant on the corner of the square with lots of green foliage protecting the clients from passersby and prying eyes. Cassian was greeted like an old friend and they were led to a table that afforded views of the outside terrace and the piazza.

'This is lovely,' Lili remarked as the waiter took her napkin and flicked it open but before he could lay it on her lap and just as she realised what he was about to do and had started tensing up, Cassian had reached for it with a smile and took it, handing it to Lili when the slightly bemused-looking waiter walked away.

Cassian had nipped something in the bud before she'd even had a chance to realise that the waiter was going to invade her space like that, by placing the napkin across her lap. Lili felt shaken. But not in a bad way. Up until this moment, she realised that she'd never ever had anyone notice her fear or watch out for her, because of it.

It felt disconcerting. She forced herself to look at Cassian. 'You must think I'm very strange.'

He took a sip of the wine that the waiter had poured. 'No, not at all. We all have our…issues. Me having an obsession with cars and becoming a racing driver after watching my family die in a tragic accident is no less strange than your fear of being touched after whatever happened to you.'

Lili felt strangely comforted. 'Maybe.'

The food arrived—local and seasonal—and Lili found that she felt pleasantly relaxed, eating and conversing with Cassian. He poured her some more wine after their main courses were taken away, saying, 'I have to drive home.'

Lili might have protested but the truth was that she was enjoying the feeling of something tight unwinding inside her.

By the time they were walking back to the car she felt deliciously relaxed. The combination of the overload of adrenaline from earlier and then the wine at lunch. She wasn't used to feeling so languorous.

It wasn't surprising then that she fell asleep in the car on the way back and only woke up when her head jerked against Cassian's shoulder as they came to a stop outside the villa.

She sat up. 'I'm so sorry, I had no idea I was that tired.'

He remarked dryly, 'It's a long time since I put a woman to sleep without even touching her, thanks for the reality check.'

Lili's face flamed as Cassian uncoiled himself gracefully from the car and came around to help her out. This time she put her hand in his without even thinking about it.

He said, 'Coffee?'

She nodded. 'Coffee would be good. I'll make it.'

He shook his head. 'You don't have to, we have Eloisa.' Who had just appeared as if summoned by a genie—exactly as Lili would have been doing if she were still housekeeper.

She smiled at the woman weakly and even though it went against the grain she said, 'Could we have some coffee, please?'

Eloisa smiled. 'Of course, Signora Corti, I'll bring it out to the terrace, it's a lovely evening.'

They went up to the terrace. The sun had set and the sky was fading from pink and oranges into dusk. Magic hour.

Eloisa appeared with coffees and some biscotti. Cassian said *grazie* and told her they wouldn't need dinner as they'd had a late lunch. He looked at her after Eloisa left. 'I'm sorry, I assumed you wouldn't be hungry too.'

Lili took a sip of coffee and welcomed the return of clarity to her brain. This had had been an entirely unexpected day from that first very frank phone call with the doctor to the racetrack and lunch...

She shook her head. 'No, it's fine, I couldn't eat again.'

'It's nice to see a woman enjoy her food.'

Lili tried to fight the blush of self-consciousness. 'As you can see I'm not someone who is shy of food.'

'You're not overweight, Lili, by any stretch. You have a perfect figure. I think a lot of people, men and women have forgotten what a body looks like.'

'Your body is…fine too.' That was the understatement of the year. Lili was glad of the fading light hiding her hot cheeks. She hid behind the coffee cup.

Cassian said, 'I'm lucky, I've always been into fitness, but it was very apparent early on that I didn't have the right physique for racing…which only made me more determined to prove people wrong.'

'Maybe you should have been a boxer.' Lili could see him, bare-chested, in silk shorts, weaving around an opponent, muscles bunching and—

His voice cut off her vivid imagination. 'That certainly could have been an option, it would have satisfied my need for danger and channelling anger.'

Lili shook her head. 'I can't imagine what it must have been like to lose everyone you loved at such a vulnerable time in your life.'

Cassian's hand stopped en route to his mouth but then it continued, as if nothing had happened. He didn't look her directly in the eye though. 'It was what it was. It's in the past now. We have more pertinent things to discuss than my tragic past.' He did look at her now. 'Specifically, our future.'

Lili's insides clenched. 'We do need to talk about this.'

Cassian put his cup down. 'I've already told you, I find you very attractive, Lili. It would be no hardship to take you to bed.'

Lili found Cassian's directness both shocking and a little thrilling. She wasn't sure if she'd entirely believed him this morning when he'd told her he found her attractive.

But her body seemed to, her insides liquefying with a kind of heat that was totally new and alien. Exciting but also a little terrifying. He was looking at her so steadily. 'You're a beautiful woman.'

The platitude sank like a heavy weight inside her. Surely he said that to every woman? But in her case she knew it wasn't true. She felt acutely self-conscious and a little disappointed that he was going to try and persuade her to consider going to bed with him. Had the whole day been a prelude to this? 'You don't have to say these things, they won't work, I won't change my mind.'

He shook his head. 'I'm not trying to change your mind, I'm stating facts. And I'm curious...why do you hide yourself?'

Now Lili wanted to squirm. 'I don't like eyes on me.' When she'd been kidnapped, she'd been blindfolded and so she'd felt the men's eyes on her and it had made her skin crawl.

Her skin didn't crawl when Cassian looked at her though. It got hot. Even if he might be trying to seduce her. The nascent suspicion that this man was doing something to heal those awful memories was a little overwhelming.

'Do you mind me looking at you?'

Could he see right into her head? Was nothing she thought private anymore? She shook her head. 'No... I don't mind.'

'You never really answered me earlier...do you find me attractive?'

CHAPTER SIX

Cassian found he was holding his breath. He'd never asked a woman before if she thought he was attractive because he usually didn't need to. But with Lili…he could feel the sexual tension between them but he wasn't certain that it wasn't all on his side.

Now she blushed and ducked her face. He could tell she was used to her hair falling around her face but it was still tied back.

'Lili?'

She looked up and there was something a little defiant in her expression. It made his pulse trip even harder.

She said, 'I thought you already established this earlier… you're an experienced man, you can tell.'

He almost felt sorry for her. 'So, you're saying, yes, you do.'

She looked like she might pop a blood vessel. He could see her veins under the delicate skin of her temple. Eventually she got out a slightly strangled-sounding, 'I mean, doesn't everyone?'

She gestured towards him. 'You have to know how gorgeous you are.'

Cassian did know he'd been blessed physically but he'd never taken it for granted. 'As flattered as I am, I don't think everyone finds me attractive and really, the only person's opinion I'm interested in right now is yours.'

'Why?'

'Indulge me. Maybe I'm insecure and need an ego boost.'

She looked at him, eyes going wide and then let out a sharp burst of laughter. She clapped a hand over her mouth almost immediately but it was too late. Cassian had seen her face transformed again, like earlier after the karting, and she was…more than beautiful. She was stunning.

She took her hand down from her mouth. 'You really want me to spell it out.'

'I do.'

She sighed and rolled her eyes but then said, 'Fine, for what it's worth, I do…find you…attractive.'

Why did that feel like such a ridiculously huge triumph to Cassian? Her cheeks were burning. It was endearing. And also a serious turn-on. Cassian couldn't help but think about how she might look after making love. Hot and dishevelled, cheeks flushed from pleasure.

He had to try and curb the heat in his body. This was a non-starter. And maybe the fact that she was so unavailable was making her more alluring. Cassian cursed himself. He'd had too much of getting his own way, never being denied anything. He'd grown complacent. And arrogant. Lili was a dose of reality and fresh air. And he needed to get some air to his brain now, because if he didn't his mind was starting to spiral into the fact that he couldn't think of another woman he'd ever wanted more and that had never happened to him.

'Look, Lili, we're obviously attracted to each other but I respect your boundaries and the fact that you've made it very clear you don't want to be physically intimate. If IVF is as far as you're prepared to go to try for a child then that's what we'll do. You're sacrificing a lot to give me my inheritance and I appreciate that.'

Now the smile was gone, she looked tortured. 'You're being more than generous already and it's not that I don't want to, it's that I really don't think I can.'

Cassian had to curb an almost overwhelming urge to stand up and go to her, pull her out of her seat and bring her close to his body where she could feel the heat between them. He hadn't even kissed her yet. She'd avoided that on the wedding day. But he could still remember how her cheek had felt under his mouth, soft, silky.

He said, 'I've decided to stay for a few days to catch up on some of the villa's administration and I promised Ricardo that I'd go to the track again. Whatever happens is your choice, Lili. No pressure. I mean that.'

After a long moment she said, 'I thought you were going to try to seduce me.'

Something inside Cassian twisted. He could be ruthless when he wanted but there was an air of vulnerability about Lili that he'd never really noticed in other women and he found himself battling the desire he felt with another desire, a need to protect.

She's your wife, it's an entirely natural instinct. That was it. Their marriage didn't need to be a real one for him to want to protect her. She was his family now. He wouldn't let any harm come to her, from him or anyone else.

He said, 'No. I wouldn't do that. I respect your boundaries.'

She looked relieved. 'I'm sorry it's not more straightforward for me.'

'It's not something to apologise for. Something happened to you and you can't help your response.'

'Thank you for being so understanding.' Lili stood up. 'I think I'll go to bed. Goodnight, Cassian.' She picked up the empty coffee cups.

'Leave those, Eloisa can get them.'

'It's no trouble.'

Cassian stood up too. 'Goodnight, Lili.'

He watched her walk away. Her shirt had ridden up a little and the jeans lovingly cupped her bottom, high and perfectly shaped. Desire gnawed at Cassian. He sat back down and smiled mirthlessly to himself. No doubt this was some form of karma being visited on him for all the times he'd shut down emotionally and pushed lovers away, not wanting to risk any kind of involvement beyond the superficial.

A couple of hours later Lili still couldn't sleep. She blamed the coffee. A bad idea. But also, something else was playing on her mind. She'd brought the coffee cups down to the kitchen to be helpful and found Eloisa there. She'd immediately said, 'I'm sorry, you didn't have to wait for us, I'm sure you've a family to go home to.' Eloisa lived in the small village nearby.

The woman had smiled a little and said, 'Thank you, Signora Corti, actually no, we don't have a family yet, but we are trying.'

Lili had guestimated Eloisa to be in her early thirties and could read between the lines to register a faint sense of weariness and desperation in the woman's voice. It obviously wasn't happening easily for them. In Italy children and family were everything. She could only imagine the heartache of everyone expecting you to have children and nothing happening.

She had a sense that the woman wouldn't want to hear some kind of platitude and so bid her goodnight.

But now the conversation replayed on a loop in Lili's head and she was feeling increasingly uneasy. Giving up any hope of sleep, she got out of bed and took off her nightclothes. She pulled out the white swimsuit and grabbed a robe.

A swim. That usually helped her to sleep and would hopefully quieten down her mind. She got to the pool and dropped the robe. The air was a little cool but she dove in anyway and surfaced at the other end and started doing laps.

When she could feel her muscles protesting she stopped and floated on her back. An image of Cassian finding her here that first night came into her head. Had she come down here now because she was hoping to run into him again? Hoping for him to…what? Try to persuade her to try and conceive a baby naturally? After accusing him of doing that? When he hadn't at all. *I respect your boundaries.* She believed him. It would have been so easy for him to try and seduce her.

She knew she was susceptible to him even as she battled her inner demons.

Lili swam over to the edge of the pool and hauled herself out, sitting for a minute on the edge. Did she *want* Cassian to make it easy for her to confront something she thought she'd never have to?

You really planned on being celibate your whole life? asked a little voice. Lili didn't know. She hadn't really thought too far ahead. Her main objective had been to put distance between her and her family and find a place of sanctuary to feel safe.

Maybe you should have joined a nunnery. Lili scowled at the voice. But it wasn't far off the life she'd built for herself.

And she couldn't help thinking about Eloisa and all the other people out in the world who she knew had trouble conceiving. Lili didn't even know if she would have trouble. As the doctor had said, there was every indication that she and Cassian would have no problems.

And could Lili, in all conscience, use IVF because her husband could afford it and because she was too crippled by her phobia to even try to overcome it?

She felt ashamed. And yet the thought of allowing Cassian to come close...touch her...made her feel sheer panic. But it wasn't just panic. It was laced with excitement. Because he was the first man who had broken through something to reach a part of herself that she'd locked away a long time ago.

Even before the kidnappers. Maybe when she'd first reached for her mother's hand and had been brushed aside with a sharp response. Her parents hadn't been tactile. Her brothers had pushed her around. So then maybe the kidnappers doing the same but in a far more terrifying situation had finally made her close down completely.

She thought of how she'd felt earlier after go-karting. The exhilaration. The way her mind had had no option but to focus on the task at hand. How much lighter she'd felt afterwards. As if she'd reclaimed some aspect of herself long denied. Cassian had given her that.

Lili shivered a little in the night air. She got up and pulled on her robe. Her hair was damp. She walked back into the quiet villa, but instead of going to her own room she kept walking until she got to Cassian's bedroom door.

It was slightly ajar. She knew that she could turn around now and go to her room and as promised, Cassian would let her dictate how this baby would be conceived. Or, she could take a giant step out of her comfort zone and change the script. The script she'd been blindly following for years now.

Did she want to risk not being able to touch her own child? Passing on to them the same treatment she'd been subjected to? If she couldn't contemplate having a child naturally with its father then how could she hope to lavish it with all of the physical affection she'd never experienced?

She stood hovering like that for so long that she felt pins and needles in her legs. This was ridiculous. She couldn't do it. It wouldn't work. She would freeze on Cassian and make a fool of herself and—

The door was pulled open at that moment and Lili's vision was filled with a bare-chested Cassian, messy hair, silver eyes. She didn't dare look down. He seemed like the kind of man who would sleep naked.

'Lili?'

She swallowed. 'Um, yes, sorry... I couldn't sleep...went for a swim.'

That light gaze dropped over her body now, taking in the short robe, bare legs, damp hair. He looked back up and his eyes had turned darker. 'You went for a swim?'

She nodded. 'And I... I'm not sure what I'm doing here... but I think I would like to try...to...do this...naturally.' Her heart was beating so fast now she felt light-headed.

'Are you sure?'

'Maybe if we talk about it first? Like...what would happen?'

Cassian frowned. 'Lili...are you a virgin?'

She nodded. There was no point denying it. She thought he might have guessed that already.

He had a slightly arrested look on his face and something occurred to her. She took a step back. 'I'm so stupid...it's probably a total turn-off to sleep with a novice...' After all it wasn't as if this was a real marriage where a husband might value his wife's innocence.

But he put out a hand and was shaking his head. 'No, it's not...' His voice sounded a bit rough. 'It's not that, it's just a surprise, that's all, and it means that we'd have to take things…slowly.'

'That's okay.' Then she blurted out, 'I might not be able to go through with it but I was talking to Eloisa earlier and I think they're having trouble having a baby and it just made me realise that perhaps it's selfish to use artificial means if we don't need to.' She stopped. She was babbling.

Cassian stood back and opened the door wide. 'Why don't you come in and we'll just talk, hm?'

Lili took a hesitant step over the threshold. There was one low light on near the bed. Sheets rumpled. French doors open, letting air in. She welcomed the faint breeze over her hot skin.

She turned around to face Cassian. She could see that he was wearing low-slung pyjama bottoms. They looked like they were hanging onto his narrow hips very precariously.

He had hair on his chest. Masculine.

He said, 'Lili, you're trembling. Are you sure you want to try this? I meant what I said earlier… I don't want you to feel pressured.'

Lili lifted a hand. It was shaking. If anything, this evidence of her fear made her even more determined. She couldn't let her past cast its shadow over her future, especially if she wanted to do it differently for her child. They deserved her bravery. She shook her head. 'No, I want to try. At least.'

'Okay, wait here.'

She watched as Cassian walked out. Not sure what to expect, Lili turned on another low light and then sat on the edge of the bed. Cassian's scent tickled her nostrils. Earthy. With a hint of sea and citrus. Uncomplicated. She had to concede that wasn't unlike him. He was turning out to be direct, open. Not some selfish, louche party boy.

She wondered about that just as his shadow fell across the door and he came back with two half-full glasses of what looked like wine in his hands. He came over and handed her one. 'I thought this might help, a little.'

Lili was touched by his consideration. 'Thank you.' She took a big sip and then put the glass down on a bedside table.

Cassian sat on the bed too, but at a distance. He took a drink of wine and handed the glass to Lili. 'Would you mind?'

She took it and put it down beside hers. She turned back. He was looking at her. 'So, you've never had sex. Have you done…anything else?'

Lili could feel heat rising. 'Not really. I developed early… and I was self-conscious. My mother used to tell me to hide my breasts. That my hips were too big. She's like a little bird.'

Something crossed Cassian's face, it looked like irritation. 'That's when you learned to hide.'

'Maybe. I went to an all-girls school. Men…boys, kind of scared me. My brothers were…rough. They treated me like them.'

'And then…something happened to you.'

Lili could feel the heat draining out of her face and body. She felt cold and wrapped her arms around herself. 'Yes.' Clipped. She silently begged Cassian not to ask her about it because she didn't want toxic memories ruining this moment.

Thankfully, he seemed to sense her plea.

'Okay. And you do…know what happens?'

It took a second for Lili to register his meaning and now the heat was back. 'Of course, I'm not completely naive. My brothers watched a lot of porn.' Her face was burning now.

Cassian said dryly, 'They sound absolutely charming.'

They had been spoiled tyrants and Lili had never been so thankful that she was no longer anywhere near them. And never would be again.

And then she blurted out, 'I saw you…in the shower. I didn't mean to. I came into your room on the first day and you were still in the bathroom.'

Cassian said, 'That's okay. Did you like what you saw?'

The image of his broad back, tapering down to lean hips and then firm, muscular buttocks flashed into Lili's mind. She nodded. She was so gauche. If Cassian still found her attractive after this then it would be a miracle.

He stood up from the bed. 'You can look at me now if you want.'

Lili's curiosity overcame her embarrassment. He was simply too beautiful not to look at. Her gaze roved over his broad chest and shoulders. Muscled arms. Pectorals. Taut belly with the delineation of muscles.

Just above the waistband of his pants, she could see the indentation where his thighs met his waist. She didn't know what to call it but it made her fingers itch to trace it.

She wanted to touch him. Her gaze jumped up to his. Had she spoken out loud? He was looking at her steadily. Completely unfazed. Something about his acceptance of this situation was incredibly empowering. What other man would so patiently hand themselves over like this?

She stood up. 'Can I touch you?'

His eyes widened. 'Of course, if you want.'

Lili went and stood in front of him. She'd stopped trembling now. Maybe the alcohol had worked. But her mind had never felt clearer. She was aware of Cassian's gaze on her and walked around behind him. She lifted her hands and held them away from his back for a few seconds. She could almost feel his body heat radiating against her palms.

And then, very gently she brought them closer and laid them on his bare back. The feel of his skin under hers was so shocking at first that she pulled them back again, but then she put them back, leaving them there, absorbing the sensation of his skin, warm and silky.

She spread her fingers, encompassing as much as she could, and then slowly moved them, up and down, tracing the way his back got narrower towards his waist.

She moved back around to stand in front of him and avoided looking in his face as she put her hands to his chest, his hair tickling her palms and fingers. Softer than she had imagined. Springy.

His nipples were two hard nubs under her palms and instinctively she moved her hands down, nails grazing against them. She heard a sharp indrawn breath and looked up. 'Did I hurt you?'

Cassian shook his head. 'No...but you are killing me slowly.'

Lili could see the faintest sheen of perspiration on his face. It was more than astounding to think she was having an effect on him. But then she looked down and she could see where his pants were bulging slightly.

Her mouth was suddenly dry. She looked up again. 'Can I undo your pants?'

'By all means.' His jaw clenched.

Lili saw a button. She put her hands to it, slipping it free. The top of his pants opened revealing dark hair. Suddenly she was a little overcome.

Cassian said, 'Do you want me to take them off?'

Without looking at him—too ashamed of the hunger she was feeling and all of the new sensations swirling inside her, she nodded and took a step back. She'd forgotten the bed was right behind her and ended up sitting on the edge again, watching as Cassian put his hands to the sides of his pants and pushed them down. Stepping out of them.

He was naked. Lili's eyes had to be as big as saucers. She was transfixed. He was a study in perfection. He wasn't fully erect but even at that he was beyond intimidating. Thick and hard. Veins running along the shaft. It twitched under her gaze and Lili really, really wanted to touch it.

Cassian said, 'You can if you like.'

She looked at him. She must have spoken out loud. She wasn't sure if she was dreaming all of this up. Time seemed to have slowed or stopped completely. There was just them in this room and this taut bubble of energy between them.

'You're so beautiful,' she couldn't help saying.

Cassian wasn't sure how he was standing so still when every nerve in his body was pulled so tight that he could feel his heart thumping. The way Lili had just touched him, as reverently as if he was made of china…he'd never experienced anything like it.

She stood up again and he gritted his jaw as she came close again. She looked down at him and that was all it took for his body to get even harder. He couldn't remember when he'd been so turned on.

She was biting her lip now and he had to clench his hands to fists to stop himself from reaching out. *You can't touch her.* Uncharted territory. It made him think of all the women who'd given themselves to him so willingly over the years, all but pushing themselves into his hands and he'd taken without even thinking. Gorging himself but coming away feeling increasingly dissatisfied.

From where he stood, he could see a tantalising glimpse of Lili's cleavage. The robe had fallen open slightly. He could also see the white of the swimsuit. The most innocuous piece of clothing and yet it had assumed almost mythical proportions in his imaginings.

But all of that was eclipsed when he felt her stroke a finger down the length of his penis. He had to close his eyes. *Madre di Dio*...and now, she was closing a hand around him, fingers shaping his flesh, moving up and down slightly.

Cassian could feel sweat break out on his brow. He opened his eyes. Lili looked up, cheeks flushed. Eyes very blue. 'Is this okay?'

He nodded. 'It's amazing...but if you keep doing that I can't guarantee that I'll be able to maintain my dignity.'

She took her hand away and Cassian almost cursed out loud. But it was good, because he didn't really want to spill into her hand like some hormonal teenager.

'I'm sorry,' she said, looking genuinely anguished.

Cassian cursed again, silently. He shook his head. 'Nothing to apologise for. It's a sign of the effect you have on me.'

'What...what should I do now?'

There was something so endearingly trusting about her that Cassian almost wanted to take her by the hand and lead her out of his room and villa and put her on a boat and send her off to some other man who would handle her with kid gloves and not want to devour her like he did. He felt like a hungry wolf with little innocent Red Riding Hood.

But even just the thought of her with another man was enough to make him also want to lock every door in the place and never let her outside again.

He took a deep breath. 'Why don't you take off your robe?'

She undid the knot in the belt and opened it. The robe fell open and she pulled it back, letting it fall to the floor. Now she only wore the swimsuit and Cassian's gaze was full of her glorious body.

The full, high breasts. Nipples pressing against the taut fabric. Soft belly. Small waist, curving out to her hips. Strong thighs.

'Will I...take it off?'

Cassian sent up a silent prayer for control. 'If you feel comfortable.'

She put one hand under a strap and pushed it down over her shoulder and then the other one. Then she tugged them down. He held his breath for an infinitesimal moment before she kept going and peeled the material down, over her breasts to her waist.

Cassian felt a rush of blood to his head. She was stunning. The most beautifully shaped breasts he'd ever seen in his life. Full and heavy. Nipples hard and pink. His mouth watered.

She kept going, shimmying her hips a little as she tugged the swimsuit down all the way and let it fall at her feet.

Cassian moved his gaze down, taking her in. Awed. A dark thatch of hair between her legs. She put a hand there and ducked her head, as if suddenly embarrassed. 'You're probably used to—'

'No.' His voice came out harsher than expected. She looked up.

'No,' he said, more gently. 'You are exquisite.'

'What should I do now?'

'Can I look at you?'

She nodded. Cassian stood back. A chance to try and get some air to his brain. To keep the fire in his blood at a level where he didn't feel like he was going to explode.

He let his gaze rove over her, every inch. And then he started to walk around her. Her back was almost as tantalising as her front. Long spine. Pale skin. The way her waist curved out to her hips and her bottom. Full and plump.

But then she turned around abruptly. 'Actually, I don't like you being behind me... I can't see you.'

He could see that she was breathing faster. The fear in her eyes. What the hell had happened to her? But he pushed that aside now.

He said, 'Okay, I won't do that again. How about if I lie down on the bed?'

She nodded jerkily, damp skeins of dark hair slipping over her shoulder, reaching down as far as her breasts.

He lay down on the bed. He felt as though his whole body was throbbing. 'Why don't you sit on the chair over there?' He indicated to a wide chair near a chest of drawers.

Lili looked at it. 'Okay.' She went over and sat down on the edge and looked as if she was waiting for his next instruction.

Cassian came up on one elbow. He knew that if they were going to do this, she would have to be fully ready and if he couldn't touch her...he asked, 'Have you ever touched yourself, Lili?'

CHAPTER SEVEN

Lili's entire body flushed. She couldn't believe she was in Cassian's room, naked. Like him. Sitting on the edge of a chair having a conversation about—she got out a garbled-sounding, 'Um, no, I haven't.'

She wondered faintly why she had started this again. She could be asleep in her bed right now. But something was awoken inside her and she knew if she had a choice she'd stay here. No matter how excruciatingly mortifying, and a big part of that was because of how amazingly gentle and understanding Cassian was being. A revelation. And yet, she knew that unless she'd trusted him on some level, she would never have come to his bedroom like this. She'd unpack that later.

Cassian sat up on the edge of the bed. He said, 'I need you to be ready, Lili, because the first time can hurt a little.'

Lili's gaze dropped to his lap where his erection was even bigger. She gulped a little. She looked back up. 'Okay. Tell me what to do.' She was determined now, no going back.

'Sit back in the chair.'

She did, moving right into the back.

'Can you widen your legs?'

After a moment of hesitation, Lili did, slowly. She could see a flush come up along Cassian's cheekbones. His erection twitched. He said a little hoarsely, 'Like that.'

'Okay, now, cup your breast...feel its weight and texture.'

Lili felt silly but she did as he asked. She'd never taken note of her breasts before, always wanting to hide them. It felt firm in her hand now. Soft. Silky. The nipple a hard nub that tingled when her finger brushed it. The tingle connected with a point between her legs and she could feel a kind of tension building in her lower belly and between her legs.

'Very good. Trace your nipple...pinch it between two fingers.'

Lili didn't take her eyes off Cassian as she followed his instructions.

'Squeeze it harder...'

His voice was sounding a little breathless. She dropped her gaze for a moment to see that he had a hand on his erection and she felt a gush of liquid heat between her legs. It almost made her close her thighs together but she resisted the urge.

'Now, drop your other hand, down over your belly...to between your legs. Stroke yourself and find what you like.'

Lili wasn't sure what he meant but she did as he asked and let her fingers delve between her legs. She was shocked to find how hot she was. And damp.

'Very good.' Cassian was stroking his erection now, face flushed. Lili felt sweat trickle down her temple. She was breathing faster as a wholly new sensation was coiling tight in her body. She was fixated on making her fingers stroke deeper, harder. Her other hand was squeezing her breast. She'd moved down the chair, legs wider.

Cassian said, 'Why don't you put one leg over the arm of the chair.'

Lili did so and found that opening herself up made it so much easier. It was second nature now to follow the dictates of her body and let her fingers slide in between the folds of her sex, inside where she felt so hot and achy.

'That's it, Lili, keep going.'

She was hardly listening to Cassian's voice now, an instinct as old as time taking over her body as her back arched and her buttocks squeezed to try and chase this elusive peak she had to find.

And then suddenly it broke over her, wrenching a gasp from her mouth, as she soared high in a violent burst of pleasure. She could feel the rhythmic clasping of her muscles around her fingers. She was squeezing her breast hard. She let go, breathing fast. Stunned into silence, as she floated back to earth.

Cassian's face was stark. He looked like he was in pain. Lili took her leg down from the arm of the chair, tried to sit up again when she felt as if her limbs had become hot jelly.

'Are you okay?'

His voice sounded a bit strangled. 'Not really... Lili, I need to be inside you or I think I might die...'

He moved back on the bed and said, 'I think I know how we can do this without you feeling claustrophobic.'

'Okay,' Lili said, feeling incredibly languorous.

He was lying back on the bed now and said, 'Come over here, and I'll show you.'

Lili wasn't sure if she could stand but she attempted it and even though her legs felt like wool, she could manage. She walked over to the bed and tried not to ogle at Cassian's body. His very *hard* body.

He said, 'Straddle me, Lili, sit over me.'

Her heart palpitated. She knew they'd have to touch, obviously, but it felt very real. Her nerves were back. Could she actually do this?

He said, 'I won't touch you. Look, I'll keep my hands out to the sides. You're in control here.'

She looked at him. His arms were stretched out. 'You promise?'

'You can restrain me if you want, there are ties in the dressing room.'

The thought of this man in all his glorious masculinity being totally at her mercy was heady enough to make her sway. But then she said, 'No, it's okay.'

She got on the bed and maneuvered herself so that she was over Cassian, her legs either side of his hips.

'You're going to have to…come up a little and help me…'

He looked down at his body and she followed his gaze to his erection. She could see a bead of moisture at the tip. She took him in her hand. So much bigger and harder than before. His skin slipped up and down the shaft and when she glanced at him his jaw was hard and his eyes were glittering.

'Lili, please.'

She had never felt so…in control and she realised in that moment that it wasn't so much about being touched that she feared as not feeling in control, but that was too revelatory for her to try and analyse now.

She came up over him and using her hand on him, positioned herself so that she was hovering over the tip of his body. Slowly, she sank down, taking him inside her.

Cassian's head was thrown back now, tendons straining in his neck. Lili put her hands on his chest and she could feel his heart thundering and his skin slick with perspiration. She kept sinking down until there was a moment of discomfort. She stopped.

Cassian's hands were gripping the sheets. He looked at her. 'I'm going to push against you, okay? It'll hurt for a second but then it'll get better, I promise.'

Lili nodded.

Cassian clenched his buttocks and surged upwards and Lili felt that very sharp acute pain as his body pushed even deeper into hers. She gasped out loud.

He stopped and she'd never felt so full.

'Okay?' he asked.

She wasn't sure. She moved experimentally and the discomfort eased. She said breathlessly, 'I think so.'

'Okay...now find your rhythm. Move up and down.'

Lili did as he said, finding the passage of his body within hers easier and easier as she moved up and down. The same sensation she'd felt before, the delicious tightening deep down in her body was building again. She moved faster, instinctively. Her fingers were digging into Cassian's chest. She could see the whites of his knuckles out of the corner of her eye gripping the sheets, but all that was beginning to matter right now was the fact that she had become pure sensation and fire and he was stoking that fire higher and higher every time he moved against her and in her.

She moved against him and he bucked up and into her. Skin slick. Hearts pounding. Cassian let out a harsh groan and said, 'I'm sorry... I can't...'

His body jerked up against hers and she could feel the the rush of his climax inside her, just as her own body was held in a state of suspended bliss before cracking open and exploding into pleasure so intense, it made her cry out, back arched, every muscle pulsing and contracting in endless waves of pure ecstasy.

When Cassian woke it took a long time for consciousness to return. His body felt weighted down. He felt...a deep sense of satisfaction and for a minute his brain was blank...*why?*—and then it came back in glorious Technicolour.

His eyes opened and he squinted in the dawn light. He lifted his head. The bed was empty. Sheets rumpled. He was laying splayed out as if he'd been used in some sort of ritual sacrifice.

And Lili…his body twitched at the memory of her sitting astride him, her glorious curves, those perfect breasts. Her skin sheened with perspiration, nipples hard, cheeks flushed.

And more…even before that, how she'd obeyed his instructions to pleasure herself, biting her lip, and frowning with concentration as if this was a very important task he'd set her.

And just like that, Cassian's body was fully hard again, pulsating with need. He groaned and sat up. Last night had been completely unexpected and easily the most erotic experience of his life. Hands down.

The effort it had taken not to reach out and touch her—he hadn't even known he had that level of control. He'd ached to cup those beautiful breasts and bring them to his mouth so he could explore their hard peaks with his tongue and suck them deep. To put his hand between her legs and feel for himself how ready she was.

He'd seen it in the slick glistening folds of her sex after she'd touched herself and how he hadn't spilled there and then…would be a mystery for the rest of his life.

He squinted against the light again. Where was she? Something inside him clenched. Was she okay? He'd blacked out after the most intense orgasm he'd ever experienced. He had a vague memory of her breasts touching his chest and maybe he'd stroked her back but then…blankness. A pleasure induced coma.

Cassian usually welcomed waking alone in a bed after making love but this time, he felt uneasy. He was pretty sure it had been as amazing for Lili, he'd felt her body clamping powerfully around his with her climax, almost inducing another climax from him...but it had been her first time.

He got up from the bed, muscles protesting and went into his bathroom to take a cold shower, and then he would look for his wife. His very unexpected and surprising wife.

Lili had just taken a shower in her own room and was standing on the terrace outside her bedroom in a robe as dawn rose, still grappling with everything that had happened. She felt as if her brain had been taken out of her head and then reinserted.

Was this the same planet? Everything felt a little altered. Like she'd been recalibrated.

She still didn't fully have words to explain the events of the previous night. She'd passed out in a haze of pleasure, and had woken not long before, her body draped over Cassian's chest, boneless. And lying there, feeling his heart pounding under her cheek...had been the singularly most profound moment, even more than the sheer physical heights she'd experienced.

His hand had been on her back and she'd recalled how just after making love, with a very gentle, light touch, he had caressed her, up and down and it had felt...so amazing. Comforting. Seductive.

To Lili's horror she'd felt emotional, a mass of tangled feelings rising up within her for all that had happened. And so as he'd slept, she'd fled, in case he'd wake and look at her, after already seeing her more exposed than she'd ever been before.

And now...as she looked out over the view, she tried her best to piece it all together. She hadn't minded Cassian's touch. In fact, when she'd been taking him inside her body, she'd craved to feel his hands on her, molding her hips, holding her so that he could thrust up even harder…she'd wanted him to cup her breasts, put his mouth on her…she just hadn't been able to articulate it because she'd been dealing with everything else.

This was huge. The fact that he'd handed himself over to her and had let her dictate everything, and feel in control… to show her that it was possible to create that for herself—no wonder her mind was blown to pieces. She'd never in a million years have imagined that a man with his kind of reputation would have that consideration, or patience.

She heard a soft noise behind her and turned around to see the object of her thoughts standing in the doorway between her bedroom and the terrace. Wearing sweatpants low on his hips. Bare chest. Hair damp. Lili was instantly jealous of his shower. He was also holding two small cups and came over in bare feet. 'Coffee?'

Lili took the cup gratefully and held it in her hands, looking at Cassian over the rim as he came and stood with his backside against the wall. He regarded her and then said, 'Are you okay?'

She took a sip of coffee to avoid answering for as long as she could. She was okay. More than okay. This man had single-handedly—emotion rose again and she blinked her eyes quickly but not quick enough to hide it. Cassian frowned and took her cup and his own and put them down on the wall. He looked concerned. 'Lili, did I hurt you?'

She shook her head and saw how he went pale and then she found herself reaching out to put her hands on his chest, as if she hadn't just broken through an epic personal barrier only hours before.

'No, you didn't hurt me. It was just…not what I expected at all.'

'Did you enjoy it?'

Lili blushed and ducked her head. She took her hands down. She'd never enjoyed anything more. She looked up again, noticing how Cassian's hands were clenched to fists as if he had to restrain himself from touching her. Between her legs a pulse throbbed to life. She felt that delicious coil of tension.

She asked, 'Can we…do it again?'

Now his face flushed a little. Eyes very silver in the dawn light. He nodded. 'If you'd like to.'

Lili felt giddy but she forced herself to sound like she was approaching this as a serious matter. 'I mean, we should really, if we're going to follow the instructions of the doctor, you know, to maximise our chances…of conceiving.' She was a total fraud. Until that moment there hadn't been the slightest thought of a baby resulting from that conflagration last night. It had been the furthest thing from her mind.

As if colluding with her, Cassian said seriously, but with a suspicious twinkle in his eye, 'Oh, you're absolutely right, we should definitely do this again if we want to make sure we're optimising our chances. We might even have to do it a few more times. Just to be sure, of course.'

Lili felt that tension spiking. 'Now?'

A muscle twitched in Cassian's jaw. 'You're not sore?'

She shook her head. She was hungry. She moved back into the bedroom and opened her robe and let it drop to the floor. She was naked. She'd never felt freer. As if a massive heavy cloud had blown away from over her head.

Cassian's gaze devoured her as he stalked into the bedroom.

She was already slightly breathless. 'I don't think I need to…you know, touch myself first. I think I'm ready.'

Cassian looked at her while his hands pushed his pants

down over his hips. He was naked underneath and when Lili looked down, she gulped. He was ready too.

He went and lay on her bed. He put out his arms, signalling that he wasn't going to touch her. Her insides liquefied even more. The healing this man had precipitated just by showing her she could trust him was overwhelming.

She came and stood beside the bed. 'Last night... I wanted you to touch me but I just couldn't find the words at the time.'

Cassian came up on one elbow and admitted, 'You have no idea how much I wanted to touch you. I don't know how I lasted as long as I did. Do you want me to...now?'

Lili nodded, biting her lip, but just as his hands reached for her, she felt a frisson of trepidation and said, 'Can we go slow...so I can get used to it?'

Cassian looked at her. 'You can tell me to stop at any point and you tell me where you want me to touch you.'

The trepidation dissolved in a wave of heat. He said, 'Do you want to be on top again?'

Lili nodded. She knew she still needed to feel that level of control. She got onto the bed and straddled Cassian. He lifted his hands and said, 'May I?'

She nodded jerkily. She could feel him under her, twitching, long and thick. He put his hands very gently on her hips and it felt good to have him steady her.

Then he said, 'Come up a little.' His hands urged her. She obeyed, and felt him take himself in his hand before he stroked himself along the seam of her body. Lili's head fell back. She leant backwards, placing her hands on his thighs. And then he was at her entrance and Lili looked down to see him feed his erection between her legs and she took him in with a gasp, sitting up straight again.

It was slower this time. Building. Lili moved up and

down, skin becoming slick. Cassian's hands were still on her hips. He was looking at her breasts. Lili said breathlessly, 'You can touch me there, if you want.'

He looked at her and then down again. His hands came up to her breasts, cupping their weight, fingers moving over her nipples, making them strain and tingle. He pinched one lightly, then the other.

Lili said a little brokenly, 'Can you put your mouth... on me.'

Cassian sat up a little and he surged deeper inside her, as he brought his mouth to first one breast and then the other. Last night had blown Lili's mind but she was discovering a whole new level of pleasure to have Cassian's hands on her and his mouth...and that exquisite sucking heat, stroking her into a paroxysm of pleasure so intense that she was falling over the edge before she'd even realised what was happening.

She looked at Cassian as the waves subsided. 'I'm sorry... I couldn't help it.'

He just shook his head. 'You are so responsive...'

He was still hard inside her. Lili moved experimentally, and he groaned a little. 'Lili, you don't have to, we can stop now if you like...'

She shook her head, hair falling over her shoulders, 'No, you didn't...you know.'

He huffed a laugh. 'Come?'

Lili wanted to bury her head in his neck. He must think she was so gauche. But he just said, 'Are you sure?'

She nodded. 'Tell me what to do.'

He lay back down and put his hands on her hips, holding her firm, but it didn't scare her, it thrilled her. He said roughly, 'Just keep moving, like that...yes... *Dio*... Lili.'

He bent his head back, she could see the tendons in his

neck standing out, and she felt his body surging within hers over and over again and slowly but surely, she could feel her own body reacting again and her eyes widened. 'Cass... I think I'm going to—' she stopped talking as he hit a spot so deep inside her that she saw stars.

And then he was clenching his buttocks, driving up and into her and with a harsh shout, she felt his body release inside hers and that alone was all it took to send Lili back over the edge, her own body pulsating along with Cassian's, and they both spiraled down into endless waves of pleasure.

'You called me Cass.'

'Hm?' Lili responded sleepily. She was lying on her back, sheet pulled up to her waist. Cassian was on his back beside her. She wasn't sure how long they'd lain there after that last time. She couldn't move but she forced her eyes open and turned on her side to face him, pulling the sheet up and holding it to her chest.

She ogled his bare chest shamelessly. The sheet was tangled around his hips, low enough to give her a glimpse of dark hair. Her insides pulsed and she squeezed her thighs together. They could have made a baby by now. But somehow the thought left her feeling a little...hollow. What would happen once she got pregnant? Would that be it? No more sex? Because as flatteringly appreciative of Lili as Cassian seemed to be, she was sure it was part his innate charm and part novelty factor. It wouldn't endure.

He turned his head to look at her. 'You called me Cass.'

She had. In the throes of passion. 'I'm sorry, I wasn't thinking—'

He shook his head. 'I don't mind. Not many people call me that.'

'You don't encourage...familiarity?'

'As a rule? Not really.'

'Because of your family?'

He didn't answer. He didn't have to. Lili asked, 'Who took care of you afterwards?'

He turned his head away, looking to the ceiling. 'I had no immediate close family so my care was handled by a board of trustees and guardians who had no clue what to do with an eight-year-old kid who'd just lost his entire world.'

Lili's chest contracted at the thought of a small bewildered boy. 'How did that work?'

'I was sent to boarding school in the UK and then a series of nannies took over in the holidays. And counsellors, lots of counsellors to make sure I was dealing with my grief.'

'Did it help?'

He let out a short, harsh laugh. 'I went to sessions and tuned out, I developed a morbid fascination with cars after the accident and became obsessed with racing. As if I wanted to do all that I could to join my family. I didn't care about anyone, or anything. But I had to learn to care about the family business once I turned twenty-one and realised that thousands of employees across the globe now depended on me for their livelihoods.'

'The playboy thing…is that all a bit of an act?' Lili remembered the picture of him with a beautiful woman at an event on the evening before he'd come back to the villa. Her chest constricted even more. Had he slept with her?

He looked at her again. 'What makes you think it's an act?'

She lifted a shoulder minutely. 'Since you've been here you haven't been behaving like a spoiled brat. Wrecking the place. Hosting debauched parties.'

His mouth twitched. 'Is that what playboys do?'

Lili blushed and shrugged. 'I wouldn't really know, it's

just what I've seen in the papers. But I get it, maybe it suits to have everyone believe you're not interested in anything permanent or serious.'

'Says my wife,' he responded. 'You can't get more permanent than that.'

'Yes, but it's not real, is it?'

'What wasn't real about what happened last night? That's the most real thing I've felt in a long time.'

Lili looked at him. Messily, sexily tousled hair. The short beard hugging his jaw looking deliciously unkempt. Silver eyes. That twitch on his mouth. Maybe she was the fool here, and maybe he was as debauched as the next playboy, laughing at her earnestness and already planning his escape back to his exciting world, after he'd done the deed to protect his inheritance.

'You mean since the night before you came back to the villa?'

He frowned at her and then his expression became enigmatic. 'You looked me up.'

'Of course I did. You're my boss.'

'*Was* your boss. And what did you find?'

Lili was sorry she'd started this now. But there was no escape. She was literally naked, beside an equally naked Cassian. *Cass.*

'I saw pictures of you at an event in Rome, with a woman.'

'And you put two and two together and came up with five.'

'Are you saying you weren't with her?'

'Oh, I was with her…as my date. But the truth was that she bored me to tears. We left the event separately.'

Lili hated how the constriction in her chest eased. 'It's none of my business.'

'No,' he agreed. 'But as my wife now you're due a certain consideration.'

Lili's heart thumped. 'You're saying you'll be discreet… the next time you take a lover.' Because of course he would be taking a lover. Hadn't they already agreed to this? *But that was before you slept together,* pointed out a little voice.

'Right now there's only one lover in my life and contrary to popular opinion I'm not in the habit of taking multiple lovers at the same time.'

But then he said, 'I meant what I said, Lili, I made a vow to myself a long time ago to not let anyone get too close. That hasn't changed. I know that your first time can be… intense. It's easy to imagine that emotions are involved and what happened between us was powerful.'

Lili went cold inside. He was telling her not to fall for him. Because she was gauche and inexperienced and naive. She pulled back a little and affected as airy a tone as she could. 'You're forgetting that I walked away from my own family, I made a choice not to let anyone close too.'

'Good, then we're on the same page.'

But in spite of her brave words, Lili had a feeling that she wasn't so sure of anything anymore.

Cassian reached over and held his hand over where Lili was clutching the sheet to her chest. He said, 'May I?'

The coldness inside her started to melt. Weakly she nodded her head. Cassian pulled the sheet down, exposing her to his gaze. He looked at her belly. Her very average and slightly soft belly. His eyes flared with heat.

He looked into her eyes. 'Can I put my hand on you?'

Lili nodded. She lay back. Cassian put his hand on her belly, fingers spread out. Then, he leant forward and put his mouth on her shoulder and then on her breast…finding her pebbled nipple.

Meanwhile his hand moved down, over her belly and down further, between her legs. Fingers seeking and finding the secret folds of her flesh where the pulse throbbed and where an ache was already building. She parted her legs, allowing him full access.

Her back arched as he inserted two fingers. And this time, when he moved over her body and she looked up at him before he joined them, Lili realised that she felt no fear at all, just a growing insatiable hunger.

None of this was remotely linked with emotion. She'd cut off her emotions long ago too, when she'd learned that she wasn't lovable. Not even Cassian Corti could change that. No matter how amazing the sex might be.

CHAPTER EIGHT

LILI WASN'T ACCUSTOMED to having nothing to do, now that she was mistress of the villa and not its housekeeper. She felt redundant even though she knew that part of the marriage agreement was a bank account set up in her name with more money than she could possibly spend. In spite of her insistence that she didn't want anything from Cassian.

She had her own money, saved carefully over the years since she'd left home and turned her back on her inheritance. She'd started out as a cleaner and then one of the houses where she'd cleaned regularly had been looking for someone to live in and become a housekeeper and that's how she'd become a housekeeper, eventually ending up in a position where she'd been able to interview for the job at Villa Corti.

Her restlessness and feelings of redundancy had led to trying to do some housework only to be shooed away by Eloisa and now she was engaged in the very genteel practice of cutting some blooms in the garden so she could fill vases full of flowers.

Cassian had gone to the racetrack in Monza to do some more tests on the car. Lili welcomed the space to try and process everything that had happened between them since she'd gone to him two nights ago…but she still couldn't get her head around it.

After making love again the previous morning, they'd

woken at lunchtime, scandalising Lili who had never slept at the villa much after dawn. But Cassian had insisted she stay where she was and he'd gone and brought back a tray full of antipasta and salad and bread. Sparkling wine.

They'd eaten on the terrace of Lili's room. And then afterwards, they'd taken a shower together and Lili had been able to indulge in the fantasy she'd had that first day she'd seen him, running her hands over his formidable body. She'd revelled in exploring him, fascinated by the effect she seemed to have on him.

And he'd only touched her if she let him and increasingly, she was finding that she didn't even want him to ask her.

He'd helped to rewire her brain and make her hungry in a way she hadn't ever imagined could be possible. *He'd helped her heal more in the last forty-eight hours than the last eight years.*

That thought was monumentally overwhelming. She now knew that it wasn't exactly *touch* that she feared as much as the thought of being powerlesss. Like she had been with the kidnappers. So even if Cassian was touching her now, once she felt as if she was in control or held the power, she was fine.

She trusted him. And on that seismic revelation, she heard a sound behind her and turned around to see the object of her very raw thoughts standing a few feet away. Wearing jeans and a T-shirt. Hair tousled. He really should come with a health warning, thought Lili and suddenly she felt shy. When this man was the one person in the world who knew her more intimately than anyone else.

He looked at her, up and down. 'I thought the days of wearing those shapeless dresses were over.'

Lili flushed. She'd found herself reaching for comfort from her dressing room. Eloisa had faithfully hung up all of her old clothes alongside the newer ones. Dressing differently had felt like a step too far after everything else that was happening to her. *In her.*

Feeling defensive, Lili pointed out, 'There's no one here to see me.'

'I see you.'

Cassian's words landed like a blow to her belly. He did see her. He had seen more of her than anyone else.

He waved a hand. 'You're obviously entitled to dress however you please, Lili. Come with me, I have something for you.'

Perversely, because he seemed to be saying she should feel free to dress like this, now Lili felt uncomfortable and regretted not wearing something a little more form-fitting. Maybe he was looking at her and wondering what on earth he'd been doing for the last couple of nights.

She put down the basket of flowers and took off the pruning gloves and followed him, curious. He led her around to the front of the villa where a gleaming car was parked. Dark metallic silver. Not a sports car but it looked very zippy. But also roomy. She recognised the world-famous make of the car.

Cassian held something out to Lili. She looked and saw it was a key. She looked back up. 'What's this?'

'A car. For you. The Fiat is the run-around for the villa so you'll need a car of your own.'

Lili shook her head. 'But I can't possibly accept this, it's too much.'

Cassian walked towards her. 'It's not, really. You'll need a car to get around and if...there's a baby.'

Lili still didn't take the key but she walked around it now, taking in the fact that it was roomy enough for a baby seat in the back. A large boot. Practical but stylish. She noticed something else.

'It's electric?'

Cassian nodded. 'There's an electrical point in the garage housing the cars, you can use that and there are pretty good charging points in the area.'

Then he said, 'Why not try it out and then decide?' at the same time as he lobbed the key at her and she had no choice but to catch it on reflex.

Lili couldn't really argue. She unlocked the car and got into the driver's seat. Cassian got in on the other side. The dashboard wasn't unlike how she imagined the cockpit of an airplane to look, but she figured out the basics.

'It's fully electric and automatic. Head out of the estate and I'll direct you.'

Lili did as he asked, too bemused and surprised not to. Cassian directed her away from the little local village and in the other direction, heading north along the lake.

The car was smooth and quiet and comfortable. Lili liked driving. Sometimes she took the Fiat out and went off on little trips to places along the lake-side, exploring. But always within her comfort zone. Something about that now irritated her. The years of feeling fearful. She was was starting to see that so much more had been taken from her than she'd even realised.

Cassian sat easily beside her. Relaxed. She remarked, 'You don't mind being driven by a woman?'

He shrugged. 'Why would I? You're a good driver.'

A little burst of pride lit up her chest. She said, 'It's a little intimidating to be driving a man who makes a living driving the fastest cars on the planet.'

'I like being driven. I'm not a control freak.'

Lili snuck him a glance. He certainly looked relaxed. She looked ahead again and concentrated on not driving them into the lake.

After a short while they came into another village. Cassian said abruptly, 'Are you hungry?'

Lili considered this and realised she hadn't eaten much at all. Too busy in her head. She said, 'I could eat.'

'Good, because I'm starving. There's a great restaurant here. Let's find a parking space.'

Lili soon found out that the only other thing more intimidating than driving a racing champion was parallel parking with one in the car. But she managed it without disgracing herself.

People were emerging for the evening *passeggiata* and suddenly Lili was acutely aware of her loose dress and top and really regretted not dressing in the new clothes. Every other woman looked so elegant and put-together. And she stood out even more with Cassian at her side. She vowed to put them in a bag for a charity shop when they got back to the villa.

Cassian said, 'It's just here.' And Lili looked to see a small doorway almost entirely obscured by twining vines. Cassian stood aside. 'After you.'

Lili ducked her head slightly and went in to find a charming restaurant, much larger than she might have suspected, opening up into an airy courtyard full of greenery and flowers. Cassian was behind her, she could feel his presence and heat and it didn't unnerve her at all. In fact she felt an urge to lean back against him.

The waiter approached, face wreathed in smiles. 'Signore Corti, what a pleasant surprise. Welcome. For two?'

'Yes, Alfredo, thank you.'

The man led them through and Lili saw couples looking up and their eyes widening when they clocked Cassian. And then looking at her. She avoided their eyes.

Just before they were led to a table in one discreet corner of the courtyard though, a deep voice said, 'Corti!'

They stopped and Lili watched as Cassian greeted a tall and very handsome slightly older man with hints of grey at his temples. Then she saw that it was a family. The man's wife was standing up now too. She was petite and very pretty, with long curly blond hair. Dressed in a very simple but cool silk jumpsuit accessorised with stylish gold jewelry in an effortlessly elegant look that Lili immediately envied.

There was a gangly tall boy of about seventeen who looked just like his father, then a girl of about fourteen who also took after the father and a younger girl of about ten with curly blond hair like her mother.

Cassian turned around. 'Lili, I'd like you to meet the D'Aquannis. Dante and his wife Alicia have been friends of the family for a long time.'

Alicia came around to greet Lili who braced herself for the inevitable unavoidable handshake but she found that it didn't cause her to tense as much as usual. She was too distracted as Alicia attempted to introduce her to all the children. Allesandro, Poppy and Cara. As far as Lili could make out.

And then Alicia turned and picked up a smaller child Lili hadn't noticed, a little boy who immediately stuck his thumb in his mouth. He had to be about three years old and had a mop of unruly curls and dark eyes like his mother. She was wry. 'And this is Olli, who as you might deduce was a very happy surprise.'

Lili couldn't help respond to the other woman's infectious and easy friendliness and smiled.

'Please, join us?' Alicia's husband was saying. Lili looked at Cassian who was already shaking his head, but she put a hand on his arm and he looked at her. 'I don't mind, if you'd like to.'

'Are you sure?'

Lili could tell he was concerned that this might be a bit much for her, all the people, and shook her head again. 'It's fine.'

'Oh good,' responded Alicia. 'We're all very bored just talking to each other.'

Within minutes the waiters had organised it so that Cassian was on one end of the table and Lili at the other. Cassian was shooting looks at Lili and she did her best to reassure him that she was fine. She was seated with Alicia on one side and her oldest son on the other and they were charming company. It made her even more aware of how much she'd cut herself off from other people.

Cassian was deep in conversation with Dante at the other end of the table and Alicia remarked, 'A handsome pair, hm?'

Lili blushed. 'Yes, they are.'

'You're newlyweds, aren't you?'

Lili nodded. The older son was now attending to one of the younger children and something about his easy tenderness and tactility plucked at her insides, because it was a dream she'd always had, of a loving family, that she hadn't witnessed.

To avoid any more personal questions Lili observed, 'You're English?'

Alicia nodded and took a sip of wine. 'I can't seem to get rid of my accent no matter how much I try and my husband insists on speaking English to me. Mostly to annoy the kids into learning so they can understand what we're saying.'

Lili laughed. 'That's one way of doing it.' Then she said a little shyly, 'I love your style.'

Alicia's eyes widened comically. 'Oh believe me, this is after years of trying to keep up with innate Italian style. I now stick to some core basics and that's it. But if you ever want someone to go shopping with give me a call. I loathe shopping but I love making new friends and drinking coffee.'

Lili smiled again. Food was ordered and eaten. Lili had a little wine, mindful of driving. She couldn't help stealing little glances at Cassian and once or twice their eyes met, sending little electrical charges into Lili's blood.

And then she felt her dress being tugged and looked down to see the smallest child, Olli, looking up at her with such an adorable and cherubic expression that she couldn't help but reach for him. He came willingly and sat easily on her lap.

Alicia immediately said, 'Oh no, you don't have to hold him, he's covered in chocolate sauce.'

'It's fine.' Lili smiled, relishing the heavy weight of the child. This was a revelation because as much as she knew she wanted a child, she'd always harboured a doubt that when it came to it, she might not be able to get over her fear of being touched but this felt like the easiest thing in the world. He was no threat to her.

The trust that the child had, to come to her and let her hold him, humbled her too. She felt emotional.

'Are you okay?' Alicia asked.

Lili nodded and blinked furiously. 'Fine, just something in my eye.'

There was a lull at the table and then Alicia's husband looked from Lili to Cassian and said, 'I assume you both know that there is a clamour of interest in knowing more about the new mysterious Signora Corti?'

Lili looked at Cassian, alarmed. Was there? He avoided her eye and said, 'Well, I'm sure they'll soon lose interest.'

'You know how they can be if they sense a story... I'd be careful. Maybe a couple of appearances just to curb the interest might be no harm. After all, your new wife is utterly charming, Cassian, it's a crime to hide her away.'

Lili squirmed and as if sensing her discomfort the child, Olli, reached out for his mother who took him onto her lap. Cassian looked at her and she tried to communicate, *sorry for not being more normal*, with her eyes.

He just said easily, 'Maybe I just don't want to share her with the world yet.'

Dante laughed. 'Well, my friend, I can understand that. Enjoy it while it lasts because I have a feeling the world will come knocking.'

The dinner broke up soon after that. Olli the toddler was getting tetchy. They said their goodbyes and Lili was genuinely sad to see them go. The older boy took Olli in his arms as they left and Dante and Alicia had arms wrapped around one another. Lili saw them steal a kiss as the kids went ahead and felt another disturbing lurch of emotion bordering on envy.

'Do you want anything else?' Cassian asked as he came and took the seat to Lili's left.

She shook her head. 'No, I'm full. Your friends are really nice.'

He nodded. 'They are. Dante became a friend once I came of age and whenever I was at the villa he'd insist on taking me out or I'd go over to visit them. They're good people and very loyal.'

'They seem like a genuinely happy family too. Close.'

'I guess.' Cassian's voice was a little clipped. He avoided her eye.

'What do you mean, *you guess?* It's obvious they're a really solid unit—' She broke off suddenly as something occurred to her and she cursed herself silently. 'I'm sorry, I'm an idiot. They must be a reminder of what you lost.' And what she'd never experienced.

A bleak expression crossed Cassian's face. 'I won't lie. I like spending time with them but each time I do, I feel nothing but terror.' He looked at her. 'Don't they realise how much they have to lose?'

Lili's chest ached a little. There was no reason why he couldn't have what his friends had but she could understand even more now why he would choose a scenario with a child that put him at a distance.

Lili had to remind herself that she'd been perfectly happy at the thought of being a lone parent with a child. And now…*what?* she asked herself. Now she wanted more than that? That thought was so disturbing and provocative she changed the subject. 'Do you think it's true about there being speculation about…me?' The thought of people she didn't know wondering about her made Lili's skin crawl a little. She imagined thousands of hands reaching out trying to touch her.

Cassian made a face. 'Much as I hate to admit it, he's probably right and Dante loathes the press about as much as I do so he wouldn't say we should court it, lightly.'

Lili's insides twisted. 'And if we didn't, would it get worse?'

He looked at her. 'It might…especially if there's not much else going on.'

The waiter came by with the check and Cassian settled up. He stood up and held out a hand and then at the last moment he pulled it back and said, 'Sorry, I wasn't thinking.'

But Lili had an image in her head of watching Dante and Alicia kiss and she said, 'No, it's fine.' She put out her hand and let him take it. And kept holding it as she stood and they left. Walking down the street he interlaced his fingers with hers. A more intimate hold. A shot of pure lust went straight between Lili's legs. She blushed.

Cassian was looking at her. 'What are you thinking about?'

She shook her head. 'About how you affect me...' She sent him a quick glance. 'Is it normal? To feel so...needy?'

Cassian stopped walking and looked at Lili. All evening he'd found it hard to take his eyes off her. She'd looked like she was concentrating so hard while talking to Dante's wife, Alicia. And then she would smile and it lit up her face in a way that stopped his breath.

And then when she'd had their smallest child on her lap, a look of pure awe and wonder had come over her face. He'd never known a woman like her.

But now she said, 'Actually don't answer that, you've probably already lost interest and I wouldn't blame you, I mean, I'm completely inexperienced and not elegant and—'

Cassian put a finger very gently to Lili's mouth. He ached to replace it with his mouth but they hadn't kissed there yet and for the first time in his life he realised why it was considered such an intimate act and he marvelled at how easily he'd kissed women before. Without even thinking. Taking it for granted.

She'd stopped talking, eyes wide. He said, 'Yes, it is entirely normal, when the chemistry between two people is as strong as it is with us. And yes, I still want you, Lili.'

'Oh.'

'I can show you when we go home if you like?'

Her cheeks coloured and she sounded a little breathless when she said, 'Okay.'

Cassian led her back to the car and he said, 'I'll drive if you like, I didn't have much to drink.'

'Okay.'

They got into the car and navigated their way out of the village and back along the lakeshore to the villa. It struck Cassian then that this was the longest amount of time he'd spent in the villa since his family had died. And it had crept up on him without noticing.

Obviously circumstances had led to this but he found that driving back to the villa now with Lili in the car beside him was the closest he'd come to a sense of peace in a long time. If ever.

That revelation was disconcerting but not enough to distract him from how much he wanted to be naked with Lili as soon as possible. So he focused on that and not on the fact that his life seemed to be deviating alarmingly far from its course.

When they reached the villa, before they got out of the car, Lili turned to Cassian and said impulsively, 'If it would help to be seen in public at a couple of things, I don't mind.'

He looked at her, frowning. 'You don't have to, it's not part of the agreement. Something else will come along to take the press's interest.'

Lili shrugged a little. She wasn't ready to fully admit that there was something deep inside her that felt almost compelled to out herself as Cassian's wife. That maybe she wasn't prepared to hide herself away in the villa like some sort of secret wife.

'I'll leave it up to you. If you think it's necessary, I'll do it.'

He considered her for a moment and then said, 'There's an event in a week, in Milan. I have a board meeting and then there's the charity Corti ball, a philanthropic event we host every year. There'll be a lot of people there, Lili, a big crowd.'

The thought of it sent that tendril of fear down her spine but she forced herself to say, 'I haven't been such a recluse all the time. I've navigated crowds, I've just avoided them where possible but I don't want to spend my life in the shadows anymore. If I have a child I don't want to limit their life because of my...issues.'

Cassian looked at her. 'You're brave, you know that?'

Lili felt like squirming. 'I'm not really,' she protested.

As if reading her mind he asked, 'Will you tell me what happened to you?'

Lili's insides constricted. He might not think her all that brave if he heard her story and deemed it to be not worthy of those *issues*. She thought of spilling out the terror of those few days and how she'd really believed she might be raped, or die, and of her family's indifference. She couldn't bear the thought of Cassian's reaction, whatever that might be. The best would be pity and the worst would be him looking at her as if to say, *was that all?*

She shook her head. 'Not...now. Maybe someday.'

'Okay.'

His easy acceptance, and his not pressing her, soothed her a little.

Then he said a little ruefully, 'I won't lie, it probably won't hurt my reputation to be seen in public as a more settled man.'

Lili forced a smile even though she was inevitably thinking about the day when he would take another lover after he was done with her and if and when she got pregnant. She recalled holding that small child on her lap and forced herself to remember that that was what this was all about. Creating a family. And a chance for love. Except, it wouldn't be a family, would it? Because Cassian had made it explicitly clear that he didn't want to be a part of the kind of tableau they'd witnessed this evening with Dante and Alicia.

And, she had to remind herself, she'd never imagined that either. *Until now.* Her mind was getting scrambled. She forced her mind back to the moment and said, 'Well then, I'll do my best not to let you down.'

Cassian got out of the car and came around to open her door. They walked to the front of the villa and he lifted his hand, silently asking for hers. She put her hand into his and let him lead her inside and up the stairs.

Lili shivered with anticipation. When they got to his room she said, 'I'd like you to undress me.'

He stood in front of her, eyes glittering. Then he smiled, unbearably sexy. 'I thought you'd never ask. I've been fantasising about taking these clothes off all evening.'

'I don't think I'll wear them again. I was embarrassed to be wearing them in public.'

He looked serious. 'You could wear a sack and look good in it, Lili. You have nothing to feel embarrassed about.'

Something very fragile and light filled Lili as he very gently started to push open the long cardigan and pushed it off her shoulders. It fell to the floor. Then his fingers were on the buttons on the front of the dress, his knuckles grazed the bare skin of her breasts and she shivered. He stopped. 'Okay?'

She nodded and just managed to stop herself from saying, *can you hurry up please.* He kept going and pulled the dress open and pushed it off her shoulders. She stepped out of the flat sandals she'd been wearing.

Now she was just in her underwear. The new underwear. Satin and lace. Cassian stood back and looked at her. Devouring her.

'Cass, please.'

He looked at her. 'Say that again.'

She frowned. 'Please?'

He shook his head and stepped close to her, tugging her bra straps down, baring her breasts. He cupped them and rubbed his thumbs across her tingling nipples, making her legs weak.

'Say my name.'

She breathed it out. 'Cass…'

'Like that.'

Then he lowered his head and covered her nipple with his mouth, drawing the stiff peak into a vortex of damp heat. Her legs gave way but he caught her, effortlessly, lifting her against his chest. Very dimly, Lili was aware that she was moving in leaps and bounds beyond a place where she'd never even imagined before, but she couldn't think of that now.

Cassian laid her on the bed and stripped efficiently. He was hard. Ready. He reached for her underwear and pulled them down. He left her bra framing her breasts.

'Widen your legs.'

She did. And he stroked himself for a second before coming down and hooking her legs over his shoulders. He pressed kisses up along her inner thighs and then he put his mouth on her and Lili no longer cared about anything but this exquisite place only he could bring her to, where time and matter ceased to exist, replaced purely by pleasure and the pursuit of it.

Milan

They had arrived to Cassian's Milanese palazzo in the afternoon. The busy city felt a little jarring to Lili after the relative peace and quiet of Lake Como but she was doing her best not to feel intimidated by it.

The palazzo was down a leafy side street off one of Milan's main thoroughfares. It was modest from the street but behind the door lay an open cobblestoned courtyard and massive ancient door, flanked by statues and trailing vines.

The palazzo was on three levels. Flagstones in the reception hall with a massive stone staircase. Cassian had shown her into rooms with terrazzo floors, massive windows, frescoes on the walls dating from the eighteenth century.

It had all the period features with the comforts of modernity. There was a male housekeeper called Domino who Lili had greeted, still feeling a little like an imposter.

She was in her bedroom suite now with a stylist from a boutique in Milan with a selection of dresses. Cassian had gone to his board meeting.

The stylist was saying, 'I think this blue would look amazing with your eyes, why don't you put it on and I'll help you do it up.'

The friendly woman was being so suspiciously hands off that Lili wondered if Cassian had said anything to her. But she dutifully went into the lavish en suite of her bedroom and shimmied out of her jeans and top and into the dress. She had to take off her bra because it was strapless and had a sweetheart neckline. She was holding this up to her chest when she went back out and the stylist did up the zip at the back, winching in Lili's waist and pushing her breasts up.

She looked at herself in the mirror, eyes wide. 'I can't wear this.' Her breasts looked so…provocative. And her waist was tiny. Since when had it been small? And her hips, so wide. There was a slit on one side, showing the length of one pale thigh.

Her upper chest, shoulders and arms felt very bare. Because they were.

'Nonsense,' the stylist said. 'You look fantastic. It could

have been made especially for you. It's sexy and modern and you have the figure for it.'

The stylist stood back and looked at her and then said, 'Have you ever considered a fringe? I think it would really suit you.'

Lili looked at her and said honestly, 'I haven't considered much about my looks at all to be honest.'

'I used to be a hairdresser, can I try something?'

Lili shrugged and let the stylist help her back out of the dress and into a robe. They went into the bathroom and the woman put Lili on a stool and started working on her hair. It didn't take long. Then she stood back and said, 'Look.'

Lili stood up. She didn't recognise herself. She now had a long, choppy fringe that together with the layers in her hair made her look much younger and somehow…cooler. Edgy. Modern. She looked like a different person. Like the woman she was becoming. Emerging from the shadows.

'Do you like it?' asked the stylist, sounding a little worried now.

Lili turned her head from side to side. 'I think I…love it.' She felt emotional. 'Thank you.'

'Good!' The stylist looked at her watch and said, 'I'll go and pick up those things we need and be back in time to get you ready, okay?'

Lili nodded.

She sat back down on the stool feeling a little stunned. Just who was she becoming? *The woman you were always meant to be.* Ridiculously, Lili had to blink to get rid of the stinging in her eyes.

CHAPTER NINE

CASSIAN LOOKED AT his watch. He was down in the reception hall waiting for Lili. She wasn't late but he was unaccountably nervous. When no woman had ever made him nervous, not even his first lover.

The stylist had just left, saying enigmatically, 'She'll be down shortly. Wait till you see her, Signore Corti.'

He heard a sound and looked up and nearly had a heart attack. Lili was on the top step in a silk midnight-blue dress that seemed to be glued to every curve of her body.

She started coming down the stairs, holding onto the wrought iron banister but all he could see was the toned length of thigh showing through the slit in her dress. And then, up, to where the swells of her breasts looked like they were ready to spill into his hands. Plump and luscious.

Her hair was down, long and lustrous. Falling behind her shoulders. Casual but very sexy.

Like her mouth, a glossy colour just darker than her own lips. Her skin looked dewy. Eyes huge and very blue. Lashes long and dark, peeping out from behind... He frowned and managed to ask, 'Is something different?'

She touched her hair and he noticed the self-consciousness. 'I got a fringe...do you like it?'

Did he like it? She looked all at once younger and more

mysterious and sexier than anyone he'd ever seen in his life. She was going to kill him.

'I think it's lovely,' he said a little inanely, not quite able to put how he really felt into words. He'd always taken for granted feeling confident around women but now he felt like a bumbling teenager.

'We should go, or we'll be late.'

They went out to where Cassian's chauffeur was waiting for them and got into the back of the car. Lili's scent was evocative and Cassian realised it reminded him of the wild roses at Villa Corti. He noticed she was wearing a simple diamond necklace and matching stud earrings and a bracelet. And she wore the wedding rings.

'That diamond set suits the dress. They were my mother's.'

Lili put a hand to her throat and looked at him, pale. 'If I'd known I would have chosen something else, but the stylist suggested these from the collection. I wouldn't really have a clue to be honest.'

'Don't be silly, they were hers but they in turn belonged to her mother-in-law, my nonna.'

Lili's hand dropped to her lap and Cassian had to curb an urge to curl his hand around hers. She asked, 'Did you know your nonna?'

He shook his head. 'No, she died young. All my grandparents did.' His mouth thinned. 'Maybe my family is cursed.'

Lili was a little shocked at his bleak pronouncement but before she could respond he was asking her, 'Are you ready for this?'

She looked out of the car and could see the venue ahead and a stream of glittering people walking up a red carpet to the entrance of one of Milan's iconic museums where the charity ball was being hosted.

She gulped and her palms felt clammy. 'I guess so. Now or never, right?'

'I will take your hand when we get out but if you don't want me to touch you, just let me know, okay?'

The thought of Cassian not touching her sent Lili into a paroxysm of anxiety. 'It's okay, I think I'll need it.' She looked at him, struck again by his consideration. 'But thank you.'

'And if it's too overwhelming we'll leave, no pressure.'

'But I can't ruin your night, if I can't handle it, I'll leave.'

'*We'll* leave.'

Lili might have rolled her eyes at his insistence but deep inside it thrilled her. She'd never had an ally before. But now the car was pulling to a stop and her nerves took over.

Cassian got out and came around to her door and opened it. Immediately the sound was deafening. 'Corti, Corti! Over here!'

Lili put her hand in his and let him help her out, praying she wouldn't fall over in front of the baying mob of photographers. Cassian pulled her into his side and wrapped an arm around her and she'd never been so grateful for physical touch. Her hand was around his waist and gripping his jacket tight, in case they somehow might be wrenched apart.

He lowered his head to her ear and said, 'Just another minute for them to get pictures and then we'll go inside, okay?'

She nodded and somehow managed to force a smile to her face. Soon he was leading her up the steps and into the building where the shouts of the photographers was replaced by people chatting, laughing and melodic music coming from what appeared to be a small orchestra, all dressed in black.

Lili could see immediately that this was another level of the social sphere. A level that her grasping social-climbing family could never hope to aspire to. But it filled her with no satisfaction, only a sense of regret for a family who had let her down.

Cassian was being greeted by a steady line of people all vying for his attention. Thankfully he seemed to be engineering introducing her in such a way that a handshake wasn't necessary. He was also careful to try and keep space around them and Lili noticed men in black suits at a discreet distance and wondered if they were security.

Lili had been handed a glass of sparkling wine and sipped it, needing the slight sense of Dutch courage it gave her.

Before long they were guided into an even larger ballroom where a charity auction was being held. Everyone was seated at round tables and small dishes of food were being served but Lili was too afraid to eat in case she dribbled something onto her dress or cleavage.

Cassian said into her ear, 'I'll be back in a minute,' and then he was getting up and walking away. Lili felt a lurch of panic which dissipated when she saw he was only going to the podium to give a speech.

He was easily the most handsome man in the room, in his classic black tuxedo. Hair slightly less messy than usual. Dark hair hugging his jaw. Vital. Commanding.

He was also articulate and succinct and passionate, inspiring the crowd to dig deep into their pockets for the auction. His playboy reputation notwithstanding, he'd managed to retain the respect of his peers and Lili felt a little glow of pride, even though she was cynical enough to know that this world always protected their own, not to mention a sporting legend.

He said then, from the podium, 'Ladies and gentlemen, you see before you a changed man.'

The crowd laughed and some heckled playfully. Cassian put his hand up. 'No, really, I am joined here this evening by my beautiful wife and I am very happy to declare that my life in the fast lane is only going to exist on the track from now on.'

There was laughter and Cassian said a few more words before he came down from the podium to rejoin Lili. She felt eyes on her but she was surprised to find it didn't bother her too much because she couldn't take her eyes off her husband.

He said, 'May I take your hand and kiss it?'

She knew he was just acting out this role of *changed man* in front of everyone but she nodded. He lifted her hand, never taking his eyes off hers and pressed his mouth to the back of it. She felt the slightest touch of his tongue against her skin and an arrow of need spiraled down to between her legs.

He sat down as the emcee proceeded with the auction. Lili hated to admit that even she was being taken in by this very public declaration of changing his ways even though she knew it was all a lie.

He had no intention of becoming the devoted husband and family man.

But she couldn't help wondering if maybe there was a chance for—*what?* The suspicion that she was yearning for something she knew she couldn't have was not welcome.

'What is going on behind that pensive look?' Cassian's voice broke her chain of thought.

She forced a smile and said, 'Be careful not to be too convincing in your newly committed husband role.'

He looked at her pointedly. 'What's that supposed to mean?'

Lili swallowed. Why had she opened her mouth? She shook her head and forced a smile. 'Nothing, just that when you're pictured out and about again you don't want to undo all the good PR work.'

Cassian just looked at her for a long moment with no expression and then stood up and held out a hand. 'It's time to dance.'

'I can't dance, Cass, seriously, it's not pretty. My mother made me go to classes but nothing worked.'

Cassian hated the way Lili said *Cass* impacted him somewhere deep and tender. But he'd told her he liked it. Especially when she said it as he joined their bodies or put his mouth on her. He cursed silently.

He looked down and all he could see were her huge eyes, very blue, and the far too tantalising flesh of her breasts, pressed against him. He realised he was holding her very close and relaxed a little. 'Is this okay for you?'

She nodded. 'It's fine. Did you hire those security men to keep people back earlier?'

Cassian felt a prickle of exposure over his skin. 'I didn't want you to feel crowded.' He said this just as someone bumped into them and he registered stark fear flaring in Lili's eyes. He turned them so she had her back to the wall and not the people.

She looked over his shoulder and said a little shakily, 'Thanks.' And then, 'I'm sorry.'

A surge of protectiveness rose inside Cassian. He wanted to do damage to whoever had put that fear into her eyes and wanted to push her to tell him what had happened but he resisted the urge.

'Don't apologise.'

She hadn't lied about not being able to dance, she kept stepping on his feet but Cassian had to admit that he found it somewhat refreshing. He was so used to everything being seamless. Unsurprising. *Dull.*

That little conversation they'd just had replayed in his head. *Be careful not to be too convincing.* The truth was that he hadn't had to act convincing at all. When he'd spoken those words they'd fallen out of his mouth all too easily, and he hadn't even noticed. But she had. His convenient wife.

He'd already begun to concede that his fast living persona had been growing more and more tiresome and easier to see for what it had been all along. A smokescreen to hide his phobic reluctance to allow anyone close. Lili had touched on that before, at the villa, when she'd asked him if his playboy persona was all an act, not even knowing how close she was to the truth.

And maybe his entire racing career was founded on the anger and whim of a young man determined to do the thing that scared him most—get into a car and risk his life again and again. Because he'd survived and his family hadn't.

Maybe? jeered a voice, *how about not maybe, but definitely.*

Cassian almost resented Lili for this little prompt to examine where his demons lived. He'd been quite happy with them, until she'd come out of nowhere and somehow inserted herself under his skin like a prickly burr. And he couldn't quite recall how that had happened. It all seemed a little hazy, as if he'd been drinking.

But his resentment couldn't last long when all he could think about was how she felt, pressed up against him. Her curves softening against his harder body. *Hardening body.* He gritted his jaw.

Then he heard a sound, a very distinctive gurgling sound and looked down at Lili who went puce. He raised a brow, glad of the distraction from disturbing thoughts. 'Hungry?'

She glared at him. 'I was afraid to eat in case I spilled something on the dress and I forgot to eat earlier.'

Cassian smiled. 'Want to leave and get some pizza?'

He saw the relief on her face. 'Can we?'

'We can do anything we want. I'm the host.'

'But should you leave yet?'

'They'll just assume I'm taking my delectable new wife home because I can't resist her.' Which wasn't untrue. It unnerved Cassian, the fact that he wanted her as much now, if not more. Lately he'd found his desire for a lover waning quickly. Surely this would follow the same pattern? *And then what?* asked a little voice, *You can go back to your empty existence pretending to be something you're not? Taking unsatisfying lovers to bed?*

Cassian scowled at himself and took Lili's hand and led her off the dance floor, taking care to shield her from other dancing couples.

'That pizza was amazing, thank you,' Lili said as they walked back into the reception hall of the palazzo and she bent down to slip off her shoes with a little groan of relief. She caught them by the straps and before she knew what was happening, Cassian had lifted her into his arms.

He said, 'Is this okay?'

Lili nodded, a little speechless, but suddenly self-conscious with a belly full of food. She hated comparing herself to all the willowy women he was usually seen with but she couldn't help it. 'You don't have to carry me, I'm too heavy.'

'No, you're not.'

Lili clamped her mouth shut. Frankly, she felt too safe and

secure in his arms to argue. He brought her to his bedroom and put her down. It was like her room, sumptuously decorated and with period features without being overwhelming.

In her bare feet she felt a lot smaller next to Cassian. He started taking off his clothes with an efficiency that had him naked in a matter of seconds. Lili drank him in. The broad chest, wide shoulders, corded muscles. She felt like sighing in pure awe.

'Can I undo your dress?'

Lili nodded and turned around, presenting her back to Cassian as if it was the easiest thing in the world.

'Is this okay?' he asked. She nodded and pulled her hair over one shoulder. His hands came to her shoulders first, massaging gently and then harder when she said, 'That feels good.'

Liquid heat entered her veins and coursed through her body as his hands moved down, fingers tracing her spine, making her skin rise into little bumps. Then he was pulling down the zip, all the way to the top of her buttocks.

The dress loosened around her breasts and then she let it fall down and he tugged the material at her hips until it fell all the way to the floor. Now she only wore pants.

Cassian came and stood in front of her. Lili pushed the underwear down and stepped out of them. They were naked. There was something very elemental about facing each other like this. Bare skin. Nothing to hide behind.

Desire surged up inside Lili like an unstoppable force. She'd been starved of touch for so long. She said, 'Please touch me, Cass.'

He took her hand and led her over to the bed. 'Lie down,' he instructed.

He looked at her. 'Where do you want to be touched?'

'All over.'

His eyes were like molten silver. He smiled and it was pure sin, as he started at her feet and worked his way up her body. It was hard not to let emotion mix with desire when she thought of all the years she'd spent in a self-enforced purgatory of isolation, but any emotion was turned to pure molten heat when Cassian reached her thighs and parted them and that devilish glint in his eye was all she saw before he put his mouth on her and drove her to her first climax of the night.

At first, Lili wasn't sure what was happening. All she knew was that she couldn't move. She was being held immobile by rings of steel. And it was dark. Fear and panic were immediate and acidic all the way from her gut to her mouth. Adrenaline coursed through her body and she fought with all her might to be free. Her elbow landed against something soft and there was a muffled groan and suddenly the bind was released and she leapt up.

It took her long seconds to realise where she was. And that she wasn't being held captive. Moonlight shone in through a window, illuminating Cassian's bedroom. It hadn't been rings of steel around her, it had been his arms.

Another light came on, a low light. And suddenly Lili felt cold. She spotted a robe on a chair and pulled it on over her naked body. She was shivering now, trembling in the aftermath.

Cassian was sitting up and rubbing his chest. Lili was horrified to be able to practically see the dent in his chest where her elbow had hit him.

He stood up. 'Lili...what the hell?'

Too shocked and horrified, she fled blindly from the bedroom and found her way to a reception room. She saw a drinks cabinet and went and pulled out a bottle filled with what looked like whiskey. She poured some into a glass and threw it back, wincing as it burned its way down her throat.

The room was suddenly illuminated in soft light. She slowly turned around and saw a bare-chested Cassian looking at her. He'd pulled on his tuxedo pants. The top button was open. Not even that could distract her from the tendrils of fear still gripping her insides like the bind she'd imagined.

'Lili...? What just happened?'

The terror was still real. She felt even now that someone might just grab her from behind and yank her back to the awful place. She blurted out the only thing she could say. 'Can you hold me, please?' She'd felt so safe in his arms earlier. And yes, that had turned to terror just now but it hadn't been his fault.

Cassian came over and took the glass out of her hand and enveloped her in his arms. Wrapping them tight around her. Gradually, Lili's heart rate eased back to normal and the intermittent trembling stopped.

The warmth of his body seeped into hers, removing the cold tentacles. Melting the terror. Her cheek was pressed against his chest and his heart was a steady beat.

And infinitesimally, Lili felt sensation return. Awareness. And with that came a need to eclipse the terror she'd just felt. In the only way she knew how.

She pulled back slightly and looked up. Her eyes fell on Cassian's mouth. Up to now, they hadn't kissed. They'd done everything else but kiss.

Cassian spoke. 'Lili...do you want to talk about what just happened?'

She shook her head. 'I want you to kiss me.'

He made a sound—like a groan. 'Lili, believe me, I want to kiss you too, more than anything, but I think we need to—'

She reached up and pressed her mouth against his, cutting off his words. His mouth was still open and she opened hers. Their breaths intermingled and then Lili felt Cassian unlock his arms. He put a hand to her head, fingers in her hair and he pulled her even closer.

And then, even though this was the first time she'd kissed a man, it happened like an age-old dance. Her arms twined around his neck and his other hand was on her waist, gripping her through the fabric of the robe and their tongues… *Dio*…how had she not allowed herself to have this before now? It was the most exquisite pleasure she'd ever known and she was drowning in the taste of him. It was like hot nectar. It made her feel desperate. She didn't know how long they stood there kissing but she never wanted it to end.

But eventually, they broke apart. Lili opened her eyes. Everything was blurry. Cassian came back into focus. He stroked a finger down her cheek to her jaw. He said, 'Now, that was a kiss worth waiting for.'

Lili might have said something witty or flippant but she just wasn't that type of person and the faintest tendrils of her terror still lingered to remind her that her past was all too present for her liking.

She said, 'Take me back to bed, Cass.'

He rubbed his chest and she could see where a faint bruise was blooming over his pectoral muscle. She was mortified. She touched it gently. 'I did that, I'm so sorry.'

'You didn't mean to. And soon you'll tell me what happened, hm?'

Lili weakly avoided his eye and nodded and to her relief he didn't push it and led her back up to the bedroom.

Two days later Lili was back in the villa on Lake Como. For the first time since she'd started living there, she had a sense that she didn't need this place to be her safety net or sanctuary. Because something else had taken its place. Or, more accurately, *someone*. And that revelation was terrifying. Because from an early age she'd learnt not to depend on anyone.

But now she was here on her own again because Cassian had gone to Rome on business before he stepped back into being a racing driver. The race in Monte Carlo was in a week's time and he would be busy prepping for that. And Lili felt bereft.

Angry with herself for allowing this attachment to form— *Ha! Attachment? That's what you're calling it?* sneered a little voice—Lili forced herself to put thoughts of Cassian aside—*good luck with that*—and get on with learning how to be the mistress of this villa and not its housekeeper.

First of all she cleaned all of her loose and flowy clothes that she'd been using as a uniform and then put them in black bags and took them to a women's refuge centre in Como. There was a slight tussle with the bag as her hand clenched around it instinctively when handing it over but she forced herself to let go.

Then when she got back to the villa she walked around and noticed lots of areas where paint was peeling or looking shabby. The decor was tired. She'd noticed this since she'd arrived but she'd put its careworn appearance down to lack of interest on the owner's behalf. Now she knew that Cassian cared deeply about the place even if it pained him to be there.

She went online and started to do some research and welcomed the distraction.

Cassian was sitting in his office in Rome—Milan was where the board of the Corti Group had their meetings because symbolically that's where the seat of Corti power had been for centuries, but Rome was where the operational part of the corporation was run from in the modern day. Along with London and New York.

He was feeling restless, distracted. Aware that his mind wasn't really on business, or the race coming up in Monte Carlo. In fact, he hadn't fully admitted it to himself but the Corti Group required a lot more of his focus than he was currently giving it and he'd known that for some time.

Not to mention the passion he had for making motor racing more sustainable because he knew if they could do it there, then they would be blazing a trail for every other industry.

But all of those things paled into insignificance when his mind kept looping back to Lili, like a boomerang. *Passion.* He'd never known anything like it. Even now there was a banked fire inside him, just waiting for her to send it sky-high again. He felt permanently altered in some way. As if she'd retuned him to vibrate at a different frequency.

He'd always prided himself—or assumed arrogantly—that he was a consummate lover. All of the women he'd been with had certainly behaved that way. But it wasn't until he'd slept with Lili that he'd really noticed another woman's reactions. And cared that she was truly with him, all the way.

He couldn't get that kiss out of his head. That first kiss. When she'd reached up and put her mouth to his. So soft. But firm. Sweet. Mouth open. Slightly clumsy but all the sexier for it.

He'd fallen into that kiss like a drowning man searching for an anchor and the truth was he hadn't found it, he was still drowning.

There was a *ping* on his cell phone and he picked it up. A text from Lili. That was enough to make his body react. He opened it and could imagine the slightly shy expression on her face.

Hi, I hope your meetings are going well. I don't want to disturb you but I wanted to discuss doing some redecoration work in the villa? And there are some upgrading renovations that would be useful. I have all this time on my hands now, I'd be happy to take it on board, with your approval. Lili. x

Cassian couldn't take his eye off that small *x*. Filled with a sudden sense of urgency he issued an order to his assistant and then sent back a text.

I'm on my way home.

On the flight to Milan Cassian realised the significance of telling Lili he was returning *home*. A wave of ice went through his body, dousing the sense of anticipation at the thought of seeing her again.

That sense of peace he'd felt recently mocked him.

This had started out as a very clinical marriage arrangement to secure his inheritance of a property that held equal parts pain and joy for him. And yet it had turned into something else entirely.

Lili had been the one to suggest the marriage in the first place. Who was she really? A prickle of exposure skated over Cassian's skin. He might look to everyone else as if he lived without much of a care but he was pretty circumspect when it came to choosing lovers. He always made sure they were from his cynical world and didn't expect anything more than a very transitory liaison. But since he'd been with Lili, all those concerns had fallen by the wayside.

Because you're married. Yes, but it wasn't a real marriage. And yet, here he was, running back to his new bride because he couldn't stop thinking about her. *You need an*

heir, you're just doing what needs to be done. But even Cassian wasn't sex-distracted enough to delude himself that the sex with Lili was being undertaken with one focus in mind and nothing else.

It was being undertaken because his desire was unquenchable and ravenous. Any other concern was secondary. He was realising uncomfortably that he needed her like he needed to take another breath. And that's why he'd gone to Rome—because subconsciously he'd needed to prove to himself that she didn't have him in a bind. But now here he was, disproving that.

Cassian almost instructed the pilot to turn around again but his phone pinged with another text. Lili responding to his last message.

Great, I'll be waiting. x

And that was all it took for his head to be filled with tantalising images of Lili laid out on a bed, naked, inviting him to come and explore those luscious curves—Cassian threw down his phone. The ice was melting, the doubts were receding and he told himself he was being ridiculous to overthink this. He wouldn't want Lili forever and he'd never denied himself pleasure before now.

He was still the same man with the same basic motivations: to live his life on his terms, and if those terms meant pursuing pleasure at all costs and racing around a track in a structure made of mostly carbon fibres at speeds of two hundred miles per hour then nothing much had changed at all.

CHAPTER TEN

IT SCARED LILI how much she was looking forward to Cassian's return to the villa. She'd thought she wouldn't see him again until some time after the race in Monte Carlo. After all, they'd certainly followed the fertility doctor's advice fairly comprehensively.

Lili was due her period any day now and while she didn't think for a second they'd be lucky enough to get pregnant on their first attempts, she found she was torn between both wanting it to have happened and also for it not to have happened because if she fell pregnant, then what would that mean? Job done. Heir conceived. Cassian could get on with his life.

'Lili, he's on the boat, he'll be here in about ten minutes.'

'Grazie, Eloisa, I'll go down and meet him.'

Lili made her way down through the garden. Dusk was falling. So much had happened since she'd gone down to these gates weeks ago. It boggled her mind if she thought about it too much.

She'd changed. She felt lighter. Less afraid. She didn't mind people getting close. She'd bumped into Matteo earlier and before that would have precipitated a reaction close to a panic attack. She'd just apologised and brushed it off.

And she wasn't wearing one of those big loose flowy dresses. Because they were all gone. She *was* wearing a dress, but it was sleeveless and came to above her knee and it was form-fitting, with a belt around her waist and buttons down the front. She'd deliberately left the top buttons undone to show a hint of cleavage, giddy with an excitement she'd never felt before, because she'd never had a boyfriend or a lover. *Or a husband.*

She pushed open the big gates and went down the steps. She heard the sound of an engine and she could make out the tall figure at the wheel. Lili's insides fizzed and somersaulted and her blood felt thick and hot and between her legs grew damp with desire. Her nipples pebbled into hard points.

The boat came close enough for her to pick out Cassian's features. Those grey eyes swept over her body and a fresh wave of heat engulfed her. He threw her the rope and she secured the boat. Then he stepped onto the pier and she was so desperate to feel him under her hands that it didn't give her a second thought or moment of hesitation when he cupped her face in his hands and kissed her so thoroughly she almost melted into a puddle at his feet.

They pulled apart. Her hands were wrapped around his wrists as if she could keep his hands on her face. And then, without wasting another second, Cassian was taking her hand and leading her straight up to the villa and to the bedroom.

An electric urgency crackled between them. Like nothing Lili had felt before. 'Cass...what?'

'I need you. Now.'

There was a stark expression on his face and in that moment all Lili could think of helplessly was, *I'm falling in love with him.*

A dozen questions bubbled up inside her, even as they both reached for each other wordlessly, stripping off clothes and falling onto the bed in a tangle of limbs, skin already damp with anticipation: *What happens if I get pregnant? Will you still want me? Or will this all be over? Will you really just leave me and your child behind and get on with your life? And why does that not feel like enough for me now?*

But they all turned to ash on her tongue because she knew she couldn't ask them. Cassian had never promised her anything. If she hadn't precipitated making love, they could very well have not seen each other since the wedding if they'd embarked on IVF. And so, if this was all she was going to get...this desperate hungry need, then she would take it.

Lili twined her arms around Cassian's neck and revelled in the feel of his hard body against hers and as their mouths met and as he joined their bodies, she told herself this was fine. She would survive this when it was over. She'd survived a lot worse.

'And I really like this look, showcasing the original features but with a more modern touch in the decoration.'

Cassian responded by gently biting Lili's bottom. She dropped her phone and turned around. 'Hey, you're not taking this redecoration stuff seriously.'

'Oh, I am,' he said, nipping at her flesh again and moving back up so they were side by side, on their elbows. She'd been showing him online mood boards of inspiration for the redecoration. 'Very seriously. I trust your judgement, Lili. Go for it.'

She looked at him. 'You have no thoughts on what you'd like?'

Cassian flopped onto his back. 'This place hasn't been

decorated since before my parents' time. Anything would be an improvement.'

'Thanks,' she said dryly, 'I think.'

He looked at her. 'I leave for Monte Carlo later this morning.'

Lili pushed down the trepidation she felt when he said that. Not only fear for his safety but also because she had a foreboding that Monte Carlo was going to be some kind of watershed for them. He'd be back in his world, reminded of all the reasons why coming home to Lake Como was vastly more boring than what he was used to.

Lili had been a diversion. A novelty.

'Come with me. I have an apartment there.'

It took Lili a second to understand what he'd said. Her eyes widened. 'You want me to come with you?'

Something flashed across his face but it was gone so fast she couldn't decipher it. She was afraid it had looked like regret. But he nodded. 'Sure, why not? You've never been to a motor race before and Monte Carlo is the most dramatic arena in the world.'

'And,' he went on, 'there's a charity event hosted by the racing governing body in the Hotel de Paris the night before qualification. We could use it as an opportunity to appear in public together again.'

Her fizzing insides deflated a little. It was just an opportunity. But even so, she wasn't strong enough to resist. She shrugged and echoed his words. 'Sure, why not?'

He reached for her, putting his hands on her waist and urging her closer so that she lay over his body. They were welded together. Chest to chest, hips to hips. She could feel him, between her legs, growing harder. Again. Her heart sped up.

'Now, what was it you wanted to discuss about chinoiserie on the walls in the bedrooms?'

Lili rolled her eyes and pressed her mouth to his. He gripped her hair, angling her head so he could plunder her deeply and Lili pushed everything else deep down where she would ignore it for as long as possible.

Monte Carlo was an assault on the senses. Stunning location, built into the hills with the Alps on one side and the Mediterranean on the other. There were scores of people everywhere. More sleek yachts than Lili had ever seen crowding the marina. Structures set up along the race route which took place on the narrow winding streets of the municipality where Cassian was driving them in an open-top sports car. Shades on, wearing a short-sleeved polo shirt. He was every muscular inch the elite sportsman and as people spotted him they called out, 'Cassian Corti! We love you!'

Lili was glad she was wearing shades too. To hide her scowl at all the women screaming for Cassian.

They wound their way up into the streets away from the circuit and Lili could see that every building and street oozed with luxury and wealth. Tall buildings, old and new towered over them. Honey-coloured stone adding to the overall impression of extreme luxury and wealth.

Cassian slowed down and turned into an underground car park under one of the older buildings. An attendent met them and took their bags while another attendant jumped into the car to park it.

They got into an elevator and it went all the way to the top. Cassian's apartment was the penthouse and an outdoor terrace had spectacular views all the way down to the marina and over to the royal palace, at a little distance away.

Designer stores lined the streets below and there were small lush green spaces. Tourists wandered around taking it all in.

'Good afternoon, Monsieur Corti.'

Lili turned around from where she'd been looking at the view to see a man dressed in a butler's uniform greeting Cassian who said, 'Marcel, how are you?'

'Very well, ready for the race on Sunday?'

'I'm always ready, Marcel, you know that.'

Lili came back inside, feeling a little shy. She wondered if she matched up as the wife of a billionaire/playboy/motor racing champion. She'd dressed in soft worn leather trousers, slim-fitting, with a loose silk shirt. Hair up to keep it from flying around her face in the open-top car. Minimal make-up.

'Marcel, I'd like you to meet my wife, Lili.'

He bowed towards her. 'A pleasure, Madame Corti, I will do my utmost to make sure your stay is as pleasant as possible.'

'Oh, I don't need much at all, please don't go to any trouble.'

Marcel had prepared a light lunch for them and they ate it on the terrace. Cassian wiped his mouth, took another gulp of coffee and stood up. 'I have to go, the guys will be waiting for me at the HQ.'

Lili lifted her head and shaded her eyes so she could see him. She hoped the disappointment she felt wasn't on her face. It was ironic really, she'd longed for a life of solitude and security and now that she could have it, she felt lonely at the thought of Cassian leaving her for a few hours.

He frowned. 'Is that okay?'

She waved a hand. 'Of course, you're here to work. Go.'

'There's a pool and a gym here...not that I'm suggesting you need to work out...there are designer shops on every corner...you should be able to keep yourself amused.'

Lili stood up and forced a big grin. 'Please, don't worry about me, I'm not here to distract you.'

Cassian moved towards her and snaked an arm around her waist, pulling her into him. She revelled in his touch, putting her hands on his chest.

'Well you've failed miserably, I'm afraid, you can't *not* distract me but I fear you would have been a bigger distraction not being here.'

Her heart leapt a little. Then he said, 'What is it? Shopping doesn't fill you with giddy glee?'

Lili grimaced. 'I've either been cleaning houses or housekeeping since I left home, I'm not exactly used to a life of frivolous activities. And I'm still not really sure what suits me. Also, I know you gave me a credit card to use but I'm not really comfortable spending your money.'

Cassian's head fell back and he let out a half laugh. He looked at her again, smiling wryly. 'If I didn't know you already I'd assume that's a line.'

'Okay then,' he said. 'Do you want to come with me?'

Lili grinned. 'Could I? I wouldn't get in the way, I promise.'

He stood back and looked her up and down. 'In those trousers, and that shirt, it's pretty impossible for you not to distract but if it gives me an edge this weekend, I'll take it.'

He took her hand but she stalled for a second. 'Seriously, I don't want to be in the way.'

He pressed a kiss to her mouth and pulled back. 'Today is just some practice sessions and checking out the circuit.'

'Okay then.' Lili couldn't hide her excitement. This was much more fun than hanging around by a pool or shopping.

The paddock area, as Cassian had explained to Lili, was the area that housed all the different teams' garages, hospitality areas and media pens. It was a hiving buzzing mini-city and Lili was awed by the sheer level of industry.

Cassian held her firmly by the hand as they made their way through to his team's hub. People were constantly stopping him to say hello but he just greeted them and kept going.

He looked back at her. 'Okay? Are the crowds too much?'

Lili shook her head. 'No, it's fine.' Because she was with him and he was anchoring her to a sense of security.

Even when they got to his team's HQ and he had to go and do his thing, he left her in the familiar hands of Ricardo who she'd met at Monza. He told her where to sit and made sure she was looked after. Lili soaked it all in and then watched as Cassian appeared again in that close-fitting driving suit and then contorted himself into the car before heading out to the track to do laps.

Ricardo gave her headphones so she could hear Cassian converse with the engineer and just hearing his voice was enough to send thrills through her.

After a couple of hours Cassian was ready to go again. The following day would be more practice laps and then Saturday would be the day he would have to try and attain pole position for the actual race on Sunday.

Lili's mind boggled with everything.

When they got back to the apartment Cassian had to take some business calls and so Lili, feeling restless after all of the adrenaline she'd just witnessed, went out for a walk. It had been so long since she'd felt...free.

Although, she had a sharp reminder that her demons weren't altogether gone when a group of young people were suddenly behind her, crowding her, trying to get past and she had a sudden spike of panic, her heart rate zooming sky-high. She let them pass and sat down on a nearby bench, waiting for her heart rate to settle.

She'd come so far in the last weeks but this was a reminder that she still had a ways to go.

As she sat there, she saw a sign for a pharmacy nearby and instinctively put a hand to her belly. There was still no sign of her period. She got up and went over and, telling herself she was just being cautious, she bought an over-the-counter early pregnancy test.

When she was back in the apartment, Cassian was still on the phone in his office. Lili put the pregnancy test under some clothes in her bag and forgot about it.

By the following evening, after another visit to the track with Cassian, Lili was beginning to feel like a pro when it came to racing—and she had yet to see a live race! She'd met Cassian's teammate, a Frenchman who was very intense. She was being treated almost as one of the team by his team and it made her feel more emotional than she'd like to admit, another reminder of how her own family had consistently shut her out.

She could understand the allure of this tight-knit world that Cassian was part of.

She'd commented earlier, as they'd driven back to the apartment in his car, 'It's like a family. Your team.'

He'd looked at her but shades had been covering his eyes. 'What do you mean?'

'You've been with them since you started racing. It's all about loyalty and they love you. I think Ricardo thinks of you as a son.'

A muscle in Cassian's jaw had popped and he'd said tightly, 'He has a son. Two sons.'

Lili had shrugged. 'I know more than anyone that family

bonds don't necessarily mean much. You make your family and you've created a family out of this world. Your team.'

Cassian had changed the subject, clearly not enthusiastic about her take on his chosen profession. He'd been conducting some online business meetings and so Lili had taken advantage of the apartment's pool to soak up some sun and force herself to relax even though it went against the grain.

She'd found that Eloisa had packed some swimwear—not her white one-piece but a white bikini. Lili had put it on telling herself she'd look ridiculous, falling out of it all over the place but it was actually very flattering and supportive.

When she heard a sound nearby her skin prickled with awareness. Footsteps stopped abruptly. Lili opened her eyes and squinted up at Cassian who was standing a few feet away.

She stopped breathing. He was wearing nothing but snug white swimming shorts. Showcasing every delectable inch of his olive-hued and honed body.

His voice sounded a bit strangled. 'It looks like we're matching.' And then, '*Dio*, Lili, I had fantasies about the swimsuit but you've just surpassed them.'

Lili wished she was sophisticated enough to stand up gracefully and sashay over to Cassian, take him by the hand and render him insensible with her sexual prowess but she was still very much a blushing novice learning at the hands of a master.

She sat up and pulled her knees up. 'You don't look bad yourself.'

He put out a hand. 'I'm hot. Join me in the pool?'

Blood fizzing now, Lili got up from the lounger with as much grace as she could muster and went over to Cassian. His eyes were glowing. But she didn't take his hand. She kept walking to the deep end of the pool and after pulling her hair up into a rough knot on her head, she dove in and swam underwater all the way to the other end.

She surfaced just in time to see Cassian execute a perfect dive and within seconds hands were around her calves and tugging her back under. She sucked in a deep breath and met him underwater.

They kissed, floating in time and space, until they had to breathe and came up for air. Lili's arms and legs were wrapped around Cassian. He backed her up against the wall and she leaned back.

He smoothed his hands down her back, easily undoing her bikini top and dispensing with it. His gaze was hot and devoured her and then he lowered his head and surrounded one taut peak with his hot mouth, making her writhe against him.

He broke away, cheeks flushed. 'So much for taking a swim, I can think of another activity I'd prefer.'

Lili was breathless. Needy. 'Me too.'

Cassian let her go and hauled himself out of the pool, reaching her her and pulling her up. They went straight to the bedroom and within seconds he was inside her, filling her, stretching her and Lili knew that she'd never know this kind of exquisite pleasure again. It made her feel emotional.

She moved against him to make the emotion go back where it belonged, but it stayed, high in her chest and throat, stinging her eyes, as Cassian moved within her until she was arching her back against him and pleading for release. And only in that moment of oblivion was the emotion eclipsed.

Lili felt a gentle rocking motion and then prodding against her bare shoulder. She was face-planted into the pillow, unable to move. She made a sound in her throat to signify she was semi-conscious.

Cassian's voice. 'Time to get up, we have an event to go to.'

Lili made another sound that she hoped conveyed what she meant which was: *Huh?*

As if Cassian had understood perfectly he said, 'The charity event at the Hotel de Paris.'

Lili moved her head to the side and without opening her eyes said, 'It's your fault I'm not able to move.'

There was a low chuckle that had a decidedly evil edge to it. She cracked open one eye and scowled at him. He was bare-chested, hair damp, and smelled amazing. He'd just showered. A spurt of awareness sent tingles through her blood, waking her up a little.

Then he said, 'I got you something to wear.'

Lili turned over on her back and saw how his eyes went to her breasts. She shamelessly let him look, hoping she might distract him enough to forget about an event. But he lifted his gaze back to hers and said, 'Nice try, *witch*.'

He went to the dressing room and came back holding up a dress on a hanger. Lili absently pulled the sheet up over her chest and sat up, blinking. It was the beautiful green slinky dress Cassian had spotted in the window of a boutique in Como.

Strappy with the deep vee and a generous slit over one leg. It looked miniscule on the hanger. She said, 'That'll never fit me.'

'Try it. I've asked someone from a local salon to come and help get you ready.'

He hung it behind the door and then said, 'The beautician will be here in twenty minutes.'

Lili squeaked and jumped out of bed, pulling the sheet around her and trailing it behind her as she made her way to the bathroom.

An hour later Cassian was allowing himself a small shot of whiskey but this, he felt, would be permittable on a race weekend when he would obviously never normally drink.

But, he was still fizzing with an overload of pleasure endorphins after making love to Lili for the entire afternoon. Again and again until they were spent.

Contrary to that first time they'd made love—now there was nowhere he couldn't touch her. She was expressive, responsive and tactile. And generous. His mind threatened to blank just at the memory of how she'd taken him in her mouth, her eyes on his as those plump lips had surrounded him in heat and suction and mind-blowing pleasure.

She kept surprising him. And, she was the first woman he'd ever brought with him to a race. He'd always kept his personal life strictly away from the track. But he wanted her here. *He needed her.* It was as if she'd become some sort of touchstone that he had to keep near him.

And, something she'd said earlier kept reverberating in his head. Her observation about how the racing crew were like his family. When she'd said that he'd felt himself tense in rejection at the very notion.

Ever since his family died, he'd vowed never to need family again. Loving meant losing and he'd resigned himself to being on his own to avoid that horrific grief and sense of abandonment. Self-protection, yes, but also due to a sense of guilt that he'd survived and they hadn't. On some level he'd always felt he didn't deserve to aspire to that kind of happiness again.

And yet, Lili had a point that he couldn't deny. The racing crew *had* become like his family. And he'd let that happen in spite of his best efforts to shut everyone else out. Certainly lovers had never come close. *Until now.*

It was disconcerting to acknowledge that he'd found himself creating some kind of a family around him. Because they really were. He'd put Ricardo's sons through university. He'd paid medical bills for another crew member's parent's cancer treatment. He'd watched their children grow up. And, he'd stayed loyal to the same team since he'd started racing. He was invested in their care and lives in a way that he could see now was like some sort of a web of connections. Care. Interest. *Love.*

On that very disturbing note, he heard a sound and looked to the doorway and almost dropped the glass out of his hand. Lili was standing there, in the dress. It seemed to have been poured onto her body. Glittering. Every curvaceous inch was glorified and celebrated. There was a cutout over one hip. The straps of the dress highlighted the line of her shoulders and toned arms. The vee dipped between the curves of her perfect breasts. Breasts he could still taste on his tongue.

Her hair was down and loose and wild but clipped back from her face. She wore minimal jewelry. She didn't need it. She looked fierce. Cassian had the very unfamiliar urge to go and kneel before her and ask her...*what?* He shook his head to try and restore some sense of sanity and she said, 'I know, it's too tight, isn't it?'

He realised she'd misinterpreted his gesture and put out a hand. He put the glass down and walked towards her. 'No. You should never take it off again. It's perfect. You're... perfect.'

She blushed. Her eyes were huge and very blue. 'Are you sure?'

Cassian nodded. 'I have never been more sure of anything in my life.' And he realised it in that moment. And he knew he wasn't talking about her dress anymore. From the minute he'd seen this woman waiting on that small pier, his life had become...less noisy. Less about the pain of the past, even as their whole marriage was designed to preserve a part of his past.

It had become more about the present. He had to face the

fact that at no point had he felt the need to check if Lili might be pregnant yet, so that he could move on with his life. Let her move back to the villa and get on with hers. *And their child.* It was as if he was deliberately avoiding having to deal with what he would do, if she were pregnant. Because that would spell the end of this, wouldn't it? After all, that was the goal here. Nothing more.

More.

'Cass? Are you okay?'

Cassian blinked. Lili said with endearing shyness, 'You look very handsome too.'

He couldn't even remember what he was wearing. He looked down. It was a white tuxedo jacket. He remembered now. Pairing it with a black bow-tie. He looked up. 'Thank you.'

Lili frowned. 'Are you sure you're okay?'

Cassian nodded. He was losing it. He took Lili's hand. 'We should go or we'll be late.'

The charity event was being held in the Hotel de Paris—one of the world's most glamorous and exclusive hotels. Iconic. Cassian had driven them the short distance in his open-top sports car and once people—passing tourists/racing fans/paparazzi had realised who he was, they'd gone wild.

Lili had clutched his hand tightly as they went into the hotel and were escorted to the space where the event was being held. She was happy to stand beside Cassian and bask in the sense of security and safety with his arm around her. Even when people crowded behind her, she didn't feel panicky. Once he was there.

First they had drinks on the rooftop pool bar, the sky gradually turning dusky pink as the sun had set over Monaco, and now they were in a beautiful vast room—lavishly decorated—with a terrace that overlooked the road where the cars would be racing—first of all, to qualify, tomorrow and then the actual race the day after.

Lili shuddered delicately, the road looked so narrow to her. How could it be safe for cars going at impossible speeds?

'Are you cold?'

Cassian handed Lili a glass of sparkling wine and she shook her head. 'No, just wondering how on earth you do it…race on roads like this.'

'It's a rush,' he admitted. 'Like nothing else.'

Lili arched a brow. 'Nothing else at all?'

He looked at her and smiled and it made Lili's heart seem to expand in her chest. He said, 'Well, now that you mention it, this afternoon came pretty close.'

'Only close?' Lili smiled. She'd never had this kind of teasing relationship with anyone. Her heart turned over. How could someone who she'd never met before, in such a short space of time, have become…her world. Words bubbled up from deep inside. Words that she wasn't even sure what they were but they were falling out of her mouth before she could examine them or censor them, she was saying, 'Cass, I think I—'

'Corti? Is that you?'

Lili was almost surprised to find a whole vast room full of people with music playing from a dais in the corner. For a moment she'd forgotten they weren't alone. And she'd almost told him—she went cold as panic gripped her and she realised that she'd almost told him she was falling for him.

Cassian was turning away now to greet the man who'd interrupted them. An older man. Lili looked at him and smiled as Cassian introduced them. But this man didn't go back to ignoring her and talking to Cassian like most people, he stayed looking at her.

Lili felt her smile falter. Why was he looking at her so intensely? And then he said, 'When I saw your wedding picture in the papers I thought you looked familiar but now I can really see it. You were the girl who was kidnapped, weren't you?'

Lili's hand tightened reflexively around the glass she was holding. She felt herself going numb and sounds got distorted. She shook her head, tried to speak. She could feel Cassian looking at her. And then as if someone snapped their fingers—actually the man had done exactly that—everything came back into focus and now the sounds were too clear and loud.

He said, 'That's it. Lara Bagiotti. Your father is the real estate mogul.'

Cassian's voice. 'You're mistaken, Adam, my wife's name was Spirenze and it's Lili, not Lara.'

But the man was shaking his head. 'No, I'm almost certain. I was fascinated by the case. You were kidnapped for what…three days? And then suddenly you appeared at a press conference with your parents…after they'd paid the ransom.'

Lili felt sick. Blindly, she put the glass of wine down on a nearby table. She looked at the man and said, 'They never paid the ransom but they let everyone believe they did.'

The man looked confused. 'Oh, but then how did you get away?'

Lili couldn't look at Cassian. The most awful thing that had ever happened to her and the thing that had demonstrated so cruelly how little loved she was, was out in the open in all its ugliness.

She ignored the man's question. 'If you'll excuse me

please.' She made her legs move, and somehow propelled herself through the crowd, pushing through people, hearing vague noises of, *hey, watch where you're going* and also, from behind her, *Lili*...but she couldn't stop.

She got out to the foyer, blessedly quiet, and stopped. Her skin was clammy, her heart was pounding, her breathing was shallow and she was sure she was about to have her first panic attack in years but there was nothing she could do to stop it.

She saw the doors and took a step towards them but a voice sounded behind her like the crack of a whip. 'Lili.'

CHAPTER ELEVEN

LILI STOPPED. CASSIAN WALKED around to stand in front of her. She expected him to look angry but he looked confused.

'Lili? What the hell was Adam talking about?'

She swallowed but couldn't seem to make her mouth or tongue work. Ironic really, considering that she'd been about to reveal her beating heart to this man only moments ago.

Cassian was shaking his head. 'That stuff he was talking about…you having another name…being kidnapped…' He stopped and a light seemed to dawn in his eyes as he said almost to himself, 'I remember that. It was about eight years ago…the daughter of some businessman in Rome was kidnapped for a few days…'

Lili wished she could fully appreciate the fact that her father had just been called *some businessman*.

Cassian looked at her. 'Was that you?'

Lili had a brief fantasy of running out of the hotel and far away but Cassian was like a solid wall between her and freedom. A voice mocked her, *since when have you felt free*? She knew when. The moment this man showed her how she could feel free again. A helpless sob of emotion was climbing up from her chest but she pushed it back down.

Miserably, she nodded.

Cassian's eyes went wide. 'What the hell, Lili? Is that even your name? What did he call you? Lara?'

There was noise from behind them, a sound of rushing, a voice. 'That's her there! Lara Bagiotti, the kidnap heiress! Married to Cassian Corti!'

Cassian looked over Lili's head and cursed. He took her arm in his hand and walked them out of the hotel. Lili's dress swirled around her legs but she was barely aware. Somehow, miraculously, Cassian's car appeared in front of them and they were in it and he was driving away at speed.

And then, within minutes, Lili was back in the apartment and Cassian was pulling off his bow-tie and undoing a button on his shirt. His jacket was gone. Her head hurt. She sank down into a chair.

Cassian was pacing back and forth. He stopped and put his hands on his hips and said, 'Explain.'

Where to start? Cassian started for her. 'Is your name even Lili?' He cursed. 'Are we legally married?'

Lili forced herself to stand. 'Yes, and yes. I was baptised Lara Bagiotti but I changed my name legally to Lili Spirenze when I left home.'

'Why?'

'To put distance between me and my family.'

'And that was you? The girl...the heiress who was kidnapped?'

She nodded and swallowed. 'Yes, that was me. That's why... I have issues with being touched...or in crowds.'

Cassian was shaking his head. 'Why didn't you tell me about this?'

'Because I find it painful to talk about. I prefer to forget about it.'

He made a scathing sound. 'Seems like that was going really well for you.'

Lili's chest hurt. She couldn't blame Cassian for reacting like this. It was a lot to take in. But she wanted to assure him of one thing at least. 'We *are* legally married, I'm not pretending to be someone I'm not.'

'Aren't you?'

That winded her. As did the way Cassian was looking at her. As if she was a stranger. A cold breeze skated over her skin even though it was unseasonably warm for late spring. The lack of emotion was far too painfully reminiscent of her parents.

'I admit that I was hiding, or taking refuge, but I wasn't pretending to be someone else. This is me.'

'You should have told me as soon as you knew we would be married. This is going to be all over the press tomorrow. If not already.'

Lili put a hand to her head and sat down again. She looked at him, insides twisting. 'I'm sorry about that...but there's no illegality here. Or scandal, really. I'm just the girl who was kidnapped and who changed her name.'

'And cut herself off from her family. Do they even know you're married?'

She shook her head. 'Not unless they've seen it in the press. I haven't been in touch with them since I left home.'

'What on earth did they do that was so bad?'

They pledged to love and support me and they didn't. Lili couldn't figure out a way of saying that without sounding whiny. She was agitated now. She stood up and paced back and forth. She stopped. 'It's hard to talk about...they weren't...supportive.'

'They saved you from the kidnappers!'

Lili shook her head. 'No, they didn't. I did that. I saved myself.'

Cassian frowned. 'What? How?'

A slew of images came into her head, and the memory of dank dark spaces. Big hands, smelly men. Rough voices.

Suddenly Cassian asked, 'Did they touch you?'

Lili thought of being passed around, manhandled, pushed down, pulled up. She shuddered but then saw Cassian's expression and said, 'No. I told you already...they didn't do anything to me like that. They were just rough...careless. And they said things...about what they'd do.'

Cassian's brain blanked for a second at the thought of big brutish men pushing a young defenceless Lili around. Saying disgusting things. There was a maelstrom inside him. He was in shock and he recognised he was also angry and... hurt? that she hadn't confided in him before now. This was huge.

Earlier this evening, not that long ago, she'd been looking up at him and he'd been drowning in her eyes, and for a moment he'd felt such a strong and profound connection that—he shook his head. She'd deceived him. Badly. He'd taken her at face value when he hadn't done that with a woman, ever. And now he was paying for it.

'How did you get away then?'

He saw Lili's—*Lara's*—throat work as she swallowed and he had to clamp down on his body's helpless response. Even now when there was enough tension between them to cut with a knife.

'They'd taken me to an industrial site on the outskirts of Rome. They were hired by a man my father had bested in a business deal. He wanted to punish him. Make him pay. Literally. They'd left me in a room but it wasn't totally secure. There was another door leading into connecting offices hidden behind a tall filing cabinet.'

Cassian said nothing, just folded his arms.

She went on. 'I managed to get out without them noticing and found one of the cars outside. The keys were in the ignition. I guess they weren't that bright. I drove to the nearest police station and they brought me home. My parents were having a dinner party.'

'While you were kidnapped?'

She nodded. 'They'd told people that they had to be seen to be continuing as normal not to let the kidnappers win.'

'So they didn't pay your ransom...what was it again?'

'A million euros, and no, they didn't. But they let everyone believe they had.'

Cassian felt a burst of anger on her behalf. No wonder she'd walked away. What awful people.

'There's something else,' she said now, her hands twisting in front of her. 'Something that explains why they were so...cold.'

'What?'

'They had trouble conceiving at first so I was adopted. But my mother especially, she never really...connected with me. But then they tried IVF, when I was about two, and it worked. They got pregnant and had twins, my brothers.'

Cassian absorbed this. 'What about your biological parents?'

Lili shrugged and avoided his eye. He saw something in her expression that caught at him inside where it shouldn't. She looked...ashamed.

Then she did look at him and the expression was gone and replaced with one of almost defiance. 'I've never pursued tracking them down because they chose to let me go. Clearly they're not interested.'

Cassian knew that under any other circumstances with anyone else he would of course refute this but it was Lili and he'd just found out the woman he thought he knew...*wasn't*.

There was the sound of cars beeping from the streets below. The sound seemed to break him out of a trance. He looked at Lili. How had this woman assumed such an importance in his life that he was standing in front of her and feeling so many things at once that he couldn't begin to pick them apart?

He had a memory flash back to that day in his office in the villa when he'd told her they would marry. She'd been so shy, shapeless. She'd promised him that he would barely even notice a ripple of change in his life and yet here he was now and the terrain looked vastly different to anything he'd ever known before.

And the only thing he could think of right now was to cling to what he knew. He shoved down the roiling emotions and the ever-present desire. He said, 'I have a race this weekend. I can't think about this now.'

Lili looked tortured, her face pale. 'I know, I'm so sorry that you had to find out like this.'

'Were you ever going to tell me?'

She blinked. 'I know I should have. But I think when things changed between us...became physical... I started to change too and you've shown me that I can feel...normal again. And I liked that. I didn't want to go back to the past.'

Cassian could empathise and he hated that. He wanted to take Lili by the arms and tell her that of course she was normal, and what even was that anyway? He also wanted to haul her into his body and kiss her until all of this receded far into the background. But there was another part of himself that was dominating those warring impulses.

The part of himself that had been formed the day of the accident when the worst thing in the world happened. When he'd learnt that you couldn't count on anything, or anyone.

The part of himself that he had to call on now. Reactivate. So he could survive this and walk away from the emotion shimmering in Lili's eyes.

She said now, 'Cass, earlier, I almost said something to you but that was when the man came and—'

He put up a hand. He had no idea what she was going to say but he knew with every fibre of his being that he couldn't allow her to say it. Because it would threaten everything that had held him together since he was a boy.

'No. I don't want to know.'

She lifted her chin. 'I think you should know that I—'

'*I* think,' Cassian interrupted her with the very unfamiliar feeling of panic gripping his gut, 'I think that you should go back to the villa. Clearly things have escalated in a way that neither of us expected but we have done what the doctor advised—' He stalled here, his mind suddenly full of very unhelpful X-rated images of Lili touching herself and then sitting astride him and taking him into her body.

He went on, 'And so, you might already be pregnant. And if you're not, we will revert to the original plan of using IVF.'

Lili's face was leached of all colour. 'You think I should go back to the villa, take a pregnancy test and if I'm not pregnant, try to get pregnant using IVF.'

'Yes. That is what you promised me at the very start of all of this. A marriage of convenience and an heir.'

'I know I did...but that was before. I had no idea...that I would fall for you, Cass.' She went on, speaking quickly as if afraid he'd try to stop her again. Cassian was too stunned. Winded.

'That's what I was going to say earlier, that I thought I was falling for you, but I know now that it's too late. I'm already in love with you.'

'Not to mention,' she went on, 'the fact that the chemistry between us doesn't seem to be getting less. It's stronger now than ever. You know more than me how these things work but even I can tell it should be going the other way.'

Lili held her breath. Cassian was looking at her with no discernible expression on his face. As if he'd been turned to stone. She'd never told anyone in her life that she loved them. She'd loved her parents until it had become clear that they held no such feelings for her. She'd always vowed that she would never love again unless she could be certain she'd be loved back.

She'd thought the safest way to achieve that would be with a child of her own. She hadn't counted on Cassian. But what was becoming very clear right now was that what she felt wasn't remotely reciprocated.

She could feel herself curling inwards as if to protect from a blow.

Then he spoke. 'I have a race to focus on. You can stay here until you return to Como. I'll have someone get in touch to help you organise travel. I'll stay somewhere else.'

He turned to go and Lili couldn't help saying, 'That's it?'

He turned back to face her. 'That's it.'

Then he turned again and he was gone. The door closing incongruously softly behind him.

Lili breathed out shakily. After a few minutes she heard the low throttle of an engine. Cassian, getting away from here, from her, as fast as possible.

And yet she didn't regret telling him she loved him. She couldn't have contained it, once it beat within her.

But what killed her most was that she'd learnt nothing—after being comprehensively rejected by two sets of parents, at the first opportunity she'd sought out the same experience. After all those years of protecting herself.

That's only because you cut yourself off from the world,

pointed out a little voice. That made her feel sicker. If anything this just proved that on some very fundamental level, she was unlovable.

Maybe even a child wouldn't love her. Panic gripped her and she went into the bedroom and scrabbled through clothes until she found what she was looking for. The early pregnancy test.

She ripped open the packaging. Maybe it wasn't too late. Maybe she could somehow go back to the life she'd been living before Cassian had opened up her world. And her heart.

Lili went into the bathroom and hiked up her dress and did what was required to do the test. Then she sat on the closed toilet lid for a long few minutes.

When she picked up the test again and registered what was on it she swayed, feeling dizzy. *It was too late.* She stood up and kicked off the strappy sandals.

She went into the apartment and through the French doors to the terrace needing to get some air to her head. The lights of Monte Carlo twinkled at her benignly as if she wasn't experiencing a personal earthquake.

She knew that even if she hadn't just discovered she was pregnant, she couldn't go back to her old life, hiding from the world. Cassian had changed her. She'd changed herself. She could only go forward. And she could choose to take Cassian at his word, or she could do the scariest thing she'd ever done in her life, and that included surviving the kidnapping.

She could ask to be loved.

Lili hadn't returned to Como. Cassian knew because one of his assistants had told him that she'd politely refused assistance to return, saying she was staying in Monte Carlo for the weekend.

He was waiting to get on the track to qualify for the race the following day. This part of the race weekend was almost as important as the race. This is when he secured his pole position, which would ensure his success in the race.

He'd never not got pole position, or close to it. He could do this in his sleep. Which was good, because Lili's words were echoing in his head on a loop. *I'm already in love with you I'm already in love with you I'm already in love with you.*

'Cass?'

The voice in his ear. 'Yes.'

'Ready.'

'Okay.' Cassian brutally excised everything from his mind and went out onto the track.

Lili was wearing soft comfy leisure wear and curled up on a couch in the apartment watching the TV. She had a throw wrapped around her shoulders. She was aware she was reverting back to some form of shapeless comfort wear but she didn't care. Right now she needed all the comfort she could get.

She was watching Cassian on the screen and could also hear the roar of the car far below in the streets. Surround sound.

The commentators were saying things like: *So far so good, Corti is not disappointing us today, putting in his usual level of performance—*

But then suddenly something happened and the car spun wildly on the track and bounced off the hoarding at the side, coming to a stop facing the wrong direction.

'Ouch.'

Lili looked at Marcel who had come into the room to watch the TV too. She hadn't even realised she'd stood up in agitation. 'What is it? Is he okay?' Panic gripped her insides, her legs felt suspiciously wobbly.

But Marcel pointed to the screen. 'He's fine, but he's angry.'

Lili looked and could see Cassian pulling off his helmet. Every line in his body radiated anger.

'What does this mean?' she asked the housekeeper.

'It means that Cassian will be having the worst start to a race in his career.'

Lili sat back down, guilt spreading through her body. This was her fault. She'd distracted him. It was all over the press today about her identity and who she'd been. The infamous kidnap heiress. They'd dredged up all those awful pictures of her looking like a rabbit in the headlights. Too plain, too big. She hadn't fit the narrative people wanted of a damsel in distress and so people hadn't really known what to do with her. And so when the time had come, it had been easy for her to leave and take another name and become anonymous.

But she wasn't anonymous anymore. And she could never go back to that.

Race day

'Corti! How are you feeling about starting at the back of the grid?'

'Is the car going to be ready for the race?'

'Is it your injury? Did you come back too soon?'

'Is your recent marriage the reason for your poor form?'

Cassian stopped in his tracks. He turned to the press pack who all saw his face and took a step back. 'Who said that?'

A nervous-looking young man put up a hand. He was holding a microphone with his other one. Cassian went up to the barrier separating the press from the drivers in the paddock area.

He glared at the young man. 'My recent marriage has nothing to do with anything.' *Liar.*

He turned and stalked off, ignoring the pack calling out more questions. Cassian knew it would be very easy to blame Lili for his near crash yesterday. And it would feel satisfying to lay it all at her door. Along with everything else. The fact that the marriage had veered so wildly off course. The fact that he couldn't seem to slot back into the life he'd taken for granted forever.

And yet, he knew better than anyone that his life had become tedious. The past few weeks he'd felt more alive and energised than he could recall feeling since he was a young man, hurling himself at the world and hoping that somehow the pain would go away. The pain of grief and loneliness.

That insane busyness had worked for a while. But then it hadn't. And then...there'd been her. Stepping out of that pool in a white swimsuit. Fusing his brain. Rewiring it. Setting him on a different path.

Dio.

Cassian got to the pit garage and pulled out his phone and made a quick call. When he heard the answer his mouth firmed. She was still here. In Monte Carlo. She hadn't left. She hadn't gone back to the villa where she'd originally promised she'd stay. *I want peace and security.* Now he knew why. He hadn't even really allowed himself to think of the kidnapping and what it must have been like for her. He couldn't think of it. It was too much.

'Cass?'

He looked at Ricardo, his good friend. *Family.* Something inside him seemed to break apart. A wall he'd been desperately holding together. His old friend—the closest thing he'd had to a father figure—just nodded at him as if he understood everything in Cassian's head before he did himself.

And suddenly, he knew. He knew that even though he was about to get into a car made mostly out of carbon fibre and go at impossible speeds on an insanely dangerous circuit, that there was nothing brave about what he was doing. He'd been a coward for a long time while hiding behind the smokescreen of being fearless. Reckless.

Lili was brave. She was braver than he could ever be. He could let that defeat him before he even started, or he could take her bravery and hope that it might give him the strength he needed right now to do what had to be done.

Lili was pacing back and forth in the apartment. The race was at lap twenty—one of seventy-eight. She'd always thought races lasted just a few minutes. This would last for over an hour.

Cassian had somehow, completely improbably started to pass cars on one of the tightest circuits of the world, and get to a position at about halfway down the pack in the race. Which, according to the commentators was next to impossible after starting at the very back.

Lili looked at Marcel. 'I can't stay here, I have to go down there.'

'Of course.'

Lili started to hunt for shoes and Marcel pointed out, 'Maybe you should change?'

Lili looked at herself and realised she was still in the same sweatpants and top as the day before. 'Oh, right, yes, maybe.'

'I'll have a car waiting for you.'

Lili washed herself in record time and changed into jeans, a T-shirt and a light leather jacket. Sneakers.

Marcel brought her to the entrance for the teams and when they weren't going to let her in because she didn't have the security passes, he said something sharp in French and suddenly they were letting her in. She tried to ignore her trepidation at the prospect of Cassian seeing her but she couldn't ignore the impulse to come.

Ricardo caught sight of her from the pit garage and waved her over. She took a seat and watched with the rest of the team as Cassian slowly but surely overtook more and more cars on each lap to get ever closer to the front.

It was tense. He came in for a pit stop but wouldn't have noticed Lili which she was grateful for. Then he was gone again.

The crew roared when Cassian overtook the number two driver. Now there was only one car between him and the front. She could hear one of the team say out loud, 'This is *nuts*. Hardly anyone has ever come from the back to win a race.'

And then Cassian was doing it. He was overtaking the top driver. At that moment he roared past the pit garage on the track outside and everyone rushed out of the garage to go close to the track behind a barrier.

There was one more lap. Cassian stayed in front. And he won the race. Ricardo came over, beaming and pulled Lili into a bear hug and kissed her on the cheek. She barely even noticed. 'This is good?'

'It is amazing, Signora Corti. Amazing. Come.' He took her by the hand and led her out to where the crew were all behind a barrier. Cassian was coming in. Jumping out of the car, helmet still on, he threw himself at the team, hugging them and they slapped at his helmet.

Ricardo let go of Lili's hand and she let him go to the front. She hung back. Cassian took off his helmet and Lili could see the sweat on his face. His hair was flattened and messy. She'd never seen anyone more beautiful.

Things happened at warp speed. A camera crew appeared and he was being interviewed. The other two drivers who'd come second and third were behind him.

Lili found herself being jostled in amongst the crew even though she'd prefer to hang back. She didn't want to ruin this moment for Cassian. But his gaze swivelled to the crowd around her and suddenly stopped, dead on her. His mouth was still open but no words were coming out.

Lili gulped.

She was here. She is here. Cassian looked at Lili standing amongst his crew and teammates and felt something inside him dissolve and turn molten. It was the last bastion of defence he'd been clinging onto. He was, in this moment, the most raw, naked and vulnerable he'd ever been. But he'd also never felt stronger and more hopeful. It rose up within him, an unstoppable tide washing away the past and his fears and he embraced it like a drowning man finding a buoy.

'Signore Corti—that was an amazing achievement, I think we all want to know, what were you thinking about to get such a showstopping result?'

Without taking his eyes off Lili and with his voice reverberating around the winner's enclosure he said, 'I was thinking about my wife and her bravery and how she humbles me because I'm not brave at all. I've been pretending to be brave all this time but really, I'm just a fraud.'

The interviewer clearly hadn't expected this answer and while he was gaping with mouth open, Cassian went over to the barrier behind which all of his team were and he reached for Lili who came to him, eyes wide, face pale. Clearly unsure.

He put his hands on her waist and said, 'Put your hands on my shoulders.'

She did, and he easily lifted her over the barrier. He let her down slowly, relishing the feel of her body against his. 'I thought I told you to go back to Lake Como.'

She shook her head. 'I couldn't leave.'

He lifted a hand and trailed his knuckles down along her cheek to her jaw. 'Good, I'm glad you didn't. And I meant what I just said, you're brave, Lili. And I'm sorry for how I reacted…' He took a deep breath in. 'It was just a lot to take in, but I do want to talk to you about it, okay?'

She swallowed. 'About what exactly?'

'About everything that happened to you and what you've been through.'

'Oh. And what about…the other stuff?'

He raised a brow. 'The stuff where you told me you loved me?'

She nodded, her eyes flashing a little bit, some colour coming into her cheeks. Cassian exulted inside. 'There's not much to talk about there because you see, I love you too and I think I fell in love with you when you walked out of the swimming pool like a sea nymph. That's when you stole my heart and terrified the life out of me. I tried to convince myself it was all just physical and it would fade but you were right, it's only getting stronger.'

He went on, 'It does terrify me, the thought of loving you and the risk of something happening again but I'm willing to take that risk if you are.'

Lili's eyes were looking suspiciously bright. She said, 'I love you, Cass. You brought me back to life. I'll happily risk the rest of my life for you.'

He shook his head. 'No, you brought yourself back to life, Lili. Don't ever forget that. You're strong and you are loved.'

She reached up and pressed her mouth to his and he could feel her trembling and Cassian relished the feel of her under his arms and her mouth under his and sent up thanks to all and any of the gods for giving him another chance.

It was only when they eventually broke the kiss that Lili became aware of the silent crowd around them. And then a whispered murmuring started up. Jostling. The interviewer cleared his throat. 'Um, Signore Corti?'

Cassian tugged her back over to the microphone with him. He said, 'I do have an announcement to make actually.'

Lili was clamped to his side and she wasn't going anywhere. Her heart was beating fast. She wasn't sure if she'd dreamt those last few moments. But Cassian had her hand over his chest, over his heart and she could feel it thudding strongly under her palm.

Cassian said, very clearly, 'I'm announcing my retirement as a driver, as of this race.'

There was a massive collective gasp not least from the direction of his team, but when Lili caught Ricardo's eye, he just smiled. Not fazed. Clearly he'd known or he'd suspected.

There was a clamour of questions from other press nearby. Cassian held up a hand. 'My only comment on this is that it's something I've been thinking about for a while, it's not a sudden decision. Our additional driver Roberto stepped in admirably while I was out recently and he's young and full of talent and ambition, the team will not suffer, I'm sure of it.'

'But, Signore Corti, you've just proven that you're at the peak of your career! How can you walk away?'

He looked at Lili. 'Because my priorities are different now.' He looked back at the press. 'I need to focus my attention on the Corti Group and as you all know I'm passionate about making racing more sustainable.'

Cassian left the journalists and photographers spluttering and he and the other drivers were brought over to the podium. He pressed another kiss to Lili's mouth before he went up and she just managed to say, 'Cass, are you sure you're doing the right thing?'

He looked at her. 'I've never been more sure of anything in my life.' He went up onto the podium and took centre position above the other two drivers. After the presentations they opened the magnums of champagne and sprayed them over each other. Lili couldn't help a bubble of laughter and joy rising up.

He found her gaze, raised the bottle and took a big swig. Then after all the photos had been taken, he came back down with the bottle and said, 'Want to join me?'

Flutters of nerves gripped Lili's insides. She shook her head slowly and said, 'I probably shouldn't.'

Cassian went very still. He looked down at her belly and then back up. She nodded and smiled. He dropped the bottle onto the grass beside them, champagne fizzing out, unnoticed. He put his hands on her waist. 'Are you sure?'

She nodded. 'I did a test. I mean, it could be a false positive but I'm late.'

He pulled her into him and said emotionally, 'Lili, you did it.'

She put her hands on his chest. '*We* did it. We saved your inheritance.'

'None of that means anything anymore, even if we hadn't got pregnant, as long as I have you I could care less about any property.'

'I'm glad it'll still be yours.'

'Ours,' he corrected. And then, 'I want a family there

again, which is something I never thought I'd say. I was always too scared to hope I could recreate it without risking losing it all again.'

Lili put a hand to his cheek. 'I know, my love. All we can do is move forward, dare to dream and live for each day.'

Cassian took her hand and pressed a kiss to her palm. 'Then let's start living right now.'

Lili grinned at him. 'Yes, please.'

They left the pit area of the racing circuit, arms wrapped around each other and the following day that was the picture on the front of most newspapers with a headline: *Corti finds true love and walks away on a high after winning the race of his life! Is he the luckiest man alive?*

When Lili saw the headline she smiled, because she knew she was the luckiest woman alive.

EPILOGUE

Five years later—Lake Como

LILI PUSHED OPEN the big heavy gates leading out onto the lake. It was dawn and the light was pearlescent over the water. A mist hung over the horizon. The heat of the coming day was in the air but it was still deliciously cool.

All was quiet and peaceful, apart from the smallest of snuffles coming from the baby tucked against her chest in a sling, rosebud mouth in a little moue. She had dark hair like her parents and it looked as if her eyes were turning blue.

Fair's fair, thought Lili as she smiled and rubbed a finger over the downy cheek. Luca, their firstborn, had his father's eyes.

And as for the twins, in the middle, well, they took after their biological parents who had died tragically after a massive automobile accident. Lili had confided in Cassian that she'd like to adopt, it was something she had always wanted, but thought she might not get to do, if she was going to be a lone parent.

But after they'd had Luca and when he was almost two, she'd found herself feeling increasingly passionate about giving a child the experience she'd never had. Of being fully a part of a loving family. When the twins had come up for adoption—only a year old—they'd taken one look at each other and known they wanted to do it.

The twins' tragic circumstances, so close to what Cassian had experienced had touched him deeply.

The first year had been beyond challenging but they'd come through it and Luca was a happily doting older brother to Rocco and Nico. And now, they were all doting older brothers to Catia, their baby sister.

And then Lili heard it and looked up. The familiar sound of a boat approaching the pier. And the tall, broad figure at the helm. They were rarely apart for long at all now, but if Cassian had to go somewhere on his own he always came back like this and this was their ritual. Lili waiting for him at the pier.

This pier no longer felt like a precipice to her. It felt like home.

The boat came closer and she grinned at her husband. It had only been twenty-four hours but it had felt like a week. He grinned back. He cut the engine and threw her the rope. She secured the boat to the post.

Cassian leapt off the boat and first, took Lili's face in his hands and kissed her deeply, before pulling back the sling a little and regarding his daughter.

'How is she?'

'Not a great night but now you're back you can take over and let Mama get some rest.'

'Absolutely.'

Lili looked at him sternly. 'And that doesn't mean napping with benefits.'

Cassian grinned wider. 'Oh don't worry, I'll let you sleep so you have energy for tonight.'

Lili knew she was as bad as he was so she couldn't really feign indignation, or reluctance. Sometimes it came back to her, how she'd been, so fearful and isolated, scared of touch. Those days were long gone now and she was endlessly grateful.

They started back up to the villa after closing and locking the gate again, mindful of three mischievous boys. Arms wrapped around each other Cassian asked, 'How are you feeling about the weekend, are you ready?'

Lili put her hand into the back pocket of his jeans and relished the feel of his muscular buttock. Diverting her mind away from the ever-present desire that hummed between them, she said, 'A little nervous, because it's the first time we'll all be together, but really glad it's happening.'

He squeezed her closer. 'You're amazing. So many people wouldn't have bothered trying to contact their family for fear of what might happen but you did it.'

Yes, she had. With Cassian's support and encouragement. And it had gone better than Lili could have ever hoped. It turned out that her mother had given birth to her at just sixteen. Her mother's family had told her she had to give the baby up for adoption because of the scandal. But, her boyfriend, Lili's father, had stayed with her and they'd ended up marrying years later, and having three more children.

So Lili had a new, ready-made family. Brothers and a sister. Who were all lovely with strong physical resemblances. Her first meeting with her parents had been incredibly emotional because they'd always regretted having to give her up and they'd hoped that she would want to know them. She'd never fully revealed to them the pain of her adopted family's treatment of her, but they had guessed as much by the fact she wasn't in touch with them.

This weekend was the first time they would all come to visit together, her brothers and sister bringing their families too. Her children had cousins. That fact alone made Lili so happy.

And, their close friends, Dante and Alicia D'Aquanni were coming for a barbecue to meet with the family and bringing Olli who was now eight, and the ringleader of all the other children.

Dante and Alicia's two eldest children had left home and Cara at fifteen had a boyfriend which Cassian liked to wind Dante up about, mercilessly, much to everyone's amusement, until Dante had turned around one night and looked at baby Catia and said, 'Your time will come, my friend, your time will come.' Cassian had not found that amusing.

Still smiling at that memory, Lili just heard Cassian groan faintly before she realised that they were about to be ambushed by three small boys who were still in their pyjamas and had been hiding in a bush. Cassian fell onto the grass and disappeared under a tangle of limbs and calls of *Sorpresa Papa!*

The baby at her breast stirred and let out a little mewl of hunger. Lili rubbed her back, soothing her, and took a mental snapshot of the moment and the feeling of sheer joy and happiness, before she put on her stern voice and helped to untangle her sons from their father, shooing the boys back up to the house to wash and change for breakfast.

Alone again, for a brief moment, Cassian stole another kiss from his wife and then deftly extricated his daughter from the sling. He held her up and she looked at him with wide blue eyes. And smiled. Cassian's heart expanded a little bit more.

He put her in the crook of his arm and patted Lili on the backside with an explicitly lingering touch. 'Go, sleep, I'll take over.'

Lili groaned. 'Have I told you that I don't just love you, I adore you?'

Cassian chuckled and watched her back away quickly, seizing her moment. When she was gone, Cassian turned around and took a moment for himself, his daughter in his arms, and gave thanks for everything.

The endless love and passion in his life. It was so full now and satisfying, that there was no room for shadows any more.

Catia moved in his arms and he looked down and said, 'Yes, my love, let's get you fed and changed and then see about your feral brothers, hm?'

And Cassian walked back up through the gardens and into the villa that once again housed a family full of love and happiness.

* * * * *

Did Rush to the Altar *sweep you off your feet?*
Then don't miss these other dramatic stories
by Abby Green!

Claimed by the Crown Prince
Heir for His Empire
"I Do" For Revenge
The Heir Dilemma
On His Bride's Terms

Available now!

BOSS'S BABY ACQUISITION

NATALIE ANDERSON

MILLS & BOON

For Sylvie, Evelyn, Kathleen, Henry, Dave and Alfie.

You are everything to me.

CHAPTER ONE

IN A NAVY sundress and nude sandals, Phoebe Copeland ambled up the Tuscan country road, opera blasting in her earbuds, living out her *dolce vita* dreams. Money was tight but she'd made it to the second-to-last day before almost running out and, given she'd dined like a queen at her singular restaurant splurge two nights ago, the perfect plump peach she'd stuffed in the side pocket of her cross-body bag would be enough stop her stomach rumbling. She crossed the road to take advantage of the shade as she toiled up. Her parents would be appalled at her pace, but this wasn't a race, this was relaxation. In twenty minutes she'd be sitting by the small pool, eating her fruit, reading her book. In other words, she'd be in heaven.

Before she'd left London her besties, Elodie and Bethan, had joked she needed a holiday fling, but Phoebe didn't need a man to make this her ultimate overseas escape. She'd not opted for a tourist resort, or a pumping city with party-all-hours nightlife, but rather rented a small cottage on the outskirts of a small village for the week. She'd haltingly chatted to market vendors each morning and spent her afternoons reading and relaxing alone. She'd never prioritised self-care before but, when she got back to London, she was maintaining it and that was actually possible now she'd finally quit the job where she'd been taken advantage of for years.

No more push-over Phoebe. No more pleaser Phoebe. No more desperately seeking approval from her parents or employer and certainly not her cheating ex-husband. Nor any other man for that matter. No more reliance on everyone else for a sense of self-worth. *She* would value *herself.* And here she was, doing exactly that. Pleasure rippled as she zoned out in a blissful dream state.

The cannon ball came out of nowhere.

The world went black. She blinked. Three times. Then the world went blue. Bright blue.

Oh, there's an angel...

He was hovering above her, his face swimming in and out of focus, an arrested expression in his espresso-brown eyes—oh, they were rich and deep with a hint of bitter at the edge. She felt no pain. Felt nothing at all as an angelic choir sang. She'd quietly died and gone to heaven and the dude at the pearly gates was other world gorgeous.

For some reason he was also shirtless. As he leaned closer she sank beneath the spell of his bottomless eyes, sculpted cheekbones and fleetingly wondered whether his close-cropped hair would feel soft or spiky beneath her fingers. His mouth moved but she couldn't hear him. She just stared into his eyes, fascinated by their endless depths. She could stare into his eyes for all eternity. Happily, he stared back in a timeless moment of heavenly connection. But then his hands obscured her view of his stunning face and her head moved slightly.

Sensation returned and the operatic chorus was silenced. Oh. He'd removed her earbuds. She gazed at him, fuzzily trying to work out what was going on, only her limbs felt oddly weakened and the longer she looked into his eyes, the weaker her bones became. She blinked again. His facial structure really was very chiselled and the slight shadow on his jaw emphasised it. His sensual lips curved as he murmured something, but she still didn't catch what. She watched his gaze drift down and then felt every cell within her reawaken simply by that caress of attention, not even touch. More than reawaken—something intense ignited. Something hot. Something she'd not felt in ages—if ever, actually.

It took far too long to realise the blue behind him was the sky. Which meant she was flat on her back. He'd come sprinting round the corner as if the devil was at his heels. Which probably meant he wasn't an angel. And she definitely wasn't dead.

Another couple of faces appeared over his shoulder. More chiselled men. Her pulse jumped. Had she inadvertently walked into a military exercise? They looked like lean, muscled elite soldiers—though the one who'd collided with her was the only one without a shirt.

A volley of Italian began. Questions. Answers. *Orders*. None of which she understood. Her 'Easy-to-Learn Italian' app really hadn't prepared her for the speed at which the locals conversed even though she'd diligently done daily lessons for almost two years and was top points scorer in the league. But she didn't need to understand Italian to know who was in command.

And who *wasn't*. It finally registered that she was sprawled on a quiet, dusty road with her dress rucked up in front of a bunch of big, strong, potentially scary men. The non-angel hadn't taken his focus off her, despite his authoritative instructions to those guys behind him, and now his frown deepened. He said something snappy and the other faces disappeared, leaving just that blue sky haloing his perfect face.

'Okay,' he said in perfect but sexily accented English. 'Where's home?'

A tiny flat in North London. She'd bought it a couple of years ago. She'd worked so hard to get the deposit, taking leftovers for lunch, saving every penny, working an extra job at the weekend. She'd been able to give that up when Bethan had moved into her spare room. Not that Phoebe charged her much rent—Bethan had hardly been able to afford anything after her marriage had ended so badly. But the flat was hers and she was so proud of owning it.

'Where are you staying?' her non-angel asked slowly.

A slight edge in his voice brought her back to the present. She drew a breath, embarrassed by the way she'd been staring. He wasn't some celestial creature. He was a man. A good-looking one, yes, but she could get a grip. She wasn't irrevocably altered. Much. Was she?

'It doesn't matter. I can get there.' She was delighted to hear her voice sounded almost normal. 'What were you doing?'

'Sprint sessions.'

'And crashed into me.' She stared at him. 'How could you not see me?'

'How could you not hear me?' He held up her earbuds and added a damning drawl to his suddenly supercilious look. 'Oh, because you weren't paying attention. Plus, you shouldn't have been walking on this side of the road.'

So this was her fault? She didn't think so. 'Well, you shouldn't...' *Be so ridiculously good-looking.* She sighed. 'You should just carry on with your sprints.'

'Can't do that.' His gaze narrowed. 'You're white as snow.'

That was actually a normal state of affairs for her. 'I'm fine.'

'Really?' He couldn't sound more sceptical as he offered his hand. 'Stand up then.'

She froze while her heart hammered. She didn't need belated *chivalry* from him. Only there were all those guys watching, and he had an implacable expectation that she would do as he decreed, which gave her the feeling that if she *didn't* he might do something worse. As in even more embarrassing.

She compressed her mouth, hoping to hide the effect he had on her, and put her hand in his. It wasn't just electricity that shot up her arm, it was magnetism. As in the strongest pull ever. Startled, she glanced up just as his long lashes lowered, veiling his gaze as he easily helped her to her feet.

Pain lanced her ankle—the old injury came back to haunt her at the worst moment. She smothered the wince and strove for a bland expression. He didn't release her as she expected but instead drew her closer, keeping her hand in his while circling his other arm around her back until they stood as if they were about to slow dance. She didn't know where to look—into his eyes was spellbinding; into his bare chest was scorching and both options simply stoked the heat flickering in her belly. His gaze slid slowly down her again and her inner response went wild.

'Your ankle—'

'Is fine,' she lied through gritted teeth, desperate to get away and recalibrate.

'You have to walk how far?'

About another twenty minutes. She would be fine. She'd walked far further on way worse, which was how she'd incurred the weakness in the first place—but she could manage this. If they would all just move along she would crawl home in mortified privacy. But she couldn't figure out how to answer him.

Phoebe worked hard to be cool, calm, collected—most importantly, she was *measured*. She delivered—discreetly and with no fuss, no frills—because she kept her feelings under control. She'd never let the arrogant authoritarian types she worked for get to her. Admittedly, that had sometimes been misinterpreted as her being something of a door mat, but she wasn't. She just focused on managing her own reactions because extremes in anything weren't healthy. But managing her reaction to this man—one definitely arrogant and authoritarian, not to mention handsome man—was a challenge.

'Are you going to tell me or are we going to stand out here all day?' he prompted.

She couldn't unclamp her jaw to answer. He released her hand only to suddenly sweep her into his arms, throwing her so off-balance, she flung her hands around his neck.

'I apologise for my sweaty state,' he muttered. 'Your dress is dusty. I'm sorry about that too.'

'Put me down,' she hissed thinly.

'You're in pain.'

Not any more. She was in full cardiac arrest from mortification. 'I can manage. I have no desire to be swept off my feet.'

Amusement burned off that bitter edge in his eyes. 'Is that not the dream of all women?'

'By a possibly psychotic stranger?'

His eyes widened. Hell, he almost looked wounded. 'You would prefer one of the others carry you?'

She looked askance at the other men and instinctively pressed closer to the half-naked, god-like one currently holding her. She blamed the electric response she'd had, because it wasn't that she felt *safer* with him, more that she didn't want to move away.

'No? Better the devil you know?' There was the slightest wink.

'I don't know you,' she muttered dryly. 'And I don't need any of you to carry me.'

'Know this, I won't hurt you.' He cocked his head and a flash of rue sparked. 'Any more than I already have. I'll escort you home.'

Um...no. Phoebe knew she was no lightweight. 'You can't possibly carry me all that way.'

His sensual smile curved. *Wrong move.* She'd just challenged him. Here he was, pushing to run faster than all the others. She tensed. She knew this ultra-competitive type so very well. People driven to be the best were often so singularly focused they excluded pretty much anyone and anything else in their lives. Her parents were a prime example of such extremism and Phoebe had been the excess baggage they'd ditched.

'Ah,' her determined 'rescuer' murmured. 'A scrap of information at last.'

'I can manage. You don't need to perform in front of your friends.' She knew she was merely a tool to show off his superior strength to his crew now. She hated that kind of show, her ex had acted all over her in front of others. But it had been an *act*. 'There's no need to create a scene.'

'I quite agree.' He kept walking.

Phoebe tensed. Not just because he was ignoring her but because being pressed close to him was shockingly—instinctively—arousing. He was big and strong, and *never* had she felt instant lust like this. She felt a primal need to quell it. 'Are you always this authoritarian?'

'Are you always this argumentative?'

'You won't make it.'

'Watch me.'

She groaned at his bone-headedness.

'You're my responsibility,' he added.

'I'm really not,' she said stiffly.

He sighed heavily. 'I feel guilty. *All* the time. This is one mistake I can actually rectify, so please allow me to.'

Phoebe was silenced—he looked and sounded astonishingly sincere. The depths in his eyes were intense. As was his hold on her. And then she pulled herself together.

'I thought it was my fault,' she muttered.

'It was. Mostly.' He smiled disarmingly. 'You need medical attention,' he added pragmatically. 'Your ankle might be broken.'

'At most it's a sprain. You really don't need to bother.' She almost pleaded with him to release her from this searing attraction.

'It's no bother.'

Aware of all the other men—keeping their distance but keenly watching—she gritted her teeth. She felt his amusement triple and tried not to overreact more. He'd run into her—literally—and he wanted to make sure she got home safely, that was all. But her instincts warned that he posed some kind of threat.

She heard a vehicle on the road behind them, a heavy engine that sounded like it was slowing. Her non-angel paused and there were noisy shouts of Italian. More men. More laughter. They were all watching. *Great.* She should have spent way more time on her Italian app.

'We can get a ride on the truck if you would like,' he said.

Yeah, no, she didn't get in vehicles with strange men.

Her non-angel turned slightly, keeping her screened from the stares of the men. 'Luca has farmed here all his life. He has five daughters and he'll ensure you get there safely.'

So was he going to leave her with the old man?

'Or, if you prefer—' his eyes glittered '—I can carry you the entire way.'

Um… No. Because while he didn't seem to be breaking any more of a sweat, her body had decided it was all for this intimacy, and it was scraping her nerves along a very particular, inappropriate edge. She was making this whole humiliating episode a far worse spectacle than it needed to be. Phoebe wasn't like Elodie—she didn't like to put on a show or want to be in the spotlight, certainly not since her ex had put her there for his own performance reasons.

'The truck would be great,' she muttered awkwardly. 'Please thank Luca for me before you go.'

He stared at her for another second then spun and carried her to the back of the truck. One of the warriors was already there. The heavy-set man undid the tray door, spread out an old blanket and put her bag down. She must have dropped it in the melee. Her determined rescuer effortlessly carried her up with one giant step.

'You'll be more comfortable here.' He placed her on the blanket, then sat beside her and winked. 'I told you I would see you home safely.'

The relief was insane. She didn't want him to see it but as she couldn't turn away from the expression in his eyes, he doubtless did. He had a slightly smug half-smile but as she stared, he sobered. Time slipped.

Suddenly she was consumed by the crazy notion that he was thinking about *kissing* her. Worse, she was definitely thinking about kissing him. Definitely considering that perfect Cupid's bow of his top lip—considering running the tip of her tongue along the edge of it. Definitely appreciating his heat and power and wanting to feel more of it. Definitely seeing heat mirrored in his gaze. Definitely sensing his magnetism strengthen. Time slowed even more. Her head angled and she leaned—before snatching a breath, stopping herself from tumbling closer just in time. She tried to stabilise her suddenly chaotic pulse. She'd *definitely* taken a knock to the head and maybe it had triggered some loss of her personal boundaries because she'd never felt as intensely, immediately attracted to anyone. Or as willing to act on it.

'What about your friends?' she asked distractedly as the driver released the brake. Good thing she was leaving the country tomorrow because she was embarrassing herself completely here.

'They'll be fine.'

She watched the four men sprint back in the direction from which they'd come while the truck moved almost slower than her walking pace. Her non-angel wrapped an arm around her, cushioning her from the bumps. She looked anywhere but his eyes, which left her with his body. His legs were long and muscular and she noted a fresh scrape on his knee.

'You're bleeding,' she said softly. 'Pass my bag, I've got some plasters.'

'I'll live. Your stomach is rumbling.' He picked up her bag but as he did, it popped open and her now very bruised peach escaped the side pocket. 'This was lunch?' He retrieved it with a growl. 'It's insufficient.' He tossed it over the side of the truck.

Antagonism flared. She was starving and that was all she had. 'You think I can't take care of myself?'

'I *know* you were walking on the wrong side of the road on a blind corner,' he said dryly, handing her bag to her. 'You're lucky it was me coming down the hill and not a car or you'd have a lot worse than a broken ankle.'

'*Sprained* ankle.' But as much as she didn't want to admit it, he was right. 'There's not a lot of traffic on that road. I'd have heard a car.'

'We were not quiet,' he replied. 'So you'll understand why I doubt your self-care abilities.'

'I'd been nailing self-care actually,' she murmured, setting her bag beside her. 'I was enjoying the weather and the peace and the pool and I had a nice peach to eat and now you—hey, he missed the turn-off!' She glanced up in alarm as the track to the cottage receded from view. 'You need—'

'You need medical attention and a decent lunch.' His arm tightened.

Her jaw dropped.

'You're *dazed.*' He nudged her mouth shut with a gentle knuckle beneath her chin. 'You might have a concussion. You shouldn't be alone right now.'

'What makes you think I'd be alone?'

'No one who cared about you would let you distractedly wander about a foreign country all by yourself and with only a peach to eat.'

She gaped again. *What?*

'Let's get you checked out and fed properly.' He cupped her face with his hand. 'Please, I feel terrible about what has happened.'

His touch, his words, stilled her, slicing deep. 'So this is all about making *you* feel better?' she asked huskily.

His eyes narrowed slightly and he released her. 'Is it always hard for you to accept help from anyone?'

Her friends accused her of exactly that. But she managed alone very well. She'd had to and she was proud of herself for not needing anyone. 'I like my independence.'

'As do I. But I'm not averse to accepting the advice of experts when necessary. I'll take you to your cottage right away after.'

She'd been in a dream state when they'd collided. She was possibly in another now. Because she didn't say no, even though she should have. And as the truck climbed to the top of the hill and turned, she saw what awaited. A long cypress lined driveway. A castle-like collection of terracotta-coloured buildings at the top. Phoebe just stared. She'd had a beautiful week in her cottage but she'd not had access to a vehicle. She'd only walked into the village—in the opposite direction to this estate—while her one other excursion had been a vineyard tour earlier in the week and the property appearing before her now was enormous compared to that. Hundreds of vines stretched in beautifully combed rows over much of the hill, though an immaculate orchard filled one block, and as they neared she saw terraced gardens cascading from the buildings—topiary, flowers, lawn. It would have to take a bunch of staff to maintain such pristine, pretty perfection.

'You work here?'

He followed the direction of her gaze and briefly hesitated before answering. 'Yes.'

'With those guys.' Tanned, fit, dangerous, they didn't look like vineyard workers but then she really had no clue what workers 'should' look like.

The truck rolled to a slow stop. He rose and slung another volley of Italian over the side but she didn't see who he was speaking to. Then he turned back to her with a fiercely intent expression.

'You really don't need to carry me,' she said even though she knew it was pointless.

'But it bothers you so delightfully.' He grinned.

'Because I'm embarrassed,' she murmured as he scooped her up. 'You're a complete stranger.'

And was he not embarrassed by his near nudity? Clearly not. He was definitely able to revel in his physicality and good for him—he had a million muscular reasons to.

'I thought I was an angel,' he countered.

Oh, hell. So she *had* said that aloud? 'I was confused,' she mumbled.

'Which is why I'm worried you might be concussed.' He carried her round the back of the building into a huge private courtyard.

Phoebe gaped at the azure pool that came into view. 'I didn't black out.'

'No? You were pretty woozy when you were on the ground.'

He didn't take her into the main building, but a smaller one on the far side of that stunning pool. The glass doors were wide open. The room was cool with its marble tiles and he set her down in a chair, draped a soft throw across her shoulders, then crouched beside her. 'So do you mind if I check?'

'Check what?'

'Your head.'

Oh. Right. It wasn't the fall making her brainless. It was all him. She couldn't tear her focus from the rising warmth in his brown eyes. A slight pressure on her chin made her turn slightly. She dropped her gaze but encountered his chest. Broad, tanned shoulders framed all kinds of muscles she didn't know the names of but, oh, boy, they were there, they were defined, they were delicious. He really was a stunning example of masculine strength. She had to close her eyes—which only made it worse.

'Tell me if it hurts anywhere,' he muttered and began gently pressing over her scalp.

It didn't hurt, it felt far too nice. She held her breath and tried to stop the fantasies, but it was impossible.

'What's your name?' he asked huskily.

She opened her eyes but couldn't answer. He was so close, so intently focused on her, seeming to study her every feature. Spellbinding her in the process.

'What day of the week is it?'

'Friday,' she breathed.

Surely he wasn't really thinking of kissing her. Surely it was pure wishful thinking on her part. But she reacted anyway. Her breathing shortened, her body heated, her mouth tingled. She dropped her gaze to his lips.

'Right.' Those lips curved. 'But you can't remember your name. Definitely took a knock to the head.'

'It's Phoebe. My name is Phoebe,' she muttered.

'Welcome back Phoebe's memory. My name is Edo.' His smile deepened and it shot right into her. He stilled, his eyes widening.

'Everything okay?' she asked shakily after a heart-stalled moment.

'Perfect.' He nodded. 'Just flawless.'

He dropped his gaze and crouched down to slide her sandal off, now taking the time to probe her ankle. His handling was desperately gentle yet she tensed.

He immediately paused. 'It hurts?'

Mute, she shook her head.

'Liar,' he said softly, then moved his fingers even more gently across her bruised skin.

This was not an intimate act. This was him being all wannabe paramedic and her body didn't need to act as if this was foreplay. Except that's exactly what was happening—her blood simmered and secret parts of her responded in a deeply physical way.

'Where's the professional you promised?' She tried to haul herself back together. 'Or are you telling me you're a doctor?'

'Not a doctor, sorry to disappoint.' His upward glance held devilish amusement. 'But I wanted to be a veterinarian when I was a—'

'*What?*' She fired up, trying not to laugh. 'I'm not sure if you've noticed but I'm not an animal.' She pulled her ankle from his hold and waggled it carefully. 'I'm the health and safety officer at my work—'

'Are you now,' he muttered with a soft smile.

'With a current first aid certificate,' she nodded, fully ignoring his amusement. 'Which makes me more qualified than you. This is merely a sprain. Some ice, elevation and rest will sort it. I've got paracetamol in my bag—'

'Can you wriggle your toes?' He took hold of her again and with careful intensity rotated her foot from side to side then looked back up to her with a now limpid expression. 'It's just a sprain.'

'Like I said,' she drawled. 'Twenty minutes ago.'

'Some ice, elevation and rest will sort it,' he added, the corner of his mouth quirking.

Okay, she couldn't *not* laugh.

He inhaled a deep breath and suddenly stood. 'I'm going for the ice, you can freshen up in here. Help yourself to anything you need.'

His quick departure stunned her. She blinked then took several seconds to stare about the place. The 'pool house' was fancier than any home she'd entered—all cool marble, floor-to-ceiling glass, stylish furniture. She couldn't work out if the interior was more stunning than the view of the large pool, spa or the verdant vineyard beyond.

Then she caught her reflection in one of the mirrors and reality hit. *Flawless?* She was a mess. Her dress was dusty, so was her face, her hair was mussed and her pupils were abnormally large. She hobbled through the room and found a gleaming bathroom. She sponged her face and her dress, super-glad she had her bag. She dug out the small comb and lip balm she kept in the front pocket and did what she could, then went back to the lounge area just as Edo appeared in the open doorway.

He must have taken a very quick shower because his short hair was still damp. He was clothed now—the tee-shirt and low-slung jeans emphasised his tan and fitted the frame she knew very well was ripped. She grasped the back of the chair, her body weakening again because even fully dressed he was still the sexiest man she'd ever seen.

He leaned against the door jamb and smiled, as if he could read her mind. 'Thirsty?'

'I can walk,' she croaked.

'Why should you have to when you have me to carry you?'

He was too much but the wink softened the impact—until she was in his arms again and then everything was hot and hard to control all over again.

She glanced around as he carried her poolside. 'Are you sure it's okay for me to be here?'

His eyebrows lifted. 'Of course.'

Yeah, but where was the owner? Surely a place like this was owned by one of those almost royal Italian family dynasties.

'This is…' She trailed off as she took in the stunningly decorated outdoor dining table. 'Is all this just for us?'

Edo put her in the nearest of the two chairs beside which there was a stool topped with a cushion. He lifted her foot onto it and deftly secured an ice pack around her ankle. Truthfully, she didn't need the ice *there*.

She glanced away from him, taking in the crystal glasses and silverware that sparkled in the sunlight. And the food. There was so much food. 'Is this all just for us?'

He chuckled. 'Wine? Juice?'

'Coffee?' she asked. She needed the caffeine hit to sharpen up her brain.

'Certainly.' He lifted the waiting cafetière. 'How do you prefer it?'

'Black, one sugar.' She fished in her bag and pulled out the small coin purse she used to store emergency medical supplies and popped two paracetamol. 'I'm guessing you don't need that plaster for your knee now.'

'No, thank you.' He glanced at her bag with amusement. 'How very organised.'

'Thank you.' She primly ignored the fact he was mocking her and set the small purse on the table beside her.

She needed to keep what little head she had left and the only way to distract herself from his shockingly overpowering presence was to focus on the food in front of her. There so many dishes—salads, breads, pasta with glistening sauce...

'What about everyone else?' she breathed.

'They've already eaten.'

Oh, he was smooth and clearly his friends were total allies. She understood, she would do anything for Elodie and Bethan. She ate—as did he—desperate to distract herself from the tension simmering within her. Fortunately, with every mouthful she relaxed and chatted lightly as he asked her about her holiday—admitting she'd had only the week and hadn't made it to many of the big attractions.

'Not Florence?' Sounding surprised, he glanced again at the print on her purse. 'Not Venice? Milan? Rome?'

She shrugged, she couldn't do it all at once and more than anything she'd needed a rest. 'I just wanted to pretend I lived here for a little while. Like a local.'

'Because?'

Wasn't it obvious? This was Italy. 'Oh, you know...the art, the language, the food...'

And now the ridiculously gorgeous men.

'Then you'll have to come back—there's so much you haven't seen.'

'I know.' She smiled. One day, for sure.

She couldn't resist the nibbles of cheese and tomato, the deli cuts, the salad flavoured and enhanced with fresh herbs and olives. She avoided the latter. Which he noticed.

'You don't like olives?' he queried, his mock outrage growing as she shook her head.

'These are grown here,' he said. 'They're the best in the world.'

'That may be so, but I still don't like them.' She chuckled.

He put down his fork and shot her a look of reproof. 'You come to Italy and don't appreciate our food.'

That was simply not true. This lunch was better than the restaurant meal she'd splurged on earlier in the week. 'I appreciate everything here *except* olives.'

'You can't handle strong flavours?' He pressed his hand to his chest. 'What's my name?'

'Edo. Why?'

'Just double checking your concussion status given your unfathomable dislike of olives,' he purred. 'You look dazed. I remain unconvinced you should be alone tonight.'

If she had her wits she'd dive into that pool and cool off. Instead she read sensual intent in every word he spoke. 'Stop staring at me,' she muttered. 'I'm not going to faint.'

'That's not why I'm staring at you,' he replied softly.

Heat built in her cheeks. He was a prime flirt but the slash of colour building in his cheeks suggested *his* discomfort. Which couldn't be right.

'You're very beautiful,' he cocked his head. 'You don't believe I'm telling the truth?'

She didn't believe any man told the truth.

'It's *my* truth,' he said quietly. 'You're beautiful to me.'

She bit the inside of her lip. Of course this would happen at the *end* of her holiday. Elodie and Bethan's teasing encouragement rang in her ears. They'd told her to indulge and she had—in sunshine and good food—but this was a different kind of temptation.

Edo lifted the silver lid off the last covered dish. A very plump peach sat solo on a small board—not her bruised one that he'd discarded. A knife gleamed beside it. He picked up the blade, brandished it with a jump of his eyebrows and sliced off a bite-sized chunk. He put it on her side plate and sat back with a wicked gleam in his eyes.

She was unable to resist the offering. She savoured the flavour of paradise. It was pure nectar and she couldn't not smile.

'Finally, you're pleased,' he said.

Not quite, actually. But close enough.

'I didn't mean to be ungrateful,' she murmured.

'I didn't think you were. I think you're guarded.' He cut another wedge of the peach. 'There's a reason people don't like to depend on others. Usually because someone's let them down.'

Her heart skipped and her gaze flew to his face. 'And you know this because...'

He kept calmly slicing the peach, placing piece after piece on her plate. 'I let someone down, so I know the impact of that kind of pain.'

She blanched. There was absolute honesty in that admission. And he'd been honest before too. 'That's why you feel guilty all the time.'

His expression shuttered. The shrug he offered was too considered. She almost didn't want to know but she couldn't ignore that raw revelation of *hurt*.

'Regrets are part of being human,' she murmured. 'And there's not much that can't be forgiven.'

His gaze shot to hers and his mask slipped. The heat in his eyes was now snuffed, his mouth compressed into a tight line. His pain was more than visible—it was so very real.

'Have you forgiven the one who hurt you?' he asked, almost belligerently.

'One?' she noted softly.

He inhaled sharply. 'I'm sorry.'

She didn't want to dwell on the past. Not her parents'

absences, not her ex-husband's adultery. Not all those *rejections*.

'Release your guilt,' she said, pulling herself back from the verge of emotional intimacy. Of *embarrassment*. 'You've done more than enough to balance the scales. Not that I was measuring anyway.' She waved her hand about. 'I've got to see another vineyard. An amazing villa. Eaten this...' She gestured to the plates—the best meal of her life.

He stared at her for a long time before finally placing the last piece of peach on the plate for her to take. 'Then here's to enjoying the fruit when it's in season.'

'Right.' She ate the morsel and licked the tips of her fingers.

He watched, moodiness darkening his eyes. 'I suppose I ought to take you back to your cottage.'

Disappointment hit but she tried to hide it. Tried to lighten her own intensity. 'You're not carrying me anywhere again.'

He laughed abruptly. 'One moment then.'

He disappeared around the corner, but a few minutes later returned to view, riding a gleaming red Vespa. A spare helmet dangled from one of the handles while her missing sandal dangled from the other. Phoebe gave up trying to stop herself from staring at him so obviously. She would never see him again and he was too stunning not to appreciate for these final moments.

He parked the moped and grabbed both her sandal and the helmet. She froze as he carefully removed the ice pack and set her sandal back on her foot as if she were Cinderella herself. She still couldn't move as he put the helmet on her and bent to fasten the strap. The action brought him deliciously close to her again. She couldn't resist drinking in his perfect features—that sharp bone structure, those deep-brown eyes now locked on her. He was close enough to kiss and surely he was about to—

He ran his tongue along his lower lip but stepped back to offer his hand. She took it and he drew her out of the chair, which then meant she was standing too close—once more as if they were about to dance. She really wanted to dance with him.

'You ever ridden one of these?' he asked softly.

Her mouth gummed so all she could do was shake her head.

Focus.

'You need to hold tight and move with me.'

Right. Sure. That instruction was hardly helping her melting thing.

He took position on the machine and waited for her to climb behind him, his gaze simmering with challenge. Phoebe put her bag across her body and spun it so it rested on her back. She straddled the bike and gingerly put her hands on his waist but he bowed his head, firmly took her hands and repositioned them on his chest. One a little too high. One a little too low.

She inwardly shivered. So that's how he was playing it? A spurt of defiance shot through her as he started the engine and exited the courtyard. She was leaving Italy anyway and he was daring her. So she widened her fingers, flagrantly feeling more of him. Her inner thighs encased the outside of his. Her breasts and abs were glued to his back. It was intimate and intoxicating and yes, arousing. It wasn't even some fast, powerful motorcycle, all the vibrations hitting her were purely from *him*. Which was how Phoebe Copeland's formerly perfect day became—impossibly—*more* perfect.

It should have taken no time at all to go back down the hill to her little cottage but she lost all track of direction and of time. She closed her eyes, no longer caring where they were going, she just didn't want it to end. Which of course, was exactly when she heard the engine slow. She opened her eyes. They weren't at the cottage. They weren't even on the road. They were on a narrow track between tall trees and she saw the sparkle of water through the leaves. Edo killed the engine and kicked down the stand.

'Why have we stopped?' she asked.

He swiftly rose off the Vespa and turned to face her. His eyes glinted as he grabbed her arms, stopping her from moving off the seat. 'Because, Phoebe, I think you were just feeling me up.'

She relished the challenge leaping in his eyes.

'You think?' She challenged right back. '*You* put my hands where you wanted them.'

'I did,' he admitted shamelessly. 'Do you want to know where I want to put mine?'

CHAPTER TWO

EDO BENEDETTI HELD his breath as the incomparable, utterly unexpected Phoebe gazed up at him with heat simmering in her eyes. Not an English rose, but a snowdrop—an arctic blonde, so fair she'd be burned in minutes. Gorgeous, with her long limbs and not *entirely* frosty exterior, but totally out of place in this—his—part of the world.

'All right, then,' she breathed. 'Tell me.'

'Tell?' Primal lust beat out primal caution and he moved closer. 'Or show?'

Her teeth pressed on her lower lip and his tension surged to scorching. He'd felt terrible for colliding with her. How he'd managed to remain upright, he still didn't know, but he'd been felled completely in another way by the woman he'd unintentionally sent sprawling. One look and he'd wanted her. One meal in her company and he wanted her even more. He released her wrists to unclasp his helmet, then hers. He dropped them both to the ground then gently cupped her face, because along with the desire he felt an equally strong level of protectiveness towards her.

It was crazy. It was also irresistible.

'You wanted to touch my face?' She sounded amused but her breathing was choppy and colour stained her pale skin.

'To start.' Honestly, he couldn't look at her for long enough.

He knew her real wounds weren't from their collision

today but he didn't want to pry—or *prey*—on whatever the cause of the shadow in her eyes was. Maybe they were both a little broken.

For him there'd be no fixing, certainly no forgiveness possible. He didn't know why he'd even mentioned guilt. He lived a perfectly happy, shallow life ignoring his personal history as best he could. It was the only way he could live with himself at all. He couldn't change the past: couldn't bring back his brother, couldn't be anyone other than his stunted self—so he kept his distance from relationships. He'd fudged another truth with her easily enough—she hadn't realised the vineyard was his. She thought he worked there and he'd not explained because this was nothing more than a moment.

Sex. When had he had it last? Was it *that* long ago? He couldn't remember. Didn't care. He just wanted to get near to her and he'd come tantalisingly close to kissing her too many times already. It had almost killed him when he'd checked she'd not hurt her head. Her long, blonde hair had slipped like silk through his fingers while she'd stared at him with those big eyes—azure and clear, like the water of the Mediterranean's best hidden beach. Her pouty, rose-coloured full lips had parted in tempting invitation. It had taken everything in him not to kiss her then. It was taking everything not to kiss her now. But she'd taken a bad spill and that was his fault and he needed to know she was sure.

He smoothed his thumbs along her jawline, unable to resist the caress, to feel her beauty, not just see it. Her skin gleamed like porcelain but it felt soft and warm, *stunning*. And now he just wanted to touch more—*taste* all.

She was unbearably fine-featured with her feline eyes, full, wide mouth, high cheekbones and dainty—delectable—ears. He ached to nuzzle those, to tease her with a nip of her petite earlobe before whispering all the things he'd do to her. He'd make her slender frame tremble, make her long limbs quake around him, make that pretty mouth part again but this time on a scream. He could, he knew he could. Because he could feel her trembling already.

'Where are we?' she muttered but didn't take her focus off him. 'Not at the cottage.'

'You weren't watching? I just took you on a scenic tour of the area.'

Then he'd circled back to this private spot on the estate because he'd not been able to let her go yet. Not when he'd felt her hold on him—her *caresses*. Edo wasn't a worthy man. He was selfish. And he wanted this moment to last.

'I had my eyes closed,' she whispered.

'You were scared? I wasn't going fast.'

Her breathing quickened. 'I wasn't scared.'

Her luminosity intensified and he felt the warmth blooming beneath her lusciously cool surface. 'You closed your eyes to focus on something else?'

She smiled and his pulse soared to meet her fire. Yes, she'd liked holding him on that ride, and he'd *definitely* liked her pressing that close—he wanted her closer still. But while there was clarity in her eyes now, he could go only so far. He couldn't take total advantage of her shaken state.

Holding her gaze, he bent closer. She didn't pull back, in fact she leaned in, her eyes alight with desire. Smiling, he gently caught her lips with his. Hers clung. In a heartbeat he tightened his grip, needing to be nearer still. He heard her soft moan and the last of his restraint unravelled. Gentle flared to passionate. Driven to touch her, taste her, *please* her, he dropped his hands to her body, hungrily exploring the soft curves hidden by her dress. He heard her gasp of longing, felt her hungry licks and hauled her closer—

His beautiful snowdrop didn't melt. She *combusted*.

He inwardly cursed. He should have done this back at the

estate where he could've taken her to a bed. But he could give her pleasure here—because that was all that mattered now. Hearing her moan, feeling her melt, holding her while she shook in bliss—

'I'll take care of you,' he growled.

Somehow he promised her that, when he never promised anyone anything. But the spark had been there from the first. Now it exploded and now he could control nothing. He kissed her hungrily. Breath mingled as did moans, muttered half words of want. Her tongue delved, duelling with his. Hot. Willing. His arousal spiked. With increasing urgency, he kissed his way across her high cheekbone, down to her delicate earlobe where he gently pressed his teeth into the tiny treasure—insanely gratified when she groaned.

'You like that? You want more?'

He nipped down her long neck, laved the fine collarbones beneath while she ran her hands over his head, holding him to her. Not that she needed to. He couldn't tear himself from her heat if someone held a gun to his head. She'd gone from polite and restrained to wild and abandoned and he was here for it. He wanted her naked. Wanted her long legs wrapped tight around his waist while he pushed deep into her. He wanted her hot and soft and strong body around his. He didn't want to just be closer, but to bury himself completely in her.

'Yes.' She arched against him, sighing, her body like fire.

The absolute surrender in her eyes crushed him. Breathless, he unfastened the first few buttons of her dress so he could feast his eyes—his fingers, his mouth—on the pale curve of her breasts. Her straining nipples needed his attention and he gladly gave it. Her sighs were like music, the rock of her hips a command.

He grasped her waist and slid her to the edge of the seat. Her dress was long and he rucked it up to get his hand on her thigh. He growled at the satiny feel of her skin and slid his palm higher, finding the edge of her panties, flicking to get beneath. Her moans rose in pitch and volume as he nibbled and licked her breast and let his fingers circle her sensitive nub before invading her slippery heat. She was wet and hot and it wasn't enough. He wanted her wetter. Wilder. He wanted deeper. Wanted to see her, taste her, inhale everything about her in the moment she shattered—

'Edo!'

So quick. So intense. The orgasm wracked her body. Her throaty cry was the sexiest thing he'd ever heard. Satisfaction thrummed through him in a spurt almost powerful enough to trigger his own release. He inhaled sharply, gasping to retain self-control while holding her steady.

'Edo...' She collapsed against his chest. 'Oh...*my*...'

He spread his legs wider for balance and stroked her hair, trying to calm them both. He cursed his lack of preparation. The flush on her skin and the way she clutched his shirt almost destroyed the last little resolve he had but he wasn't risking her. He would keep them both out of trouble. He cradled her, listening as her breathing slowed. Then she pushed on his chest and when he looked into her eyes, he knew he was in trouble anyway.

Because she didn't look dazed. She looked alert, stunning, determined. The sensuality emanating from her actually weakened his knees. 'Edo—'

'Come on,' he interrupted.

He couldn't hear what she had to say because he couldn't deny what he knew she was about to ask.

This was absolute madness, but Phoebe didn't care. She was with a gorgeous guy who'd just given her the most intense orgasm of her life—and the fastest—so she didn't complain about him lifting her into his arms this time. No, she wrapped her legs around his waist—tightly—and heard him groan. *Yes.* She quivered with another aftershock, her body heating again as her core pressed against him as he walked. She wriggled, pressing closer to his magnificent ridge. He'd just made her feel incredible and she would return the favour. She needed to touch him the way she'd been dreaming of from the moment she'd set eyes on him. She ran her palm over his head, feeling the tickle of his short hair and pressed her face into his neck and rocked again.

'Phoebe,' A husky growl and he swore. 'Stop, look where we are.'

She stilled and looked around, momentarily worried they weren't alone. He'd taken only a few paces into the trees and now they were in a small clearing. It was lush, verdant, private—a picture-pretty mini-meadow with a clear pond in the centre.

'This is *beautiful*,' she breathed, delighted. It was shaded and quiet and she was so hot, she would happily lie with him here in the long grass.

'Uh-huh.' He inhaled deeply before setting her down and stepping back to pull his shirt off.

But then he took another step back.

'Where are you going?' She couldn't stop herself following after him, stunned to see his magnificent chest again—all that tanned, muscular perfection. But why was he literally distancing himself from her when she knew exactly how ready he was—extremely hot. Extremely hard.

'I have to cool off,' he muttered.

She slipped her hands back around his waist.

'No.'

He grabbed her arms, looking both pained and fierce. 'Phoebe, we can't, I don't have anything with me.'

She frowned, confused.

He grimaced. 'I mean protection.'

'*Oh.*' She'd not even thought about that. She'd just been driven to experience everything with him, but she wasn't on birth control and didn't have any condoms. Hell, she'd never actually *bought* any of those…

'What?' His gaze narrowed as she went completely still.

'Elodie and Bethan,' she muttered.

'Who?'

'They threw it at me before I went through the departure gate.'

'Threw what?'

She'd shoved it into her bag because she'd not wanted to hold it through the security check and had forgotten about it. Was it still there? 'A present.'

Her cross-body bag still rested on her lower back. She pulled it round and rummaged deep, smothering her reckless giggle. Bethan had told her to have a holiday fling, but not *marry* him on a whim, like she had. But there was no danger of that here. Phoebe would never marry again and Edo definitely had a 'no commitment' vibe. She finally got hold of their gift, and never had she loved her friends more. She glanced up, checking for his reaction.

He'd frozen, staring slack-jawed at the box of condoms she now held in her hand. 'You've not opened it?' he asked hoarsely. 'That's a real shame.'

'Right?' She bit her lip. 'Especially because I go home tomorrow.'

'Are you sure?' he muttered huskily. 'You really did have a knock—'

'It really wasn't that bad.' And she'd never been as sure of anything. She wanted this one moment—of togetherness, of nothing but enjoyment with no guilt and no expectation. He'd made her feel indescribably good and she wanted more, wanted him to have it too. And maybe she was just projecting but she sensed he was as lonely as she. Which was madness, because he was stunning and would surely never be short of women wanting his company.

But truly, the only *mistake* here would be *not* indulging in this with him. Why shouldn't she pursue this moment of pleasure? Hell, it would probably never happen again because she'd never felt physical desire like this. Not as instantly or as intensely and she honestly didn't really feel like this was a *choice* anyway—this was essential. Feeling anything to such an extreme would ordinarily worry her, but there would be no permanent ramifications from this... and besides, she simply couldn't resist. 'Stop assuming you know what's best for me.'

His dark brown eyes bored into her. There was a moment—who knew how long—where they stayed like statues before with a blink, the spell was broken. He stepped forward the same time as she so they collided again. Hard. It was heaven. Hands grabbed, mouths pressed. They slammed together, broke apart for a breath, only to slam again, grappling to get rid of clothes while retaining as much contact as possible. Impatient. Hungry. Hot.

'Hurry.' She stumbled out of her dress with an uncoordinated shimmy while trying to keep running her hands over his chest and discover every one of those beautifully defined muscles.

'Your ankle—'

'I don't give a damn about my ankle.'

He huffed a laugh but lifted her again, only to lower her to the soft grass a second later. She pulled him down with her and caught his mouth with hers. It was everything—having him above her, pressing her into the summer scented dell.

He kissed her everywhere, drowning her in temptation and sensation. She shivered and arched, surrendering completely to the passion he roused in her. His growls emboldened her, lending her strength, speed, confidence—*liberty*.

She drank in his curving long muscles. They bunched. Strained. She ran her tongue along the vein popping from his heated blood and smiled at his groan. She worked the zipper of his jeans and shoved them down, pressing her fingers into his tight buttocks, pushing him closer. He grunted ferally and pulled back with a sharp movement. She watched as he tore the box of condoms with his teeth, watched his hands shake as he rolled one on before dropping back to where she writhed impatiently, hot and so, so ready.

'Don't slow down. Definitely don't stop,' she muttered.

He stared back with that passionate intensity, his body heavy and insistent and heavenly. 'I couldn't if I—'

'Oh!' She arched as he pushed inside her with a powerful thrust. '*Oh!*'

He was big and strong and filled her so completely that to her astonishment she came hard. It was *everything*. She clutched and curled around him, shuddering in pleasure.

'Phoebe...' He groaned, bracing but still thrust deep, anchoring her until her ecstatic trembling eased. 'You feel really good.'

'You make me feel amazing,' she gasped, somehow rolling from that orgasm straight onto the precipice of another.

She'd felt nothing like this. *Ever*. It was quicksilver and effervescence—rare and ephemeral and she just had to ride the wave before it disappeared. There was no control now. No more words. Only movement and sensation—hot and fierce and free. He rolled his hips and thrust into her—filling her—over and over and she hovered on that delightful—*agonising*—precipice for mere seconds.

She entwined her legs and arms around him, holding as tightly as she could. Instinctively matching his rhythm, she squeezed—clutching him inside—refusing to release. He muttered in her ear—hot guttural praise and gravelly filth that made her moan even louder. She gasped as he thrust—

relentless and demanding—until a mere breath later tumbled back into that starburst and oblivion with a wild scream.

She had no idea how long it was before she fluttered back to full consciousness. The scents of summer and sex, of heat and peppery wild herbs, perfumed the air. It was mid-afternoon—the warmest part of the day—and she was blanketed by his big body and slicked in sweat. She'd never been as hot in her life. Never as satisfied.

He lifted away from her and rolled onto his side. 'Thank God they gave you a three-pack.' His groan was husky and rueful. 'That was over far too quickly.'

Um… Did he think? Because she had zero complaints. She was absolutely humming. 'I had no idea…' she mumbled, too dazed to realise what she was giving away.

'No?' He looked into her eyes and his smile slowly broadened. He reached out and lightly ran his fingertips back and forth across her stomach.

'Mmm…' She would let him keep that smug look. He deserved it. She was so blissed out.

'No idea what?'

She sighed. Whispered. 'That it could be that good.'

He kissed her—slow and gentle—but she quivered again anyway. Only then he smiled. 'I'm going to have a swim. Are you going to join me?''

She nodded but couldn't resist just watching for a moment first. It was insane how beautiful he was, how quickly she got hot around him. He stepped into the water, curved his arms and dived. Great, now she was even hotter. She scrambled to her feet. Not in her wildest dreams had she imagined she'd have sex and go skinny-dipping with a handsome stranger in an Italian woodland but there was no stopping her now.

She splashed in quickly and dove, gasping in outrage as she emerged from the cold water.

'You have to move,' he called with amusement.

She wriggled all her limbs and yes, the temperature eased. She giggled and swam to the other side, stretched out and floated on her back, watching the sunlight pierce through the trees. It was so lush. So perfect. Definitely heaven.

'Phoebe. You'll burn if you stay in the sun too long.'

She turned and saw him standing on the bank watching her. Droplets of water cascaded from his skin. It was like nature had bejewelled him but seriously, wasted effort. He needed nothing more to draw her attention. She swam closer. He watched—clearly and unashamedly aroused and definitely the most stunning thing she'd ever seen. The wry smile on his face deepened as she picked her way out of the pond while not breaking her fascinated study of him. Yes, she'd shed every inhibition ever.

'You must be tired from carrying me everywhere,' she murmured. 'Maybe you should lie down.'

He stepped back to the flattened space where their clothes had been flung and complied with a knowing smile. She knew he was only indulging her bossiness when really, he was the one seducing her all over again. He stretched out and she straddled him—splaying her thighs over his—and played. She adored touching him and did so—everywhere. It was utterly intimate and decadent and looking into his eyes, she'd never felt as wanted in all her life.

He purred, whispered, his pleasure beyond evident. And she teased—taking her time with the condom, making him swear until she laughed and then he took over—lifting her with impossible strength. Their eyes meshed as their bodies melded again. She quaked and slammed her hands on his chest to steady herself. He filled her to the edge of ecstasy and gave her the boldness to explore him even more, to find his weak points, make him lose everything, the way she did.

She feasted on his beauty, on his strength and stamina.

Riding him was the most sensual experience of her life. She felt invincible. Beautiful. Powerful. She'd not known sex could be so liberating or so fundamentally good for the soul. This was connection at a cellular level—all freedom and joy. He let her set the pace, met her with that intense ferocity, teased her back until she arched, shuddering in delight, not even knowing she was moaning...*falling*. His arms swept around her, pulling her to him, holding her safe and close as she shattered.

'Phoebe...' His voice permeated her dream and his warm hands rubbed her upper arms. 'You're getting cold.'

Not when she was curved into his heat like this. She didn't want to move, didn't want to wake. But she lifted her head, met the hunger in his eyes, knew hers reflected the same.

'It would be a shame not to use the last one, don't you think?' he whispered.

'If you think you're up to it?' she murmured.

He chuckled. 'You know I'm already up.'

She liked his smile—liked making him smile. Liked making him shudder more. 'Yes.'

She really did.

He trailed his fingertips all over her with the slowest, languorous, most complete of caresses. He was heart-achingly tender—knowing she was over-sensitive, gently kissing where her skin was reddened from the rougher exertions of earlier. They moaned, barely moved as they reconnected, going searingly slow. She didn't want it to end. Ever. It seemed he felt the same. But in the end, all too soon, there was no stopping the runaway train that was their lust. She clung, closing her eyes against the tears, and let herself go one last time.

'Are you okay?' he asked as they dressed. 'You're very quiet.'

She put her fingers on his lips. 'Words will spoil it,' she whispered.

'Spoil?'

'It was perfect. Just perfect.'

Far too perfect. And she could fall for him far too easily, so it was a good thing she was leaving. A good thing she didn't even know his last name. Her attraction was all the feel-good hormones flooding her body from the *three times* they'd just been intimate. That kind of sexual endurance was totally new to her. Actually, day-time sex was new too. As was sex with a stranger. As were orgasms as well, to be completely honest.

She shamelessly hugged close to him as he drove her right up to the door of the little cottage. But then she moved. Quickly.

'Thank you.' She slipped off the back of the moped and handed him the helmet.

'Am I allowed to speak now?'

'No.'

He gripped the handles tightly and storminess rose in his eyes—he was more serious than she'd seen him all afternoon. She kissed him the second his mouth opened. Quick, fiery, *final*.

'I'm not sorry you ran into me,' she whispered.

'Phoebe—'

'And for the record,' her heart hammered as she hurriedly stepped back, 'You didn't let *me* down.'

CHAPTER THREE

Four months later

PHOEBE TWISTED THE ring on her finger, mentally cajoling the final page of the report to hurry up and escape the printer. She was helping out her office junior because she had the magic touch with the temperamental machinery but frankly she was feeling pretty temperamental herself. She'd heard rumours that her new company might be a takeover target, but just ten minutes ago her boss George Scott hadn't just confirmed the fact, he'd told her the deal was done and she was to head to the boardroom together with their top analysts, to meet the new management.

They were even getting a new name. Phoebe was shocked and honestly, scared. She liked this job. She liked old-school gentleman George. He appreciated her efficiency and he was nice, proudly showing her pictures of his grandchildren. She liked being in the smaller, family-feel firm. There wasn't the arrogant alpha-capitalist boy behaviour she'd endured at the corporate bank where she'd worked her way up from receptionist to highly skilled PA. Making the leap to a boutique firm had been part of her rebalance. But apparently some enormously successful European entity was taking over and a rebrand was merely the beginning. There were bound to be redundancies and, as she was the most recent hire, she'd likely be in the firing line.

'He's arrived.' Megan, the office junior, scuttled back from delivering refreshments to the boardroom, and shot Phoebe a stunned look. '*Nothing* like I imagined.'

'No?'

Phoebe didn't have time to get details. She grabbed the last sheet and strode to meet Felipe Mazzoni, Head of Acquisitions for EDB International—the company she'd not heard of until now and hadn't had a chance to research. But she was determined to make a good first impression. The boardroom was full but she wasn't actually late. Just last. She walked in, head high, polite smile in place.

'Ah, Phoebe, there you are,' George waved her in. 'Everyone, may I introduce Edoardo Benedetti—'

Phoebe glanced at the dark-haired man on the far side of the table just as he looked up and caught her gaze on the full.

Short hair. Angular cheekbones—the sort that looked like they'd been chiselled by a sculptor. *What?*

'Edoardo is the CEO of EDB International,' George added.

He was *who*? Blood roared in Phoebe's ears and the floor pitched beneath her suddenly unsteady legs.

They were supposed to be meeting Felipe—not someone called Edoardo. Definitely not *this* Edoardo. *This* Edoardo was Edo and he worked on a vineyard in Tuscany. Outdoors. Which was why he had a full body tan and seriously fit muscles and slightly callused hands. He had nothing to do with *insurance*. He shouldn't have a suit that made him look every bit as sexy as when he'd been half-naked. He should be on some hill in the Italian countryside seducing all the other tourists he took to that pond.

'Phoebe?' George prompted. 'Are you going to sit down?'

What? Oh. *Yes.* She was going to snap her mouth shut too. She sank into the last empty seat—directly across from his—and couldn't stop staring. Deep-brown eyes locked on hers for a scant second before his focus dropped to the paperwork in front of him—not a flinch, not a gasp, not a flicker of recognition.

Maybe—*please, please, please, to all the deities*—maybe he didn't recognise her. Or maybe he'd had so many lovers since, he'd forgotten all about her. Better still, maybe *she* was mistaken. Maybe this guy was Edo's *doppelganger*?

Yeah, no. He looked identical *and* had the same first name. She'd never found out his surname. It hadn't mattered when it had been a perfect fever dream. She'd not tried to find him on social media. She'd kept it a treasure—close and secret. She'd not even told her best friends. Elodie had been away, Bethan had been busy at work. Phoebe had also been busy with her new job but determined to stay on her self-care plan. In fact, she'd recklessly splurged the last of her funds on a pretty ring at the airport when leaving Italy to remember that feeling of freedom and fulfilment. She'd chosen to wear it on her wedding ring finger—where Ryan's had once sat—as a proud reminder that she needed no man to buy her anything. She could get what she wanted and needed all by herself.

Okay yes, it had *also* been to remember that very particular moment she'd had on the Tuscan hill side, but it turned out she didn't need the memento because she'd thought about him *every* night since. At first it had been so seared in her mind she'd struggled to sleep, but since she'd dived deep into work at her new job she now slept like the dead. In fact, she'd snooze past a full twelve hours if she didn't set a billion alarms on her phone. But she still saw his face just as she fell asleep—and every night felt a tiny, terrifying fear that nothing and no one else could ever compare to that moment. The most incredible sex of her life. The most fun afternoon of her life. No wonder she couldn't stop staring at him now.

As George introduced everyone, Edo made direct eye

contact and nodded to each person. Phoebe's nerves tightened as her turn neared. He barely glanced at her, the split-second he did, his gaze was brutally cold. The iciness hit harder than when he'd literally knocked her down on a back country road in Italy. Not that it mattered, because sensation *scalded* her.

It was just like that day—she had a weird loss of co-ordination and hearing as once again the visuals overloaded her brain and short-circuited everything else. And then, to make everything worse, memories overwhelmed her—she'd trailed her hand down his sternum, tested his muscles, tickled him just because she could. They'd had *fun*. Heat suffused her as she remembered clinging to him as he moved inside her, pleasuring her to the point where she could no longer speak. They'd done *everything* and then some.

It hadn't been enough. She wanted more—

Her mouth was now drier than the Sahara and she couldn't swallow, let alone say anything. She reached for the nearest glass but completely underestimated how much her hand was shaking and instead of sipping like a normal human, she spilled it. The iced water splattered across her blouse—specifically across her left breast.

Could it get any worse?

Actually, yes. Because her blouse was white and the wet patch turned transparent. Worse, Phoebe had gained a little weight lately—still indulging in all things Italian. Namely pasta and gelato. So her boobs were popping over the top of her bra cups and now her all but sheer shirt had her turned on nipples on display for everyone to ogle whether they wanted to or not.

Could she die now? Quickly. Completely. Turn to ash.

Naturally she didn't. And she didn't have her blazer with her to cover up. She'd been in a hurry picking up that stuff from the printer because Megan hadn't been able to fix the jam. Phoebe was good at sorting sticky situations. She was cool and calm under pressure. Not this time. It was too much to hope that no one would notice. There was total silence in the room and she felt the squirming second-hand embarrassment of her colleagues.

She put her hand up to cover herself and risked a glance in his direction. He'd looked down but his expression was now thunderous. The ambient temperature plummeted twenty degrees. Which made her shiver. Which then caught his attention. This time it was for a timeless second that she stared right into his dark brown eyes again. Every memory flashed. Every muscle melted. He was still insanely good-looking. Still mesmerising. Still set her libido on fire even when he glared at her like this. And she was sure he'd just read her mind and knew what she was thinking about, and now he looked even more grim.

'Thank you for the introductions, George.' Edoardo broke away and ended the awkward silence. 'I look forward to getting to know you all.' He glanced around the table again but skipped Phoebe entirely. 'Unfortunately Felipe has been delayed so I'm here for a brief transition period until he's able to get here.'

How long was 'brief'? *Please be a single day. Please let this man board a plane and head back to his company's headquarters this afternoon.*

'As I'm sure you know, our focus at EDB is insurance and reinsurance. We also specialise in risk management.'

The senior analysts nodded, looking galvanised. Phoebe picked up a pen and pretended to take notes. After all, that was what she was here for.

'While we're based in Milan, we have offices around the globe.' He cleared his throat. 'As with any integration, there will be a transformation period, but we've pursued an aggressive acquisition strategy for some time, so rest assured we know what we're doing. Disruption and staffing restructure will be expedient and ideally minimal.'

Staffing restructure.

Phoebe tensed, her worst fears confirmed. He was powerful. An apparent master of *aggressive acquisition strategy*—what, like the way he conquered women? Poor George having to see his life's work swallowed up by one man's *strategy*. Her anger brewed as he smiled at the others. He was arrogant. Greedy. Disingenuous. He was supposed to be a *vineyard worker*. She couldn't trust the promise he'd just made. Especially when he didn't so much as glance at her again. Their shared moment was a liability. There was clearly no chance they were going to be able to laugh about it, but they should be able to *deal* with it. Have one conversation then never mention it again—just forget about it completely.

Only she'd already tried to forget and very much failed. And now she was utterly on edge, her body *aching*. All she had to do was look at him and it happened—reckless lust.

But she had a mortgage to pay and while Bethan's rent helped, money was tight. Phoebe was still paying back student debt from the degree she'd aborted in order to support Ryan and *his* career. Their divorce had left her worse off in so many ways. That holiday to Italy had been her first ever self-indulgent splurge. So she was not losing this job—especially not because of a man. She'd destroyed her future for a guy once already and she wouldn't do it again—she simply couldn't afford to.

Edo unfastened the top button of his shirt and ran his finger around the collar but loosening it didn't ease his strangled feeling. Nor did the back of his neck cool from the exposure to more air. He stalked to the window, wrestling with the diabolical nightmare that Phoebe Copeland, the supposedly superstar personal assistant George had raved about for weeks, was *his* Phoebe. His snowdrop—looking particularly snowy today, it had to be said. Frigid perfection in that white blouse, grey trousers, her long hair half hidden in a neat low ponytail—a world away from the vibrant summer temptress he'd tumbled with.

His innards had ignited when she'd walked in and then memories hadn't been the only thing to surge. It had been a complete brain and body response to her shining blue eyes and porcelain skin. She wasn't supposed to be *more* beautiful than he remembered—than he dreamed night after night— yet here she was, unequivocally stunning, as if she'd been dipped in a dust that had enhanced every feature. He'd not trusted himself to speak. Not trusted his own body. But as the shock receded, complications clamoured in his brain. And then she'd splashed water on her blouse.

Worst torture imaginable.

He'd almost leapt to her aid but had seen her instant mortification. Had they been alone, he could have helped. Could have teased her. Could have *touched*. One look and he'd been right back to lust-a-thon. But they hadn't been alone—they'd been in a *business* meeting—there could be no touching. It had been horrific.

He'd dragged up self-control and relied on muscle memory to deliver the introductory spiel he'd given many times. He'd not trusted himself to look at her again, certainly not smile. But he'd seen her anger flash while he'd detailed his company credentials. When he'd mentioned some smoothing of the company restructure, she'd gone tense. Which had set him on edge too.

Absorbing George's company into his portfolio would mean staff changes—that was standard with any acquisition, but he'd try to keep them to a minimum, just as he always did. Frankly, he was proud of the low turnover and high staff satisfaction rates in his company reports. But there could be no accusations of *bias* in any restructuring process.

It shouldn't be a problem. They'd shared a moment, that was all. He'd never wanted anything more—still didn't—especially now he was effectively her boss. But his libido now hit worse than it had the night after their afternoon together. They'd had spectacular sex three spectacular times in quick succession and he should have been *spent*. He hadn't been. He'd paced like a caged animal. In the end he'd drunk the best part of a bottle of whisky so he couldn't possibly go to her. So he could *forget*. Unhealthy as all hell. And he'd been unable to resist visiting the cottage the next afternoon but she'd already left. He hadn't known anything more than her first name—not where she lived or what she did for work—which was good, because by then he'd been even more desperate to forget her. The intensity of his attraction to her was too much. Knowing he couldn't find her should have helped end it. It hadn't.

He couldn't forget the snowdrop-turned-siren. And now her employment at one of his companies was utterly abhorrent. Even when he was back in Italy, he would know where she was. What she was doing. That he could get to her...

Pull it together.

He didn't want emotional entanglements. Ever. He certainly didn't want complication. He would have a direct, calm conversation with her here in the soundproof boardroom with that one wall of windows, yes the glass was frosted, but it was still better than the full privacy—*intimacy*—a smaller office would invite. It was only a few days before Felipe should get here. It was going to be fine. Manageable. He would sort it out now and restore his focus on important things. He wouldn't let anything distract him from work.

He sent an email summons and waited in his preferred position—seated with his back to the wall, table between them, eyes on the door. She arrived moments later. She'd changed her top.

Of course she would have a spare in her office. She was prepared for any eventuality—why, she'd had condoms in the bottom of her bag when she'd been on holiday, had a Botticelli print coin-purse stuffed with plasters and paracetamol as well—a miniature medical kit in case of emergency. She was the first aid queen—she probably also had a torch and batteries and who knew what else in there. She was every bit the efficient assistant George had praised. She was also stunning—her long limbs tailor-made to coil around him, her soft curves hidden now but his to reveal.

Edo didn't—couldn't—stand as she entered. Didn't offer his hand or smile. Her presence was pure provocation. He tensely battled the urge to walk round the table, pin her against the wall and kiss her everywhere until she was hot and breathless, breathing his name in that broken way she did just before she came. He didn't of course. But only just.

Appalling to be so debilitated by *lust*. It had never happened to this extent before—aside from that afternoon in Italy.

'Take a seat.' He jerked his head.

The desk was an enormous plank of wood between them. She perched on the edge of her chair and didn't smile either. He forgot how to speak, never mind what he'd intended to say. He just stared—how she had this impact on him he didn't know. But her eyes mesmerised him.

'I wasn't sure what you wished to discuss given you gave no indication in your immediate summons, so I brought a selection of senior management reports for you.'

'You know this isn't about any reports,' he said more roughly than he meant to. 'We have a situation.'

Her deep-blue eyes widened. 'I disagree.'

'How?' he muttered bitterly.

'I don't think anything that's happened prior to today needs to be relevant going forward,' she said bravely. 'I don't allow my personal life to interfere with my work.'

'Really?' Did she honestly think they could *ignore* what had happened? Even though that was exactly what he'd intended they do.

'There's nothing between us.' She added stiffly. 'In fact I'd forgotten all about it until I saw you here earlier.'

'You'd *forgotten*.'

'Yes, and I think it best we both forget it again immediately.' She shrugged her shoulders and avoided his eyes. 'I won't let some little incident from months ago jeopardise my job.'

A warning if ever he heard one. Was she thinking of blackmailing him into keeping her employed? The thin hold he'd had on himself frayed. 'Well, I won't let some little incident jeopardise my reputation in the industry.'

'Then we're in accord.' She pressed her lips together.

Yeah, no. They weren't. He couldn't sit still. He rose and paced away from the windows to the back corner of the room where he rested against the wall—trying to get as far from her as possible. Even so, he homed in on her tension. She was worried about her job and he knew he ought to reassure her.

'I'd been told you're very good,' he muttered.

She went impossibly more stiff. Yeah, that hadn't come out quite the way he'd wanted.

'Does that surprise you?' she asked coolly.

He couldn't answer. Wouldn't lean into the innuendo he knew they were both hearing.

'I *am* good at my job,' she added. 'I like my job. And I *need* my job.'

Frustration raked like nine-inch nails down his back. 'I'm good at my job too,' he growled.

Somehow this had devolved into a combat situation where

they verbally went toe-to-toe, and it was worsening by the second.

'*Your* job?' She shook her head. 'What's that, exactly? Swallowing up the little guy?' A thread of emotion made her voice uneven and she suddenly jumped up.

Edo tensed as she paced towards his end of the room but she backed off, taking the wall opposite his.

Accusation gleamed in her gaze as she hissed at him. 'George built this company from the ground up over decades and you're just going to gobble it in one bite. His name gone for ever.'

He folded his arms across his chest as grim amusement—combined with irritation—ran through him. 'Your loyalty is sweet but blind.'

Apparently she'd started working here after returning from her trip to Italy and while she'd thoroughly impressed George in these few short months, it wasn't enough for the old boy to confide in her completely. This gave him perverse pleasure—the ultimate personal assistant clearly wasn't perfect. And she certainly was willing to think the worst of him.

'George *asked* me to take over,' he said. He'd met George at industry events several times in the last decade. They'd always got on well and Edo had been touched when George had asked him for help. 'Scott Insurance doesn't actually meet my usual acquisition standards, however I'm willing to make an exception for an unwell, aging associate.'

He'd done this entirely as a favour to George, only now it had backfired in a wholly unexpected way.

'Unwell?' she echoed, her expression troubled.

'You've obviously not been working here long enough to have George's complete confidence and his personal life isn't something I'm prepared to share with you.'

Looking stung, she bit her lip. 'Is he going to be okay?'

The concern in her eyes forced him to relent. 'He's ready to enjoy his retirement.'

'His grandchildren,' she said softly.

'Yes.'

Okay so George had talked to her a little. Of course Edo had wanted to support the elderly man in his desire to prioritise his grandchildren, especially given his own grandfather hadn't at all. He'd abandoned Dante—Edo's brother—in his most desperate hour. Ignored Edo's entreaties in the most inhuman, callous of ways. And in the end, the worst had happened. Edo understood how much family *ought* to matter, which was also why he would never have one of his own. He—like his grandfather—wasn't equipped to care for and protect anyone other than himself. But Phoebe's snap judgement about this acquisition and her denial of everything between them stung. 'I'm not the bad guy here.'

He was determined never to be the bad guy. That was why he remained alone.

She glared at him. 'I thought you worked on a vineyard.'

'In my holidays I do.'

'You expect me to believe that a billionaire enjoys menial work in the *holidays*?' She lifted her eyebrows.

'It's my vineyard and, yes, I greatly enjoy working with my hands.'

She shot him a death stare. He would smile but he was too pissed off at himself to be able to. He was letting her get to him. But it hadn't been some little *incident* and no way had she *forgotten* about it. That flicked like a whip on a raw welt and pushed him to test if it were true.

He slowly crossed the floor. They were far enough from those frosted windows but in his flash of temper he no longer gave a damn about anyone seeing them anyway. He just had to get closer to her and—

'How's your ankle?' he asked huskily, skimming a glance down her body as he inched nearer.

'Fine.' She stood stiffly.

The closer Edo got, the more he drank in her features—the clarity of her deep-blue eyes, the delicate swirls of her ears, her enticing full lips. Desire washed over him, obliterating all thought. He hovered a breath away, barely holding back. He wanted to kiss her. He wanted her heat, her sighs, her softness, her sensational response to having him thrust—

No way could he work alongside her.

The electricity in his body short-circuited his brain.

'My personal assistant will fly out and work with George,' he snapped.

'You're side-lining me?' She gaped. 'Why?'

He couldn't be near her. 'Because if *you're* my assistant here, we'll have to work in close proximity.'

'And?' She tilted her head and shot him down, saltiness blooming in her eyes. 'That's no reason why we can't work together. We're adults. We're professional.'

No reason? He glared at her. Irate with himself.

'You're here only temporarily, correct?' she added. 'So, it's no problem. As I said, forget it. Or at least pretend as if it never happened.'

'You really think that's going to be possible?' He couldn't believe it.

'Of course.'

'So what, we meet in open spaces?' He tried to pull himself together. 'With other people present?'

'Are you afraid to be alone with me?'

Honestly, yes.

'It's for both our safety,' he ground out.

'*Safety?* Can you not control yourself?'

Apparently not. He stared—*appalled*—as she refused to look him in the eyes again. Suddenly he was very keen to prove that he wasn't the only one feeling this. Because her body was sending him the wildest signals. She might've changed her top but the new one didn't hide her entirely—he saw her arousal, saw her flush, saw lust in her eyes. It had strengthened with every step he took nearer. 'I don't think I'm the only one. I don't think you can either.'

'You're unbelievably arrogant.'

But not wrong. He placed one hand on the wall either side of her head and held himself back from pressing against her. Colour stained her skin, he ached to feel the warmth of it, wanting to whisper in her ear, to nip that petite lobe again, wanted to spread her legs and—

'Edo?' she suddenly whispered. 'What are you doing?'

He pressed his palms harder against the wall. He wasn't touching her. He *wasn't*. But just being this close sent chaos through his body. And—thankfully—hers.

'Proving why we *both* need chaperones. At all times.'

More colour flooded her cheeks.

'Proving that it wasn't *a little incident*,' he added huskily. 'It was wild. And I don't believe you've forgotten a second of it. I know I haven't.'

Her breath shuddered. 'Edo—'

'Don't dismiss me,' he muttered. 'Don't dismiss this.'

'But *this* cannot happen,' she pleaded.

'Exactly.'

Yet neither of them moved. He didn't want to. He cursed the situation. He'd never had an affair at work. Never even been tempted. Never ever thought he would. But right now? He was so on the edge and already behaving badly.

Her pupils surged—drawing him in until she bent her head and brushed back her hair, hiding her eyes from him and something glittered in the light.

'What's that?' He lost his self-control as white-hot fury flared and snatched her hand in his to stare at the little blue stones set in a thin band. It looked like a dainty cross between an engagement and wedding ring. 'Are you *married*?'

She'd not been wearing a ring when he'd met her in Italy. Had she removed it? Had she cheated on her husband with him? Jealousy strained his already tight leash. He had to make a conscious effort not to squeeze her hand too hard in his outrage. 'What the *hell*, Phoebe—'

'It's not a wedding ring,' she snapped.

'So you're *not* married?'

'I *was*,' she said jerkily.

Edoardo recoiled.

'Obviously I'm not any more and haven't been for a while and I never will be again, which is why I wear it on that finger, because I'm *not* available. Not that it's any of *your* business.' Incandescent, she tugged free of his grip.

Relief and fury coalesced, leaving him confused as hell. He gritted his teeth, but the curiosity leeched out of him anyway. 'What happened?'

'Nothing that's relevant to this situation.'

Right. Angry, he glared at her. But those full lips tempted him—he would lick, taste, tease—he would make her tremble and take him in with that wild abandon. He almost lost it in the urge to haul her against him and trigger her surrender to their chemistry here and now and—

He was behaving *appallingly*. He was at *work*. She was trying to put him in his place and he should already be there. He'd just done everything he'd promised himself he wouldn't. So much for self-control. Her personal life and her past *weren't* his business. Except he wanted to smack the guy. And she was staring back straight at him with a passion that she couldn't hide and he knew he was the same.

'Phoebe—'

'You're right. We need to establish firm boundaries,' she

interrupted fiercely. 'We're never alone. We only discuss work.'

It was exactly what he'd wanted, except now he didn't.

'I meant what I said,' she said. 'I need this job.'

He took a second—two—to rebuild control and nodded.

'I understand,' he said curtly. 'I'm not a jerk. Any employment decisions will be entirely merit-based.' So much for a smooth conversation to circumvent awkwardness. He didn't know what this was. *Who* he was. 'I'll be gone from here as soon as possible.'

CHAPTER FOUR

Phoebe survived the first three days without major incident. Barely. Edoardo Benedetti had taken over the boardroom as his office. Which meant George was working in there too. Which meant she was in there more often than not. Yes, working in the same space as Edo was totally a problem but she was determined to pretend it wasn't. She was ferocious in her intention to detail, put in long hours pre-empting the needs not just for George, but Edo too. No way was she letting him *wish* he could restructure her out of a job but feeling handcuffed by the fact they'd had a one-afternoon stand. She would be perfect. Irreplaceable. Her presence might be an inconvenience to him, but too bad. She kept her eyes locked on whatever was right in front of her and ensured that was almost never him. She desperately tried not to remember those moments when he'd grabbed her hand and glared at the ring she'd bought in part because of *him*. It was too ironic.

But their agreed rules had to work, they had to be enough. She had no choice. Had he thought she could just walk away from her job? He had no idea of her reality. And she'd certainly had no idea of his. Not the wealth, not the power, the connections. But she knew his body, his scent and couldn't stop herself seeing so much despite rarely looking at him directly. He worked with savage efficiency, with a level of focus that made her irrationally angry.

Though she still slept like the dead, she woke feeling more tired than before. He was the last thing she thought of and the first thing when she woke. Her body hummed even when she was beneath an ice-cold shower and clamped every urge down. It was *exhausting*.

'Is everything okay, Phoebe?' George asked in a low tone. 'You're very quiet.' He glanced towards the window and frowned. Edo was standing out in the corridor talking with an analyst. 'You know you're not to worry, I've insisted he keep you in your current position.'

Phoebe inwardly grimaced. The last thing she wanted was George putting pressure on the man to retain her. But the older man watched her with astute sharpness. 'He's very highly regarded in the industry. He's achieved phenomenal success in only a decade, you can trust him to do a good job with this.'

Oh, she was bitterly sure Edo was fantastic at his job. He seemed to be fantastic at everything. Even though she shouldn't, she couldn't resist curiosity. 'It's not his family company?'

George shook his head. 'I think his grandfather headed an investment firm but that's a separate entity. You can find out more in Milan.'

'Sorry?' She blinked. Milan?

'I want you to accompany me to the meeting there on Wednesday,' George added. 'I know it's late notice, but it would be helpful to have you there.'

Instant excitement at the prospect of returning to Italy kicked. But for safety's sake she should say no. Except she liked George, and if his health wasn't all that, she didn't want to do anything to stress him, and her latent pleaser elements were hard to shake. So she didn't formulate her refusal in time.

'I'm just checking Phoebe's ability for Milan, Edoardo,' George raised his voice.

Phoebe turned to see Edo had walked back in. For the first time in days, she looked him right in the eyes. His held a gleam that shouldn't be there.

'It would be helpful if you're able to come, Phoebe,' he said softly.

Surely there was no double entendre in that statement—she was only hearing it because of her own gutter-dwelling mind. 'I can come.'

'You can take the weekend there,' George said jovially, oblivious to the undercurrents whirling around them. 'Go see some sights.' He turned to Edo. 'Phoebe loves Italy. She had the holiday of a lifetime there just before starting here.'

Phoebe shrivelled inside. She suspected George had picked up on her cool interactions with Edo and was trying to foster common ground between them. If only he knew.

'The holiday of a lifetime? Wow,' Edo echoed dryly. 'What was so good about it, Phoebe? Did you meet some friendly locals?'

She couldn't look away from him, there was a vestige of that sly humour he'd shown that day—and there was *all* the challenge.

'It was the scenery that was spectacular, more than the people,' she countered calmly.

'Oh?' His eyebrows arched. 'You appreciate nice scenery.'

'Yes.'

His mouth almost curved. 'There's much more than scenery to be experienced in Milan. I'm sure you'll enjoy it.'

He knew she'd not been to Milan. And now she definitely wasn't going to let her feelings for him get in the way of her going. 'I'm quite sure I will.'

'Marvellous,' George said.

Phoebe smiled weakly, feeling instant regret at the wolfish expression in Edo's eyes.

She'd go on this trip and then she would find another job.

The next morning, she arrived as early as usual only to find George had yet to make an appearance, while Edo was already eyeball-deep in reports, looking like he'd been there for hours. Suited, clean-shaven, focused. Pure billionaire boss on duty. She'd looked up his company online and died when she'd seen its market valuation. No wonder that magnificent vineyard was *his*—he needed something to spend his spare billions on.

Thankfully he disappeared from the boardroom not long after she arrived. Probably waiting for the safety net that was George. Ten minutes later there was still no George. She was hard at work on a report when a tanned strong forearm entered her view and placed a steaming coffee on her desk. She reared away from the cup as if it were a poisonous snake about to strike.

'You don't want coffee?' Edo asked, eyes narrowing. 'Black, one sugar, right?'

'I've gone off it,' she blurted, so shocked she couldn't stop herself.

She'd been off it for a few weeks, actually. The smell was too strong and, despite her tiredness, she couldn't bring herself to drink it.

'Right.' He stepped back, turning away before she could even muster a polite smile.

His withdrawal was more than physical, and instant regret—*loss*—hit. She could have—should have—thanked him, because she was ridiculously touched that he'd remembered how she preferred it. But he had a third coffee on that tray—one for George too—so he'd not meant anything special by getting her one. He was being polite. Making an effort to form a more normal 'boss and personal assistant' relationship. Except she was the personal assistant and by rights *she* should be bringing the coffee. Not him. She fidgeted with her pen, wishing George would hurry up and arrive because he made the perfect chaperone. But ten minutes later George phoned to tell her he was going to work from home for the day. She met Edo's eyes as she listened to George, then ended the call. And then she couldn't look away from him with his shirt sleeves rolled back, revealing the sun-kissed skin, the muscles. He didn't move from where he stood at the opposite end of the room but suddenly she felt steamier than if she'd been in an endless hot yoga class and knew she couldn't be alone in here with him for the entire day—

'Phoebe—' But his phone rang just as he spoke and he swung away to answer it.

There was a series of calls in which he spoke in increasingly abrupt Italian. She had no hope of understanding a word of it. When he left the room she put her head down and with increasing desperation tried to focus. But she still kept watch for him as she had for all these days. She was so hyperaware and every other thought was inappropriate. It was unstoppable and as exhausting as it was exhilarating.

Towards the end of the day he approached her with a too controlled pace, his hands jammed in his pockets, his expression tense.

'George can't come with us to Milan tomorrow.' He shoved his phone in his pocket with a vicious movement.

She froze. 'Why not?'

'He's unwell. He'll fly out as soon as he's feeling better.'

'Poor George,' she mumbled awkwardly. 'So we'll delay our departure too?'

Edo shook his head. 'There are meetings I must attend.'

'I'll wait here for George.'

Edo stared at her moodily. 'George wants you to attend and report back to him. Seemingly, he trusts you very much.'

She stared at her keyboard, trying to hide the illicit thrill coiling inside her. She wanted to be alone with him. She'd wanted to be alone with him again for *months*. Having him near was torture and she couldn't even look at him for fear he'd see the desire in her eyes. But she had to get over it—prove to herself that she could control it. That she wasn't going to ruin her life again because of some man. Because of her own *extreme* reactions. She was stronger than that.

'He's right to,' she muttered defiantly. 'I'll do a good job.'

'We'll leave first thing as originally planned,' he said briskly. 'I'll send a car to collect you.'

She jerked up and glared at him. 'That's not necessary. I'm capable of getting myself to the airport.'

He inhaled sharply. 'It's an early flight—'

'But—'

'Could you not reject everything I offer?' he snapped, glowering at the coffee still sitting—untouched—on her desk from hours ago.

She gaped at him as his phone buzzed again and he turned away with a sharp movement. Phoebe stared after him, startled by his vehemence. She hadn't intended to be rude, but yes, she'd been cold for days. Even George had noticed the strained atmosphere. She'd had to be like that just to control herself—yet how pathetic that she couldn't even handle him offering her a coffee.

While Edo had kept his distance, he was coping far better than her. Was that because it wasn't as much of a nightmare for him? Was he over it already? She needed to grow some maturity. Accepting something from him might make amends. She wrote her details on a piece of paper and put it in front of him just before leaving for the day.

'Here's my address. I'll be ready first thing.' She avoided his eyes as she mumbled, 'Thank you.'

Edoardo stared at the two-storey house with grim, unwanted fascination. The property was tidy but cramped. There was no front garden and he doubted there'd be more than a little courtyard that probably never saw the sun out the back. The place seemed too grey for the sensual woman who'd splashed in the water that day back home.

He glanced at his watch and watched the door. He had the suspicion that George had contrived this unfortunate situation that meant he would be travelling alone with Phoebe. It was obvious that things were cool between them and maybe George thought they'd hash out a better working relationship on this trip. Hell, the old man had confided that Phoebe wasn't smiling as much as she usually did, and that he was concerned she was stressed about the restructure. There was no way Phoebe would have *said* anything to George, but something about her brought out the old man's protective instincts. Whereas it was Edo's predatory instincts that she fully engaged.

She was extremely good at her job. Once past that water moment in that meeting, she'd been focused, detail-oriented, ruthlessly proper. No smile. No banter. It was business and only business, and rightly so. He could see why George raved about her. It wasn't her fault that *he* couldn't stop thinking about her in every inappropriate way imaginable and at all times. But he had to suck up his impulses, especially when she was clearly—determinedly—keeping her distance. She couldn't even bring herself to drink the coffee he'd bought for her. He'd almost lost it. Almost tossed every ounce of control away to hold her, kiss her, make her admit she felt it too.

He needed Felipe back. Badly. Because he couldn't go on like this much longer. He would lose control.

The front door opened and he watched her walk towards the car. She was wearing another grey-suit-white-blouse combination, and her face was drawn and pale, as if she hadn't slept well. He knew that feeling. He missed the long navy sundress that deepened the colour of her jewel-like eyes. He missed the fire and challenge she'd sent his way that day. Her spirit had been leeched from her. Because of him.

'You should have messaged that you were here,' she said as she got into the back seat beside him.

'I was early.' He'd been nosy. He kept the partition between his driver and them down, so they weren't 'alone', but he was increasingly irritated by the way she never looked him in the eyes. Even now she had her head bent, reading from her tablet, informing him of updates he'd already skimmed, with impeccable politeness and efficiency. He wanted to throw the damned thing out the window. He didn't. He said nothing. Didn't move. It was sheer relief to arrive at the airport.

'You don't have a private jet?' she murmured as they followed the crowds into the commercial terminal.

He absolutely did, but there was no way he'd be using it today. He would not be locked in a cabin alone with Phoebe for three hours. Look at what had happened the last time they'd had time alone together.

'This is better for the planet,' he said brusquely.

To the astonishment of his assistants in Italy, he'd spent half the evening requesting all the travel plans be amended, but as they boarded the plane he realised he'd made a massive mistake. The problem with flying commercial—even first class—was that the seats were too close together, and this wasn't a huge aircraft. Plus, it was full—so he couldn't take himself off to the other end of the plane. Couldn't lock himself in the facilities either. He was going to be stuck right next to her. For hours.

The stewardess offered snacks and he snatched up the distraction, needing something salty to match his mood. Especially when he watched Phoebe pick out a plump green olive from the miniature antipasto selection and pop it into her mouth.

'What?' She shot him a questioning look as he glared at her.

'I didn't think you liked olives,' he gritted.

She paused, the next olive halfway to her lips. 'I changed my mind.'

When? *Why?* Because she'd not wanted his olives and he was absurdly put out by the fact. But worse was the torture of watching her nibble on them now. He was jealous of an *olive*. It was ludicrous. But he ached to take her hand and lick the brine from her fingers and he totally would—*if he wasn't her boss*.

Now he wanted to rage around the aeroplane like a toddler throwing a tantrum, because he couldn't sit still this long. He gripped the arm rest as they took off.

'Are you a nervous flier?' she asked awkwardly.

'I'm fine,' he snapped.

To his ever-mounting outrage she then curled away from him. A moment later she'd promptly fallen asleep. Sure, it had been an early flight but *really*? How could she possibly fall asleep so quickly and easily? She clearly wasn't troubled by desire, not bothered by their physical closeness…whereas he was increasingly unable to function for thinking about her. He'd thought she'd been distracted too—hell, she'd been avoiding him so much he'd thought it obvious. But now he was jealous as hell. And concerned. Her neck looked uncomfortable in the contorted way she was hunched. He wanted to pull her close so he could cushion her head and she could rest more comfortably. So he could feel her warm weight on him. He didn't of course. Touching her would be inappropriate. He'd maintain his distance—he'd been doing it a whole week already, hadn't he? Even if it was killing him. So then he was reduced to watching her sleep. Like an obsessive. But why was she so tired? Hadn't she slept well last night?

He'd paced for hours. Taken a cold shower well past the wrong side of midnight to douse his head and drown the memories that tormented him more and more. It hadn't worked.

He gritted his teeth for the entire flight. She didn't rouse when the imminent landing announcement was made over the plane's intercom system. Edo rolled his shoulders but couldn't ease his tension. He ought to wake her and there was only one way he wanted to do that—*if he wasn't her boss*. But he was her boss. So he'd behave accordingly.

'Phoebe…' he murmured and leaned nearer. 'Phoebe.'

She blinked, slightly dazed. Her face was so close to his and lightly flushed, and her blue eyes were luminous and warm and he was lost in them again instantly. She was just luscious and he needed a white flag. He'd give anything to kiss her right now. He sank lower, nearer.

'I'm sorry.' She tensed in embarrassment and he stilled, sitting back. 'I didn't fall asleep on you, did I?' Her breathing quickened. 'Didn't drool?'

He couldn't smile as he shook his head. He wanted her sleeping on him. He wanted her drooling over him. Something had to change. If it weren't for the promise he'd made George, he'd back out of the deal or sell on Scott Insurance—he had other, better targets on his list. But he couldn't do that to the old guy. And he couldn't let his loss of self-control force him into such drastic action.

The second they got to the hotel, he made a beeline for the concierge to ensure that their rooms were as far apart as possible. Different floors. He didn't even want to know which floor hers was on. There was no need to make temptation all the more difficult to resist. He spoke in Italian, not wanting her to know how perilous his self-control was. Then he turned back to her and broke into English.

'You have time for lunch and a rest before the first meeting this afternoon,' he said curtly. 'I will see you in the meeting room ten minutes ahead of the start time.'

He walked away before he saw the room key the receptionist handed to her. He went up to his room and stripped out of his suit. A shower wasn't going to cut it. He'd go use the hotel pool and thrash out a few miles.

He was just setting down his towel at the back of the pool area when she walked in. She didn't see him and he ducked behind a pillar—cursing his childishness—but he couldn't be in this pool with her. Couldn't bear to remember the last time they'd been in a body of water together. Yes, now his descent was complete. He was *hiding*. Worse than that, he was now watching her like some sick voyeur. But he couldn't actually move as she dropped her towel and walked to the edge of the pool.

A bikini. Blue. Heaven help him. He stared like some deranged stalker with no self-control as she slowly stepped down the stairs into the water. The image echoed the one from months ago—he remembered those exact slow steps she'd taken into the shallow edge of the pond. He remembered her laughing squeal at the temperature of the water.

She'd been naked that day, while that jaw-dropping bikini covered deeply personal parts now. But every inch of her body was so ingrained on his memory, he noted the subtle differences—her breasts seemed more full and her skin was so radiant, he could see her gleaming even from here. She was a willowy, tall blonde—more slender than curvaceous—only that wasn't quite the case now. There was a softness about her, definitely a slight curve to her lower belly that hadn't been there before. It was as if she'd blossomed like some goddess of fertility—all rich curves in deeply feminine places.

No, to coffee. Yes, to olives.

The thought hit randomly. Her different *tastes*. Then another thought hit so hard, his brain halted entirely.

Phoebe really needed to get a grip. She had no idea how she'd endured that flight—having him so near, breathing in his scent, feeling his warmth. She'd had to turn away, close her eyes and feign sleep. Until she'd suddenly and completely fallen asleep—that terrible exhaustion overtaking her again. But then he'd woken her and her heart had taken a hammering again. He'd been so close and so careful, yet she'd been certain he'd wanted to kiss her…

And now, to be back on Italian soil back beside Edo was shockingly thrilling. But he couldn't get away from her fast enough. She'd hoped the swim would siphon some of her excess energy, but she still felt *wired*. She went back to her room to shower and prepare for the meetings this afternoon. She'd been back only a moment when there was a peremptory knock on her door. She frowned. She'd not ordered room service and she wasn't due to meet Edo for another hour. She checked the peep hole. Stood back from the door and took a breath.

He knocked again. 'I know you're in there, Phoebe, open up.'

She opened the door fractionally and glared at him stiffly. 'What do you want?'

They were not on work time and she couldn't muster cool politeness this second, especially when she was clad only in a bikini and a towel.

'Can I come in?' he asked bluntly.

She hesitated. It was too intimate. 'I'm not dressed for company.'

'Please, Phoebe. It's important.'

The hard light in his eyes told her he meant it. What had happened to the 'public meetings with other people present' rule? But she stepped back, tightening her grip on the towel. 'Is something wrong?'

'Maybe, I'm not sure.' He stood in the centre of her small room.

He dwarfed the space and she became horribly conscious that her bed was only a foot away from him. She braced by the door and waited for him to elaborate.

An irritated expression flickered on his face as he turned away from the bed. 'This room is tiny.'

It was undeniably small, had a dingy view of the car park and was situated a little too close to the gym, so there was a lot of foot traffic. But she'd refused to be disappointed. She was back in Italy on a free trip. But she bet he wasn't in a shoe-box-sized room with sound-proofing issues.

He frowned as a loud ding sounded in the room. 'You're too near the lift.'

She stared as he rubbed the back of his neck and suddenly cursed.

'Edo—'

'Is there any chance you're pregnant?' he suddenly growled.

She reeled and took a step back. 'What?'

'Is there any chance you're pregnant?' he repeated. 'I realise this is awkward. But I wondered—'

'Why would you think that?' She was so shocked, she laughed.

'Because, if you are, there's a chance it might be my business. So if you could just answer—'

'You're *crazy*...'

'It's a yes-no question, Phoebe.' He stepped closer. 'Or is there the possibility?'

She was too astounded to even think. 'This is a total violation of my privacy.'

'And you're prevaricating.' He seized her shoulders. 'Why?'

'I'm not prevaricating. I'm just shocked you'd even think—'

'So you definitely know you're definitely not pregnant?' he reiterated, bending urgently towards her. 'You can swear on your life?'

She stared into his widened eyes. 'Why would you think I am?'

He dropped his hands and stepped back from her. 'You don't like coffee any more. You do like olives.' He looked uncomfortable. 'You're glowing. Your skin is radiant.'

What the actual hell? Was he noticing her *skin*? 'Maybe it's my new moisturiser—'

'No,' he interrupted shortly. 'I saw you in the pool just before. Your belly is—'

She gaped. 'Are you seriously commenting on the roundness of my stomach?'

He froze then lifted his chin and looked her directly in the eye. 'Yes.'

'Maybe I'm bloated. Maybe I ate too much bread on the flight this morning—'

'You didn't have bread on the flight this morning.'

A rush of panic rose within her because she didn't want to consider what he was suggesting. 'You're monitoring my eating habits? You realise you're bordering on creep territory.'

'Yes, and I'm sorry, but I notice you!' he exploded. 'I can't help it. I can't stop it. I notice. *Everything.*'

She was silenced by the wild light in his eyes. By the fierce response that rose within her at his admission. Because she noticed him too. She was deeply aware of his every move and she was fiercely glad it was the same for him, even though it was madness.

'You want to know what else I've noticed?' He stepped closer again.

She couldn't move as he pulled the towel from her loose fingers and left her standing in only her bikini. She felt as intimate and exposed as if it were lace lingerie.

His breathing deepened. His voice roughened. His gaze dropped. And just like that her body responded. The weakness within—heat melting while other parts tightened. Aching for attention.

'These…' he touched her with the lightest finger. Crossing the boundary they'd agreed on. 'These are bigger.'

And so sensitive. They were already straining for more of his touch. She was turned on in a second—her taut nipples aching for him. She bit back her moan. This was forbidden but also what she'd wanted for so long.

'Something's changed, Phoebe.' He pressed his hand back to her lower belly.

She shuddered, shocked again by the mad question he'd asked her. 'I've gained a little weight, that's all…'

Because it couldn't be possible. It just *couldn't* be possible. But then she felt the fluttering deep in her belly—butterflies, right? She stilled. Inwardly focused on that strangest of sensations.

'Phoebe?'

She hardly heard him. She was so focused on that tiny feeling inside. She'd felt it last night just before she'd fallen asleep. Thought it was nerves about the trip today. But maybe it wasn't? No. Surely not. And she'd had her period since Italy, right?

But only the one, now she thought about it. And it had

been oddly light even for her. And since then she'd been so busy at work, she'd lost track of time...

She stared at him in mounting horror. 'We used protection.'

The rise and fall of his chest quickened. 'Protection that you provided.'

'It was a gift. You know that.' She vented. 'And like I'd...'

She trailed off because his hand was still on her lower belly and he possessively spread his palm wider—ignoring her outrage, which now faded anyway, because she was desperately trying to just *think*. Could *he* feel those flutterings? Surely they weren't anything. Surely this was all just in her head.

'No other possibilities since?' he asked hoarsely. 'Don't tell me that's not relevant to this situation.'

There were these flutterings again.

Nerves. Just nerves. But there was the maths that wasn't adding up—the dates weren't working out the way they should.

His face paled. Then he pulled a box out of his pocket. 'Why not find out for sure.'

Her face felt like it was on fire. 'You've already bought a pregnancy test?' She quietly died inside. 'When did you do that?'

'At the pharmacy downstairs about five minutes ago. I saw you at the pool. I'd had the same idea to burn off some energy.'

He needed to burn energy too?

She took the box from him with shaking hands. 'Two lines is trouble, right?' Her mouth was so dry.

'Will you let me see the result?' he asked.

She was stunned he'd asked that. And it just showed how little they really knew each other. 'Of course.'

She'd barely left the bathroom a few minutes later when

the result began to appear. She put the test on the table between them and stared down at it.

Pregnant.

'How could you not have *known*?' He released a rush of air. 'Is it mine?'

Sudden and absolute rage consumed her. She whirled to get away from him before she did something violent only he stepped forward and spun her back, pulling her close to him.

'Phoebe!' He growled. 'Is. It. Mine?'

She was so stunned to be pressed against him she couldn't speak. Couldn't stand the surge of desire that literally stopped her heart. She stared up at him, outraged and overwhelmed. Emotion leeched her brain power. She was tempted to lie. To deny him. But she was too out of control to have a hope of deception.

'Of course it is,' she answered angrily—*wounded*. She put her hands on his chest and pushed him hard in the hope he would release her. He did. So quickly that she almost stumbled back.

He stared after her. *Appalled*. He couldn't make his horror any more apparent. Well, ditto.

She marched to the door. 'You need to leave.' She needed time alone to think, respond, plan.

'I'm not going anywhere.'

She spun back to face him. 'Yeah, well I don't want to talk about this right now.'

'Then what do you want to talk about?' He stalked towards her. 'Work?'

All the frustration that had coalesced over the week morphed into a rush of primal force that couldn't be denied. 'I don't want to talk at all,' she snapped. 'I'm not in the mood.'

The ferocious energy coiling inside her needed an out. She was furious. It was more than four months since they'd been together in Italy. Which meant she must be more than four months' pregnant, and her baby would come sooner rather than later and that was—

No. She slammed on the brakes. She couldn't think about it. At all. Not all the ramifications or complications of the total nightmare that was this situation. *Every* emotion overwhelmed her. It was too much. She wouldn't *think* at all. She just wanted to forget. To feel better for just five minutes.

And there was a fire in his eyes that was utterly dangerous. Utterly undeniable. He took another three steps. Stopped an inch too close. An inch too far. He slammed his hands on the door either side of her head. Sensual force emanated from him, impacting her even more. Her body was already aflame and the primal edginess in his tense stance, in the sharpened angles of his beautiful face, in the wildness of his eyes—destroyed her.

She couldn't even breathe as he demanded, 'So what are you in the mood for?'

CHAPTER FIVE

ABSOLUTE RAGE CONSUMED HER. Phoebe grabbed his shirt with the intention of shoving him away, only somehow the message between her brain and fist got confused and she pulled him to her instead of thrusting him from her. The screaming tension of the last few days snapped. He took the last step and smashed his mouth on hers. Lost to sensation, she opened. Moaned. He twisted a hand into her hair, angled her head for better access, raked his tongue deep into her mouth. It was everything she'd wanted for months. She arched, banging against his body, desperate to get closer. He pushed her back, pressing her against the door with such pleasurable pressure, she almost came on the spot.

'Damn it Phoebe,' he immediately braced, pulling an inch back. 'We have to be careful—'

'No.' She wouldn't take it easy…she would take what she *wanted*. 'Don't stop.'

She needed to feel better. To feel *him*. Now. He stared into her eyes so she saw the moment he sank beneath the same wave of need surging through her—swamping all reason. It was unstoppable madness and so fantastic that she sobbed.

'Please…please…' She pushed up his shirt.

He got his arms out and tossed it to the floor. She gasped at the sight of him. He pressed his hot lips to hers, then roved along her jaw.

'Don't stop… Please don't stop…'

He didn't. The hot kisses became scorching. He trailed a searing path down her neck, across her collar bone. Her nipples peaked—aching painfully against her bikini top. She needed his mouth there, his tongue. Needed him lower still. Whimpering, she rocked her hips and hooked her leg around his. She ached for his hands and mouth and weight to be everywhere. All at once. She'd wanted this for so long and they were so close now that all she had to do was push his trousers down just enough—

He gripped her wrist, stopping her. 'I don't have anything with me,' he growled.

'I'm already pregnant.' She groaned.

He paused, panting, temptation clearly tearing him apart. 'I haven't done this since you.'

'Same.'

There was another snatched moment as he looked into her eyes. He released her and finished the task of pushing down his pants. Fierce pleasure surged as a wildness too raw to endure swept over her. He was beautiful. She had to indulge in this, just *once* more. That was all it would take. She just had to get closer—get the high of having him again.

She didn't know how, but in a second she'd been stripped of her bikini bottoms. He lifted her and she wrapped her legs around his waist. He growled her name and thrust hard.

'Yes!' she shrieked.

This was what she'd needed. What she'd *missed*. Him lodged deep inside her. He looped his arms around her, trapping her between him and the door, and pumped into her with feral grunts that only turned her on more. She tightened her arms and legs and flexed every sexual muscle she could, so full of frenetic energy that she simply had to expend it—push him faster. But in an instant she was shaking, endlessly lost in the throes of the most intense orgasm of her life, soaring higher as she heard his shout as he joined her…

'Phoebe.'

She couldn't answer. Panting, she rested her forehead on his shoulder as he carried her to the bed. But she refused to release him and he grunted as she took him down with her.

'Phoebe.'

She heard the serious edge in his voice and chose to ignore it. 'I still don't want to talk about it.'

They'd be forced to face reality soon enough. They might as well feel good about something now—prolong this pleasure. His pupils dilated and he rolled onto his back, taking her with him. She straddled him, immediately stretching out her hands to caress his lean, hot, hard body. Every one of his powerful muscles was hers to enjoy again and she did. Until he lifted her and slid lower until it wasn't his thighs directly beneath her but his mouth.

He held her steady—one hand on her hip, one on her breast—thumbing her nipple. She gasped as he intimately kissed her, as he suckled and nibbled her sensitive nub. Moaned as he made her quake all over again. And then he lifted her again, only to scoot back up so he could slide her wet, hungry body onto his. To the hilt. Energised by the ecstasy, she rose and sank onto him over and over again, throwing her head back in unbearable pleasure. And then she couldn't move for the bliss, but he flipped them both again and pressed closer, closer, closer, filling her once more with his fiery energy until she forgot absolutely everything.

Edo sat on the edge of the bed and gently pulled the coverings more closely around her. He rubbed his face, failing to ease his resurging tension. Her cheeks were flushed, her lips full from kissing him so passionately, and she was fast asleep.

He cursed beneath his breath. Long and vicious and entirely directed at himself. The chemistry between them was unbelievable. He couldn't believe how *desperately* he'd lost control. His only consolation was that she had too—*entirely*. She'd completely taken him by surprise. He couldn't have stopped her. Part of him felt feral pleasure that there hadn't been anyone else for her, while at the same time he felt appalled as guilt twisted. That had been extremely passionate, extremely physical, and she was *pregnant*. He couldn't comprehend that either. And he needed to. Fast. Because it was the worst thing. *Ever*.

He rolled his shoulders and stood. Maybe they'd just needed to get rid of that tension so they could discuss the future like rational adults. Except he still had all the sexual tension. He just wanted her again. Now. They needed to get away from a bedroom. Neither of them could keep their hands to themselves when they were alone. It was avoidance, he knew. Pure avoidance to escape the horror of this reality. He couldn't be responsible for her. Or her child. But he had to be.

He was certain she would sleep a while yet which gave him a window in which to act. Her room was too small for him to talk freely on the phone and he needed to brief his lawyer. Security. Staff. He'd go to his suite so he didn't wake her too soon.

He glanced at her shoulder bag on the table and glimpsed her passport tucked in there. Edo was already—with very good reason—a distrustful man. Phoebe was in denial. She didn't want to deal with this—hell, she couldn't even have a conversation with him about it yet. Which meant she was a flight risk. He braced against another prickle of guilt, quietly slid the passport from her bag and crept out of the room. Of course he would return it to her, but right now he needed the insurance.

Then he moved. The most immediate issue was her safety. Security arrangements needed to be made before anyone found out about her. He'd never wanted the responsibility of caring for anyone. Of *protecting* anyone. He'd failed Dante and he couldn't fail again. But he didn't have time to panic, to gnash his teeth and shake his fist at fate. He had to fix this as best he could. But what was best for Phoebe wasn't him. Yes, she needed his outward symbol of support and strength, but his personal support was severely limited. Because it wasn't only his brother he had failed.

His mind raced, sifting through the possibilities. Only one option satisfied the anxiety rising within him. The right thing. He would stand with her—keep them safe—but at the same time keep his distance personally. Because he was his grandfather's heir and the failings of that old jerk resided within him too. He would keep his cool and propose—but it would be like any other acquisition, a business deal for security and convenience only. He could do that—explain it coolly and rationally and she would understand. She would agree.

Back in his suite, he dictated instructions to assistants, swiftly repacked his bags and summoned a bell boy to collect them. He'd get her somewhere safe and alone so he could explain what needed to happen and why. She was smart enough to work with him on this. It would be completely manageable.

Less than an hour later, he strode back down to her room, hoping she was still asleep, but just as he got out of the lift, her door opened. He paused where he was while she paced towards him, dressed again in the bland shirt and trousers. It took her a moment to glance up. When she did, she skidded to a halt and paled.

'You're awake.' He shoved his hand on his hips, trying to contain the rage that instantly surged. 'Where are you going?

'For a walk.'

'With all your luggage?'

She bit her lip.

'You don't want to go to the meeting?' he added when she still didn't answer.

'As if you haven't cancelled it already.'

'You're right. I've cancelled all of them.'

Her eyes widened. She wasn't pleased. Nor was he.

'We need to work this out,' he growled. Her behaviour fully justified the action he'd felt bad about. But he wasn't absolved, he was irate.

'You don't have to have anything to do with it.' She matched his anger. 'You can just walk away. Right now. Go on. It's obvious you want to.'

'What makes you say that?' He tensed.

Her gaze dropped. 'You left.'

'Did you think I wasn't coming back?' His stomach dropped, stunned she'd think that. Instantly defensive because he'd failed already. He curled his hands into fists, needing to vent the emotions rising within him. '*I'm* not the one currently trying to run away. Where were you going?'

His anger mushroomed in direct correlation with her silence.

'Well, you weren't going to get far without this.' He pulled her passport from his back pocket.

Her jaw dropped. 'You stole my passport?'

'Stole' was harsh. Borrowed was better. He'd needed the information.

'Good thing I did, given you were about to leave without even talking to me.' He put her passport in the inner pocket of his jacket.

'Because I *really* don't want to talk about it right now,' she snapped with low voiced fury.

'We have to discuss the future—'

'Not now. I need space, I can't think clearly—'

'You can have space without walking out on me.' He lost

his temper entirely, asking everything that had been bothering him the last hour. 'How could you not know you were pregnant? Have you been taking care of yourself? You've been working long hours.'

'There's nothing wrong with working long hours. You do that too.'

'*I'm* not pregnant,' he gritted.

'Edo.' She closed her eyes and sighed. 'I just want to go *home*.'

He steeled himself against her sigh. There was no choice—he needed to ensure her safety. He'd already made a mistake by leaving her earlier and she was even more vulnerable than he'd realised. 'And so you shall.'

Phoebe could only stare as Edo grabbed her luggage. He guided her downstairs to where a massive car waited. One heavy set guy held the door for her while another two sat in the front behind the thick glass screen. Had he requested extra bodyguards? Why? As well as taking her passport? *What the actual hell?*

'Are we going straight to the airport?' she asked tensely.

He watched her fasten her seatbelt before fastening his, taking his time before answering. 'We don't have a huge amount of time, Phoebe, we need to make secure arrangements.'

His concept of time clearly differed from hers. 'It might be later than is ideal to learn I'm pregnant, but we do still have *months* before this baby arrives.'

A frown furrowed his forehead. Apparently he couldn't stand to think of it being an actual baby.

'Once word gets out, it'll cause problems,' he said.

She flinched. 'What business is it of anyone else's?'

He rubbed the back of his neck. 'How can you go from writhing in my arms to running away the second my back is turned?' He dragged in a breath. 'I'm getting whiplash.'

She could hardly explain it to herself. Maybe it was just the culmination of tension over the last few days, or the need to delay the realisation of what had happened. But it wasn't even lunchtime, she was pregnant with his baby and the first thing she'd done when finding out was sleep with him again. Her attraction to him was unstoppable—even now she was burning with desire to move closer to him. But he'd left her. Alone. And he'd taken her passport. And she didn't understand anything.

'What happened this morning was just a primal reaction to the pregnancy news,' she murmured vaguely. 'I wanted to forget.'

'Sex is a stress release for you too.' He nodded acceptingly. 'We're good at it.'

Phoebe masked her flinch. Maybe that afternoon in Tuscany had been carefree fire because it had been meaningless. They'd not shared surnames let alone thoughts of any future. It was meant to have been one time—merely sexy hijinks with supposedly zero consequences. But Phoebe suddenly realised that what had happened this morning had been hugely different. She'd ached for him on a level that was actually terrifying. That need had been too much—too undeniable. And their encounter had been too good not to mean something—to her.

He regarded her from hooded lids. 'Marry me and the stress-release sex can continue indefinitely.'

She stared at him for a long moment. 'Are you joking?'

'It would be for the best.' He cleared his throat. 'Marry me, Phoebe.'

She couldn't believe he was even suggesting it. 'Edo, neither of us want to get married.'

'This isn't about either of us any more.'

She tried to ease her breathing, but she was beginning to feel like she was into the fourth hour of an ultra-marathon and each inhale hurt. 'We can parent this baby perfectly well without some piece of paper.'

His jaw hardened. 'Doesn't it deserve to have legitimacy and social acceptance?'

'What archaic world are you from?' she whined, ignoring the steel hardening his gaze.

'It needs the security of my name and the protection I can provide.'

'The *baby* can have your name,' she snapped. 'But there's no need for *us* to marry.'

She focused on staying measured and not screeching at him. But she saw the implacable set to his mouth and, heaven help her, it was intensely attractive. Worse, what he was offering struck deeply at some primal level within her. She lost her mind—hell, her *will*—around him. She was so tempted to say yes, to go all in—to indulge her weak desire to leap to the extreme. And she couldn't let that happen. Not on this.

'You don't want my name?' he asked softly.

She shook her head, denying the curling lick of pleasure inside at the prospect of having something so deeply personally *his*. The possessiveness inside her—the greedy part she couldn't shut down—wanted that. But it was madness. She wouldn't lose herself again. Certainly not in some man she barely knew.

'Do you think that just because I slept with you again that I'm going to say yes to everything you want?' She wouldn't give in to everything for a guy ever again. 'You're too used to getting your own way, and you can't keep me here against my will.' She glanced out the window and saw they were still in the city. 'We are going to the airport, aren't we?'

'No, we're going somewhere private to thrash out the plan for our future.'

'There's no need for a plan. It's straightforward. We're having a baby and we'll cope.'

'You said you would never be married again—why, what happened the first time around?'

She shot him a scathing look. 'You want me to spill my guts about my first marriage now?'

'It's as good a time as any,' he shrugged. 'The sooner we understand where we're each coming from, the sooner we can smooth our differences.'

Stunned, she stared at him. He was calm, while she was chaos. She had to pull herself together and fight. She drew another steadying breath. 'If we marry, I assume you want us to live in Italy?'

His lashes veiled his eyes. 'Initially, that would make most sense.'

'Am I to give up my job?' she followed up.

'Phoebe—'

'Are you going to give up your job?'

'Is that the problem—'

'Of course you won't,' she interrupted again. 'Because it's too important to you. Because *you're* more important than me. Because you earn more and have more power and more people working for you or something like that, right? So the *problem* is that *I'm* the one who'll make all the sacrifices—'

'Biology dictates some of this Phoebe. You're the one literally growing the baby. You need rest.'

'Seriously?' She glared at him.

'You can hardly stay awake for more than a two-hour stretch now. It's only likely to worsen.'

He thought it was impacting on her work? 'But—'

'I can ensure you have everything you need,' he growled impatiently.

Money maybe, but other things? She wasn't so sure. 'Everything?' she questioned. 'Are you promising to take care of my *every* need?'

His gaze skittered from hers.

'No, I didn't think so,' she muttered. 'This isn't what you want, Edoardo.'

'What either of us *want* is irrelevant. We need to do what is *right*. I cannot put this child at risk.'

'From me? Will I not be a good enough mother?' She was desperately wounded.

'Of course not,' he said harshly. 'I'm sure you'll be an incredible mother.'

She blinked.

'You're thorough. Organised. Conscientious.'

'I don't think parenting is like paperwork.'

He breathed in sharply. 'Phoebe—'

'I have a job I like and a home I like in London and I'm not giving them up just so you can feel as if you've done "the right thing".'

It was so obvious he hadn't wanted to propose—it had slipped out in some half-hearted effort and now he was digging in because he felt he had to.

'You live on the ground floor of a cramped flat with no yard. You don't even own the entire building. There's no freedom to play outside, and with that other flat above, your front door isn't properly secure.'

She stared at him—how did he know all that? And while he might not consider her work valuable, it was meaningful and rewarding for her. She didn't want to be 'kept'. She didn't want to lose her identity and become virtually nothing again. Because then she could be tossed aside like rubbish, as she had been before. Discarded once she'd lost her apparent value. So she would protect herself—her work, her home and her self-worth.

'Don't dismiss my achievement just because it's in a different league to yours,' she said. 'Maybe I didn't have a wealthy family to give me a leg up the financial ladder.'

He stiffened. 'What makes you think I did?'

'George said your grandfather was a financier.'

'I focus on insurance,' he snapped. 'My success is my own.'

She gritted her teeth. Really? He didn't have all kinds of privilege from growing up around that wealth—with education and connections and opportunities? But it wasn't worth the argument, there were bigger points to win here. 'Ditto. So don't diminish it. I love my flat. It might not be a mansion, but I worked so hard to buy it. It's *mine*.'

'It's mostly the bank's,' he retaliated coldly. 'And you know it's not good enough to raise a child there.'

'It's more than good enough for me,' she argued proudly. 'I'm happy there. Bethan is happy there. And my baby will be happy there. Just because you have a bunch of houses means nothing. Beautiful places are horrible when there's no warmth at their heart. Same with beautiful people.'

'No warmth?' He laughed derisively. 'There's fire between us.'

'That will die,' she said coldly. 'This child doesn't need to be saddled with parents stuck in a toxic relationship.'

'We won't be toxic. We can manage this like sane adults if you'd stop for a second and listen to what I—'

'Oh, so this is my fault for not *listening*,' she marvelled acerbically. 'Meaning not immediately agreeing to everything you want.'

'Phoebe.' He sighed heavily. 'You're right, this passionate phase between us will pass. Same with the marriage. We will eventually separate and divorce.'

She stared at him all over again. He hadn't meant marry for life? 'Then why marry at all?'

He pulled his seatbelt, loosening it from his chest and then letting it snap back against him. 'Eventually you and the child will live in London. Of course you can work if you want. You can do everything you want.' He didn't answer her question. 'You can have nannies, staff—'

'Wow. Where are you going to be?'

'I can't be the father you had.'

'Well, thank goodness for that, because my father sucked at dad duties.' So the Italy thing would only be temporary? She was so confused. 'You don't want your child to grow up here?'

'It will be safer with you.'

It again. And safer how?

He tensed. 'The bond between a baby and it's mother—'

'Shouldn't necessarily be more important than the bond it has with its father,' she said shortly. 'Look, I gave up everything for my first husband. I moved cities. I quit my studies. I blindly followed him because I was so in love and thought he felt the same. But he didn't. I'm not doing all that again, so don't ask me to.'

She'd thrown herself headlong into believing Ryan loved her utterly and unconditionally. But he hadn't. She'd been an irresistible, temporary accessory who'd suited his style at the time. Once he'd succeeded there, he'd been ready to level up with a better model.

Edo looked at her directly. 'The difference here is that you're not blindly in love with me. We'll have a contract, Phoebe. A written guarantee that you *will* be taken care of. You won't have to give up everything you want. In fact, you'll get far more than you ever would have dreamed.'

He meant *financially*. But money didn't buy happiness.

'You can write up a contract,' she nodded. 'Go right ahead. But it still doesn't require us to be *married*.'

'Phoebe, I'm an extremely wealthy man.'

'And? Is that supposed to impress me? Are you telling me to snatch you up now before some other woman does?

Sorry, Edo. You're a controlling jerk who's taken my passport. Right now, you're the *last* man on earth I'd marry.'

He pinched his nose and released a heavy sigh. 'I don't blame you for being angry. But we have little choice.'

'Why? Who's holding the gun to our heads? It's just you and me who get to decide this.'

'No. It is not.' He closed his eyes momentarily and released another breath. 'There was an abduction in my family and I'm more wealthy now than my family was then. Which means *you* are even more of a target. Fortunately, I also now have more deterrent power.'

Stunned, she gaped. 'Someone in your family was abducted.'

'My brother.'

'What?'

'He was thirteen.'

Shocked, Phoebe's breathing shortened. 'What happened? Is he okay?'

'We got him back eventually, but he was never the same,' he said stiffly. 'I won't take the risk of it happening to you.'

'No one is going to want to abduct me,' she whispered.

'Unfortunately, you're very wrong.'

So many questions raced through her head. Why had they targeted his brother? Had they caught the kidnappers? Where had he been held? But the one that popped out was fully needy. 'Why didn't you tell me sooner?'

'I hadn't the chance before you tried sneaking out of the hotel,' he snapped.

'I wasn't running away entirely,' she said defensively. 'I just needed space to think.'

Space from him because he was overwhelming—at least, that was how she felt around him.

'How was I supposed to know that?' He breathed hard.

'This is why we need to talk. And we can't make arrangements without consulting the other first.'

'Okay, then tell me where we're going now.' She shot him a sharp look.

He hesitated again. 'Back to the vineyard. There's both space and privacy there.'

'It's also isolated and difficult for me to get to an airport.'

He rubbed his hand over his head. 'I thought you liked it there.'

She'd loved it there. But returning to the scene of the crime would be a risk to her self-control. This really was about safety. Duty. Not any kind of desire. He didn't *want* the baby. He wanted to do what was *right* for the baby. She felt the rejection deeply personally. 'No one needs to know it's yours,' she said softly.

'What?'

'I can leave the father's name blank on the certificate.'

'You would deny my paternity?' He looked outraged.

'If it makes my child safer, then yes.' Phoebe lifted her chin. 'You're the one saying they're in danger. The fact is *you're* the source of that danger.'

She didn't really mean it. But his high-handedness infuriated her. He was railroading her. Rushing her. She'd worked hard to rebuild her life and she needed to retain her independence because he was powerful. He had money. And how he made her feel was terrifying.

He paled. 'I'll do whatever it takes to ensure the child's safety. And your safety.'

'What does that mean?'

'It means don't get in my way, Phoebe.'

She glared at him. 'You're threatening me?'

He sucked in a sharp breath, clearly trying to calm down. 'No, I'm telling you that I will keep you safe.'

'Well, I don't feel particularly safe, given you're effectively holding me *prisoner* here.'

'I'm not,' he growled and set her passport on the seat between them. 'Truce, okay? Let's start over.'

She took back her passport. 'Difficult for me to use the thing when I'm locked in an armoured car.'

He breathed in and out again. Twice. Then turned to her. 'Would you mind terribly if we remain in Italy for a few days while we work through this issue?' He ground out the question with aggravatingly false politeness. 'Or do you wish to return to London immediately and we'll make our plans from there.'

Phoebe stared at him, suddenly aware of her own flip-flop thinking. Because she needed time to absorb the shock of all of this, and either way *he* wasn't leaving her alone. And at least the privacy here was a bonus and honestly the last thing she felt like was getting back on board another plane.

'We can stay here for a little while,' she muttered. 'I do like your vineyard.'

He blinked. 'I appreciate your accommodating my difficult demands.'

She'd accommodated his demands really well a few hours ago. And he hers. And that heat was building in her body all over again.

But she realised that half of his problem was that he was worried. He didn't need to be.

'Just so you know, I'm sure everything is fine, I've been ridiculously healthy,' she muttered. 'Maybe I had a little nausea a few weeks back, but I put it down to new-job nerves. I've not been out partying or anything.'

His mouth twitched. 'Do you usually go out partying?'

'A while back my friends and I went through a phase,' she declared loftily.

Elodie had made a deliberate point of it, while Bethan had

seriously needed some laughs when she'd first come back from her hellish honeymoon in Greece.

'I've always had quite light periods,' she added with excruciating awkwardness, but she had to explain it. 'Honestly, I've just been really busy and distracted, and didn't pay attention to it.'

'The incomparable, efficient PA doesn't keep a spreadsheet to track all that data?'

'I have enough spreadsheets at work. Life outside of the office is messier.'

His eyebrows lifted. 'Do you leave the towel on the floor? Dishes in the sink? I don't mind if you do.'

'Why would you when you have staff to clean up after you,' she drawled. 'You get to make messes and pay other people to fix them for you.'

'Not this time,' he countered. 'I'm sorry that your liaison with me has put you in this position. It's the last thing I wanted to happen.' He fiddled with his seatbelt again. 'Do you have family support? Will your parents be helpful?'

No way was she telling her parents. It would never be a good time, but it was competition season. They were miles away on a training camp—helping others in a way they would never help her. They certainly wouldn't drop all that and come to her aid.

'They're very focused on their own lives,' she fudged. 'What about yours?'

His mouth compressed. 'They've both passed on.'

A hit of pain whistled through her. 'Oh, Edo—'

'It was a long time ago.' He dismissed her sympathy before she could even express it. 'So you don't have any support.'

Right. Nor did he. And he definitely didn't want to talk about *his* family either.

'I have *friends*,' she said stoutly. 'I'm going to tell them once we've worked the basics out. They're more my family than my mum and dad are.'

'I would prefer this didn't hit the press any sooner than can be helped.'

'They won't say anything, they're my *friends*,' she repeated bullishly. And the press wouldn't even be interested. His obvious scepticism needled her.

'You don't trust your friends?' she asked.

'I don't have friends.'

'None at all? No work buddies? No old schoolmates?' She didn't believe him. 'What about those guys you were running with on the day—'

'They're my bodyguards.'

'But you were laughing with them. You were talking like—'

'A boss banters with his employees,' he said bluntly. 'We work out together. We compete. But we're not friends. I pay them to protect me.'

Her breathing went choppy again. The man was very fixated on protection.

'There's no one else?' she asked. His parents were gone but what about his brother?

His lips curled into a mirthless smile. 'Why do you look so appalled? It's a deliberate choice.'

'I don't believe you don't like people. I don't believe you're not social—'

'I like seeing people *sometimes*. I like sleeping with beautiful women *sometimes*. None of them are friends and none are permanent fixtures in my life. None ever will be.'

'So everyone has a use-by date?' She was shocked. 'Where does that leave your child?'

'With you.'

She sucked in a breath. Was he really that cold? 'If you're really not interested in either of us, and have little desire to have any real involvement in our child's life, why insist I stay here now?'

'Because we need to ensure your safety. We need to ensure you have the best healthcare for the remainder of your pregnancy. For the birth. We need to prepare the property in London—'

'With what—a panic room?'

'That will be the least of the alterations.'

Seriously? 'And in this grand plan to keep me safe in every way possible, am I to be all alone all day?'

His jaw tensed. 'Would you like to invite one of these amazing friends to stay for a while?' He looked like it was the worst thing imaginable.

Oh, hell, no. Firstly she needed to get her wayward hormones under control. Secondly, she didn't want anyone to see how non-existent her relationship with him was. She was pregnant by a virtual stranger who didn't want to be involved with the baby in the long term.

'What if I meet someone else?' she asked tartly. 'What if there's another man who wants to be more of a father than you're willing to be?'

'If it ever arises, we'll deal with that situation,' he said stiffly.

'You don't think I'll ever meet anyone else?' She was really hurt by that.

'I thought you said you had no intention of marrying again,' he said shortly. 'Was that a lie?'

'No. I'm definitely not getting married again. Especially not to you.'

CHAPTER SIX

EDOARDO GROWLED, FRUSTRATED by her repeated rejections of his proposal. Not that he could blame her. He'd made a total mess of it—the words had slid out before he'd had a chance to prepare her properly. He didn't know what he'd been thinking—it had been flippant as hell, but she'd just looked so damned luscious, and it had been his sex-drive talking. But, as they'd both agreed, that fire would fade.

Mentioning his wealth to convince her had been a worse move, but he'd thought he might get her to understand by telling her a fraction about Dante. Apparently not. So much for being a master of negotiation—of strategizing difficult deals and getting the win. He'd never failed more spectacularly than he had with Phoebe just now. He just couldn't think clearly. He didn't want to talk about family or friends or anything *personal*. All he wanted was to haul her close and kiss her until she said nothing but *yes*—repeatedly.

'We should get a paternity test.' She added insult to injury. 'You'll want to be absolutely certain the baby is yours before you commit yourself to something you really don't want. Let's not discuss the future until you're sure.'

'I'm already sure and so are you,' he growled. Delaying this was pointless when they both knew the truth already. 'Stop trying to slow things down, that's not how things work with us.'

He was driven by an imperative, primal need to keep

her close. For now he needed to know she was *safe* and that meant not letting her out of his sight. His world had tunnelled down to only that one thing. He would do almost anything to ensure her safety. And, yes, he'd swerved dangerously close to keeping her passport. But that would be abduction and he knew how destructive that was.

Which was why he needed to start over—*ask* her to stay. It was shocking to feel such an inhuman impulse to keep her with him whether she wanted it or not. But he wasn't willing to compromise on them getting married. The more she resisted, the more he was convinced. Aside from social rights and legal privileges, marriage would project a unified exterior. He didn't want her vulnerable and she was extremely so. Clearly she had no family to turn to. No money either—she needed her job for a reason. She was almost flat broke with mortgage payments eating most of her monthly pay. Having a few friends was not good enough. Her vulnerability would only increase once people knew about her association with him.

He would arrange it so if anything happened to him they would be cared for. Once married, there would be no question about her priority. Eventually he'd install them in a fortified home in London where there'd be the best security systems, bodyguards, secure schooling—*not* her flat. He just needed time to arrange all that. And he couldn't arrange anything when he felt overwhelmed by this unrelenting need to know she was safe *now*.

'It doesn't need to be that big of a deal for us *personally*,' he pushed, increasingly desperate to recover his form. 'But marriage will show the world that you have my protection.'

'I don't need your protection.'

He gritted his teeth. She still didn't understand. He could respect that she wanted to keep her independence. Hell, he would support her to keep working if that was what she wished to do. He wasn't a complete Neanderthal. But he needed her to understand just how serious the risk to her was. Instead she was looking at him like he'd gone off the deep end. He rolled his shoulder, unable to ease the tension. He didn't talk about what had happened but maybe he should show her—*shock* her. He pulled out his phone and went into a file he never looked at.

'This is Dante on his thirteenth birthday,' he clipped unemotionally and flashed it at her.

Her face whitened. He steeled himself and swiped so another photo filled the screen and turned it back to her.

'This is him when he was finally found.'

He didn't need to see the photo. The image was branded in his mind. His already lanky brother had lost several kilos, leaving him almost skeletal by the time he'd been recovered. Starved and hurt, he'd still been wearing Edo's jacket and that devastated Edo every time he thought about it.

'Why did they take him?' Phoebe whispered, stricken. 'For a ransom?'

He didn't answer. Couldn't. Because it hadn't been Dante they'd wanted at all. It had been Edo. And it had been his fault they'd made the mistake. His fault his younger brother had suffered so much.

'Is he okay now?'

Edo went hot and cold, unable to answer her. He never should have mentioned it. But then he steeled himself all over again because he needed to get her to agree to his protection. By whatever means necessary.

'Won't it be awkward to be back at work in London with everyone knowing you're expecting my child?' he muttered.

'They don't need to know.'

'I'll tell them,' he said unemotionally. 'I'll tell everyone. How safe will you feel, knowing this is what happens to vulnerable members of my family?'

Her jaw dropped. 'You wouldn't—'

'Can you imagine your vulnerability? Maybe now you can understand just a fraction of the fear I feel for you in this instant.'

Her breathing quickened. 'Edo, this is emotional blackmail.'

'Yes, and I'm not about to apologise. You'll stay here where you are safe, where you can be cared for. You have the child. Once we've arranged proper security, you'll both return to London.'

'But all of that can be done without any need for us to *marry*—'

'There will be no other child for me,' he exploded. 'No other heir. You carry the entire burden—'

'What happened to your brother was terrible, but who's to say it will ever happen again?'

'Who's to say it won't?' he shot back. 'We have to take precautions.'

He didn't like thinking of the baby. He felt guilty that he couldn't be the kind of father any child deserved. He couldn't be supportive. Strong. He wasn't those things. He'd failed his brother. He'd been irresponsible and distracted and he had no right pretending that he could be anything otherwise. So he wouldn't. Yet he didn't want the child to feel he was entirely indifferent.

'Wouldn't it be nice for the child to believe it was created in a caring relationship?' He hopelessly grasped at straws. 'That it was wanted?'

'It *is* wanted.' Raw emotion—hurt—flickered on her face before she glanced away from him. 'Regardless of our relationship at the time of conception.'

She wanted this baby. But he didn't—*couldn't*—want it in the same way, because he could never care for it in the way he realised she already did. But he didn't want either of them to suffer. Frightening Phoebe wasn't ideal. Kidnapping her completely not okay. Maybe appealing to her tender-heartedness towards the infant was the key.

'Do you want it to think it's the accidental product of a random sexual encounter or would it be better to believe it was born out of a grand passion between its parents?' he asked.

For the first time she had no immediate comeback. He froze as he realised this mattered to her. This *different* sense of security.

She looked down at her hands and her hair fell forward, covering her face from him. 'You would lie to our child?'

'Is it so much of a lie?' He brushed back her hair, quelling his rising adrenaline. He'd finally found the right pressure point to exploit. 'Wasn't it a desire that couldn't be denied?'

He still wanted her, and if this morning had been anything to go by, she definitely still wanted him. 'Wouldn't it be better for the child to believe its parents couldn't resist each other?'

Phoebe couldn't look at him. What he'd just said made her crumble inside. To be wanted like that, madly—deeply— was such a tempting fantasy. It was the one thing she'd ached for all her life because neither of her parents had wanted her. She'd been an inconvenience, not a joy. She'd had to fit around them—not hold them back. All she'd wanted was to be the centre of their world—even just *sometimes*. She didn't want her child to dream of that in the way that she had. It had left her with a constant weakness and because of it she'd made bad choices.

For all his doomsday predictions and fear mongering and showing her his poor brother's picture, *safety* was something that could be arranged for them outside of marriage. But she did want this child to know it was wanted. She wanted that more than anything.

His attitude towards the baby confused her. He wanted the wedding, wanted to keep it 'safe', while at the same time he wanted to remain personally distanced from the child. Why? Didn't he want to take on that responsibility? Was it that he didn't believe he *could*?

When she'd been a child, her parents hadn't just insisted upon her being self-reliant, their absence had dictated it. She'd tried to be strong like them—to push through pain and carry on. And when she'd fallen and hurt herself, they'd not kissed it better. They'd not even been around. She'd learned to carry her own plasters.

The afternoon they'd collided, Edo had taken *care* of her. He'd been commanding and compassionate and yes, funny. Maybe it was only because he'd wanted to get into her pants that afternoon, but it showed her that he was capable of care. In his way he cared now—constantly feeding her, providing safe shelter—he nailed the basic necessities of life. She had no doubt that he *could* be a good father, the problem seemed to be that he didn't want to be.

'I want the baby to feel wanted,' she breathed. 'To believe in that fairy-tale.'

She wanted it to feel secure in *that*. Her parents were passionate—focused, driven extremists. They had their dreams and didn't let anyone get in the way of them. Not even their child. Phoebe could understand it, but she didn't want to be the same. Because she'd fallen into that extremism in her relationship with Ryan—submerged herself in a dream that wasn't real. She couldn't let that happen again. And she knew she couldn't go to her parents for help with having this baby. They wouldn't deviate from their path for their grandchild either. She would break that cycle. *She* would put her child first—ahead of her own discomfort. And she would take the time—the resources—that Edo was offering her to make a better plan for both her and the baby's future.

And the child deserved its birthright as his heir—to have a connection with him. She did want it to think it had been conceived, if not in love, at least in passion. Its father wanted to do his best for it, even if his best wasn't all *she* would desire from him, this wasn't about her. Their marriage would only be for long enough to cement that security and that story.

'Then let me arrange the fairy-tale,' he said gently. 'You can always back out at the last minute.'

'What, jilt you at the altar?' She glanced at him.

It was a mistake. His looks alone were stunningly seductive. How could he look intensely determined but tender at the same time? She didn't want to sacrifice anything in her life to follow a husband who cared little for her, but this wasn't that. There was no lie here, he wasn't promising her the moon.

'It's not for ever, Phoebe, but it will create a solid foundation and give you both security on several levels. And me too.'

Maybe she shouldn't make such a mountain out of the marriage molehill—it was another form of extremism, right? Maybe she could compromise. She just needed to be careful—not confuse lust for anything else. Not *fall* for him. But to make a sacrifice for her child? Then yes, she would consider that.

'Okay, then. We marry. *Briefly.*'

He released a long breath. 'Can I arrange ante-natal care for you while I'm at it?'

She should have known he wouldn't stop there. 'I'm the picture of health and you know it.'

'Even so. You're months along Phoebe, you need to be checked out. There are things you might need.'

'You really worry that bad things might happen.'

'Bad things do happen,' he said calmly. 'So we take precautions and alleviate as much risk as possible.'

'Hence why you work in the insurance industry.'

He was all about preparedness...preparing for worst-case scenarios. He ensured he had the ability to cover all kinds of costs—even to pay a ransom.

'You trying to figure me out, Phoebe?'

'Maybe some things are falling into place.'

He shrugged. 'You should have a check-up. Don't you want the best for the baby?'

'Don't use that to get your way in everything.'

'Don't you want what's best for *you*? Your health matters,' he growled. 'At least let me do what I *can*.'

There it was again, that implication that there were things he couldn't do. But this was a shock to him too, right? Maybe, given time, he might want to do more than he currently thought he did. And he was right, her health did matter—even more so now. 'Fine.'

He picked up his phone and tapped a brief message. Next second the car pulled into a side street, turned around and went back in their previous direction. Phoebe frowned and glanced out the window. Now she thought about it, it had been taking them for ever to leave Milan. It looked like they were still in the central city. Shouldn't they be on some motorway by now?

'You said we're going to the estate, right?' she asked.

'We're seeing a doctor first.' He kept his focus on his phone. 'Heading there now.'

She stared at him, anger blooming. 'Have we been going in big circles this whole time?'

When had he made a doctor's appointment—was it *before* he'd asked her? Before she'd said yes? And was this doctor happy for them to show up whenever Edo felt like it? She didn't bother asking any of the questions. She already knew he'd done exactly that. All of it. And judging by the clenched tilt of his jaw, he wasn't sorry.

Less than ten minutes later the car parked outside a sleek clinic. She unfastened her belt but before she could reach for the door handle Edo gripped her wrist.

'You wait for them to check the area first.'

She stared at him, then at the bodyguard who'd exited the front passenger seat and was scanning the pavement. 'There's no one—'

'You need to get used to them doing their job,' Edo added firmly. 'It will become normal.'

To have people monitoring her every move? To never have to open a car door for herself ever again? Phoebe's tension grew as his bodyguards walked them to the door, went in first and then dropped back to wait and watch at the exit. It was only a moment before a nurse signalled for Phoebe and Edo to follow her. Which meant the doctor had indeed been happy to be flexible on time. Phoebe stepped into the large consulting room, blinking at the older woman who stepped forward to greet them—she was the ultimate in academic refinement with her tailored suit, perfectly styled hair and air of brilliance and assurance. She and Edo spoke in such fast Italian Phoebe had no hope of following along. She glanced at the framed certificates adorning the wall—the science degree, medical degree, surgical specialties, awards. Everything about this place—especially the doctor—was impressive and yes, reassuring. She did want to know everything was okay. Did want to know if there were things she ought to be doing.

'Dr Di Lello would like to take your medical history.' Edo interrupted her reverie. 'I'll give you privacy.'

He wasn't staying in here to listen? She'd expected he'd want to be here for everything, what with being a control freak and all.

A cynical smile curved his mouth, as if he'd read her mind. 'You can't get out of here without my knowing, but I appreciate you'll feel more comfortable without me breathing down your neck. Your health is the most important thing right now. I'll have my cheek swab for the paternity test while you talk. Be honest with her and find out what you need to know.'

With perfect English, Dr Di Lello questioned Phoebe at length while she got her nurse to do a blood draw. She was calm and supportive. Phoebe relaxed, asked all her questions, gratefully took the pregnancy guide the doctor gave her, together with a prescription for pre-natal vitamins.

'We will do a scan now,' the doctor said with a smile.

A what now? Phoebe stared hard at the doctor. 'You mean, see the baby?'

Her heart pounded. Suddenly this was *very* real. But what about Edo—she glanced at the door—would he want to see the baby too?

'Shall I see if he wants to step in?' the doctor asked.

'Yes. Okay. Thank you,' she babbled breathily, a chill sweeping across her skin. This was so awkward. Her stress grew as she waited for ages before Dr Di Lello returned— alone, her expression neutral.

'He's on a call.' The doctor moved to the examination area. 'We'll go ahead without him this time.'

Phoebe stilled, tried to regulate her breathing. Edo couldn't come see their baby for the first time because he was on a call? Giving her privacy in the doctor's room wasn't him being sensitive, he just had other more important things to do. She could understand that his work was more important than *her*, but to consider it more important than their baby? That angered her. He'd really meant it when he'd said both she and the baby would be better off without him in the long term.

She lay on the narrow bed and the doctor touched the sonogram wand across her belly. An amorphous grey mess appeared on screen at first, then very clearly a head emerged, a body. A *baby*.

'There's a really strong heartbeat,' the doctor said in her measured, reassuring way.

Phoebe stared at the grey swirling outline on the screen and listened to the scurrying beats. Her heart raced too.

'I'm just taking some measurements,' the doctor murmured.

It seemed to take for ever, but Phoebe just stared at the screen, *awed*.

'Everything is looking really good,' the doctor said softly. 'Do you want to know the gender?'

'You can tell already?' While Phoebe could see the head and body, identifying more tiny details seemed impossible, even if she squinted.

'Yes, would you like to know?'

A lump blocked her throat, making it impossible to speak. She shook her head slightly. It didn't matter as long as everything was okay.

The doctor smiled. 'Then it shall be a surprise.'

Edo tried to concentrate on what Felipe was telling him, but he had to get him to repeat every other sentence because he kept zoning out, which meant the call had taken far longer than necessary. He couldn't stop wondering about Phoebe. Had she had a blood draw? What had she told the doctor? Was she healthy—was she well and strong enough for this pregnancy? Uncertainty stressed him—he didn't know the first thing about pregnancy or child birth and honestly didn't want to. But nor did he want Phoebe suffering, didn't want her unwell or at risk. There was risk with this and he just didn't—

Someone coughed behind him and he turned. His focus arrowed to Phoebe but apparently she'd developed an obsession with the floor. He abruptly ended the call and addressed the doctor.

'Is she okay?' he asked in Italian as he stared at Phoebe. Why wouldn't she meet his eyes? What was wrong? He stilled, filled with strained energy. But the doctor assured him everything was as it should be—Phoebe was healthy, the foetus developing normally, its growth aligned with the possible conception date he'd given her. He fidgeted, impatient with her focus on the infant. He already knew it was his, he wanted to know more about Phoebe. But as the doctor promised to email through the test results urgently, Phoebe stalked to the door and pointedly glared at the waiting bodyguard. Edo jerked his chin and the bodyguard moved to escort her to the car. He shot a glance at the doctor, ignoring the cool hint of condemnation in her eyes as he thanked her, then swiftly followed his reluctant fiancée out. She was already strapped in and staring out the window by the time he got in.

'You okay?' he asked once they were underway and heading to the estate at last.

'You mean the doctor didn't tell you everything?' Phoebe muttered icily. 'Clearly you leaving the room was purely performative.'

'She only told me about your health in relation to the foetus.'

Because he didn't trust Phoebe to tell him if there were problems. But the doctor had confirmed that there were none—everything was exactly as it should be, and frankly the relief flooding him now obliterated the fact that she was angry with him. Volatile emotions were only to be expected, given this was a huge shock with huge ramifications. But Edo could now breathe more easily. He would leave her alone to process things and progress his own plans. He pulled out his laptop, determined to finally finish the reports he'd been stalled on since seeing her again in London.

'Do you want to know if you're having a son or daughter?' Her icy voice sliced into the silence.

He froze. His mouth gummed.

'Does it matter to you?' she added when he didn't—

couldn't—respond. 'It doesn't to me, so I didn't find out, but you might be able to work it out if you study the picture.' She placed a photograph over the laptop keyboard in his lap. 'The doctor printed it, seeing you didn't want to be present for the scan.'

Edo blinked but there was no avoiding the image—a head, a little body, even littler limbs. A baby. An indefinable emotion slammed into him. He tensed, rejecting it. He didn't want to know *this*. He didn't want to feel *this*. Whatever *this* was. It just made his blood run cold.

He picked up the photo and only just stopped himself from crumpling it in his fist, instead he shoved it into the front pocket of his laptop bag. He couldn't look at it. Couldn't consider what was coming. Not now. Not yet. Not ever. Cold sweat slicked because he knew it wasn't good enough. And that was the problem he couldn't overcome. *He* couldn't give her the fairy-tale she *really* wanted. And he could never be all that child needed.

'Are you hungry?' he asked huskily after a moment.

They'd not had lunch but honestly, he didn't want to stop, he just wanted to get her to the estate. To where he knew they could be safe.

'No.' Her reply was brutal.

He glanced at her but she'd turned to look out the window and he couldn't see her eyes. Didn't need to. She was angrier than ever. She was right to be. But nothing he could say would make this better, he would focus on what he could do. That was plan—yes to the panic room, to the twenty-four-hour protection team, to the best medical care that could be bought. And he would ignore the photograph peeking out of his bag for as long as he could.

Phoebe stared out the window, stewing for hours. How could he not even look at the picture of their child? She shouldn't have agreed to marry him. He obviously wasn't interested the baby. Or her. Only in their security. It was shocking. And it hurt. She remained silent for the rest of the long drive. So did he. But the view—the countryside—changed. Just as dusk darkened the sky, it became recognisable.

'This is your estate,' she murmured.

He glanced up from whatever it was that had held his attention for so long and nodded. 'I'm sorry I misled you that day in summer. I didn't think it was important.'

He didn't need to apologise about *that*. That wild, warm afternoon was supposed to have been a single moment—light, free, fun—*neither* of them had intended to get close for long. But now they were stuck with each other. Even if their marriage would be temporary, their lives would be permanently entwined because they were having a *child* and at some point he'd have to face that fact.

When they pulled into the estate, she dutifully—*pointedly*—remained in the car while the security team got out and checked the compound with alert experience. Two more hefty men came out of the main building to join them. How had she not noticed this insane security that day he'd brought her here? How had she not worked out that his running mates weren't mercenaries but bodyguards—that, while there'd been banter between them, they were employees? Because Edo had seemed relaxed and fun, and she couldn't reconcile the man she'd met then with the grimly distant one waiting by the car door for her now. But, as she took the hand he extended, that silky desire swept through her—as strong as it had been all those months ago, as unstoppable. It sent her pulse racing and her awareness sharpened. She needed to work *that* out as well. But Edo lacing his fingers through hers didn't help.

'Isabella runs the villa. She'll provide anything, you only

have to ask.' He jerked his chin towards the middle-aged woman who now stood just outside the large doorway.

Phoebe smiled at the soft-eyed Isabella but didn't get a chance to speak because Edo's hold on her was tight and he kept walking. She'd not entered the main building back in summer but she didn't get time to truly look around now because he pushed on too fast, clearly determined to get her...where?

Her breathing quickened. Did he want to get her alone? Want to explain? To her horror that treacherous part of her desperately wanted to be alone with him. Even when she was mad with him.

He led her up a flight of stairs, opened a door and drew her inside before releasing her hand. 'We have admin to do.'

Phoebe stepped into the vast study and stared at the perfect piles of papers set out on a large table. Disappointment slammed, adding to her anger. He didn't want to get her alone to ravish her, he wanted legal certainty.

'Apparently so,' she gritted.

Some poor assistant had been working hard to have printed and sorted all these forms and documents. She snatched up a pen and signed the first super-quickly in a pique of fury, barely scanning the text because she, who prided herself on paying attention to details, was utterly distracted—and appalled—by the overwhelming urge to touch him. Her anger only seemed to make it worse—hell, her want for him now was wilder than that afternoon they'd shared. It seemed she increasingly lost control of herself when she spent too long near him and spending several hours trapped in the back seat of a car with him was *definitely* too long.

They both silently, furiously, filled in and signed everything.

He set down his pen then glanced at her, his brow furrowed. 'You need food. We shouldn't have missed lunch.'

Food would be good. Food would be a *distraction*. She really needed that right now. He didn't take her hand to lead the way again. Just silently escorted her. The dining room was sumptuous. The view from the window showed the pool, the verdant countryside. The table was laden—linen cloth, sparkling crystal and silverware, fresh flowers, so *much* food. Clearly Isabella was an extraordinary housekeeper. Her mouth watering, Phoebe sank into the chair Edo held for her, abandoning both anger and attraction in the need for sustenance. She didn't speak, too engrossed in sampling every dish.

But Edo talked—about nothing of significance. Seemingly his mood had lifted now all those documents were done. He explained the history of the region, how the dishes they were eating were prepared, the kinds of grapes they grew. He was determinedly charming but Phoebe saw through the facade that it was. He didn't want to discuss anything heavy or intimate.

But a refuelled Phoebe increasingly couldn't think of anything else. She couldn't comprehend the *magnitude* of today's events. She rubbed her hand across her forehead. How had this happened? How had she ended up here? How was any of this *possible*? How was she going to survive spending this time married to him for a while when she already liked him more than she should—and how was she going to manage the fact that he didn't really want any of this at all? Because she couldn't quite believe that last bit. Because she was a fool.

'Phoebe?'

She glanced up at his soft change of tone and realised that she'd not heard a word he'd said in the last few minutes.

'You're tired.' His eyes narrowed on her. 'I'll show you to your room.'

She tensed, trying to push away the instant knock of disappointment. But of course she would have her own room. They weren't a couple. They were strangers who'd had wild sex a couple of times. He didn't guide her physically. There was no hand on her back or across her shoulders, no fingers laced though hers.

'I thought you'd want your own space.' He led her into a large room that she couldn't even look at, because he turned towards her. 'No?'

She couldn't break away from the scorching heat now filling his eyes. From the tempting smile curving his lips. The polite dinner facade dropped and she saw his desire. Oh, she was definitely a fool, but she *couldn't*—

'No?' he repeated softly with a half-laugh.

She *couldn't*. Not answer, not resist. When he put his hands on her waist she just curled her arm around his neck and pulled his head down to hers—hungry for the pure, fiery escape again.

'Are you tired of talking?' he teased, his mouth an inch from hers. 'Thank God. So am I.'

CHAPTER SEVEN

PHOEBE RECLINED ON a sofa in the pool house feeling like a sybarite indulging in her favourite things. She had a dish of nuts beside her, a glass of juice and a book in her hands. She'd woken alone—to her disappointment—but in fairness, it had almost been lunch time when she'd finally come back to consciousness. And, with even more fairness, this time Edo had left a note informing her he'd be working in his home office.

She'd gone to the window to check the weather—and the view, and next moment Isabella had gently knocked on her door to deliver a delicious brunch tray. Phoebe's Italian app had been all vocab, not much verbal practice, but they made it work. She'd offered profuse thanks, babbling with embarrassment.

That was when Isabella had said Phoebe was the first guest to stay the entire time she'd worked there. And she'd worked there for years. That nugget had fuelled within Phoebe a need to move and expend her over-thinking energy. She'd pulled on her bikini and taken a swim in the pool—it was heated and could be used year-round. Then she'd come into the pool house with its smaller, more private feel. She'd been in here for all the hours since—mulling her future.

'The results of the paternity test are in.' Edo dropped into the chair beside her.

'What?' Phoebe took a moment to put down her book, hiding how her heart leapt at his appearance. 'That was quick.'

'They were expedited.' He picked out a pistachio from the dish. 'And we've been granted a special licence to have a civil service at the family chapel for security reasons.'

Her mind just blanked. 'You have a family chapel?'

'It's on the property.' He cracked the shell and clarified. 'It was the chapel for the family I bought the estate from.'

'So this isn't a property you've had in your family for generations?'

'No.'

She waited but he didn't elaborate. Where had he grown up with his family, then?

'I'm divorced,' she pointed out eventually. 'Can I even get married in a chapel?'

'It's a venue, that's all. There will be a civil officiant. Crucially, it's private.' He chose a cashew then. 'The ceremony will be at three tomorrow. Everything's arranged. You only need to show up.'

Tomorrow? She was aghast.

'You've planned the whole wedding just like that?' When had he had the time to do that?

'Vows, paperwork, pretty much everything.' He fished in the nut dish again. 'We can change any details you don't like.'

'Such as the actual wedding bit?' she mumbled, disconcerted.

Hell, she'd thought *she* was efficient. Edo was next level and moving *fast*.

'Do you want any friends or family to attend? There's time to fly them out first thing.'

'No thanks.' She swallowed.

'So, no family present for either of us.' He shot her a grin. 'Like an elopement.'

Yeah, an elopement in some other family's chapel.

What about his brother? He wasn't coming to the wedding? Was Edo ashamed of her and their shotgun wedding? Why didn't he want to tell her anything? But she could hardly question him about his family when she didn't want to talk about hers either.

'Do you have something to wear?' he asked.

'You mean you haven't organised that as well? Edo, how inefficient,' she mocked. 'Never mind, my work suit is suitably funereal.'

'Indeed it is.' He chuckled a little too loudly for her liking. 'Why do you insist on that grey automaton outfit? It's boring, and we both know you're anything but boring.'

'Are you commenting on what I wear at work?' She leaned towards him. 'Maybe it's a way of blending into the background so I don't get harassed by rich, arrogant jerks who think they're entitled to anything or anyone they want—'

'Someone harassed you? Who?' His smile vanished.

She arched her eyebrows and handed him the entire dish of nuts.

'I kept my distance. It nearly killed me but I kept my distance,' he muttered. 'What are you going to wear tomorrow?'

'Apparently nothing, given I've no chance of finding anything in the village,' she grumbled.

'Nothing.' His grin returned. 'I look forward to it.'

She rolled her eyes.

'What did you wear last time?' he asked. 'Got any photos?'

'I deleted them all and burned the dress.'

'It was that bad, huh?' Edo tossed one of the nuts into his mouth. 'Tell me about it?'

'It was from a second-hand store. A simple slinky number. White,' she answered blandly. 'Inexpensive, because I was a student. I thought I looked good, but honestly, I cringe about it now. I must have looked like I was playing dress-up.'

She'd been a kid, so eager to be grown up and desired.

He stopped with the nuts. 'I meant tell me about your marriage, not the dress.'

'You mean you want us to have a *personal* conversation?' she mock-marvelled. 'Because generally you avoid such things. Or at least, like the information to travel one way only.' She took a cashew from the dish he'd just almost dropped. 'You're a closed book. One with an appealing cover but impossible to open.'

'I told you something personal in the car yesterday,' he pointed out softly.

'Only because you were desperate to convince me to marry you. You know we'll both need to do better. We need to work out how we want to raise the baby—'

'Eventually,' he interrupted. 'Let's focus on the immediate issues.'

'Like my wedding dress?' she muttered sarcastically.

She didn't have time to trawl the shops, even if there were any. Besides, she hardly wanted to face petite assistants when her belly was becoming more obvious by the hour.

'I'll wrap up in a sheet, toga-party style.' She shrugged. 'Problem solved.'

'I've got a selection arriving shortly.' He smirked.

'What? Sheets?'

'There's a reasonable variety of *dresses*, hopefully you'll find one you can endure just long enough for some photos.'

'Photos?'

'For the baby's album.' He grinned at her. 'You can indulge your inner fire-starter and light a bonfire immediately after.'

'You're not worried I'll burn down your entire estate?'

'You're the office fire warden, far too responsible to make such a catastrophic error.'

'Fire warden?' She shook her head. 'First aid certificate.'

'Same thing.' He shrugged. 'Can you cope with a wedding band? You can melt that down later too, remake it into something you prefer.'

Oh, she needed to take him down. But before she could even try to answer she heard heavy wheels out in the courtyard.

'That will be your dress delivery. Do you want help choosing?'

She stood. 'I can manage.'

'Naturally,' he muttered acerbically.

Her refusal wasn't about independence, if Elodie or Bethan were here she'd fall over them in desperation for help. But she did *not* want Edo alongside her in this moment.

By the time she made it upstairs, Isabella was hanging several garment covers in the walk-in wardrobe of Phoebe's room. The housekeeper's eyes sparkled and Phoebe swallowed all pride. 'Do you want to look at them with me?'

There were several options but it didn't take them long to find a favourite. It was the colour of the crème in a crème caramel, long, with a delicate lace layer. Phoebe liked the long sleeves and the way it flowed about her body—masking her belly. She still couldn't believe that she—supposedly so practical—had an unplanned pregnancy. Worse, that she'd not realised for so *long*.

Isabella fussed about her gently, smoothing parts and adjusting the hang of it. Then she met Phoebe's eye and smiled. Phoebe didn't go back downstairs but asked Isabella if she could have her dinner brought to her. No problem, of course. Edo didn't disturb her and she tried to relax enough to sleep. The pregnancy hormones helped—she was asleep in seconds.

* * *

Isabella woke her with a breakfast tray. Without Phoebe having to ask again, she stayed to help—drawing her a bath and providing beautiful toiletries. Moved and grateful, Phoebe sat still as Isabella swept her hair into a half up, half down style. She took deep breaths and reminded herself this would only be temporary. She wasn't going to lose herself. This was different, she could keep it on *her* terms. She just needed not to let her lust for him get the better of her.

In the early afternoon a bodyguard drove Isabella and her down the hill to the chapel. Phoebe gazed at the small stone building with its circular window. Phoebe walked in slowly. It took a moment for her eyes to adjust to the light inside. Edo was already there, unbearably handsome in his dark suit.

Ceremony. Vows. Rings.

It passed in a complete haze because she could hardly hear above her heartbeat. She could hardly look at him either. He was too gorgeous. Too serious. And she was all thumbs, putting the wedding band on his cool finger. She'd not had to do that before. Ryan had refused to wear one.

Isabella and the bodyguard witnessed, taking time to sign the paperwork. As Edo talked with the official, Phoebe took the chance to walk about the chapel, trying to clear her fuzzy head. The floral array smelled gorgeous. Someone had put time and effort into making this tiny, already beautiful building even more stunning. She moved slowly, studying the old memorial plaques, reminders of the family who'd once owned this property. There were generations of them. A glint in the further back corner caught her eye. Half-hidden by flowers, the bronze plaque was incongruous because of its shine. It was newer. She brushed the petals to the side to read the inscription and froze.

Dante Benedetti

Was this his *brother's* memorial stone? Phoebe's breathing

became choppier. She frowned and moved closer to read the dates, confused. Edo had said they'd got Dante back. He'd shown her that awful photo of him when he'd been freed. He'd said that Dante had never been the same but he'd never told her more. According to these dates, Dante had been nineteen when he'd passed. Five years after the abduction. What had happened? Why had he died so young?

Worried, she glanced back at her husband—serious and focused as he and the official talked. He'd lost both parents. She still didn't know how. Now she knew he'd not been wholly truthful about his brother. She'd joked about him being a closed book, but he truly was. Of course he didn't *have* to tell her anything personal—certainly not anything deeply painful as this clearly was. But she worried for him—and now wondered what *else* he'd kept from her. This had all happened so fast because she'd been swept along by his intense insistence on *security*...

Was there worse that had happened? What *had* happened to his parents? And what was the impact of all this on Edo himself? He must be so very hurt. It made her heart ache. Badly. Had she just made a massive mistake? Because she'd thought he might come round to the reality of their baby, to choosing to be more involved than he'd said he intended to...

Far too late she realised that she knew almost nothing about the man she'd just married.

CHAPTER EIGHT

'PHOEBE?' EDO STRODE towards his wife, his blood chilling. 'What's happened?'

The stunning woman who'd walked up the aisle towards him looking like something out of a dream only twenty minutes ago now looked atrocious. Her skin was the colour of chalk and there was a stressed sheen in her eyes. He wound one arm around her waist and pressed the backs of his fingers against her forehead. 'Are you unwell?'

A tremor rippled through her. 'Just a little tired.'

Guilt twisted into a rock-hard knot beneath his ribs. 'I shouldn't have kept you waiting, I—'

'I'm fine.'

She didn't look fine. She looked scarily ethereal. Was this a reaction to the wedding? Was she overwhelmed? Had she not slept at all last night? She couldn't have, even though he'd deliberately left her alone to rest. Now he ushered her into the car and drove it himself up the track to the villa.

'What about the photos?' she asked.

'We have enough already.' He glanced and saw her confused expression. 'Taken during the ceremony.'

'Oh.'

She hadn't noticed one of his assistants taking photos? Always efficient Phoebe was shaky. He'd have carried her inside but knew she'd resist if he tried. And maybe she needed to feel some modicum of control in this moment—control was important to her. And fair enough.

He led her to the lounge inside and fetched refreshments. He'd banished the staff from the villa, needing to be alone with her. But he couldn't touch her now.

He'd been edgy all morning—hell, he'd cut himself shaving, been dressed hours ahead of time. In the end he'd been reduced to strewing flowers everywhere in that chapel just for something to do to pass the time. And then she'd finally arrived. She'd looked beautiful as she'd walked towards him—he'd not been able to take his eyes off her, not been able to breathe. He'd got what he wanted, but now he questioned the cost. Because the radiant flush in her cheeks had evaporated. He'd sapped her vitality. So he would stay away.

He *should* stay away—it was what he wanted, right?

He barely ate. Nor did she. He gritted his teeth to stop himself from nagging her about it. He needed to do better. The vibrant woman who'd walked into that meeting in London less than a fortnight ago was now a pale shadow of herself.

'I might go rest for a bit,' she murmured barely ten minutes later, pushing away the plate she'd barely touched.

'Of course.'

He stood as she walked out but didn't follow. He couldn't trust himself to enter a bedroom with her and not succumb to temptation. He'd already made too many selfish demands on her and she obviously needed rest.

But she didn't reappear in the evening. It took everything in him not to go to her. He paced in his room. Paced around the villa. Saw light beneath her door at some awful hour of the morning—but he still didn't go in.

The next morning he paced around the patio—waiting for her to surface. Finally she appeared. His stomach curdled as he saw her pallor. Not to mention her reluctance to look him in the eyes.

'Did you not sleep well?' He poured himself a coffee to stop himself going to her.

She sat at the table and chose a piece of fruit. 'I slept fine, thank you.'

A complete lie. His discomfort deepened.

'What would you have me do today?' She sliced a single piece from the apple and didn't nibble.

'I'm not your boss any more, Phoebe.'

She set the small paring knife on the edge of her plate. 'You're my husband. I'm your wife. So, anything you need me to do today?'

The words 'husband' and 'wife' provoked his unease and she knew it.

'Rest,' he muttered dryly. 'It seems you need it.'

'So I'm reduced to being an incubator…'

He dragged in a breath, refusing to fight with her when she was clearly still exhausted. 'What would you *like* to do today? Tell me and I'll arrange what I can.'

She was beautiful even with those shadowed eyes and drawn features. He just wanted to pick her up and take her to bed and pleasure her. Slake his lust. Ease his guilt. They would both sleep for hours then. But that method of relaxation was in *his* best interests, not hers, and he'd already been selfish enough.

'I'll have a think about it and let you know,' she muttered tightly.

Edoardo nodded and left the table before he did something rash.

Wrapped in a robe, Phoebe curled up on her favourite sofa in the pool house and tried to suck up her intense disappointment. She *should* consider this as a holiday of her dreams.

After all, she was back in Italy—her fantasy destination—ensconced in a stunning estate with a heated pool and privacy and an endless supply of amazing appetisers provided by the sweetly attentive Isabella. She didn't even have to ask the housekeeper for anything, the kind, discreet woman just *noticed* and quietly delivered.

No doubt she also noticed that Phoebe's new husband was hardly showering her with attention. In fact, he was fully MIA. Phoebe had no idea where he even was. It was mortifying to be such an obviously unwanted wife, especially when she ached for the hedonistic escape that sex with him brought. She didn't know when or how the ache was ever going to ease. She'd waited awake for hours alone on her wedding night and he hadn't come anywhere near her—not even checking in to see if she was okay.

It had taken her almost all the long, lonely night to work out that maybe he'd slept with her earlier only because she'd *demanded* it. Hell, she'd absolutely launched on him like a wild tigress in the hotel in Milan after discovering her pregnancy. Maybe he'd gone along with her because he'd wanted her to accept his plan. And now he had what he wanted—her married to him for the birth of the baby—he didn't *have* to sleep with her any more. He didn't have to tell her anything more about his life either. Because he didn't really want her in it.

It was horrific. Worse, she was still extremely frustrated. Not that she'd let him know that. She wasn't going to be accused of being *needy*. No, she was going to focus and fix her future. *Immediately.* The sooner she got herself independent, the better.

She'd brought her laptop from her bedroom and now she brainstormed. Given she could do a lot of her work remotely, she would set up a service as a virtual assistant. If she started now, she'd be well placed for when this sham marriage ended. By the time the baby was born, she could have clients and even an independent income. She wouldn't need to be entirely dependent upon him. He could help with the baby's needs but she could have her own income.

'Have you had lunch?' Edo interrupted.

Phoebe stiffened. He didn't take the chair next to her this time.

'I haven't stopped eating all morning.' She nodded towards the plate of crackers and cheese on the table beside her and didn't meet his eyes. 'I've resigned from Scott Insurance,' she added before he walked off. 'I've let George know. It's effective immediately. I'm keeping this laptop, consider it my outstanding holiday pay.'

She braved a glance up. He stood three feet from her. Rigid. Faint tiredness shadowed his eyes.

'Okay,' he said slowly.

'I'm starting an online business.' She maintained her cool bravado.

'Great.' He coughed. 'Doing what?'

'I'm going to be a virtual assistant.'

'You don't want to take a break before establishing a new venture?'

'I'm not cut out to do nothing for weeks on end.'

His mouth pinched. 'It hasn't been weeks, it's barely been a day. And you're not doing nothing, you're growing a baby.'

'Are you taking time off?' she queried before smiling glacially. 'It's something to distract me while I'm stuck here.'

Although yes, this was a stunning place to be stuck, and she wouldn't mind it if *he* were to distract her. But he clearly didn't want to do that.

He crossed his arms across his chest. 'What can I do to help?'

Leave her alone. Let her salvage a little pride. But instead of staying polite, her anger started to seep out. 'You're not going to stop me?'

He met her gaze for a charged moment. 'You'll need a work space. I'll have it arranged.'

Phoebe sucked back her self-control. 'If you insist,' she muttered.

He left the room with unseemly haste, apparently uninterested in discovering any further details of her plans. *Great.* At least now she knew where she stood and she wasn't going to let it get to her. Much.

She nibbled on Isabella's treats, sipped water, worked solidly on her business plan for several hours, forcing concentration with sheer will power. She even made a start on a web presence before realising she'd become totally stiff from sitting still. She'd stretch out with a swim. She shrugged off the robe and went to grab one of the large, fluffy beach towels.

She stopped just shy of the shelves, shaken by her own reflection in the large mirror on the back wall of the room. She'd not dared look at herself properly since learning of the baby—she'd half ignored those signs, those sensations. Now in only her bikini she moved nearer to her reflection, astounded by the rapidity of the changes in her body. The reason for her belly's curve had somehow swiftly become utterly undeniable. She really was *pregnant*. Shyly fascinated she tugged on the string of her bikini top and let it fall to the floor. She stared—her nipples had a slightly darker blush and were unbearably sensitive. She cupped one breast, testing its weight—

She heard a rough drag of breath but it wasn't her own. She glanced up and caught Edo's gaze in the mirror. He was only a few feet behind her and she'd been so focused on her self-exploration, she'd not heard him arrive. Embarrassed, she slid her hands across her chest to hide her nipples.

'Don't stop,' he muttered.

Her breath stalled. Did he think she was pleasuring herself? Her anger flared. Maybe she'd let him think that. Let him believe she wasn't hurt by his distance. She let her hands drop to the band of her bikini bottoms and watched his tension ratchet. She studied his reflection then—saw the stark hunger in his eyes, his clenched fists, the bulge in his trousers—and her heat rose. He was undeniably aroused. And that made her even more angry.

'Don't you want to join in?' she muttered.

Why was he holding back from touching her? What had happened after their wedding? Because she'd spent the last twenty-four hours with her ego destroyed believing he didn't want her any more but it seemed he did. So why was he over there doing nothing?

'I can't.' But he edged closer, tension now streaming from him.

'Why?'

'You look exhausted,' he growled. 'You have since the wedding. You don't need me making extra demands on you.'

A rush of relief swept through her but it didn't diminish her anger. Those 'demands' were the sole personal benefit to *her* of this arrangement.

'Why don't you try *asking* me what I need instead of assuming that you know best,' she growled back.

'Can you be trusted to know what's best for yourself? You didn't even know you were pregnant.'

She glared at him. 'Yeah, well, maybe I don't need you to take care of me. I *can* take care of myself.' She widened her fingers, caressing her breasts, displaying her nipples to the air—and his fierce stare. 'You didn't have to sleep with me again just because you thought it would get me to agree to the wedding.'

'What?'

'It's obviously all you wanted.' she goaded. 'You've kept your distance since easily enough.'

'Because you're *exhausted*,' he argued harshly. 'And it's only been one night. And it's been anything but *easy*!'

The man was infuriating. He'd been *thinking* of her, but not communicating with her, and how could she be so pleased and so annoyed at the same time?

'Well, it was a stupid idea,' she flared. 'I didn't sleep at all last night and now I'm even *more* exhausted.'

His eyes widened but his mouth suddenly twitched. 'You need orgasms to get to sleep, that's what you're saying?'

'I can get them on my own,' she shrugged sulkily. 'Don't trouble yourself.'

He took three paces and wrapped his arms around her. A tremor wracked her body as he pressed hot and hard and huge behind her. She didn't want to be wrapped in cotton wool or treated with kid gloves. And, honestly, he could just *please* her.

'Phoebe,' he growled hotly, his teeth scraping her earlobe. 'How could you—'

'How could *you*?' She slammed her hands on the mirror and pushed back against him.

'This bikini…' He shoved her bikini bottoms down and swept his hand up her inner thigh, testing her slickness and heat.

He didn't need to. She was on fire—so very ready for all he could give her.

'*You*—' he growled, switching to Italian.

She didn't know exactly what he said, but she knew to her bones it was dirty and *hot*. When she heard him unzip, she quivered—ridiculously close already. He nudged her feet further apart and slipped his fingers into her folds, intimately positioning her for his invasion.

'How can you think I don't want you?' He thrust, burying deep inside her while not taking his gaze from hers in the mirror. 'Never think I don't want you. I can't *stop* wanting you.'

But he wanted to. Frankly the physical need she felt for him was too much for her too only she couldn't stop it either. She leveraged against the mirror and arched, locking him deeper, closing her eyes in the exquisite agony.

'Eyes on me,' he rasped. *'Look at me.'*

Her eyelids fluttered. In the steamy reflection she saw his wildness—felt it in his fierce pumping, heard it in his throaty mutters of desire. It was *insane*. Pleasure wrung through her—wave after wave of untamed rapture.

'I can't get enough of you,' he muttered, the admission almost desolate.

She was suspended somewhere between ecstasy and oblivion. He carried her to the sofa, kissed every curve of her body, filled her again—made her writhe and sigh and sweep her limbs around him. Desperately holding him closer and tighter, she sobbed, needing him nearer still. Until on the very edge of darkness she heard his gruff whisper.

'Sleep, you need it.'

Phoebe stepped into the shower, hoping the steam might clear her fuzzy head. She soaped her sensitive body and as impossible as it ought to have been, lust flickered. She closed her eyes, willing herself to keep both arousal and tears at bay. But she'd never felt pleasure of the kind she did with Edo. She'd never wanted it—*him*—more. Which was dangerous. Wanting anything this much—be it someone or something—put her at risk. Extremes were unhealthy. She only had to think of her parents to know that. She had to take control of herself.

Ryan, her first husband, had been her only other lover and for him she'd dived headfirst into being the *perfect* wife.

She'd tried so stupidly hard for months. Until the day she'd found out he was cheating. When she'd confronted him he'd said it was because she was boring—with no education, no hobbies of her own. She had no colour or vibrancy. So it wasn't *his* fault he'd had to go elsewhere to find it.

His attack had crushed her because every word he'd said—up till that point—had been true. She'd changed herself *for* him. She'd given up the things she'd wanted because she'd put Ryan's wishes before hers. She'd *craved* the emotional security she'd thought he offered, had been so desperate to hold onto it that she'd done everything to keep his attention. To keep him happy she'd agreed to whatever he wanted. She'd made it so easy for him to treat her like a door mat because she'd become one. Never arguing, never denying him. As she'd sensed his distance increasing, she'd become more desperate to please. Less like herself. So never, *ever* could she do that again.

Except the lust she felt with Edo was a billion times more powerful. She couldn't let herself fall for him in other ways. Especially knowing he didn't want to actually include her in his life. He kept so much of himself from her, it was obvious he didn't want to deepen their intimacy beyond the physical. He didn't want to be a husband, and not a father either. Ultimately he wanted their base to be far from him.

But part of her still wished for more for the baby. Maybe there would be magic when Edo met his child for the first time. Maybe then he might want to offer it more than physical and financial security. For that reason, she had to remain here. Her child deserved that chance. But she could claw back *her* emotional safety—protect herself. She would be careful and controlled, and not let Edoardo Benedetti sweep her off her feet. She would not agree to everything he asked. She would keep far enough away.

And at least, unlike Ryan, he was honest. He wasn't pretending to be in love with her. Sex might be nothing more than a stress release for him, but she was now certain he enjoyed it as much as she. Maybe she would ask for just enough. Maybe that would help cure her of this desire—a little something for herself during these few months.

Because she would be true to *herself*. She would build her business. She would have what she wanted. Ask for it. Take it.

Even from Edo.

She found him sprawled on the sofa in the house, a drink in hand, a dish of olives on the table at his side, clearly ignoring the pile of papers beside him.

He cocked his head as she walked towards him. 'You would like dinner?'

'Not particularly.'

His eyebrows lifted. 'Then what would you like?'

She waited as he sipped his drink. 'A honeymoon.'

'Pardon?' He choked.

'I have an insatiable need to have sex with you.' She pilfered an olive from his dish to hide her smile. 'I'm sick of how insatiable it is. I want you to pleasure me until I'm over it.'

He stared at her as if she'd just grown three heads.

'Do you need me to repeat that?' She popped the olive into her mouth and savoured the burst as she bit.

'No.'

'Do you have a problem with it?'

'No.'

'Great. So can you arrange it please?'

He set down his drink and cleared his throat. 'Rome? Paris? Manhattan? You want sights, nights out dancing?'

She wrinkled her nose. 'No frills is fine by me. Just a bed and pool will be sufficient.'

He covered his mouth with his hand, his eyes widening more. 'You want a "no frills" honeymoon?'

'Mmm-hmm.' She swiped another olive. 'I'm sure it's just pregnancy hormones. Time will take care of it. Honestly, we can stay here if it makes you feel safer,' she said. 'I just want the sex.'

'That's your ideal honeymoon—sex on demand.'

'Well, you'll want to work as well, right? So do I. And I know you don't want company most of the time, so if you like I could have a call bell.'

'A *what*?'

'To summon you when I need servicing.'

He didn't move. 'I can't tell if you're being serious.'

'Well, maybe the bell was a step too far, but really, the plan is pretty solid, I think. Don't you?' She studied the floor for a moment before glancing back up to meet his astonished gaze. 'I'm tired of not getting what I want.'

CHAPTER NINE

FOUR DAYS LATER Edoardo ran back up the hill, chastising himself for being increasingly bothered by the not so arduous task of satisfying his lustful wife. It ought to be the best deal ever. He had the freedom to focus on his work while having sex on tap—except his focus had disappeared the instant she'd walked into that boardroom in London and hadn't yet returned. He was starting to worry it never would.

Phoebe had been beautiful and proud when she'd pushed for this 'honeymoon', but he'd thought there'd been vulnerability in that jut of her lower lip. Apparently he was wrong, because his determinedly independent wife was bold and passionate and increasingly *vital*. She appeared when she wanted 'servicing', and he leapt to his feet like her slave and—depending on the location—either swept her into his arms there or took her to his bedroom.

At night—after—she retreated to her own room and presumably fell into a deep sleep while he lay awake most of the night. She was definitely well rested, given her radiance and clear eyes. She'd got what she wanted—*all* she wanted. He was little more than a *stud*. It was utterly wonderful and absolutely annoying at the same time. Of course he was happy to be used but, contrary to what he'd thought, he increasingly wanted beyond the barriers they'd willingly built.

In the small hours he'd set up an office space for her—one way of dealing with the insomnia and burning some of the excess energy he was struggling with. He'd even fetched flowers from the chapel to put on the desk. He'd been oddly nervous when he'd showed it to her the next morning. She'd stared at it and then asked him to thank the staff. He'd opted not to tell her he'd done it himself. He'd walked out and quietly closed the door. She'd put hours of effort in there since. And as pleasing as that was, part of him regretted setting it up at all.

Dinner was the only meal they shared and aside from their moments in bed—or the pool, or the shower—was the best bit of his day. Conversation centred around work—she'd already built herself a website to advertise her services and he'd heard her phone calls, canvassing for clients.

Conversely, he was struggling with working from home—working at all, to be honest. His mind constantly drifted to those moments in the chapel when she'd walked towards him, when she'd whispered promises he didn't want her to keep...

His only salve was that her business-like exterior dissolved the second he gently bit one of her delicate earlobes, when he kissed his way to her collar bones, when he cupped her gorgeous curves. She melted in his arms, so he took her in them more and more—not waiting for her summons.

Even so, it irked that she spent more time talking to his staff than him. He heard their laughter in the villa. *Her* laughter. Somehow he felt more distanced from her than he'd been a week ago when they'd been avoiding eye contact in George Scott's office. And instead of focusing on that latest business acquisition, he wondered about Phoebe. About her family. Her friends. Her first marriage. What had gone wrong? Had she been in love with the guy? And why did that make him feel as if snakes were squeezing his vital organs? How could he feel jealous when she was with him now?

Because she wasn't really *with* him.

Curiosity relentlessly smouldered through skin to bone, finally becoming impossible to ignore any longer. He glanced up at the villa and saw she'd appeared on the terrace. She usually took breakfast out there. He went to join her. But when he arrived, he saw she wasn't alone. Isabella was sitting beside her, while Mattia, his best bodyguard, stood too near. All three of them were laughing.

He stared at the short silk pyjama set he'd never seen her in before. He didn't know what she wore to bed because she so determinedly vanished on him. Hell, they'd never actually spent an entire night together—the first night here he'd left her early, now she left—always. And this whole scene was far too intimate.

'Leave us,' he said curtly.

Both Isabella and Mattia vanished inside.

'That was shockingly rude,' Phoebe frowned as soon as they were out of earshot.

'They're employees.'

'Not mine,' she said. 'I like talking to people.'

Oh? Just not him.

'You distract them from their work,' he replied defensively. That was what she was doing to him.

'They've been helping me practise my Italian.'

He took the chair Isabella had vacated. 'I'll practise with you.'

'I'm going to need a wider vocabulary than, "yes, yes, harder, don't stop, please".'

He gaped, heat shooting to his loins while a small smile curved her mouth.

'Besides,' she added blithely, 'You usually work out now.'

He gritted his teeth. She knew his routine and was avoiding him as much as she could—outside of the bedroom. He noticed goose bumps peppering her upper arms and picked up the soft rug hanging on the back of his chair, rising to tuck it about her bare shoulders.

She stiffened. 'You don't need to—'

'Don't say it,' he said gruffly, looking into her eyes. 'Or I swear there'll be consequences.'

That vixen spark burned brighter in her. Yes, the uncontrollable edge of their passion turned her on the most.

'Of course, you want the consequences,' he muttered huskily.

He was suddenly so close to setting her on the table and eating *her* for breakfast because their fire raged out of control. But he couldn't. Hell, his staff were around—one might appear any moment with more damned food for her. So he sank back into the seat and poured himself a coffee.

'Have you been in touch with your parents at all?' he asked.

'Why do you want to know that?'

'Can we not make idle conversation?'

Her gaze narrowed. 'You don't do anything idly. You have an underlying motive for everything you do.'

'I'm your husband. Can I not ask you about your family?'

It wasn't the first time he had and he still knew little.

'You're not really my husband.'

Irritated, he waved his hand so the ring on his finger caught the early sunlight. That irritated *her*.

'Are we not going to have a child together?' he added belligerently.

Her eyes flared with an emotion that wasn't desire. But was as hot. 'I didn't think we wanted any intimacy other than sexual,' she said coolly.

He closed his eyes, battling the urge to take her to bed, tease her until she was taut, but then withhold orgasms from her until she answered his questions. Trouble was, he wouldn't be able to go through with it. Making her come was too much of a pleasure for *himself.*

Moreover, he wanted her to actually *want* to talk to him. That she might lower her guard enough to grant him a little insight. He didn't want to have to manipulate or *bully* her—he'd already had to drag her up the aisle and the prospect of *dragging* more from her was distasteful. For once in his life he had no idea how to go about getting what he wanted. Usually it was easy. Usually *he* just rang a bloody bell and issued orders. But right now he didn't even know quite what it was he really *needed.* He was just uncomfortable as hell and it was because of her. Yet weirdly, she was also the balm.

'You okay?' she asked after a few minutes of awkward silence.

'I'm irritable.' He breathed out.

She sipped her juice then carefully set it on the table. 'Want to talk about why?'

Discussing how he felt was an anathema to him. He didn't do it. Ever. Frankly admitting his irritability just now was a first.

'This isn't easy, I guess,' she added softly.

He ran his fingers across his brow. How could she go from being pricklier than a porcupine one moment to being gently understanding the next? 'I can't get a handle on you.'

Her lips curved. 'I think you get a handle on me very well.'

'I'm not talking about sex, Phoebe.' He huffed a reluctant laugh. 'I know we have that nailed.'

'What else is there for us to nail?' she muttered.

This time it wasn't a coquettish flirtation and it hit in a way he didn't expect.

'I would like us to be...' He didn't know what.

'Friends?'

He didn't have friends. But he'd like her to talk to him, laugh a little. That day by the pond, she'd laughed a lot. Now things were different. Difficult. Increasingly so. He'd thought marriage would be the way to ensure both her and the child's safety. He'd thought it would be simple. He'd set his limits. She'd made her demands. It should be settled. But it still wasn't right.

Phoebe stilled at the uncertain expression in Edo's eyes. Was the man saying he wanted to talk to her? Her heart pounded. She was unbearably interested in everything about him. Ring-fencing her curiosity to the bedroom this last week had been extremely difficult and keeping emotional distance even more so—especially when she'd learned that *he'd* created that beautiful office for her, not the staff. Isabella had told her he'd rearranged the furniture and set everything up on his own. He'd even put flowers from the chapel in a vase on her desk. She hadn't been able to say anything about it for fear she'd get emotional.

'I'd like to understand you,' he said slowly.

'Okay,' she said. *Not quite friends, then.* She wasn't going to be hurt about that. She could keep this cool. 'I'd like to understand you better too. But—'

'Closed book. I know.' He cleared his throat. 'I should explain why.'

'Not if you don't want to.'

A muffled snort of frustration escaped him. 'Can't you be even a little curious? I'm crazy curious about you.'

'Really?' She stared at him, surprised. 'What do you want to know?'

He regarded her for a long moment. The question, when it came, was almost a whisper. 'Where did you go on honeymoon with your first husband?'

Prickly heat crawled over her skin, making her itch. That was the first thing that had come to his mind?

'We didn't have one,' she said. 'He had a new job and I followed him there.'

She'd been naïve to think she could be some perfect wife, that Ryan had really loved her. 'I left him less than a year after we married. I wasn't enough for him. He cheated on me.'

Edo looked so shocked she actually smiled when normally she'd have a stab-in-the-heart feeling right about now.

'What more could he possibly want?' Edo muttered.

Her mortification rose. Sex with Ryan hadn't been amazing, but it was way too icky to discuss that.

'He was selfish in bed,' he guessed with mortifying accuracy. Because of course Edo wouldn't think it ick. 'Didn't give you what you needed?'

Shame swamped her, but Edo calmly waited for her reply as if this wasn't anything embarrassing. He had a healthy, playful attitude to sex—he made it fun and pleasurable and not bound up with any emotional burden and he'd never once left her unsatisfied. Frankly, he now knew her body better than she knew it herself. So if there was anyone she could talk to honestly about this, it was him.

'I didn't give him what he needed either,' she admitted, spilling intimate secrets she'd not even told her best friends. 'I didn't know what I needed, let alone how to tell him. I don't think he'd have appreciated my trying to tell him anyway. I'd saved my virginity for so long and he took it so quickly. Literally so quickly. It didn't get better from there.'

Edo's jaw tightened. 'I'm sorry he didn't prioritise you,' he muttered.

She pulled the rug more tightly around her shoulders and shook her head. Being prioritised wasn't something she held much hope for any more.

'How did you meet?' he asked.

She shrank at the rising memories. Her emotional weakness back then was actually more embarrassing than her less than stellar sex-life. But maybe it would be good for their child if she and Edo understood each other better. Besides, she couldn't deny him—she wanted this fragile moment of communication to last—even if she was the one doing all the talking. 'First you should know I was an unplanned, unwanted only child,' she muttered. 'It's partly why I ended up so...'

His eyes widened. 'So what?'

Needy. Beneath the rug, she scratched her arm and tried a different way to explain. 'Dad's an adventure racer.'

'A...' Edo frowned. 'Pardon?'

'He travels the world competing in ultra-long-distance endurance events. Mum was an athlete too before she had me. Since then, she's been his coach and support crew. They prioritised his career.'

'Endurance events?' Edo looked confused. 'Like running?'

'It's their passion. Purpose. Everything.' She nodded. 'Neither of them particularly wanted to parent me. Eventually I went to boarding school, shuttled between grandparents in the holidays. I raced for a bit but I wasn't good enough. I injured my ankle the one time I tried to be like him and push through anything and it's been weak ever since. Then I was a support person to try to stay involved.' She'd thought if she showed an interest in what they loved, they might show more of an interest in her.

'That explains your organised survival kit with the meds.' Edo shot her a half-smile.

'Right.' She nodded. 'I get that it's more than a career for them, it's a lifestyle, but I wanted attention and affection from my parents. Only there wasn't space for me. I know to achieve at an elite level you have to be that extreme, but it leaves no room for other things.' She absently scratched at the itchiness more. 'School was seriously average, but for whatever reason when I went to university, I suddenly had guys paying me attention—'

'Whatever reason?' Edo reached across and grabbed her wrist, stopping her from scratching too hard. 'Phoebe, you're stunning.'

She shot him a grateful but disbelieving smile. 'For a while I wasn't interested in any, but Ryan was in his final year, and he was very charming. He was the man on campus, you know? Suave, popular, persistent. He picked me out, started walking me to class, popping up in places, brought me coffee and cake, then other presents. I was so flattered. I couldn't believe he paid me so much attention...'

'He swept you off your feet,' Edo said quietly.

'Love-bombed me, yeah. Made me feel like a million dollars. And he loved how I reacted. But it was all about the reactions. He fed off people's admiration.'

If Ryan had kitted out a home office for her, he'd have done the big reveal with a full audience in tow. And he'd have expected a ticker-tape parade and balloons spelling out *Thank You* from her. Whereas Edo hadn't even admitted to her that he'd done it all himself. Maybe that was because her reaction didn't really matter to him, but honestly—it still meant more to her.

'He wanted to win me. Publicly,' she explained. 'Then we were the cute couple on campus. I didn't realise how performative it was. The wedding was his idea—a rush job in a registry office—it was so-old fashioned it was "cool", and we were for ever, and he wanted everyone else to want to be us...which in hindsight was very cringe. But I just believed in it—in him—when he said he loved me. I finally felt *wanted*. I thought I had the whole dream and I just fell so hard.'

He'd been someone to pour all *her* love into.

'He got an internship up north and I dropped out of university to follow him. I took an office job to help us financially. But then he changed, he needed someone equal to him to climb the corporate ladder with—not some low-level office administrator. And he found her in less than six months.'

He'd needed a more perfect partner for his next phase. He'd found a new target, relentlessly pursued her, acquired her. Phoebe had only found out when his lover confronted her in the street. She'd rushed home to beg Ryan to deny it. He hadn't. Instead he'd blamed her—for holding him back, being boring and having no ambition. That had hurt a lot. Because he'd wanted her to support *his* ambition. Phoebe had felt completely betrayed and unwanted again.

'I gave up everything,' she said. 'I left my friends. My university plans. Most of all I lost myself in trying to be what he wanted.'

She'd not been enough to hold his attention—just as she'd not been enough for her parents. She would never trust anyone would ever commit to her again. And Edo *wasn't*, was he.

Edo's grip on her wrist gentled. 'Phoebe, to give up everything for someone else shows a kind of generosity and courage most people never have. You're passionate. You're all in. That's not—' He shook his head. 'He didn't know how lucky he was.'

She smiled at him sadly. Edo was wrong. Being 'all in' had been her mistake. To dive into anything in such an extreme way wasn't healthy. It had blinded her and she'd made bad choices. 'But I should have held onto the things that were important to me. Not got so lost—and not lost so much time. Because the stupid thing is I don't know if I really loved him or if it was just that *I* wanted to be loved. *I* was so *needy* I was willing to do anything to be sure of that love,' she confessed. 'It took so little for him to convince me, and nothing for him to have an affair.'

'You weren't wrong in everything—you just picked the wrong guy. He was an idiot not to appreciate you.' He frowned and rubbed his head. 'What did you do?'

Her parents had been overseas, of course, and she'd not told them. Not asked for the support she knew wasn't within their capabilities. She wasn't doing that now either.

'I went to London. I was alone but it was better. I worked so hard—I did evening classes and upskilled. I met Elodie when I took a bunch of accountants to an escape room for a team building exercise. She was the manager there, and she hired Bethan, who then became my flatmate. We formed our divorced wives club—we were never, ever going to marry again.'

She chuckled hopelessly and stared down at his hold on her wrist. 'Only I just have. But only so none of this stuff happens to this baby. This child is going to know they're wanted and loved. Absolutely, unconditionally and *always*.'

She looked up after a moment. But Edo didn't move, didn't answer. She'd just done all the talking again and now he didn't even seem to be breathing.

Edo sat like stone, too busy processing to think what to say.

Two rushed weddings. Two rubbish honeymoons. Two terrible wedding nights. She deserved so much better than what either he or the ex had given her. She'd given everything up for love once and she didn't want to lose herself again so no wonder she'd been reluctant to marry him. Frustration filled him because he'd basically made her. The least he could do was help her understand why he was the stunted creature he was. Why her security was so vital to him.

She tried to pull her wrist free. 'Anyway, I should—'

'When Dante was kidnapped, my grandfather refused to pay the ransom,' he blurted.

'What?'

He couldn't look at her. He released her wrist and gripped the edge of his chair instead so he couldn't walk off this time. She deserved more from him. Deserved as much of the truth as he could actually manage.

'My father died when I was ten—speedboat accident.' He glossed over the fact his father had been a spoiled thrill-seeker. 'Mother, Dante and I moved in with his father. My grandfather worked deals that were on the edge—he made a lot of money, but a few enemies as well, and he flaunted his excess. His intention was for me to take over the company and everyone knew it.' But Edoardo had never wanted to take on his business. 'He said if he gave in then the demands would only escalate and that the risk of it happening again would also increase.'

He breathed out. 'Dante was held for almost three weeks.' Twenty endless days and nights of terror and guilt. So much guilt.

'I hated my grandfather for it. Fought him. Tried so many other ways to get the money. I couldn't understand why he wouldn't do everything possible to get Dante back.' He still felt sick—he'd been so powerless.

'You would have gone to the ends of the earth,' she said softly.

'I would have done anything.' He hid his face as the guilt consumed him. Because he'd then made the same mistake. He'd been as blind as his grandfather. 'It was a miracle that Dante was recovered alive but he was never the same. Nor was my mother,' he said heavily. It had crushed him. It had crushed his mother. And it had destroyed Dante.

'I was determined to care for Dante after that—without

needing any input from our grandfather. I refused to be his heir, refused to go into his business. Instead, I started my own. But I got fixated on financial security, on building a reserve.'

'A safety net,' she said softly.

He jerked a nod. He'd wanted to make things better for his brother, but he'd been blinkered. 'I thought I was helping. I didn't notice that Dante started to self-medicate. Alcohol, drugs. I was working such long hours I wasn't there for him. By the time I realised he was…' he shook his head. '… I got him into the best clinic I could but…'

Edo had been heartbroken by his failure to help Dante, to not give him the emotional security he'd needed. And it had been his fault from the beginning.

'When he was nineteen, he overdosed. I don't know if it was deliberate or accidental.'

Phoebe leaned closer. 'I'm so sorry.'

'I never forgave my grandfather.' He'd never forgiven himself.

She nodded slowly. 'Where is he now?'

'He died a couple years ago. I didn't go to the funeral. Didn't see him after Dante, but I inherited…' *Too many things from him.* He inhaled sharply. 'I sold his company as soon as I could.'

Her eyes widened.

'The money's in a charitable trust.' He couldn't have a cent of the man's money when it was far too late to help Dante. 'It supports various addiction groups.'

He couldn't look at her. He didn't want her thinking that was particularly good of him or anything. It was simply that he couldn't bear to have anything to do with it. 'There was something fundamentally missing in my grandfather.' In *him* also. A workaholism, a blinkered focus, obliviousness to true needs…

Edo had failed his mother. And he'd failed his brother. Twice. Because they'd meant to take *him* and it was Edoardo's fault they'd got Dante instead. But he couldn't ever tell her that. 'I can't go through anything like that again.' He finally met her eyes. 'It's why I never intended to marry.'

Her gaze filled with immense sadness. 'But you're going to be a father.'

His chest ached. 'I never intended for that to happen either.'

'But it has,' she whispered.

He couldn't even nod. He knew what he was saying was hurting her. He wished he could make things better, but he was fundamentally *limited*. He wasn't good enough. He was too poorly equipped to be responsible for anyone, let alone a fragile child. He could never offer anyone emotional security and he needed her to know that. And he couldn't stand to be near her a moment longer. 'I'd better not miss my conference call.'

Shame filled him as he walked away. But he'd meant it. He couldn't allow anyone close. He couldn't bear to *fail* like that again.

The only thing was that she didn't want that either. She'd never wanted to marry again—she wanted to be her own person. To do the things she wanted. Her face had lit up when she'd talked about her business plans. Same as when she talked about supporting her friends. And it was good their child had her because she was amazing. Phoebe *flourished*—even in a less than ideal environment.

He connected to the scheduled call, listened idly as a security consultant listed off initial possibilities to enhance security of her flat in London. He stared at the date on his desk calendar, distracted as something stirred in the back of his brain. In the end, he waved off the consultant, letting him know he'd be in touch. But he didn't want to fix deadlocks to the doors and install cameras and panic buttons. It still wouldn't be secure enough. He wanted her safer. He wanted *more* for her, even though he knew *he* couldn't be enough. But he wanted to make her life better in however limited a scope he could.

He rubbed his face, frustrated. She'd wanted the experience of living in Italy for a week, but she'd chosen quiet village life over other touristy or cultural experiences. Maybe that had been a money thing, but she shouldn't have had to *choose*. He could never let her fall in love with him, but she could love Italy. Maybe that would be something more. Because his estate could be a safe haven for a young child to grow up in—space, sunshine, a swimming pool.

Phoebe could be queen—hell, the staff already adored her—and she could run her business with brilliant efficiency from here. She could have her friends come to stay any time. Surely her life in London would pale in comparison to that?

He breathed out, invigorated. Maybe the least he could do was give her everything *Italy* had to offer.

CHAPTER TEN

'CAN YOU TAKE a break for a couple of days? After all, it's the weekend.'

Phoebe glanced up from the document that might as well have been written in gibberish for all she'd taken in. She'd been unable to stop stewing about what Edo had told her at breakfast. He was all she could think about and now here he was in the doorway, bringing all his intensity to her. And such trouble.

'It's Thursday,' she answered blandly.

'So we make it a long weekend.' Edo flashed a smile but his eyes held a slight wariness. 'Neither of us should work all the time. You've hardly seen Italy. Come see more of it.'

'Why?' she tried to query lightly even as her pulse leapt.

Because she knew he didn't want to be a father, didn't want to be a husband. So it was spending more time with Edo that would be dangerous for her. Already she was trying not to fall for him and pretty much failing. She'd be *safer* staying right here, glued in front of the enormous computer screens he'd set up for her, only allowing herself to enjoy the physical relationship that he'd assured her would end soon enough.

'I'll show you some of our greatest treasures,' he added. 'Art, fashion, culture. There'll be the best *gelato* of your life.'

He was almost playful, offering just a glimpse of the man

he'd been the afternoon they'd met. So seductive. And she knew there was so much more to him.

'Work-life balance,' he added lightly, taking a single step into her office. 'We'll leave in the morning, so you have time to clear your paperwork.'

Well, *she* hardly had that much to sort before she could walk away from her desk. But if someone in the room failed at work-life balance, it was the heartbreakingly handsome man tempting her right now. She didn't really understand why he was asking her to do this—but if anyone needed a break, *he* did, and she wanted to be the one beside him while he did.

'Okay,' she said.

He nodded and walked away, leaving her staring after him. What he'd told her this morning was horrifyingly sad. Poor Dante. Poor Edo. But he'd wanted to be there for his brother, he'd wanted to do all he could, which showed he was loving. He was just desperately hurt. So no wonder he preferred superficial pleasures with temporary play mates. His wasn't a raw wound but an infection to the bone and maybe it could never heal. But he was offering her another moment—and she simply couldn't resist. Of course she wanted to see more of Italy. *Especially* with him.

They flew first thing, accompanied by three burly bodyguards. Phoebe gazed out of the helicopter window, enthralled by the view of the changing countryside. They walked slowly through the heart of Florence. Edo selected the café—he had coffee, she juice, and they nibbled on *cornetti* and he then took her to the Uffizi.

She stood in front of the enormous paintings and stared, her heart so full.

'She's not as beautiful as you.' Edo's whisper tickled her neck and pierced her thin-skinned heart.

Phoebe rolled her eyes. 'You're not suggesting I'm more beautiful than a Botticelli?'

'I'm insisting you're more beautiful than Spring herself.' He took her arm and led her out of the gallery. 'Come on, we need to get to Milan and find an evening gown.'

'Why do you need an evening gown?'

He grinned. 'You need one for the opera. Have you ever been?'

She shook her head.

'We are the home of opera,' he declared. 'We are the best at it.'

'You think you're the best at everything—food, music, fashion, sex—'

'And am I wrong?' He pressed his hand to his heart. 'You love Italy. You wanted to come here for years. Not to attend an opera while you're here is a crime.' He swept her along with his infectious energy. 'In the summer I'll take you to the outdoor theatre in Verona. The nights are hot and sultry and it will stir your passion. You will love it.'

In summer? Had he forgotten that by next summer they would have a child? That—according to his plan—she and their baby would be in London. *Without him*. But she blinked away that reality, because right now he was smiling and charming and sliding her easily into a little more trouble.

A different set of bodyguards greeted them in Milan. First stop was a couture fashion store. She took one look at the window and refused to get out of the car even when the bodyguards gestured that it was safe to emerge.

'The dress code is this formal?' she half-wailed.

'It is the opening night of the season and we have prime seats.' Edo chuckled.

'But I can't—'

'You can pay me back once you've made your first five

figures,' he pre-empted her primary concern. 'I'll know where to find you.'

As they walked in, the assistants immediately straightened, shooting charming smiles at him and slightly widened eyes at her. Self-conscious, Phoebe instinctively covered her belly with her hand, but then the assistants became impossibly more attentive and charming, fussing over her with wide smiles and promises to find the perfect outfit. Shooting her an amused glance, Edo took a seat near the rear of the store.

'You're not going to stay and watch?' she whispered, appalled.

'What else would I do?' He smirked. 'I'm looking forward to the fashion show. Besides, they've offered me coffee and apple cake.'

There were several possibilities but in the end it was a toss-up between a midnight-blue and a floral.

'You choose.' He shook his head when she appealed for his opinion. 'You get to please yourself.'

The asymmetry of the blue appealed, with its one dramatically feathered sleeve and one bare arm. It was loose enough around her middle to hide the blooming curve of her belly while showing off her legs. One assistant found delicate shoes to match and both they and the dress were tissue-wrapped and bagged before she'd even glimpsed a price tag.

Fifteen minutes later, their driver stopped outside a strikingly modern apartment building.

'Is this a private hotel?' she asked as his security team moved them through.

'No, this is my place. I was only in that hotel for the convenience for the meetings.'

Phoebe's curiosity was uncontrollable but she tried not to go bug-eyed as the lift opened on the top floor, revealing a luxurious apartment. It was as beautifully furnished as the vineyard estate—comfortable but revealing little about him personally. There was art but no personal photos, no small trinkets anywhere. But there was a massive home office. The man worked all hours, all the time.

'Do you want a beautician appointment before the opera?' he muttered as he followed her into his sumptuously spacious lounge.

She turned to face him. 'Is that what people do?'

He shrugged a shoulder. 'You could have a rest if you'd rather.'

She half-smiled at his supposedly relaxed amiability. This was a very well-behaved Edo. He was offering her options instead of backing her into a corner, into her 'choosing' the one *he* wanted. But she knew what he wanted. The same as what she did. They'd not been alone like this all day and she'd not gone to his room last night, so it had been a while since she'd kissed him. She ignored the inner alarm sounding that she was in more than a *little* trouble. That this was now more to her than a release, that it was a need to connect with him in a more than physical way. Oh, she worked to ignore that.

His eyes gleamed as he watched her gaze linger on his lips. 'Rest?'

She could only nod.

There was no rest; in fact, they ended up rushing to get ready in time for the opera. Phoebe swept her hair into a high bun and rubbed on lipstick.

'Thank goodness for this dress, it gives me enough drama, right?'

'Yes, but would you like a little extra sparkle?' He strolled towards her in his elegant suit and unfurled his palm.

She gazed at the stunning drop earrings. They were probably real diamonds, not crystals, and she couldn't think. 'When did you get those?'

'I saw them online, thought you might like them.'

'You online-shopped?' She was stunned. *When? Why?*

'From a Milanese jeweller, they were couriered here this morning. It's not that big of a deal.'

She bit her lip. 'You don't have to buy me things.'

That wasn't what they were doing. This was all—and only—happening because of the baby and he didn't want this.

'Not even for your birthday?' he said softly.

She gaped and gazed into his guarded face.

He shot her a knowing smile. 'You didn't realise?'

'I've lost track of the days.' Her heart pounded and confusion tumbled through her. 'I didn't tell you it's my birthday.'

'I'm aware.' A fleeting smile lit his eyes. 'But I had your passport, and all the paperwork for our wedding, and I'm a details person.'

'So you got me these as a birthday present.'

He nodded. Then she realised that this whole *day* was a birthday present.

'Phoebe?' He froze. 'Why do you look like you're about to cry?'

Because she was about to cry. He had no idea how barren her birthdays had been. It was partly why Ryan's gift-giving had overwhelmed her. But in hindsight she saw it had always been a performance—he'd given her things in front of others. To impress everyone. But this was just Edo and her, and no one was here watching. She blinked rapidly, desperate not to embarrass either of them.

It's not that big of a deal.

He'd not meant this to be emotional. Not meant it to *mean* anything. But she didn't know how else to take it. Maybe he was just so wealthy that whisking dates across the country for food and culture and sex was just normal. Except Isabella had told her he never had guests to stay and she knew he worked all the hours and suspected he didn't spend such time with any one person.

'Why are you doing all this?' she muttered.

She'd married him already. They were working out their physical chemistry. He didn't *need* to do anything more. These weren't the actions of a convenience-only husband and it made her wonder—hope—for more. Even when she knew she shouldn't. Because this was also a man who wouldn't—*couldn't*—open up to her.

'I thought you might enjoy it.' He looked wary. 'You were listening to opera the day we met, it was blasting in your earbuds. You have delicate earlobes and I thought the earrings would be nice.' He reached out and touched one. 'You kept your paracetamol in a Botticelli coin purse, but you hadn't been to Florence to see the original paintings.'

He'd noticed those things? Remembered them? He'd *personalised* this whole trip for her. Because he was a *details guy*. But more than that, he was a *nice* guy. A prickly, overprotective, deeply pained, nice guy.

'This was unbelievably thoughtful of you,' she said huskily.

'It was nothing,' he said quietly, his wariness intensifying.

She shook her head. It was too late for him to backtrack now. He'd done it and he couldn't deny it—his actions told her things about him. He might not have meant this in any romantic or intense way, but it did still mean something. To her.

'I never had a birthday party as a child, so while this might be nothing to you, I truly appreciate it.'

She took the earrings from him and turned to the mirror to put them on.

'No party ever?' He leaned close and watched her.

'My parents were always away for my birthday. It's peak racing season.'

'They're away now?' he said. 'What about presents? Did they bring you one when they got back?'

She shot him a twisted smile. 'It wasn't a priority.'

Since they'd learned about all that, Elodie and Bethan had made a fuss of her on her birthday. But Edo had done all this without knowing a thing about her pitiful birthday past.

She looked at her reflection then met his gaze in the mirror. 'The earrings are beautiful, Edo.' She would treasure them. 'This whole day has been lovely. Thank you.'

He met her gaze for a long moment. 'I'm glad you like them.'

Yeah, it wasn't just the earrings she liked. Honestly, she didn't need accessories when she had him standing beside her. She was really, truly, deeply in trouble.

'We'd better go,' she said huskily.

Three bodyguards escorted them into the foyer of La Scala.

'This is ridiculous,' she hissed as people parted to make way for their entourage. 'It's not like we're royal.'

'You look it,' he muttered, wrapping his arm around her.

He stole her breath so easily. A second later it was stolen again as she stepped into the theatre. She'd entered a red and gold, luxurious world. Their private box had just the two gilt chairs and delicate refreshments. It was desperately intimate and romantic. Until she glanced down and saw a bunch of upturned faces.

'People are staring,' she murmured.

'Stare back haughtily,' he instructed with a wink. 'The audience is here to be seen as much as watch the opera—or at least, until the curtain rises.'

Was that why he'd wanted her well-dressed and bejewelled—to be seen? No. Edo *wasn't* Ryan. This was different. Edo had brought her out in public only because he'd guessed—*correctly*—that this was an experience she'd dreamed of. This wasn't a generic night out, this had been considered—tailored, for her birthday. And as lovely and touching as it was, she couldn't let herself read more into it. But that was a new battle.

'It's a spectacle, yes?' he asked.

Absolutely. She forced her focus away from him and onto the scene before her. In moments she was fascinated by the fashion, the hauteur, the hum. Beautiful people of all ages streamed in. Phoebe watched one elderly couple slowly walk to their seats. They kept holding hands as they waited for the performance to begin. They looked like they'd been to many performances together and suddenly she was wistful as anything.

'It's a tragic love story,' Edo explained as the orchestra tuned. 'Tosca will do anything to save her lover, even sacrifice herself.'

It didn't matter that her Italian was limited, the music was overwhelming, the story epic. Phoebe lost all sense of time in the intensity of it. In the second half, the lead tenor sang a solo that savaged Phoebe's heart. Not only hers—the entire audience was silent for several long seconds after the singer ended.

When the applause finally thundered throughout the theatre, she turned to Edo—and froze. The man was *ashen*. There were beads of sweat on his brow and, while he was staring at the stage, she was certain he wasn't even seeing it. She put her hand on his but he didn't respond. This was more than being swept up in the emotion of the opera—something was actually wrong.

'You need some air,' she said.

Keeping hold of his hand, she stood before he could answer. Or argue. She led him out to the quiet foyer, gesturing for the bodyguard to stay back. Edo leaned against the wall and drew in a deep breath. She waited, watching the colour slowly return to his cheeks.

'I forgot it was this opera,' he muttered gruffly. 'That clarinet solo at the start of that aria…' He drew in a deep breath. 'It reminds me of him.'

It took her a second to understand. 'Of Dante?'

'My mother was a music teacher…did I ever tell you?' He rubbed his forehead and grimaced ruefully. 'No, I know I didn't. She was a musician before she married Dad. Dante inherited her gift. She taught him several instruments but the clarinet was his love. He was extraordinary. The aria reminded me of him.'

But—given that reaction—he didn't want to be reminded. Phoebe's heart ached. 'He played that piece?'

'Beautifully.' He bowed his head. 'I'm sorry.'

'You don't need to apologise.'

'You're missing the end of the opera.' He forced a smile. 'Spoiler alert. Everyone dies.'

'I know.' She nodded. 'Big drama. Maybe we should leave before the rest of the audience comes out.'

He sighed. 'You don't mind?'

'Of course not.'

The doors were opened by those silent men who kept a distance even as they formed a protective ring around him—and, for now, her. They kept people away. Kept him isolated. Because he insisted on it. He didn't want comfort or support from anyone. Yet the irony was he gave it so well. He was *caring*—he had been with her the afternoon they'd met, and since. He had been to George by taking over his business. He just didn't *want* to be.

Deep pain like this didn't magically get better. So Phoebe couldn't let herself be confused by his generous actions today. She couldn't let herself think that he wanted anything more with her beyond this temporary marriage. He *wasn't* trying to convince her to stay. He'd explicitly told her he didn't want her close—not long term. He couldn't even look at the sonogram picture of their baby. He wanted them safe but ultimately far from him because he wanted to remain alone.

He thought he'd let his brother down. He'd lost pretty much all his family and he didn't want to build a new one. All of which broke Phoebe's heart. He *should* have more. And yes, she wanted him to have that more with *her*. But she had to stop thinking in that direction. She had to protect herself and her baby and couldn't let herself fall any further than she already had. She had to keep her distance too, right? Because she'd also been hurt. And she couldn't trust her own feelings—she'd believed in someone's kind gestures before and had been wrong to.

As soon as they were back in his apartment, Edo poured himself a drink. Phoebe watched him splash the whisky and mutter beneath his breath, and couldn't remain silent.

'What was he like?' she asked softly.

She caught sight of his crumbling expression as he abandoned the glass and turned away. Instinctively she stepped forward and wrapped her arms around his waist. She pressed her head against his back. He didn't have to answer, but in this moment there was no way she could leave him alone with this agony.

Edo held her arms around him so she couldn't pull away. Her warmth at his back was about the only thing keeping him standing. And he didn't want her to move to be in front of him. He couldn't bear to see the compassion he knew would be in her eyes right now. He thought about Dante daily but he hadn't talked about him properly in *years*. 'It's painful to think about him,' he muttered.

'But you can't stop, right? You loved him,' she said softly. 'He deserves your thoughts of him. He was your *brother*.'

That clarinet echoed in his head, and he needed to mute

that sad melody, so he talked to cover it. 'He was two years younger than me,' he muttered. 'Totally different. He was music. I was maths. He daydreamed and was always late. I was school captain and on time.'

'But you were close.'

He nodded. 'We fought each other but teamed up against everyone else. I carried our grandfather's expectations, while he carried our mother's. We both knew pressure,' he interrupted. 'We both wanted fun. He wanted a Vespa. I wanted a Ferrari. The nearest either of us got to either were the die-cast models we had as kids.' God, he hadn't thought about those in for ever. 'They were red, of course.'

'So the Vespa you took me on that afternoon...'

'I bought it for him,' he said tightly. 'Years too late.'

Phoebe's arms tightened and Edo couldn't stop speaking—admitting things he'd never told anyone.

'Our mother died a year after Dante was kidnapped,' he whispered. 'She was just broken. Her death traumatised Dante even more and I...'

'None of it was your fault, Edo.'

Oh, but it *was*. He stiffened, pulling back, trying to compress the feelings that spilled out regardless. What was he doing? He couldn't spoil more of her night with his selfishness.

'I'm sorry, this is your birthday.' He loosened her arms and turned to face her. Tried to step up. 'And you're tired.'

She looked so beautiful. 'You miss him,' she ignored his diversion.

'Always.'

'And your parents—'

'Not my grandfather.' Not the workaholic automaton who'd cared about money most of all. The one he was most like.

She cupped his face in her hands. He didn't want her sympathy. That wasn't why he'd told her. But honestly he didn't know why he'd told her any of this, didn't know why everything was bubbling up inside him now when for so long—for *years*—he'd been perfectly fine. Great, in fact. Until she'd stormed into his life and changed everything. She'd accused him of emotional blackmail before and he'd deserved it. Now he didn't want to play on her tender-heartedness either.

He tried to step back but she was stronger than he realised. Or maybe he was weaker. Too weak to resist gazing at her, taking in the depth in her eyes, the parting of her lips, the fineness of her features. The emotion in her expression, in her hold. Her soft warmth invited him and was irresistible. Once more, he stood still in that timeless, overwhelming moment of want.

He would kiss her. He couldn't *not* kiss her. But it wasn't to release tension. Wasn't to submerge all these awful emotions in pleasure. He just wanted to kiss *her*. Wanted to touch *her*. Be close to *her*. He wanted to give to her.

But he couldn't talk any more. He could only act. She said nothing as he led her to his room and unzipped her dress. She was beautiful. Sweet and soft and with that quiet, dignified strength that felled him. He gently unhooked her earrings, then let down her hair. He didn't deserve this bliss, but *she* did. He dropped to his knees. Caressed her. Worshipped her. Because this was all about her, not his own escape. Not this time. He kissed her as she ought to be kissed. Loved her the way he would if he could. And she didn't just let him, she met him. Her legs pressed close around him, her arms tight, her kisses endless. But he couldn't hold her gaze. And she buried her face in his shoulder as she came. Hiding part of herself from him too. He couldn't call her out on it when he was doing the exact same thing. Hiding how important this had become.

He held her as she slept—for the first time staying with

her for the entire night. He curled around her, drawing her close and resting his arm over her waist with his hand splayed on her burgeoning belly. Until now, they'd never spent an entire night together. Except now, despite feeling an exhaustion that was more than physical, he couldn't sleep. He measured his breathing, slowly counting in a futile attempt to fall into the abyss. Her fresh scent filled him. Her body was warm against his, her breathing was slow and peaceful and he was almost asleep when he felt a bump against his palm.

He stilled, confused. It happened again. A tiny nudge. A sharp one. He froze, processing. And then a wave of emotion hammered him. How could she sleep while a little person was apparently practising football kicks inside her belly? He gently smoothed his fingertips over her stomach, back and forth, wondering if there was any way to lull the acrobat inside. He'd barely been able to think about the reality of the baby. But here it was, a shocking reminder of the responsibility for which he would never be prepared—a tiny, playful poppet that would soon become a small playful child. A child who ought to have a little brother or sister to play with—to tease, to *protect*.

His heart felt horribly full, horribly near to bursting. But there could be no sibling for this baby unless Phoebe met someone else once *he* let her go...

His guts twisted. He'd seen her watch that elderly couple as they'd made their way to their seats at the theatre tonight—they were clearly a life-long love match. Edo was stopping *her* from finding one of those. She was sacrificing those chances in her life now when she should have so much more. He'd not even been able to give her a birthday without selfishly lowering the mood. He could never give her all she *ought* to have, could never be the man she deserved. Frankly, aside from money and security, all he could give her was good sex.

But that was all she'd wanted from him anyway, wasn't it? She'd had less than average with her jerk ex and all she'd actually wanted from Edo was a thrill that afternoon back in the summer. Then just her no frills, sex-on-demand honeymoon. Nothing more.

The problem for him was that she was dangerously irresistible—and not just sexually. He liked being around her. Liked how he felt when she was near—when she was working alongside him, dining opposite him—talking and laughing.

But he'd unintentionally pulled on her heartstrings, and he didn't want her staying with him out of pity. He would do them both a favour by letting her go.

But the thought of her meeting someone else savaged him all over again. Edo knew loss. Intimately. He knew it again now. Mourning not what had happened but what might have been. For the future that he might've had if he were a different person. If he weren't damaged. If he were actually good enough, *for her*. But he wasn't. He'd been unable to properly support his mother. He'd failed his brother repeatedly. He couldn't fail Phoebe too. And never their baby.

He had to fix all this. Somehow get his distance and perspective back. But in this smallest of hours, and at this darkest time of night, he was so damned tired. So he stayed curled around her—pressing his chest to her back, entwining his leg with hers, stroking his fingers gently across her belly. And, as exhaustion swallowed him into sleep, he accepted how awful he really was.

Because he didn't want to let her go at all.

CHAPTER ELEVEN

PHOEBE STROLLED IN the autumn sunshine, slowly winding her way back to Edo's apartment. It was a beautiful morning, with beautiful people everywhere, and she watched them all—desperately needing the distraction from her racing over-thinking. Edo had been so deeply asleep he'd not stirred when she'd left the bed. Still hadn't stirred while she'd eaten, showered, dressed, then paced in his lounge. In the end she'd had to get out. Had to breathe. Because she *had* to get a grip on herself.

Yesterday had been intense, while last night had been unforgettable. He'd opened up to her. He'd held her. All night. He'd been tender and caring and more vulnerable than she'd ever imagined. He had demons and doubts and while she couldn't wave some magic wand and make them all go away, maybe she could support him. If only he wanted her to and she couldn't help hoping that maybe he did. She couldn't stop that hope from growing. Maybe they could be *more*. Maybe they could *last*. Because she was more than half in love with him.

But she'd been wrong before. So wrong. So she was particularly wary of facing him. Perhaps if she just gave them more time, if she stayed near, then maybe his defences might lower... She wanted that so much, it terrified her. Her nerves grew with every step she took back, multiplied when one of the bodyguards raced up to her about a block out from his building and insisted she come with him urgently.

'Has something happened?' she asked, suddenly breathless.

The man didn't answer, merely muttered something short and sharp into a discreet microphone and set a punishing pace. Her heart pounded as he escorted her into the building—past another man who held the door, another who was holding the lift doors open. He pushed the buttons but let her enter alone.

The ride to the penthouse took too long.

Edo stood right in front of the lift door. His stormy expression pushed Phoebe's pulse higher but before she could ask what was wrong he stepped forward and pulled her from the lift.

'Where have you been?' he rapped.

'For a walk,' she said, trying not to react to the tension screaming from him. 'You were sleeping so soundly, I didn't want to disturb you.'

'You escaped your bodyguard,' he snapped.

'I didn't *escape* him, I—'

'He's been dismissed.'

'Edo, that's not fair.' She snatched a breath. 'I told him I didn't need him—'

'And *I* told him to watch you at all times. You can't just wander off.'

He couldn't possibly be serious. 'I was only gone an hour.' She stared at him, pained to see him struggling with his emotion. 'Can I not just go out? Would you have me electronically tagged, like a prize heifer?'

He didn't laugh and suddenly she was too strung out herself to handle him well. 'I simply explored your very posh neighbourhood in the sunshine. Is that so terrible?'

'It's not safe.'

'It's *ridiculously* safe.' She inhaled sharply again. He was upset because he'd been worried—*irrationally* worried—and she had to make him see that. 'Edo, what happened to

Dante was so awful, I can't imagine it. But he wouldn't want you worrying like this for the rest of your life—'

'They never caught them.' He cut her off.

'What?' She stilled.

'The fiends who took him. Never caught. Dante was too traumatised to give much information and they never—' His breathing heaved. 'For all I know, they're still out there.'

'Edo.' She leaned back against the wall, her legs suddenly weak.

'You didn't take the most basic precautions,' he growled. '*Basic*, Phoebe. When you are so vulnerable. You're *pregnant*.'

She gazed at the wildness in his eyes, the pallor of his skin. Her walking in the sun for an hour had been torture for him. Because of the baby.

'You can't live like this,' she muttered sadly.

His expression turned thunderous. 'Like "this"?'

She was heartbroken for him. He was so isolated. So fearful. So burdened by the belief he had to protect her that he couldn't enjoy even the little things in life—couldn't let her, either.

'You can't control *everything*.' Her emotion got the better of her. 'Not the weather. Not random things. Not life. Not me either. And I don't want our *child* to be *afraid* to go for a walk in their own neighbourhood.' She didn't want *any* of them being afraid to go further than three feet from a tribe of bodyguards. 'We can't condemn this baby to a life of *fear*. It'll be damaging—'

'You think I'll *damage* our child with my concerns?' He jerked back. 'If that's the case, then perhaps its best if you return to London sooner rather than later.'

'What?' She froze. She hadn't meant to make him snap. But he had. Just like that.

'You'll be better off there. As will the baby.'

She struggled to understand what he was saying—to be sure whether he meant it. 'Have you changed your mind about me staying here in Italy until the birth?' *Truly—just like that?*

To her horror, he jerked his head in assent.

'You're right, I can't control you here. I don't want to. More importantly, you don't want me to. So I'll step back. But I'll make sure you're safe in London.'

Wild hurt rose within her. 'I can keep myself safe. Case in point, this morning.'

'What you do with my security plan when you're there is up to you.'

'Your security plan?' Was he really only concerned with keeping her physically *safe*? Was there really nothing more to what he wanted for her? Or for their baby?

'Yes.' He met her gaze steadily. 'But you also need your friends, Phoebe. Their support. You need your place.'

So *he* wasn't a friend? And her place wasn't here with him. Because he didn't want to support her.

She reeled, desperately cut. Because, despite her best efforts, she'd still fallen for him. She'd still believed they might have a *chance*.

'Why did you even bother with this in the first place?' she asked angrily. 'Why not just leave me and your unwanted offspring to fend for ourselves?'

'I wanted what's best, but—'

'So do *better*,' she said. 'Don't just throw money at the problem and walk away. Are you really not going to be there for your own *child*?'

Their baby deserved *everything*. And, heaven help her, *she'd* wanted everything.

'I'll see it when I visit,' he muttered tightly.

It. How was he back to *it*? 'And how often is that going to be?'

He didn't answer. But Phoebe already knew. It would never be often enough.

'Our baby needs you.' Agonised, her heart was shredded. '*I* need you—'

'No.'

Edo turned away, unable to keep looking at her. She was right. It wasn't good for either her or their child to be around him, but not only because of his security concerns. He would let her down and he would let the child down, and it was better for her to know that now. It was better to make this mess certain.

When he'd woken alone this morning and couldn't find her in the apartment, nightmare moments had become minutes. Honestly, he couldn't survive another moment of that kind of agony, so his close involvement had to end *immediately*. He'd lost his cool with his security team, but he was *irate* with her. She'd shrugged off her protection so casually, so *carelessly*. He'd told her about Dante and she still didn't get it. Didn't factor in his feelings.

And why should she when his feelings clearly weren't her primary concern. God, he'd *wanted* her to factor them in. He'd *wanted* her to care. But the emotion he'd thought he'd seen in her eyes just then hadn't been *real* because she'd gone out regardless. And, even if it was real, then it wasn't right—she wouldn't be happy with him because at some point he would fail her. And he wanted her to be happy. But, more importantly than anything else, he wanted her to be safe. She would be safer in so many ways without him.

'Edo—'

'It was my fault,' he said brusquely.

He was as bad as his grandfather. As blind. He would screw them up in an unforgivable way.

'What?'

'Dante's abduction was my fault.' He spun back to face her. 'It was raining and we were late. I was impatient and wouldn't wait for him. I tossed him my jacket and told him to walk. I didn't mean it, it's just that he was slow. Always so slow. I pushed ahead and was idling at the corner when the van swung in. They thought he was me.'

'Edo...' She paled. 'And you saw it?'

'From too far away to do anything,' he muttered. 'I let him down that day. Again when I couldn't convince them to pay the ransom. And again when I focused on making money to help him instead of just *being* there. My grandfather was emotionally inept and I'm the same. We're missing something vital, Phoebe. Like I already told you, I'm not fit to be a father.'

White and breathless, she looked as worried as he'd felt five minutes ago. 'That's not true.' She moved closer. 'It wasn't your fault. *None* of that was your fault.'

She was wrong.

She stepped closer. 'And you're not alone in this. We can do this together, raise this baby together—'

No. Pain whistled in Edo's lungs. Because he saw it then— the caring he wanted. The caring he couldn't let her give to him. 'You and me are good together in bed. That's all.'

She stilled.

'It's all it is, all it's ever been,' he pushed, needing to make her *want* to leave. 'Stress release. You said it yourself. It's all you wanted from me.'

There was a sharp silence before defiance sparked in her eyes. 'It's all you wanted to let me have.'

That hit. Her mouth opened but he wouldn't—couldn't— let her say anything more. 'I thought you weren't going to give everything up for a guy again.'

Phoebe flinched at his caustic vehemence. 'I'm not, I'm—'

'No?' He stepped forward, his words acidic and mocking. 'Then you're what? What were you about to *offer*?'

Anger poured from him now and pushed into her. What had she been going to offer? *Everything.* Because that was what she did. And you know what? That was okay. That was her and it was what she'd do for anyone—everyone—she loved. Including him.

'I'm not going to apologise for how I *feel*.' She thrust back into his space. 'I'm not going to apologise for who I *am*.'

She couldn't believe what was happening. He didn't just struggle with loss but with guilt, and it was too much for anyone to bear. But he didn't have to do it alone—she would be with him. Only he was determined to push her away.

'I'm a passionate, caring person, right?' She threw back his description of her. 'Willing to go all in for someone.'

'Willing to stay in my compound, surrounded by bodyguards, secreted away for ever?' He pulled her to him, squeezing out what little breath was left in her lungs. 'Phoebe?'

He gazed into her eyes and pressed her closer. He could mould her to him so easily. She shivered as he all but rummaged through her soul. And then—even more easily—she melted.

Yes. She *was* willing. She quite desperately wanted to be with him.

His sharp inhalation pierced the warmth permeating her. 'Only because you can't get enough of *this*.' He harshly released her. 'Chemistry. Great sex, Phoebe. There's nothing more to us than that.'

He flipped from sizzling to stone-cold in less than a second.

'Last night *wasn't* a stress release,' she threw back at him, sliced. Not for her. It had been connection and giving. And of course they were more than great sex. Her demanding that 'honeymoon' had been little more than bravado. She'd thought she could remain emotionally independent, but she'd been wrong. Everything had changed for her and honestly she couldn't believe it hadn't changed for him as well. Because he'd been unable to stay away from her too.

'You're willing to give everything up for me, Phoebe?' he taunted cruelly. 'Lose yourself for a man who'll never give you what you want or what you deserve?'

She didn't want to *lose* herself in him. She wanted to build a *life* with him. This relationship was utterly different to the one she'd had with Ryan. Because this was Edo, and he was kind and thought *beyond* himself. 'You have more to give than you—'

'No,' he interrupted. 'I told you, Phoebe. I *can't*. I never promised anything more.'

It slapped. Hard. Edoardo Benedetti would never love her. He wanted her—temporarily—but wouldn't love her. He didn't want to attach to anyone. He deserved to love and be loved every bit as much as she did, but he'd encased his heart in stone. The way he'd played her just now was *excruciating*.

'And you won't even try?' she asked even though she knew the answer. Not for her. Not for anyone. And that was *not* good enough for their *child*.

'Why would you sacrifice everything to settle for so little?' he said.

'It's not what I'd be doing,' she said, with sudden clarity. 'The person I'm willing to sacrifice everything for is our child.'

His mouth thinned. 'Don't use the baby to blackmail me into what you want.'

'As if you didn't do that to me?' She shot back. 'And for what? A piece of paper you're going to do nothing with. You're abdicating your responsibilities. Well, you don't get to choose which little parts of parenting you get to perform.'

'Actually, that's exactly what I get to do.'

'Not with me. Not with my child.' She snarled. '*My* child should have *more*. Not suffer a thousand cuts while trying so hard to get their father's approval or attention, and never being able to, because you'll never stay long enough, never visit enough. You'll never *be* enough for this baby because you're not actually *interested* and I don't want my child going through that.'

'All or nothing, is that what you're saying?' He glared at her. 'Is this an ultimatum?'

She tossed her head. 'Yes.'

His eyes were like ice chips. 'Then it's nothing.'

'Just like that?' She chilled. He would walk away from *everything*?

'Yes.'

Wow. She steeled herself. She'd suffered rejection so many times, but this was the absolute worst.

'I got you something. Not that you're going to need it.' With shaking hands, she took the cheerfully wrapped present from her bag and set it on the table. She'd seen it when walking past the boutique shops this morning and had been unable to resist buying it for him. She'd been stupidly nervous about it, actually—had hoped he'd understand her intention.

But he didn't even look at it, let alone open it. He just stared at her.

'Get me on the first flight to London,' she said. She wasn't sticking around to suffer for a second longer. *'Now.'*

CHAPTER TWELVE

SHE DIDN'T HAVE to wait for the first flight because Edo sent her back on a private jet only two hours after their horrific argument—that was how determined he was to get her out of his life as quickly as possible. He'd removed himself moments after their fight and reappeared only when all arrangements had been made. That meant two bodyguards went with her. No softening. No apology. No kiss goodbye. He'd just brusquely told her he'd be in touch. Her present had still been on the table as she'd walked out.

She felt sick the entire flight, appalled that she'd lost it so completely. That he had too. It had been a monumental blow-up and she reeled from the destruction—it was impossible to process it properly.

The first thing she did on landing back in London was lose the bodyguards. Threatened to have them charged with stalking if they didn't back off. Not that it stopped them following her taxi in one of their own. But they couldn't come into her house. She slammed the front door behind her, so relieved and *so* devastated. The tears she'd been holding back for hours overwhelmed her. She stepped forward and promptly tripped over the hallway rug.

'Damn.' She collapsed in a heap, her ankle throbbing like fire. *'Damn!'*

'Phoebe?' Bethan burst out of her room. 'Are you back? Are you okay?'

No. She couldn't even get into her own house without screwing up.

Bethan sank to the floor beside her and put her arm around her. 'What's wrong? What's *happened*?'

Between sobs, Phoebe confessed everything—she'd not told her friends about the wedding or the baby, wanting to tell them face to face. Now it spilled out in a sorry hiccupping mess of confusion and heartache, and her ankle was *agony*.

They spent hours at an emergency clinic. Her bone had never healed properly from the break when she'd been young and this injury was far worse than the one in Italy. While she didn't need a cast, she was going to have to wear a moon boot for a few weeks to keep her ankle still, and she would have to remain housebound for a little while. No doubt Edo would probably be thrilled about that last bit.

'Shouldn't you let him know?' Bethan eventually asked as they waited for the cab to take them home.

'There's no need,' Phoebe muttered.

Bethan frowned. 'I think you should—'

'Please, Bethan, I need space to get over him—it's too soon and I don't want him coming here out of obligation. I'm fine.'

'Okay.' Bethan's face softened and she leaned against her. 'I'm sorry it didn't work out.'

'Me too.'

She spent a couple days on the sofa dealing via phone with the security consultant who wanted to change the locks, install alarms and cameras. She didn't argue, she didn't want to make Edo worry from a distance. She would do enough to set his mind at rest on that.

A courier parcel arrived—the laptop, her notebook. No

personal message accompanied them. Her marriage hadn't lasted as long as the first and that hadn't exactly been long. Knowing neither of her husbands had ever actually loved her didn't do a lot for her sense of self-worth. *Never, ever again.* That was the one—only—thing in which she could let herself go to the full extreme. But her ultimatum to Edo—that extreme reaction—that hadn't been fair.

That's what she felt sick about. Her ultimatum—her extreme reaction—had been rash and hurtful. She could never ban him from their child's life. She felt awful for even implying it. No, she would compromise. She would try as hard as she could to ensure her child had a relationship with its father. Something would be better than nothing.

Edo wouldn't let himself grow close to anyone but she would have to manage that for their baby. Besides, she still believed that Edo wouldn't be able to help himself—his caring would come out for the child. He couldn't quite hold it all back—couldn't not act. She ran a protective hand over her belly. Her baby would be loved. She would ensure it grew up free and confident and yes, safe. She would work that out somehow. But she needed a little time to heal her own heart before trying to build some kind of trade-off with him.

She shouldn't have told him about her past, then she wouldn't have heard him say those soothing things that revealed he had a soul. She wouldn't have learned about his brother and known just how desperately Edo had loved him. She would never have known how big his heart was beneath the defensive exterior he fought to retain. It was why he was so protective—and afraid—for their baby.

She would have been better off not knowing any of that. It was actually cruel, how kind he could be. How thoughtful. He didn't want it to mean anything. But it did. It couldn't not. He was capable of total and complete love. He just had to *let* himself. But he was stuck and determined to remain so.

***

It had been the right thing to do. Edo felt guilty about his cruelty, but a little more guilt was nothing compared to the constant burden he would feel if she stayed. If something worse happened. He could never give her everything, so she was better off away from him. As was the baby.

He'd phoned Isabella and gotten her to courier Phoebe's laptop to her. Then he'd buried himself in work, but struggled to stay submerged. Concentration was elusive. Sleep impossible.

He didn't return to the estate for four days. When he did, he told Isabella that Phoebe wasn't coming back at all. The housekeeper hadn't spoken to him in the three days since. He still couldn't sleep. Still couldn't work.

He should've got her to pack up Phoebe's rooms but it didn't feel right to have anyone else touch her personal things. He went into the office he'd set up for her. She'd rearranged the stationery implements he'd bought for her and she'd printed some photos that she'd stuck beside the large screen. There was one of her with her friends outside her flat in London.

He rubbed his chest as he stared at it. The owner of the flat above hers had finally accepted his outrageously high purchase offer. Ideally, he'd convert the two flats back into the one. Then he'd work on acquiring the houses on either side—one could be the staff residence and he could knock the other over and create a garden. None of which he told her. She couldn't have made it clearer that she didn't want anything to do with him now. So he would go through the lawyers.

He steeled himself and went into her bedroom. He'd rarely entered it, even when she'd been here. He'd taken her to his bed—it was bigger. Now he saw she'd pulled a large armchair to the window—he briefly took in the view of the hills and vines but his focus was caught by the brightly coloured throw across the arm rest. It was from the pool house, the one he'd wrapped around her shoulders the day they'd met. A short pile of books was stacked on the floor—a few novels, but a beginner's guide to pregnancy and child birth was on top. That she hadn't mentioned it to him hurt. As did knowing she would now go through it alone.

He whirled away and glanced at the bed, at the few things on the bedside table. He couldn't bring himself to touch any of it. She'd made it *cosy*. She really was a snowdrop—the first flower to bloom in winter when the snow was still settled. Undefeated and undaunted, she just determinedly blossomed despite an uninviting environment. With the scarcest of encouragement—of *attention*—she came wonderfully alive.

While all he'd done was try to keep his distance—supposedly focused on keeping her safe, when really he'd been keeping *himself* safe. Except he'd been unable to resist circling back to her, because she was warm and loving and generous.

She had so much love to give and she'd hardly been given the chance to. But she was going to be fine. She was better at coping than he was—already she lived a more rounded life—she had friends, a home, connection. And he knew she would make a wonderful mother for their child. She would do everything in her power to ensure that.

Edo's powers were far more limited. He'd imposed boundaries. She'd accepted most. Demanded more, but not everything. Until he'd pushed her out completely. He'd known just how—what wound to press on. He'd denied the truth and let her think there was nothing between them but sex.

It was all you wanted to let me have.

He went back to work in his office. Still couldn't focus. It was worse than when she'd been there and distracting him all the time. The still-wrapped present sat in the bottom of his bag. After Dante's abduction, Edo had never opened the presents his grandfather had sent him. He'd never wanted another cent of the man's money. He hated him with every fibre of his being. Because there was the fear there, that he had a little too much in common with the selfish old jerk.

And now Edo couldn't bring himself to open Phoebe's present either. Yet nor could he throw it away. It fuelled his anger. It had been *her* birthday, not his. She'd had hardly anyone buy her any presents and yet there she was, *giving*. He didn't want to accept anything from her. Except he had already taken so much more. And she just kept giving, didn't she? Even when the odds were against her. She would do anything for the ones she loved.

So would he, right? That meant making this sacrifice. That meant sending her away and letting her be both safe and free. Edo deserved—needed—to be alone. But Phoebe didn't. She *should* meet someone else. Probably would. Some smart guy would see her. Would love her. Would give her everything. His blood bubbled and arrogance surged at the thought. No other man could give her what *he* could give her, and he didn't mean wealth and riches. But he'd *chosen* not to.

His grandfather had withheld Dante's ransom—he'd been afraid of having more taken from him. More money. Edo had withheld his heart from Phoebe. Why—when their time in Tuscany had been the best days of his life? Because of exactly that. She'd gotten too close and he was terrified fate would rip his heart from his chest. He'd been such a coward. He'd let her think that she was something *less*. Crushed her when he should have offered unconditional support. Let her believe in his indifference. He'd been terrified of letting her down and he totally had.

He'd stopped her from saying whatever she wanted. Dismissed her feelings for him. Minimised her when she was the only thing that really mattered to him. He'd told her that what they had was less. He'd denied his own feelings. And hurt the woman he loved.

He stared sightlessly down at the pool house, unable to stop the memories surging. He'd not admitted how much he wanted her to stay. How much more than sex they were. He'd let anxiety conquer him. *Silence* him.

He'd not supported Dante either. He'd let silence grow when he should have tried to reach out. He'd not known what to say. He'd done what he thought he had to—got them financial security and independence. And it wasn't enough. Regret almost sank him now.

He glanced at the bright wrapping paper peeking out from the bottom of his bag. Irrepressible. Optimistic. Hopeful. Phoebe wasn't a quitter. He couldn't be either. Not now. She didn't know how important she was to him and, whatever else happened, she ought to know that. She deserved to know that.

The sonogram photo of their child was still stashed in the side pocket. A different kind of gift. One altogether too precious. He pulled it out, made himself look. Made himself face the feelings he'd been trying to deny for days. He was going to be a father. And he wanted to be a good one.

He drew in a deep, painful breath. He could never get forgiveness from Dante and, while he could ask Phoebe for hers, more important was what *he* could give *her*. And that was honesty. Full, complete, honesty. Despite his fears, he needed to offer her his whole heart—*unconditionally*.

CHAPTER THIRTEEN

'You don't need to hover over me all the time,' Phoebe reassured Bethan for the thirtieth time in five minutes.

'I don't want to go on this date. I don't even like him like that. I'm not ready for anything new.'

'I know,' Phoebe sympathised before turning pragmatic. 'But you've not been on a date in centuries, so just consider it practice. A small step to getting over the Greek.'

Bethan fidgeted with her bracelet, repeatedly opening and closing the clasp. 'Didn't we agree getting involved with men was a bad idea?'

'You don't have to get involved with him. You're just going out to remember what having a social life is actually like. And because you *really* want to get over the Greek.'

'Okay.' Bethan nodded, nerves still evident in her eyes. 'You're right. I need to move on, and nothing else has worked. This might.'

'Worth a shot, yes?'

Bethan bent and hugged her. 'I won't be late.'

'I'll be here.'

Phoebe had only been back in London ten days and Bethan had already knitted a stunning merino baby blanket and was onto an array of tiny singlets. She and Elodie had both been accepting and excited about her pregnancy and were helping keep her chin up most of the time. But honestly Phoebe was looking forward to having tonight entirely alone. She planned to sink into the sofa, watch back-to-back tear-jerker movies, eat pizza and ugly-cry. But, only a few minutes after Bethan had left, someone thumped on the front door. Whoever it was didn't stop.

'Hold on!' Phoebe limped into the hallway as quickly as she could and assumed it must be Bethan, because she'd not even ordered the pizza yet. 'Did you forget your key?'

She opened the door and froze. It wasn't Bethan filling the frame. Edo's glittering gaze raked her from head to toe and stayed there.

She wasn't wearing enough. Not nearly enough. And nor was he—because that black jacket did things to his eyes that ought to be illegal.

'What are you doing here?' she croaked.

'What happened?' He stared at her foot and a white ring appeared around his mouth.

'Noth—'

'What *happened*?' he repeated in a harsh whisper that hit more than a roar ever could.

Phoebe gasped. He really didn't have the right to storm in there and demand to know things when he'd said he didn't have emotional support to give. But his devastated expression destroyed any resistance she had.

'The baby is fine,' she muttered.

'I don't—' He broke off sharply and bawled out another question. 'Are *you* fine?'

'Yes. I only twisted my ankle.'

'The same one?' His voice rose. 'We should have got you proper treatment that day.'

'It's *fine*,' she said sharply. The last thing she wanted to hear was more guilt from him.

His expression flared. He took two steps forward and scooped her into his arms.

'Edo!'

He hefted her closer, kicked the door shut and stomped through to her lounge.

'Put me down,' she ordered thinly. 'Now.'

He did. Very carefully. She snatched the gaping halves of her robe together and pressed as far back into the sofa as she could while fighting to recover her breath. How was it possible for her heart to thunder so hard and her hope soar so high? It made her dizzy. But it was stupid. *She* was stupid. He'd set her 'getting over Edo' progress back in less than a second.

'Why are you here?' she demanded tremulously. 'I don't want you here.'

She couldn't bear to be this near to him. Every intention she'd been trying to foster—to be measured and reasonable, to work towards some kind of compromise with him, fled. She could be nothing but emotional, and it was awful. 'You need to leave. *Now.*'

Edo obstinately took the chair beside the sofa and looked around her flat because he couldn't bear to see the vulnerability and pain in her eyes. He needed a moment to breathe after having her in his arms again, because his brain wouldn't work, and his body just ached with the fear that that might've been the last time he might hold her like that. It took everything in him not to pull her back into his arms. To throw all his words into the air and just kiss her—but that was their problem. They fell into physical abandon when they needed to communicate deeply. Words first. Then actions.

Calm before that.

So he looked around. Her home wasn't what he'd have once expected. It wasn't organised and neat and perfect. It was full of colour and comfort—a completely maximalist, cosy nest with cushions and photos and interesting objects everywhere. It was full of heart. Maybe it didn't look much on the outside, but he should've known it would be this brilliantly warm on the inside. She'd not had a home she'd felt secure in as a child, so she'd made one for herself here, and he was a jerk for assuming it wouldn't be good enough. For forcing her away from it.

What he'd provided wasn't the same at all. Couldn't even compare. His estate was horribly empty now without her. Polite and efficient, never flustered Phoebe craved this sort of stimulating and creative and warm kind of home. Kind of *life*—actually. Intense and varied and rich. Which was what she'd demanded from him, in bed at least.

'Edo?' Her prompt sounded less angry. More uncertain.

Because he was clearly losing it—he'd been sitting here silently for minutes, and she was probably starting to think he was deranged. He pulled the present from his pocket and set it on the low coffee table at right angles to them both. The wrapping was crumpled and it looked somewhat sad.

'You haven't opened it?' she whispered. 'You came all this way to give it back to me?'

She looked so hurt, his heart broke. She thought he'd behave that awfully? It was a sharp reminder that he needed to do better—to be fully honest with her.

'I wanted to be with you when I opened it,' he explained huskily, turning to watch her beautiful face. 'I was ungrateful and rude when you gave it to me. I overreacted really badly to *everything* that morning.'

She pressed further back into the sofa, her mouth pinched as she bit the inside of her lip.

'I overreacted to everything about you. I couldn't handle my feelings and I pushed you away,' he said. 'But I can't resist you any more.'

'You don't have to resist me,' she answered stiffly, avoiding his gaze. 'You just need to stay in Italy.'

'But I don't want to stay there without you. The last week has taught me that. I don't want to stay *anywhere* without you.'

Her eyes filled with even more vulnerability and twisted his heart. She didn't believe him.

'Edo—'

'Please let me say it,' he hurriedly added. 'I should have said it so much sooner, but I was scared, Phoebe.'

'What does it matter?' She swallowed. 'When we're just sex.'

He deserved her anger—her doubt.

'We do have the most incredible chemistry,' he said softly. 'Neither of us can deny that.'

Phoebe didn't want to hear any more. She didn't want to hurt any more. 'But it will die eventually, so you don't need to apologise—'

'I do. And it's not all I need to do.'

She was frightened. Really frightened. Her heart was so fragile right now. With one word he could shatter her. All. Over. Again. So she closed her eyes. Tight. 'Please leave.'

'I can't,' he whispered. 'Phoebe, I'm sorry I pushed you into a marriage you didn't want, but I just had this primal feeling that I had to tether you to me. That I needed you near me. I thought I had to protect you and the baby, but it wasn't really that. Phoebe…' He groaned. 'Look at me, *amore. Please.*'

She couldn't resist him. Never had been able to. Never would be able to. She opened her eyes and her heart tore. He was on his knees in front of her, his beautiful face pale and every muscle in his jaw clenched, but his espresso eyes were filled with wary hope.

'I thought if you fell in love with Italy you might stay,' he muttered, watching her so closely. 'I wanted you to want to stay.'

'You never thought I might fall in love with you?' she asked helplessly.

'Deep down that's *exactly* what I wanted. I tried everything to keep you close except *tell* you why. But I couldn't be honest about why having you near mattered so much to me. Phoebe, you're wonderful.'

He took her cold hands in his, rubbing his thumbs across her knuckles. 'You're warm and funny and beneath your calm exterior hides the most passionate woman I've ever met. But you scare the hell out of me. I cannot bear the thought of losing you, I cannot bear the thought of failing you.'

She squeezed his fingers, holding him tightly. 'You won't.'

'I have already,' he said sombrely. 'I let you think I didn't care. I shut you down and didn't let you speak and I sent you away. I'm the one who fell that day on the road. I *fell*—instant and hard and then spent for ever trying to deny it. You're everything I thought I couldn't have and I was a coward. And I was cruel. I'm sorry I couldn't say it before. I'm sorry I let you go. But I love you, Phoebe,' he breathed. 'Give me the chance to prove it.'

'You don't need to prove *anything*,' she argued fiercely. 'I already know you, Edo. You were kind to George. Kind to me that day all those months ago. I know you've done so much for me since. You put that office together for me…you left me flowers—'

'You knew about that?' He snatched a breath.

She nodded. 'And I began to hope you might care about *me*, but then…'

'Then I let you down,' he cupped her jaw. 'I'll make it up to you. I'll spend my life—'

'Just stay with me,' she mumbled. 'That's all I need. You *with* me.' She didn't ever want to be alone—not abandoned, not sent away—but *wanted*.

'Always. I'll move here. I don't care where I am as long as we're together. I want everything with you, Phoebe. Everything you want.' His voice broke and the last emerged as a desperate whisper. 'And I really want our baby.'

Her eyes watered at the genuine desire in his words. He cared about her desires, her needs and their child. Happiness surged in an unstoppable rush and truthfully, she desperately missed the warmth and beauty and space of his Tuscan estate. 'Thing is, I do really like olives these days. Can't seem to get enough of them.'

He dragged in another jerky breath, but his gaze softened. 'So it might be good to live near an endless supply?'

She smiled tremulously and, the second she did, he kissed her. It was the messiest, most emotional, sweetest kiss of her life.

'Edo...' Her breath shuddered as the reality of his return hit and she blurted her most terrifying secret. 'I'm totally in love with you.'

He picked her up, holding her tightly as he bent his face to hers. 'I was really hoping that.'

'It scares me,' she whispered, snuggling into his neck because she wasn't close enough. Not yet. 'What I feel is so huge—'

'I know.' He carried her through her flat. 'Me too.'

Phoebe didn't want him to put her down, not even onto her bed. She couldn't bear to be more than an inch apart from him, almost cried when he stepped back to strip, even though he did it with world-record speed. She tried to move towards him but her moon boot made her attempt clunky.

'It's okay.' He came back to her and frowned at the slight bruising at the top of the casing on her ankle. 'You're going to have to lie back and let me love you.' He pushed her down with gentle, implacable force. 'Let me take care of you, okay?'

She quivered. There was nothing she wanted more. She wanted him to love her—the way she loved him. And to her utter delight he did. He kissed her—everywhere—over and over. He gently caressed her until his hands tightened and his body tensed. He held her in his strong arms, reassured her, and in the end claimed her with all his power, all his passion. So there was no uncertainty, no doubt. He'd truly come back and he wasn't letting her go. *Ever*.

'Are you going to open your present?' she asked eventually.

He'd propped his head on his hand and was tracing patterns over her skin, a soft smile curving his mouth as he gazed upon her with open adoration.

'I thought I just did,' he teased.

But he slid from the bed, returning to her room only a minute later, her gift in his hand. Phoebe sat up, fluttering nerves returning, and watched him tear the wrapping before setting the contents in his palm. The die-cast toy was vibrant red and she could only hope that it didn't upset him.

He stared at it for a long time, then looked at her with a soft, sad smile. 'You remembered what I told you about Dante and me.'

'I thought you and the baby might play with it together,' she whispered.

'I would love to do that.' His voice cracked, but with a teasing flourish he ran the little toy moped across her stomach. It tickled and she smiled at him, even as tears sprang again.

He swiftly leaned forward and kissed her. 'Thank you for bringing love back into my life,' he said huskily. 'You're vibrant, Phoebe. Don't hold back on me. Stay passionate, be as extreme as you want—you're everything to me.'

'And you're *mine*.' Possessively, she wrapped her arms around him again as all her emotions unleashed.

'Yes,' he promised simply. 'And I always will be.'

CHAPTER FOURTEEN

Two years later

PHOEBE PEEKED OUT through the window even though Edo had challenged her not to. Fairy lights were festooned over the interior courtyard while several tables adorned with linen, fine china, floral arrangements and sparkling crystal glasses were set out in rows. It was Phoebe's twenty-fifth birthday and details guy Edo had turned party planner extraordinaire.

Last year they'd celebrated with quiet contentment—remaining holed up, getting to know their baby and just indulging in the joy of being together. But this year, Edo had gone all out to give Phoebe her first proper birthday party. She'd been busy with a client most of the week, and hadn't kept track of all the preparations, but the sumptuousness and generosity didn't surprise her. Isabella had helped, of course, enjoying the chance to go big.

Their guests milled downstairs as the musicians played and their staff offered them delicate nibbles. Edo's olives of course. And his wine. Bethan and Elodie were there, several of their staff, even George, her former boss. He was in remission and enjoying his retirement and had brought his wife and grandchildren over for a family holiday.

Edo was still ridiculously protective but gradually becoming more relaxed. He now even allowed their security to follow at a more discreet distance. Working with a counsellor, processing the losses, the trauma, of his youth had helped. Phoebe sometimes went too, supporting him when he asked. Just as he supported her—with balance. And with dreams.

Much of the time they were here at the estate, loving family life. Edo had stepped back some from his work, while her business was thriving—she'd even taken on two employees, which was good, given she too now wanted to pull back her hours.

She went to the mirror to put in her diamond earrings and give herself a final check.

'You look stunning.' An awed whisper came from the other side of the room.

She turned. The tenderness in his expression melted her heart. She was wearing the lace dress she'd worn at their wedding and yes, she'd hoped he'd react to it.

'Phoebe.' He stalked straight to her, hauled her into his arms and kissed her hard. He didn't react. He combusted. Phoebe simply melted against him. Again.

'Happy birthday my love,' he growled before kissing her again. 'I have something for you.'

She didn't need anything more than him right here with her. But Edo pulled a chain from his pocket.

'You're spoiling me.' She gazed at the beautiful locket dangling between them.

'You deserve to be spoilt.'

'Everyone does.'

'Maybe.' He shrugged. 'But you most *especially* do.'

She smiled. He was as intense as ever but now he didn't hide a thing about how he felt. He expressed it all and she loved him all the more for it.

'Alessio is downstairs keeping Elodie and Bethan busy,' he said.

Her friends doted on her feisty, fast-on-his feet son. So

did Edo. Alessio Dante Benedetti had changed their lives. She opened the heavy locket and saw the picture of him—and Edo. Her husband. Her son. Her *family*. 'Put it on for me?' she asked shakily.

She turned and held up her hair so he could fix the chain around her neck. She watched his beautiful face in the mirror.

'It's a good thing there's room for another photo…' she murmured.

He glanced up to meet her gaze. His face flushed and his eyes gleamed.

'We need another photo?' He swept his hands down her sides and around to settle on her lower belly.

She leaned back against him. 'You know already.'

'I do pay *very* close attention to your body.' He nipped her earlobe the way they both loved, stirring her blood with such ease.

'You can read it like a book?' She watched his reflection with misty eyes. 'Play it like an instrument?'

'My beautiful snowdrop is blossoming again,' he muttered huskily.

'The first brother or sister for Alessio.' She shivered as he caressed her.

'First of several,' he agreed hungrily.

She chuckled in delight and then moaned with reluctant rejection. 'Edo, we have guests…'

'But we can steal a few moments before going down there.'

'Is that all you need?' she teased archly.

'It's all *you* need,' he countered with a grin. 'I can wait 'til later.'

She shimmied back against him. She didn't want him to wait until later. She wanted to have all of him now. She always did, always would. With a chuckle, he turned her to face him and teased her with the unstoppable, passionate recklessness they'd always shared. He carried her to her bed, lifted her skirt and used his tongue till she burst like fireworks. While she was still recovering her breath, he took her with tender possessiveness and did indeed play her like an instrument—making her vibrate and hum with pure pleasure again, before with a growl he succumbed to their passion too.

'I've dreamed of having you in this dress since our wedding day,' he rasped.

'Edo!' She sobbed against him as he rocked hard into her.

'I'm here now...' He growled. 'Here always.'

Deeply, irrevocably. He was *hers*. And she was his—the one he was building a whole family with, the one he *wanted*. And he told her, showed her, like this. Every. Single. Day.

Long minutes later, she turned back to the mirror and caught sight of her flushed reflection. 'I have to redo my make-up,' she squeaked, overcome with embarrassment.

'You're perfect as you are,' Edo said softly as he tucked in his shirt and rubbed his own flushed face. 'What does it matter if it's obvious to everyone how much you are loved?'

Her tears rose again. It didn't matter at *all*—they had passion. They had love. They had each other. And it was everything.

* * * * *

MILLS & BOON®

Coming next month

HER ACCIDENTAL SPANISH HEIR
Caitlin Crews

Something else occurs to me. Like a concrete block falling on me.

Something that should have occurred to me a long time ago.

I count back, one month, another. All the way back to that night in Cap Ferrat.

I stand up abruptly, gather my things and stride toward the front office.

My mind is whirling on the elevator down and I practically sprint out the front of the building then down a few blocks until I find a drugstore. I give thanks for the total disinterest of cashiers in New York City, purchase the test and then make myself walk all the way home to see if that calms me.

It does not.

I throw my bag on the counter in my kitchen and tear open the box, scowling at the instructions.

Then I wait through the longest few minutes of my entire life.

Then I stare down at the two blue lines that blaze there on my test.

Unmistakably.
I simply stand there. Maybe breathing, maybe not.
The truth is as unmistakable as those two blue lines.
I'm pregnant.
With *his* child.
With the *Marquess of Patrias's* baby.

Continue reading

HER ACCIDENTAL SPANISH HEIR
Caitlin Crews

Available next month
millsandboon.co.uk

Copyright ©2025 by Caitlin Crews

COMING SOON!

We really hope you enjoyed reading this book. If you're looking for more romance be sure to head to the shops when new books are available on

Thursday 19th June

To see which titles are coming soon, please visit
millsandboon.co.uk/nextmonth

MILLS & BOON

FOUR BRAND NEW BOOKS FROM
MILLS & BOON MODERN

The same great stories you love, a stylish new look!

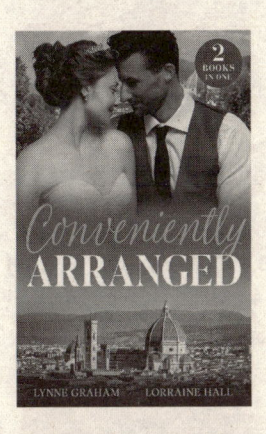

OUT NOW

Eight Modern stories published every month, find them all at:

millsandboon.co.uk

afterglow BOOKS

Afterglow Books is a trend-led, trope-filled list of books with diverse, authentic and relatable characters, a wide array of voices and representations, plus real world trials and tribulations. Featuring all the tropes you could possibly want (think small-town settings, fake relationships, grumpy vs sunshine, enemies to lovers) and all with a generous dose of spice in every story.

@millsandboonuk
@millsandboonuk
afterglowbooks.co.uk

#AfterglowBooks

For all the latest book news, exclusive content and giveaways scan the QR code below to sign up to the Afterglow newsletter:

SCAN ME

afterglow BOOKS

NOT SO FAST
He's on track to win her heart...
KAREN BOOTH

Much Ado About Hating You
They're enemies at work...but can love write their happy ending?
Sarah Echavarre Smith

- Sports romance
- Enemies to lovers
- Spicy

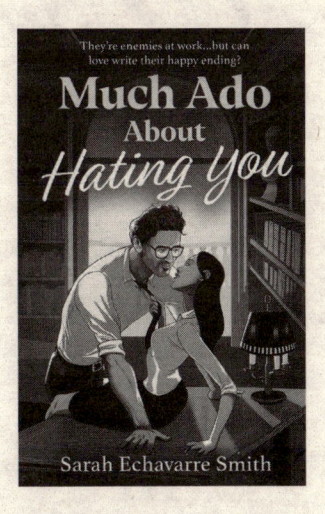

- Workplace romance
- Forbidden love
- Opposites attract

OUT NOW

Two stories published every month. Discover more at:
Afterglowbooks.co.uk

LET'S TALK

Romance

For exclusive extracts, competitions and special offers, find us online:

- **f** MillsandBoon
- **X** @MillsandBoon
- **◉** @MillsandBoonUK
- **♪** @MillsandBoonUK

Get in touch on 01413 063 232

For all the latest titles coming soon, visit
millsandboon.co.uk/nextmonth

OUT NOW!

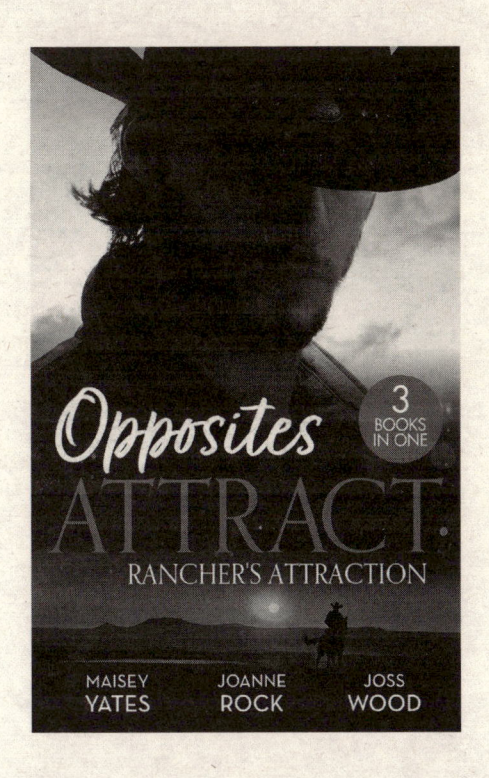

Opposites Attract: Rancher's Attraction

3 BOOKS IN ONE

MAISEY YATES · JOANNE ROCK · JOSS WOOD

Available at
millsandboon.co.uk

MILLS & BOON

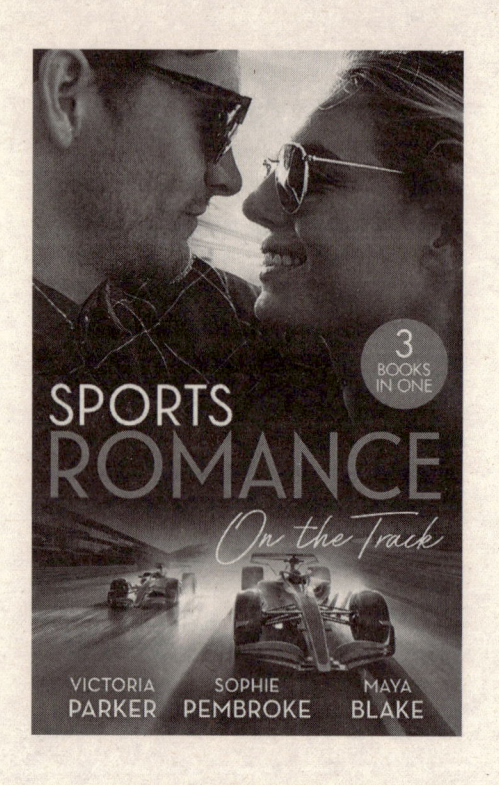